Testimonials for *The Invaders*

"Rick Wilkinson knows how to keep readers turning the pages. With deft story-telling he weaves three narratives together and takes us into the resources industry and into areas of Australia's defences during WW11 that are rarely explored in fiction. The Invaders pulls off the difficult trick of being both entertaining and informative."
—Robert Gott, crime novelist

"When do explorers become regarded as 'The Invaders'? This theme intrigued me personally on reading this impressive novel by Rick Wilkinson. Rick evokes the beauty — and lurking menace — of a remote part of Australia, steeped in mystery. He entwines indigenous traditions with the first thrust of European scientific exploration, the very real threat of armed invasion in WW2 and the need to balance humanity's need for vital resources against preservation of the land. Emerging from this complex interplay of cultures and characters is that even the best intentioned of people are prone to prejudices that can lead to tragic consequences. Throw in the 1987 stock market crash – here is a tale that will keep you engrossed up to its denouement. Highly recommended."
—Reg Nelson, Vintage Energy

"Wilkinson cleverly interweaves sub-plots that move powerfully backward and forward in time. Some of the characters nimbly spill across those boundaries. It is a story that does not rely on popular history. Nor does it depend on established formulas. It is an engaging read for casual observers of history because it covers so many areas that are not well known: as such reader interest is piqued. One for any bookshelf."
— **Christopher Beck, Media Dynamics**

"Set in the Northern Territory, *The Invaders* is a Tour de Force where damaged individuals cannot escape a past that embraces a breathtakingly vivid history from the voyage of the *Beagle* to the Japanese threat in WWII to oil exploration in the eighties."
— **Kerry Cue, author, journalist, mathematician**

"Rick Wilkinson is a worthy successor to Ion Idriess, the adventurous author of tales from Australia's wild deep north. Rick's tragic story is informed by his vast personal knowledge of the geography and geology of the region, the petroleum exploration industry and of historical events."
— **Noel Bushnell, veteran journalist, *The Traveller* blogger**

"Rick Wilkinson's *The Invaders* is a ripping yarn of interlinked endeavour, intrigue, high drama and repentance spanning three epochs in remote and beguiling northern Australia — early British exploration, the invasion threat during World War II, and the modern-day exploitation of natural resources. The constant throughout is the rise of Aboriginal engagement, understanding and more latterly, empowerment."
—**Barry FitzGerald, Resources Columnist**

THE
INVADERS

THE
INVADERS

RICK WILKINSON

Published by Brolga Publishing Pty Ltd
ABN 46 063 962 443

PO Box 452
Torquay Victoria 3228
Australia

email: markzocchi@brolgapublishing.com.au

All rights reserved. No part of this publication may be reproduced, stored in a retrieval system or transmitted in any form or by any means electronic, mechanical, photocopying, recording or otherwise without prior permission from the publisher.

Copyright © 2022 Rick Wilkinson

National Library of Australia
Cataloguing-in-Publication data

        Rick Wilkinson, author. ISBN: 9780648697084
        (paperback)

A catalogue record for this book is available from the National Library of Australia

Printed in Australia
Cover design and typeset by WorkingType Studio

BE PUBLISHED

Publish through a successful publisher
National Distribution to Australia & New Zealand
International Distribution to the United Kingdom

Other books by Rick Wilkinson

Resources industries:

A Thirst For Burning—The story of Australia's oil industry
Speaking of Oil & Gas—Introducing the petroleum industry
Rocks to Riches—The story of Australia's national geological survey
Well, Well, Well—Behind Australia's wildcat names
Where God Never Trod—Australia's oil explorers across two centuries
Once Upon a Wildcat—Images from Australia's petroleum story
The Oil Shale Initiative—Ian McFarlane's quest to develop a new energy source for Australia
Knights, Knaves & Dragons—50 years inside APPEA and Australia's oil and gas politics
Twists in the Sand — 50 years in the turbulent life of Beach Energy

General:

The Bellarine…via Rambler's Road—People and stories of the Bellarine Peninsula
Return of the Phasmid — Australia's rarest insect fights back from the brink of extinction

For children:

The Stones of Fire series (fiction)
Book 1: *The Ancient Secret*
Book 2: *Teeth of the Storm*
Incredible Journeys—Adventures into the unknown (non-fiction)
Endangered! Working to save animals at risk (non-fiction)
It's True! Animals are electrifying (non-fiction)

Prologue

Item 1:
Archives: Timber Creek Police Station Museum, Northern Territory

Police incident report No.106, dated 14 June 1947
Thomas 'Nugget' Reardon, stockman on Bradshaw/Coolibah Station, Victoria River District, stated that while looking for stray cattle in the far north of the run early in the month, he discovered wreckage scattered along a beach opposite Quoin Island near the mouth of the Victoria River. The debris appeared to Reardon to be from a timber vessel and included part of a mast as well as a fragment of a transom on which he could discern the letters 'e d a'. Reardon reported the find to the Bradshaw/Coolibah Station manager who passed it on to Sergeant Jeffries of the Timber Creek constabulary. Sgt. Jeffries subsequently visited the site and confirmed the report.

No vessels have been reported missing in the region recently. Investigators think the wreckage is older and may have been dislodged from under the reef shelf in Quoin Island passage by cyclone *Winifred* and accompanying tidal surge that occurred in February this year. This hypothesis is backed by the Bureau of Meteorology, Darwin.

A search of the records raises the possibility the wreckage is from the lugger *Frieda* which vanished without trace from its mooring at the Lutheran mission on the Fitzmaurice River in January 1943 along with the mission superintendent Pastor Hans Müller. Müller, an Australian of German birth, was briefly interned under the provisions of the National Security Act in 1940, but judged no threat and allowed back to his work at the Fitzmaurice Mission. Despite his release, his presence in the region was linked to rumours of collaboration with Japanese forces poised to invade the Australian mainland. Pastor Müller's disappearance gave strength to the rumours. His body was never found and the disappearance remains unresolved.

Signed: George Jeffries (Sgt, Timber Creek Constabulary)

Item 2:
Article from the *Territory News*, Saturday 5 December 1987

Who left the 303?
Mystery surrounds the ownership of a .303 rifle left on the steps of the Timber Creek police station this week. The weapon was found by the duty officer when he arrived for his shift early on Monday morning. There was no note and nothing to indicate why it had been left deliberately unattended. The rifle was not loaded, but residue in the barrel suggests it had been fired recently.

A police spokesman said markings on the rifle identified it as a Lithgow SMLE No.1 MkIII* (short magazine Lee-Enfield made by the Lithgow Small Arms Factory in New South Wales) universally known as a 303 and used by Australian troops during World War 2.

Of the serial number, only the letter D, followed by the

numbers 79 were legible. Firearms experts say the 'D' signifies it was manufactured in late 1941 or 1942, but a search of army records has failed to trace its precise provenance. Police are appealing for anyone with information about the weapon to come forward.

(J.L. Stokes – Journal entry 10 November 1839)

… We were very cautious in choosing our sleeping berth for the night, to avoid a surprise during the dark; we therefore selected a friendly hollow beneath the stem of a straggling and drooping old gum tree, large enough to conceal the whole party, ….

Chapter 1

October 1987

Bradley Dixon flinched at the sudden loud reports, two in quick succession that seemed to be just outside his room.

Gun shots? Bloody hell! Surely no one would fire a gun so near the camp.

Putting the journal down, he rose from the bed and opened his door a chink to listen. The familiar background rumble of the drilling rig filled the night, but nothing seemed amiss. He stepped onto the boardwalk skirting the line of Atco accommodation huts and looked about, squinting in the glare of the floodlights.

A tousled head and bare torso appeared in the hut doorway two along. Ethan Williams tweezered sleep from his eyes with thumb and forefinger. 'You hear it too? What's goin' on?' His voice husky.

Brad shrugged. 'Nothing at the rig anyway. Sounded like shots out in the scrub. Roo shooters, station hands maybe?'

Williams grunted and shook his head. 'No panic then.' He glanced briefly at the derrick dominating the brightly lit camp before retreating into his room without further comment.

'Surly bastard,' Brad muttered at the closed door.

Chapter 1 October 1987

The drilling supervisor had been on the plane from Melbourne with Brad. He hadn't said much then either, apart from the fact that he'd been up earlier to examine the well site before the rig moved in. The rest of the flight Williams divided between reading James Michener's *Texas* and snoring in rasp-like bursts, his head pressed into a pillow against the window.

Brad, a new chum to the Bonaparte Basin, would have appreciated a bit more local background to the Stokes-1 wildcat. As a geological contractor he was used to well-sitting jobs at short notice, but this one had been exceptionally swift. The previous geo had been evacuated with acute appendicitis. Able Exploration was a private company—a one-man band with no staff geologists.

Brad moved back to his own doorway, then changed his mind. Stokes' journal lay open on his bed, but a coffee seemed a better plan. He sauntered along the boardwalk towards the mess hut. The night air was warm and still, with a touch of mugginess that signalled the build-up to the Wet.

Brad glanced across the drilling pad to the rig, its constant rumble a reassurance of the norm, like the clacking suburban trains passing the back fence of his childhood home in Melbourne. The oblong layout for the Stokes-1 well program was much the same as for other land rigs he had worked on in his five years with the consulting firm, but less claustrophobic than the offshore rigs and platforms in Bass Strait where he spent the first seven years after graduation. One thing though, all rigs boasted a kitchen stocked with good food and ample helpings, open around the clock.

Brad pushed the mess door and went in. No one at the tables, but he heard the clatter of pans in the galley. Preparations for the day-shift breakfast and the end of night-shift 'evening' meal. He crossed to the coffee station, threw a spoonful of instant grounds into a mug, added hot water from the urn and took a sip, wrinkling his nose.

'I'd kill for a decent coffee,' he said to the urn, thinking of the cappuccino parlours he could frequent in Melbourne.

'Complaints go to management, not the kitchen staff.'

Brad swung round, sloshing coffee on his wrist. A girl leaning across the servery grinned at him. A white kitchen tunic hid her figure, but he caught the mischief of blue eyes and pretty dimpled cheeks. A wisp of blond hair escaped from under the regulation elasticated white gauze bonnet.

'No complaints about the food,' he said, 'but a proper coffee machine would be nice.'

'You've only been here three days and already you pine for city service.'

'How do you know it has been three days?' Brad had not noticed the girl before.

'You see a lot from behind here.'

'Well, come out and join me. I'll pour you a cup and you can convince me it's as good as the city.'

'Love to, but I'm tied to the bench back there.'

'Lucy! Carrots to chop. Back to work.'

'See what I mean.'

The girl pouted and pushed back from the servery as the large frame of the camp chef-cum-catering manager loomed into view. Wearing a tall white hat, blue and white checked trousers and a white tunic stretched tight across his ample belly, Charlie Camilleri was everyone's vision of a cook. His friendly, garrulous nature and laugh lines etched into a swarthy complexion completed the caricature.

Chapter 1 October 1987

'Go see the Malteser,' everyone said when Brad first arrived at the rig. 'He'll give you all you need to know… and plenty you don't.' And they'd been right. Charlie had immediately launched into his experiences in Malta as a child during the privations of the war years in the 1940s; how he helped tend the garden in the family plot. 'Mama would say go get dinner. Turn over some rocks. I would find snails and put them in a tin 'till they shitted out their stomachs, you unnustand what I mean? Otherwise they taste bad. Mama boiled them up and we have with bread and garlic. My first lesson to prepare food!'

He then talked about his emigration to Australia in the 1960s and his travels all over the country since. 'Been right round—never same road twice, you unnustand. Then I can make another line for my map.' Charlie had pointed to a battered Texta colour-filled Shell Road Map tacked onto the mess hut wall. A camp wag had labelled it "Travels with Charlie." 'This a good place here. Your first time? You'll like it.'

Now Brad watched as the chef playfully flicked a towel in Lucy's direction before making his way over to Brad's table.

'Cheeky monkey,' he said. 'I can sit down?'

'Where have you been hiding her?' Brad asked.

Charlie pulled out a chair and took off his hat, revealing a bald central patch between tufts of greying hair about his ears.

'Don't get ideas. I see you look,' he said, wagging a fat finger. 'I want no kitchen troubles. Anyway, take the Malteser's warning. She boss's niece. Unnustand what I mean?'

'The boss—Able?'

'Yes.'

'How did that happen, her working here with you I mean?'

'Oh, I know Abel a while. I fix his wheel along the road one time. We camp. I make meal. He like it. We talk. Then he offer job as rig cook for a well he is drilling in Queensland. I been cook on all his wells since.'

Brad had trouble picturing Able as a road traveller. Private jets seemed more his style, but maybe he did in earlier days.

'Anyway,' Charlie continued, 'he ask me for taking Lucy on this well—kitchen experience before she go to cooking school next year. Why not? She works good. But she not for you, unnustand? Bad enough to keep rig boys away.

Brad grinned. 'Got it.'

'Reg Able pretty smart guy,' Charlie said. 'In resources game all his life. Sharebroker first, then his own companies. You know him?'

Brad shook his head. 'Half an hour, tops. But he came across as a bit of a maverick.'

He'd received the call a week ago, rushed into the city to meet Reginald Able for lunch and was boarding the plane at dawn next day. He had planned a fortnight off after the last job in western Victoria, but he couldn't decline the consultancy's urgent request. Debra had been incandescent, especially when he couldn't tell her much about the work or the company, only that it was in far northeast Western Australia near the Northern Territory border.

Able had sped through lunch with Brad before he too caught a plane—to London. In his fifties, short and slight, prominent nose and penetrating eyes, he'd been dressed casually for travel: slip-on canvas shoes, jeans and an open-neck check shirt. Brad wished he hadn't taken the trouble to put on a coat and tie for the meeting. On arrival at the rig he soon learnt that the entrepreneurial company founder and CEO was always on a plane to somewhere, making the rounds of company offices, doing deals and shaking the hands of politicians, financiers,

Chapter 1 October 1987

dignitaries, even royalty on some occasions.

Charlie tapped the side of his nose. 'I learn to have faith in Reg. You unnustand.'

This time it wasn't a question. Brad decided not to pursue it. Instead he brought up the disturbance earlier. It still puzzled him.

'Charlie, you know these parts pretty well, do the station hands often go hunting at night?'

'Not here. Homestead too far. Too far for town boys also. Why you asking?'

'Oh, I thought I heard a couple of gun shots tonight. They seemed pretty close to camp. I don't think it was anything to do with the rig.'

Charlie leant back in his chair. 'Ah. You hear them. Yes it has connection with the rig, a little bit I think. Same thing when we first arrive and again last week.'

'They were shots then?'

'Yes. The old bloke, but in the air. Not serious at anyone.'

'Doesn't sound friendly. Who's the old bloke?'

Charlie came forward again, placing his elbows on the table. 'Some old bush man. Locals call him scrub bull 'cos he acts… how you say … cantankerous when you go near. He has shack off the station track to mustering yards. The road for rig passes close. You maybe seen his place on the way here.'

Brad shook his head. 'I noticed some yards, but no hut.'

'It's nearby. Anyway, the old bloke doesn't like intruders. He fire off his gun one time when young jackeroos try to spook him after night in town. Silly buggers. The station manager says leave him be. He do no harm.'

'So what's his beef with the rig?'

Charlie shrugged. 'Some older town peoples say he was

Nackeroo in the war.'

'A what!?'

'Nackeroo. I forget the proper name—Northern Australian Brigade—something like this. Soldiers sent up north in case of Japanese coming. Maybe this was his place for patrol. Station manager say some rumour of a trouble for him from back then. No one is sure and no one gets close to find out.'

Charlie stood up. 'Not to lose sleep for this. No terrorists in the night. Anyway, for me there is meal to prepare.'

Brad watched the Malteser's large backside disappear into the kitchen before he too rose and made his way back to his room, his curiosity aroused.

Chapter 2

September 1942

Corporal Douglas "Ash" Ashmore slapped his cheek and examined the smudge of blood on his palm. His blood. 'Blasted mosquitoes. Swarms of them.' He moved closer to the fire to get his body into the smoke. His eyes began to water, but it was better than being eaten alive.

Beside him Sam Greenwood laughed. 'You'll have to get used to them Corp. This is their territory.'

'Theirs and the bloody crocs,' drawled the lanky Queenslander, Stretch Middleton, from the other side of the flames. 'We ought to let the Japs have it. Serve them right.'

Ash grunted. They could make light of it but the reality was much darker. Since the Japanese incursions into New Guinea, all Australia from the Prime Minister down was spooked by the thought of invasion through the country's defenceless north. Entry anywhere from Cape York to Onslow was a logical next step. So here they were, three Nackeroos and an Aboriginal tracker, patrolling down the Victoria River in the Northern Territory waiting for them.

Ash wiped his eyes. It was ludicrous. They were hardly equipped to stop any invasion. In fact they had been ordered not to try—a directive from the top. Major Stanner had made it crystal clear when the whole force paraded in Katherine. They were not to engage the enemy unless it was absolutely necessary. Instead, their job was to observe without being seen; let the invaders pass, then follow and remain behind enemy lines to report their movements. The task of the North Australia Observation Unit, Stanner had said, was to set up coast surveillance and reconnaissance patrols on horseback. They were to carry their own supplies, including wireless equipment, and stay out in the bush as long as was called for. They had to be bush shadows, blend in and live off the land.

The NAOU's Katherine parade had been at the end of August. After that the force split into three companies—four if you counted the men who stayed in Katherine general headquarters. The soldiers quickly dispensed with the clumsy unit name and proudly referred to themselves as the Nackeroos, an irreverent combination of horse knackery and jackeroo. Corporal Ashmore and a group of about 140 others were assigned to B-Company whose patrol area encompassed a wide arc around the southern Bonaparte Gulf, including Timber Creek and the Victoria River district and west into the Kimberley as far as the Ord River catchment and Wyndham at the bottom of Cambridge Gulf. B-Company headquarters was established at Ivanhoe, south of Wyndham, but Ash found himself assigned to the eastern area base at The Depot at Timber Creek.

To get there, the men and their equipment had been stacked high on to what had seemed an endless convoy of blitz wagons for the tortuous trip along the dirt track out of Katherine towards Victoria River Downs station, then up to Timber Creek. The men took it in turns to sit on the front mudguards

Chapter 2 September 1942

out of the dust. On some stretches the trucks sank to their axles in it. The men had to get down to lighten the load. The journey reminded Ash of his earlier contribution to the war.

Born in 1910 and brought up on his father's gut-wrenching tales from the trenches of the Great War, he had vowed he'd never willingly get involved in such a bloody conflict. But he forgot that in the early fervour of the new call to arms, leaving his fiancé and his job as a motor mechanic in Melbourne to join the AIF in 1940 and shipping off to the Middle East. He saw plenty of action, but not his father's sort. Instead Ash fought the steering wheel of a three-ton truck weaving around shell holes in Palestine and, later, out from Cairo into the desert. Short and slightly built compared to the broad shoulders and brawny arms of many of the drivers, his experience with engines tipped the scale, a knowledge that came to the rescue more than once for make-shift repairs on the road. It suited him to have a roving mission, not confined to the static discipline of the ranks. He carried loads of whatever was needed to and from the front lines: medical supplies, food, munitions, even stretcher cases when field ambulances were busy elsewhere.

Suddenly it was over. Ash was on a troop ship back to Australia, the AIF recalled by Prime Minister Curtin in mid-1942 to defend home ground. Arriving in Melbourne, he found his fiancé enjoying the favours of an American lieutenant and immediately broke off the engagement, feeling strangely relieved yet bemused at his lack of remorse. He spent his month of leave alone, borrowing a car for a few days from his former employer, cadging extra petrol coupons and driving to the ocean at Anglesea. Strolling along the empty beach, the war seemed unreal even though he knew it was just over the northern horizon.

Most of the returned Australian troops anticipated service in New Guinea. Ash did too. It seemed the only place to be to stop the Japanese advance. He realised there would be no call for drivers outside Port Moresby and resigned himself to a return to the rigidity of the infantry ranks. Watching the sea hump into crests of foaming white rollers that swept froth across the sand to his feet, he had no inkling that fate had something else in store.

Returning to the city, Ash retrieved his kit from the boarding house and set out for the barracks. Soon after reporting for duty, he saw a cluster of men around the unit's notice board. The memorandum causing all the fuss called for volunteers for a unit to operate in northern Australia. The idea intrigued him. Applicants had to be medically fit, have bush experience, horsemanship, initiative, the ability to handle weapons. A knowledge of signals would be an advantage. In the panicked aftermath of the bombing of Darwin and the more recent Japanese midget submarine infiltration of Sydney Harbour, all talk in newspapers and in the barracks was of impending invasion. Ash thought the new unit was likely to be right in the thick of the action. He'd always wanted to see the Australian north and he liked the sound of the NAOU outfit's free-wheeling commando-style. He reckoned he'd qualify even if his bush experience only amounted to some rabbiting weekends in the Dandenongs and a trip to Wilson's Promontory. He'd never ridden a horse, but steering a bucking truck through the Middle East would surely count in his favour.

Ash received his selection notice one Sunday morning accompanied by orders to move out immediately. Four hours later he was on a train to an interim training camp at Ingleburn southwest of Sydney. Within weeks the new unit moved to

Chapter 2   September 1942

Katherine. Then Ash found himself in Timber Creek with a pair of stripes on his sleeve, given because of his age and overseas experience. Many of the other recruits, like Privates Greenwood and Middleton, were 10 years younger. They'd spent the first part of 1942 in army camps in the south, frustrated because they were being used as casual labour at the docks and railyards instead of being in a fighting unit. For them, volunteering for the NAOU had been an attractive way out.

Ash had serious doubts there'd be much restraint if they did happen on any Japanese during their patrols. Most of the men were itching for a chance to fight. They didn't join up to just look. Ash wasn't even sure what his own reactions would be if they encountered the enemy. As the nominal leader of this little party, he had to ensure that the hide and seek policy was upheld. He kept the relationship casual. Rank and seniority hadn't cut much ice when it came to catching, saddling and riding the horses bought or requisitioned from the local cattle stations. Ash had numerous spills before he started to get the hang of it. Greenwood and Middleton were country boys and much more adept. Sam was a farm hand from the wheat-belt near Clare in South Australia and Stretch had been cutting cane around Proserpine before joining up. Horses were part of everyday life to them. Ash remained a novice and had the bruises to prove it. Still, it beat walking. He leaned back again, away from the smoke and reflected on the day's traverse.

The Lieutenant in command at The Depot had sent a separate patrol overland to Wyndham to requisition a boat for transporting men and supplies up and down the Victoria River. Before its arrival the Lieutenant wanted Ash's group to reconnoitre the Victoria region because the available maps were sketchy and unreliable. His orders were to make a sweep north along the river from The Depot to Bradshaw station homestead at the junction with the Ikymbon River, then on to Blunder Bay where the Victoria widened as it approached the sea. That was generally accepted as the closest point navigable by large boats. The enemy would likely establish a base there before probing up-stream in shallow-draft vessels and sending foot patrols into the hinterland.

Ash's party had to scout for any signs of Japanese incursion, find the best places for the Nackeroos to set up satellite bases to keep a watch on the river and be in radio communication with The Depot. Few Europeans had been in the region apart from some early explorers and, more recently, those connected with the cattle stations on either side of the river. Most of the Aboriginal inhabitants were now congregated at the mission on the Fitzmaurice River to the northeast or were employed as stockmen on the surrounding runs.

Ash climbed a sandstone knoll above The Depot camp on the morning before they set out. He gazed at low-lying scrubby country of yellow grasses and scattered white-trunked gums, thickest along the banks of the broad, dirty-blue band of river that curved across his vision in a series of wide arcs. The Pinkerton and Yambarran Ranges drew an uneven line along the horizon, indistinct in the heat haze that hung like a cloying wet curtain. Ash thought about trying to cut across country to short circuit some of the river's meanders, but decided against it. They might miss some evidence or clue of a foreign presence. When the patrol moved out next morning he left the lead to Gabriel, their Aboriginal guide, trusting the local man to find the best path.

Ash estimated they'd made about 25 miles that day. It had

Chapter 2 September 1942

been hard going across tidal mud flats where their passing sent basking crocodiles sliding into the water. The soldiers eyed these reptiles nervously. Gabriel continued, unconcerned, and it was only when the horses broke through the crust into syrupy ooze that he led them to higher ground.

They moved out onto the plain where the grasses brushed their boots and pot-bellied boab trees stood like sentinels with straggly arms reaching for the sky. They crossed waterless gullies carved into the plateau where creeks ran into the Victoria during the wet season. One, packed with dense undergrowth laced with vines that snagged legs and saddles and equipment, was fed by a natural spring where they thankfully replenished their flasks. As the day wore on the temperature rose and shirts darkened with sweat. For Ash it was a sobering introduction to the free-wheeling bush life he had let himself in for.

At Gabriel's suggestion, he called a halt in mid-afternoon. They unsaddled the horses and threw their bed rolls in the shade of acacias on a rise overlooking the river flats, a safe distance from the crocodiles that lay like a row of logs at the water's edge. He was surprised when Gabriel immediately set off down the slope with the horses. The others watched for a moment, then followed warily, rifles in their hands.

Gabriel led them around a bend to the head of a narrow gully where a trickle of water slid down the rock into a shallow pool blocked off from the river by a stony bar. 'Good water boss,' he said. 'No tide long here.'

'You knew this place Gabriel?'

The Aborigine grinned. 'Yes boss. Been plenty time.'

As the horses drank their fill, Ash stood guard while an emboldened Sam and then Stretch splashed about, shirtless and knee deep. Sam's fair hair and tanned, muscular torso contrasted with his mate's dark thatch and tall, wiry, but equally sun-browned frame.

'Your turn Corp.'

Conscious of his white skin below the neckline, Ash contented himself with dunking his shirt and hanging the dripping cloth around his shoulders. When he stepped out Gabriel handed over the reins and retrieved the .22 rifle he had lain on the gravel.

'Get tucker, boss,' he said and walked further around the bend. About an hour later Gabriel returned holding up three limp, long-necked birds. 'Magpie goose. Good tucker, boss,' he said, obviously pleased with his haul. It had been good tucker too, cooked in the coals and torn apart in their hands. The only thing missing was a cold beer. They'd made do with tea, the leaves flung into a billy of boiling water hung over the fire.

Night fell before they had finished, intensifying the mystique of the land in the darkness beyond the camp perimeter. The occasional bird call, a rustle in the undergrowth and, nearer at hand, a snort from the horses hobbled in the shadows were the only sounds as the soldiers sat watching the flames. Gabriel stayed a little apart even though Ash had urged him to join the ring.

It had not been Ash's place to choose the members of his party. Gabriel had been selected as a guide for the patrol by the Lieutenant who had assigned Greenwood and Middleton. In B-Company a group of Aboriginals were attached to the ranks to fulfil various tasks like tracking, guiding and horse tailing. In the main, the Nackeroos treated them as integral members of the Company, providing them with the same food

Chapter 2   September 1942

and sleeping quarters as the soldiers. The few instances of white race superiority were quickly stamped on.

Some of the Aboriginals, like Gabriel, spoke English and they were called in as interpreters when communicating with local tribes. Ash guessed that Gabriel had been educated at the mission where most of the children were given Christian names related to the Bible. Gabriel was in his early 20s, tall and surprisingly broad-shouldered, unlike many of the gaunt Aboriginals seen around The Depot. The characteristic broad nose and lips of his race were well proportioned in an oval face set with intelligent brown eyes and fringed with dark, straight hair cropped short around his ears; his dark chocolate skin lightened to tan on his palms. He held himself erect, proud of the task entrusted to him; his manner respectful without being servile.

Ash was impressed with Gabriel's quiet confidence, unhurried and sure of his surroundings. In the bush his skills would be invaluable if they did come across a Japanese force somewhere along the river. Gabriel would have to lead the Nackeroos in close so they could study and report on the enemy's strength and movements. It would be torture and death if they were caught. Ash wondered whether he, or the Nackeroo command in general for that matter, had the right to ask the Aboriginal scouts to take such risks when in civilian life they were treated as anything but equal.

The thought troubled him as he looked across at Gabriel stretched out on his swag on the other side of the fire. Ash lifted his gaze to the shadows of the surrounding scrub, acknowledging the bond of the Aboriginal to his land. The Japanese had no place here. The Nackeroos were invaders too when it came down to it.

Ash slapped his cheek as the mosquitoes resumed their attack. He glanced at the sprawling branches of the trees flickering in the firelight near his bedroll.

'I'm going to turn in,' he said quietly. 'A lot of ground to cover yet, so a dawn start tomorrow.'

Chapter 3

September 1987

Brad Dixon stared into the mirror over the basins in the ablution block. Blue eyes, straggly fair hair, bushy eyebrows and prominent nose set in a pale face looked back at him. A well-proportioned mouth was spoilt by the beginnings of a double chin. He'd tried to grow a beard once, in the bush because he couldn't be bothered shaving. It turned out to be wispy and gingery. He'd shaved his cheeks and chin clean after two weeks and resigned himself to the daily chore he disliked. A razor blade left a rash on his skin, so he carried a battery job now.

Brad had never tanned easily either. In childhood his mother hounded him to use sunscreen and wear a hat. Then later, in her letters: "I'll bet the sun is hot enough to wear two hats out where you are" and "I saw in the chemist that a 50+ cream is available now. I'll send a couple of tubes if you can't get it out there".

Cancer was a horror word in his family. His father died of it, although it was smoking and lung cancer that got him— brought on by the trauma of war the Legacy people had said. Brad was never sure if they meant his dad smoked to soothe memories of the war or that the war experience weakened his lungs and made him more susceptible to the tar. He was a 50-a-day man and died a month short of his sixtieth birthday. Brad had been on the Mackerel gas platform in Bass Strait when he got the call. The company had immediately given him compassionate leave and he was home on the next chopper. 1980. Not that long ago really. Brad was 35 now, the only one left.

His mother died two years ago. There was no such thing as a broken heart, but she never got over the loss of Brad's brother. James didn't see his first birthday, born and gone in the year after his father returned from the war. Brad always wondered if sorrow was the reason his mother had waited so long to try again. He remembered the times when she withdrew with tears in her eyes at mention of his brother's name. Sometimes, especially when she was angry with him for a misdemeanour, Brad took it into his head that she didn't love him; that he might be second best in her affections. The impression stuck with him through childhood. Brad compensated by constructing a shell, steeling himself not to rely on or worry what others thought. As he grew older he began to comprehend her sorrow. He realised he had been unfair and hurtful. Gradually the relationship with his mother warmed. But his crust of self-preservation remained and, when the time came, he had no compunction in leaving the nest.

Looking back, his father's passing must have upset the already delicate balance—no one else at home for his mother to care for. Heart attack the hospital told him. Once again he was away on a job. And he felt guilty all over again, even though no one ever blamed him for his absences, not to his face anyway.

Brad broke off his reverie as Wingnut, one of the roughnecks, entered the shower block, a towel over his shoulder and a calico

Chapter 3 September 1987

sample bag containing his toiletries in his hand. An amiable youngster in his early twenties, his large ears sticking straight out of his skull had earned him the lasting nick-name. He took it in good part, laughing about trying to find a hard hat with a wide enough brim to protect his upper extremities. Wingnut flung the towel on a hook and walked into the shower recess.

'Gotta get spruced up a bit for breakfast. You seen that little honey in the kitchen?'

Brad laughed. 'Good luck. You'll need to get past the Malteser first.'

'Yeah. Don't know why he's so protective. Probably wants her for himself, the old bastard. Well I can look anyway … and dream. Makes the shift go quicker. Only a week now and I'll be back in Perth on the shag. The most willing sheilas in the country down there. They like to guide me in by my handles.' Wingnut's cackle drowned in the gush of water from the shower head.

Brad smiled and left the roughneck to it. Wandering over to the mess, he found himself next to Ethan Williams in the breakfast queue. After filling their plates they headed over to the same table. Two roustabouts pushed back their chairs, nodding a greeting before leaving Brad and Williams to themselves.

'You hear any more from the shooter last night?' Williams' face twisted in a smirk.

'No, but I got a bit of a rundown from the Malteser. Did you know about him?'

'Yeah. The old geezer's done it before. He's got a chip on his shoulder about anyone intruding on his patch. I asked the police in town after the last time. They said he's harmless. The best thing is to just ignore it.'

'Charlie said he was up here during the war. And there was some sort of trouble he'd got into.'

'So I've heard. Could be bullshit, but who knows. I don't give a damn as long as he doesn't get serious with that gun. Hopefully we'll be out of here pretty soon anyway. I don't fancy getting stuck here for Christmas in the Wet.'

Brad watched as Williams stabbed a sausage, his beefy hand grasping the fork near its prongs. The drilling super had just delivered the longest speech that Brad had heard him utter since sharing the plane ride in. He seized the moment.

'I've been meaning to ask. Back in Melbourne Able gave me a copy of John Lort Stokes' *Discoveries in Australia* about his voyage in the *Beagle* around northern Australia in the 1830s. So I've figured out the well is named after him. But I can't find a connection. Stokes was exploring around the Victoria River. That's over in the NT. Not close enough for a name association. Any idea why Able chose it?'

'Didn't you ask him?'

'No. The book was left for me when I checked in at the airport. I can't think why. His note just said I might find it interesting.'

'God knows. That's Able for you. He'll have a reason, but he likes his intrigues.' Williams gave a cynical grunt, drained his coffee and got to his feet. 'Anyway, back to work. We'll be tripping all morning. The formation at the moment is a bastard on bits.'

Brad watched the drilling super make his way across the mess. Near the door he stopped to have a word with the night-shift driller before continuing through the exit. The rig crew seemed to tolerate Williams' brusque manner. They grinned and called him Sourpuss out of his hearing, but his

Chapter 3 September 1987

authority was respected. Not an easy job being responsible for maintaining discipline and deadlines and keeping an unpredictable character like Able happy at the same time. Rather him than me, Brad mused. He had no ambitions for any command. Some of his contemporaries from university were chief geologists and one was already an exploration manager. Brad had equal experience, but he preferred the unshackled, if less certain, life of a consultant. He persuaded himself that he wasn't just drifting.

He finished a second coffee before adding his dirty mug and plate to the pile on the servery. Outside, he headed to the mud-logging hut. Aaron Davey looked up from a microscope as he entered.

'Getting ready to begin the trip out,' he said. 'This limestone is tough. It knackered the last bit quick time.'

'Where are we?' Brad asked.

'480 metres.'

'A way to go yet then. Let's have a look at the log.'

'I reckon we might be flying blind.'

'What makes you say that?'

'Well, I've been looking at these limestone cuttings under the microscope. The composition doesn't tally with what we are expecting.'

Aaron, with his shock of black hair and olive skin was junior to Brad and a recent graduate from the University of Western Australia, but he was keen. Brad stepped over to the microscope and peered at the dark granules on the glass tray underneath.

'You could be right. But the nearest well is 100 kilometres away, so correlation is iffy at best.' Brad shrugged. He picked up the mud log and moved over to the desk to write the day's report. That done he yawned, stretching his arms over his head. Aaron looked across.

'Those gunshots last night keep you awake? You hear about our local nutter?'

Brad related his conversations with Charlie and Williams.

'I've never heard of the Nackeroos,' Aaron said. 'My uncle was in New Guinea. Funny thing, he was in Bougainville near the end of the war and he told me once that the Japs would come up close in the hills around the base at night to watch the movies the Yanks put on the big screen in camp. It's kinda like this old bloke watching the rig from the shadows. Pretty creepy stuff.'

'Yeah, well I hope he doesn't make a habit of it.' Brad got up and took his hard hat off the peg by the door. 'Think I'll get this report sent off and wander over to the drill floor.'

The ground across to the rig, churned to a pale yellow powder by the constant vehicle traffic, puffed up around Brad's ankles with each step. He saw Lucy sitting in the sun outside the mess with one of the kitchen hands. Freed of the constricting bonnet, her blond hair fell below her shoulders. She caught sight of him and waved. Brad waved back, but didn't stop although he was tempted. No point in provoking Charlie's displeasure. He moved on past the pipe racks and the mud tanks to the steps leading up to the drill floor.

The rig wasn't new, but it did have a relatively fresh coat of paint. The derrick gleamed white, the substructure a royal blue, and the railings a canary yellow. Brad wondered idly whether someone had deliberately invoked a Mediterranean feel. He mounted the steps, saluted the driller busy with his winch levers and lent on a rail outside the open door out of the way. The noise of the rig motor made talk impossible anyway. The

Chapter 3   September 1987

pitch increased as the winches took the strain of lifting 400 metres of drill pipe out of the hole.

From the drill floor Wingnut winked at Brad as he and his fellow roughnecks got ready to handle the next 30 metre length of pipe. As the pipe joint came into view the driller applied the brake. One of the roughnecks quickly wrapped conically-shaped metal slips around the pipe below the joint. The driller lowered the pipe back down until the slips jammed it firmly in the rotary table. Then two of the men swung the pair of heavy tongs across to snap shut on the pipe—one above, one below the joint to pull in opposite directions and break the seal, enabling the top length to be screwed off and swung clear. Immediately a gush of drilling mud spilled from the bottom of the freed pipe and the drill floor was awash with slippery grey fluid. One of the crew grabbed a hose to sluice it away while the others pulled the detached pipe to the side for stacking. At the same time the derrickman working high in the rig mast unshackled the top of the pipe length and pushed it into the rack beside him. The driller released the brake and the winch block rushed back down to the drill floor where the roughnecks quickly attached it to the pipe in the hole and removed the slips so that lifting could continue.

Brad never ceased to be amazed at the speed and coordination of a good rig crew during a tripping operation, choreographed like a working man's ballet—not that the tough roughnecks would like to hear it described that way. There was strength involved, but you didn't need to be Atlas. An equal measure of fitness and good balance was required. Experience also helped, but danger always lurked.

Wingnut worked the upper tongs. After breaking the next

seal, he detached and swung them away. Somewhere in that motion he lost concentration, his boot caught and his upper leg continued round with the weight of his body. Yelping in pain he fell backwards, flinging his arms into the arc of the detached pipe that was haemorrhaging drilling fluid. Caught by surprise, the roughneck guiding the pipe lost his grip and the full weight of the pendulum caught Wingnut's right arm against the steel handle of the tongs. Brad didn't hear the bone snap, but he saw the unnatural bend of the limb between the elbow and wrist. Beside him there was a blur of action as the driller leapt out of the doghouse, skidded across the greasy drill floor and grabbed the swinging pipe before it could complete a second arc. One of the roughnecks rushed forward to help him steady it. The other took Wingnut under the shoulders and tried to pull him clear, but the cascading mud made the task impossible on his own.

'Give us a hand, for Christ's sake!'

Brad broke free of his inertia, reached across to take hold of Wingnut's good arm and together they dragged the limp body to the landing where Brad had stood a moment before. As the rig crew regained control and secured the detached pipe, Wingnut stirred and gasped.

'Fuck that hurts.'

Brad squatted and wiped the mud off his face. 'Stay still till we know how bad it is.'

The driller joined him. 'Shit! This is gunna need more than first aid. Old Sourpuss will go ballistic. And I'll have to roust one of the night crew.'

Wingnut grimaced. 'Sorry boss.' He turned to Brad. 'I guess I'll get to Perth sooner than I expected.'

Chapter 4

October 1942

Corporal Ashmore squinted across the river through the midday haze at the conical shape of Endeavour Hill sloping down to the curve of Blunder Bay. In the middle distance the Victoria split into two channels around Entrance Island, then re-joined in a wide expanse that flowed on towards open sea in the Bonaparte Gulf.

'We need to get over there for a look around. What chance of crossing here Gabriel?'

'Alright when tide low Boss. Might be little bit swim.'

Stretch Middleton swore. 'Bugger that! What about the crocs?'

Sam laughed. 'I thought you Queenslanders were up for anything. Don't worry, I'll fire off a few rounds before we set out. Scare them off.'

'You reckon? Well, I sure as hell aren't going to be tail-end Charlie.'

At slack tide, the horses waded up to their bellies most of the way and then swam across the deepest channel with the men beside them holding on to the saddles. For the last half mile they floundered through thigh-deep mud, stumbling over mangrove roots to reach firm ground above the level of high tide.

'Blunder Bay; Blunder in. Bloody well named,' Stretch grumbled as he scraped the mud from his legs. 'So much for a cleansing swim.'

'This way Boss.'

Gabriel led the way through the scrub, the ground rising gradually towards a low ridge.

'Well, I'm jiggered!'

Sam spoke for them all as they came upon a creek running fresh water. Following it upstream for another hundred yards they were even more surprised to find the spring bubbled down the rocks into a shallow waterhole bordered by Pandanus palms, stringy barks and several large boabs. Nearby, a wall of sandstone provided a natural shelter, the level ground in front of it sufficient to accommodate a camp of five or six men screened from the air by the surrounding scrub; behind them a clear view of the river rapidly engulfing the mud flats on the incoming tide. They went back to fetch the horses and afterwards stripped off to sluice themselves clean in the waterhole, relishing the knowledge that here at least it was croc-free.

Later, Ash sat with his back against the wall making mental notes for his report. Gabriel came up beside him.

'A good place, Gabriel. You have been before?'

'Yes Boss. Sometimes. Water not always so much.'

'You mean the waterhole can be dry?'

'Little bit. Maybe too much horse.'

'Too many horses. Are there brumbies round here?'

Sam laughed. 'Spoken like a true city boy, Corp. I think he

means there's not enough water for us to sustain horses for very long. The level went down quickly just with our four.'

Stretch grimaced. 'You're talking foot patrols only, then. Christ, that'll be fun in this heat.'

Ash weighed up the pros and cons. The place would serve well as The Depot platoon's forward post. Horses weren't essential, but it did mean the coast watchers would be confined to the immediate surrounds for several months at a time, a radio the only link to the outside world. Except by boat, presuming the Wyndham party had secured one. Some men would handle the solitude without going stir crazy. Some wouldn't. Boredom and loneliness could be as much an enemy as the Japanese.

The Nackeroos' equipment, including the heavy wireless set and several months of rations, would have to be ferried downriver and manhandled through the mud and mangroves to reach firm ground. Not a pleasant task in the baking sun and increasing humidity. With the Wet season approaching, any prolonged exertion would bring even the strongest man to a standstill. Ash thought it might actually be better when the rains began. But the Lieutenant wanted the forward base established before then: camouflaged shelters, wireless aerial deployed for best reception and observation nests in various spots.

Ash knew that Bradshaw, fifty miles to the south, would be a comparative paradise. He hadn't delayed the patrol long there because the station homestead and its plentiful fresh water piped from a spring in the nearby Yambarran Range were obvious attributes for a Nackeroo camp. It was within relatively easy reach of the platoon's headquarters at The Depot and could support any number of riding horses and pack animals.

Ash had marked Bradshaw as an ideal place to begin land

patrols inland to the east across to the Fitzmaurice River mission. A forward base at Blunder Bay would enable foot patrols to the west, with the proviso that the men be relieved at regular intervals.

* * *

Early next morning from the summit of Endeavour Hill the Nackeroos scanned the vast expanse of brown water swirling around an S-bend in the river below. The tide was full, the mud banks covered. They looked across Blunder Bay to where the wedge shape of Entrance Island sat mid-river and Queens Channel shimmered in the haze to the north. No vessel of any kind could anchor or pass unnoticed, during the day at least, if the coast watchers were doing their job. Entrance Island would be the place for a base supplied from the sea. Ash knew his report would not be complete without scouting the island for any signs of the enemy, past or present.

To the south the rugged terrain they had traversed in the last five days resembled an enormous wrinkled green, yellow and brown tapestry. In the middle distance the long strait of river marked on the map as Holdfast Reach had cut through a series of low ridges—eroded remnants of tilted folds sweeping across the land in broad arcs defined by bands of trees, dark green against the yellow grasses. Closer to hand the country was dominated by a flat-topped range, some parts whittled into a series of mesas whose sloping approaches were capped by dark cliffs that rose above the plain like prehistoric forts. The city boy in Ash saw the landscape as primeval, daunting, yet strangely enticing.

'Christ.' Sam swore as he came up beside Ash. 'Talk about

Chapter 4   October 1942

isolated. You could have the whole Jap army out there and no one would know.'

'I don't want to draw the short straw for this post,' Stretch Middleton added, flopping down on a rock outcrop. 'A man could go mad staring out at nothing all day. And you break into a sweat if you so much as blink. No wonder the place is empty. What do you say, Gabriel? No one lives in this area?'

'Not empty, Boss,' the Aborigine said softly. He swept an arm wide. 'Plenty life all around. Rains come soon and you see him come out. My people stop here long times before that Captain Cook come. Good country for hunt, fish.'

'Cook was never here. Where'd you get that idea?'

'He didn't mean it literally Stretch.' Sam corrected. 'Cook is symbolic of European arrival. Wickham and Stokes were first here. I read about it once. The Victoria was the big hope for a way into the supposed inland sea. It wasn't of course, but ships still came up this far and offloaded cargo onto smaller vessels to go further – the way we've come. The Depot at Timber Creek is as far as they got… by river anyway.

'Well, aren't you the educated one. It still looks bloody uninhabited to me.'

'Yeah, well I'll stick with Gabriel's version.'

'You do that. Anyway, I'd prefer a bit more action than sitting around like some frog in a swamp waiting for something that won't happen.'

'Shut it!' Ash cut in. 'Or I'll recommend you both for the post. If navigators could get up river last century, it'll be a piece of piss for the Japs now. Maybe it won't happen. There's hundreds of places they could come ashore if they want to. But Entrance Island and Blunder Bay are made for a landing, so someone's got to watch. This is one spot to do it from.'

Ash heard the irritation in the voices. It had been a hard five days and there'd be another five at least on the way back. The Depot was 100 miles up-river. His orders were to scout and report back with recommendations as quickly as possible. They hadn't brought a radio because that would require pack horses and slow them down. They'd carried essentials only, relying on Gabriel's expertise to live off the land. So far so good, although it took a bit of willpower to eat snake and goanna.

Ash stood up.

'Okay. Let's get back down to the horses. I want to get across to the island at low tide.'

'What's there that we can't see from here?'

Stretch didn't try to disguise his annoyance, but Ash kept his voice calm.

'I don't expect to find the place crawling with Japs. HQ will want to know if anyone's been there though. Maybe a scouting party looking for a landing. You both know what a Jap boot print looks like. The mud would preserve it if it's above the tide line. Or any other sign. They would leave something.'

* * *

The search of Entrance Island didn't find any evidence of occupation or visitation. Ash had split the patrol into two, keeping Gabriel with him. Both parties spent an uncomfortable, fireless night listening to the sounds of the river and the whine of mosquitoes. When they regathered next morning Ash pooled the information to draw a rough sketch of the terrain, marking likely vessel landing places and camp sites, most of them on the northern, seaward side.

At the crossing point back to the Blunder Bay shore, much

Chapter 4   October 1942

of the river bed was exposed by the ebbing tide. It was time for the return journey—either that or wait another twenty-four hours. None of them fancied it during the night ebb. They set out in single file with Gabriel leading. Ash followed, attempting to direct his horse in the same track even though the marks disappeared immediately in the sucking mud. The horses floundered fetlock-deep through the cloying ooze. Ash swayed uncomfortably in the saddle, trying to synchronise with the uneven gait. Even his truck journeys along shell-holed roads in Palestine were more comfortable. The patrol's progress seemed agonisingly slow. Behind him Stretch swore.

'Hey Corp, what's the chance of the army building a bloody bridge? A gateway to bloomin' paradise.'

As Ash twisted his head to reply, his horse stopped abruptly, nearly unseating him. He clutched the reins to steady himself. Gabriel had halted, gazing seaward and listening intently. Ash frowned.

'What's the matter, Gabriel?'

'We too slow. Tide coming quick time. We hurry now boss.'

At that moment, Ash heard a faint rumble and saw a dark line extend across the estuary.

'Bloody hell! Let's go.'

The four riders urged the horses forward, willing them to lift their hooves out of the mud, to lengthen their stride. In moments the rumble changed tempo to a roar. Ash looked again. The dark line had become a brown wall of water five feet high—maybe more—charging towards them. The bank was still forty yards away. Ash registered that they weren't going to make it. After that, he lost track as events merged into a frightening blur.

The tidal bore smashed into the stranded patrol with a force that made the horses stagger. The water rose up to their bellies and the current tore at their legs threatening to carry them on the surge into Blunder Bay. Ash fought with the reins to keep his mount heading to the bank, but the horse lurched sideways in panic. He felt himself sliding from the saddle. Desperately he tried to stay upright, but one foot slipped from the stirrup and, still holding the reins, he fell into the river. As the water closed over his head a searing pain in his other ankle caused him to gasp and swallow. He let go the reins. His rifle slipped from his shoulder, the sling catching for a moment around his neck before it wrenched away and sank.

With flailing arms Ash struggled back to the surface, coughing and choking. The horse was still beside him, but he couldn't get free. He was being dragged along, his foot caught in the stirrup, the pain in his ankle excruciating. He tried in vain to reach and grasp the girth. Each time the current buffeted him away. Desperation gave way to panic. Then came a cold fear as he went under once more. This is what drowning was like. His fate to die in a flood tide of the Victoria River. Nowhere near a battlefield. Dimly he became aware of something grasping the front of his shirt. A support round his shoulders pushed him upwards and his head rose out of the water. He sucked in air, gagged and spluttered, sucked in more air ready for the next plunge. It didn't come. Instead he felt pressure on his foot, his leg fell free and he turned upright in the current.

'You right now boss,' Gabriel said in his ear. 'You stand up. Not too deep.'

Ash put his sound foot down into the mud and stood. The water came up to his neck. But as soon as he put the other foot down, pain lanced through his leg. He cried out and almost toppled over again. Gabriel acted quickly.

Chapter 4 October 1942

'You hold im good around neck,' he said.

Later Ash couldn't say how long it took Gabriel to reach the bank piggy-backing him through the swirling tide. An eternity. He was dimly aware of hands taking him by the shoulders, lifting him up the slope and laying him down on firm ground. He turned over on his side, vomiting a spout of muddy water and bile. Then he flopped back and lay still.

'You okay Corp?' Sam bent down beside him. 'You must have swallowed half the bloody Victoria. I wouldn't have believed it could come so fast. Like a bloody train. Here, get this down you.'

Sam handed him a pannikin of hot tea. Ash clawed back to consciousness and coughed his thanks.

'Everyone else okay? The horses?'

'Yeah,' answered Stretch from beside the small fire he had made. 'We jumped off and grabbed the reins while Gabriel grabbed you. I gotta hand it to him. He was like a fish the way he swam back when you went under.'

Ash moved to a sitting position and immediately winced as his left foot dragged across the ground.

'Shit!'

Sam moved down and gently felt around the top of Ash's boot.

'That's going to be a bugger,' he said. 'It's swollen to hell. No way of telling if it's broken or just a bad sprain. In any case, I think you'll have to keep the boot on. If you take it off, you'll never get in it again.'

Stretch laughed. 'One way of getting out of camp chores,' he said, kicking dirt on the fire. 'You'll need a lift up onto the horse next.'

* * *

The Nackeroo reconnaissance patrol made its way back to The Depot along the west bank of the Victoria. Ash's orders had been to survey both sides of the river. He was determined to make a comprehensive report, despite his incapacity. Not comfortable in the saddle at the best of times, he spent much of the five-day trek trying to minimise the pressure on his throbbing left ankle. The tensed, awkward posture made his back ache, but mounting and dismounting caused most pain. Each time, Gabriel appeared by his side to help. The others shrugged and after a while they treated it as another of the Aboriginal's routine tasks.

Ash reluctantly accepted this service, but it was not until the second night camp after hobbling, half hopping across to the fire that he appreciated Gabriel's genuine concern. The Aborigine handed him a crutch cut from a sapling, the forked end stripped of bark to fit snuggly in his armpit, a cross piece lashed on at arm's length.

'This fella help walk better,' he said.

From then on Ash rode beside Gabriel whenever he could, sending Stretch or Sam to the lead. He was careful not to pry. He realised Gabriel would be offended, maybe even alienated by direct personal questions. Instead he conversed with him about the land they were travelling through, its features, its stories and characters of the creation.

Probing gently he learnt that Gabriel had been born in the bush, but brought up at the Lutheran mission on the upper reaches of the Fitzmaurice. There he had attended the strict regime of the mission school for a few years, learning English and Bible stories in between tasks like carting water and gathering wood for the cooking fire. He began riding at the mission, later improving his skills when working as a stockman on surrounding cattle stations. Then the army moved in and Gabriel was one of the first local Aborigines to be incorporated into the ranks of the Nackeroos.

These snippets emerged bit by bit as the patrol moved south. As they talked, Ash saw the countryside in a new light. There was no need to fight the land and try to tame it; rather it made more sense to accept, even revere its presence and learn to use what it provided. He began to feel an empathy for the Aborigines' way of life. Never one for rank or authority by right of birth or office, he appreciated Gabriel as an integral and indispensable member of the patrol—more than that, an equal. He dared to think that the loyalty went both ways.

Chapter 5

September 1987

Brad kept a firm grip on the steering wheel as the Land Cruiser lurched over the corrugations. He had to concentrate to keep out of the deep grooves gouged by the rig trucks. Beside him Wingnut winced with each jolt, but kept his eyes closed and said nothing.

'Sorry,' Brad said. 'These bloody vehicles weren't built for comfort. We'll be on the bitumen soon.'

The roughneck nodded as he tried to cushion his broken arm against his body and hold on to the side door with his good hand at the same time. His wrenched knee gave him only one leg to brace against the Toyota's bucking metal floor.

Brad glanced across. Wingnut looked haggard and in pain. Probably shock had set in too. The Malteser, designated the rig's medic besides his role in the galley, had put a splint of sorts on the forearm and steadied it in a calico sling. He'd also bandaged the swollen knee, but said immediately that the roughneck needed hospital treatment.

Ethan Williams had exploded, his stream of abuse directed at the drill crew lasting several minutes. The drilling super stopped short of telling Brad his presence on the rig floor had

Chapter 5   September 1987

been an unnecessary distraction, but the shake of his head made this message clear. Then he'd said Brad was the only one who could be spared to take the injured roughneck to town.

Brad winced himself as he steered around a particularly rough section of road. Chest-high dry grasses stretched out on either side, interspersed with tall bloodwoods, boabs and the occasional Pandanus palm. Small mobs of Brahman cattle stared at him from the shade. One, closer to the verge and more skittish than the rest, lumbered away with ears back and hump jiggling—not a beast he'd want to encounter on the road at night.

Further on, he passed outcrops of dark grey limestone, the remains of an ancient barrier reef system formed when northern Australia was under the sea. Rounding a bend Brad saw the mustering yards. Lengths of old drill pipe, no doubt scrounged from some earlier rig operator, had been used as rails, slotted into stout wooden uprights. Remembering Charlie's directions, Brad scanned the other side of the road and saw faint wheel tracks leading off to the bushy's hut nestled against a limestone mass. There was no sign of life. He drove on, wondering what the old bloke did with his days.

Finally, after another half an hour of jolting and weaving, Brad passed over a cattle grid and saw the green forty-four gallon drum by the side of the road that marked the station boundary. Much to his own relief as for Wingnut, he turned onto the bitumen highway. Fifty kilometres down the road he passed the town speed limit sign, eased off the accelerator and looked for directions to the hospital.

'Any idea where it is?' he asked.

Wingnut remained silent. Brad saw that his passenger was still tense.

'Must be somewhere central.' Brad tried to sound casual.

'I don't like hospitals,' Wingnut muttered.

'Better than leaving you to Charlie. He'd likely amputate with a meat cleaver. Besides, think of the pretty nurses you'll meet. Ah. Here we go.'

Brad turned into a long driveway bordered by a line of stately palms set in a manicured lawn verge. He swung around the turning circle and stopped at the entrance to let Wingnut out before continuing on to the car park. Walking back, he took in the single-storey building with its iron roof, brick walls and glass front entrance—more like a large house than a hospital. Wingnut was waiting outside. Brad sighed.

'Come on. The sooner you get this sorted the sooner you'll be enjoying yourself in Perth.'

Inside they were met by an atmosphere of hushed calm. The receptionist looked up as Brad approached with Wingnut limping beside him.

'You must be Mr Felix Honeyman… from the oil rig,' she said.

Brad looked blank till Wingnut muttered 'yes'. No wonder the roughneck didn't reveal his real name. What the drill floor crew would do with Felix Honeyman!

'A Mr. Charles Camilleri phoned to say you were on your way. Some paper work first and then if you wait over there someone will be out to get you.'

Wingnut grimaced at Brad and flapped his sling.

'I'm right-handed.'

Brad took the pen and filled in the forms with personal details the roughneck divulged reluctantly. The rows of plastic-padded seats in the centre of the entrance hall reminded Brad of an airport lounge. Wingnut slumped in his seat and gazed at

Chapter 5   September 1987

the strip lighting in the ceiling. Brad let him be and contented himself with watching the people who came and went to the reception desk. The last time he'd been in a hospital it was to see his mother. And he'd been too late. He pushed the memory away.

'Mr Honeyman? Come this way please.'

Brad looked up to see a blue-uniformed nurse standing before them, her manner businesslike, abrupt. She moved aside as Wingnut struggled to his feet, but made no attempt to help.

'Do you want to come and hold his hand?'

Penetrating hazel eyes fixed on Brad—her expression coolly assessing, challenging, like an athlete staring down an opponent. A wisp of dark hair over one ear had escaped from the locks pulled back from her face and coiled behind her head. The style drew attention to her high cheekbones and fair skin. Brad rose, puzzled at the hint of sarcasm.

'No thank you, ah…,' he read the name-badge pinned to her breast pocket, '… Sister Frost. I'll wait here.'

He watched her walk away, trying to reconcile the curt demeanour with the trim figure and shapely calves. When Wingnut hobbled through the swing doors after her, Brad shook his head and crossed to a nearby table that held a stack of magazines. Flicking through the titles he selected one that featured rural articles and went back to his seat. His interest waned within a couple of pages, so he re-visited the stack and pulled out two more. They also failed to capture him. After the fourth trip in half an hour he gave it up and slumped in his seat. Patience had never been one of his virtues as Debra often reminded him. Well, she wouldn't any more. Brad wondered if she had carried out her threat about changing the locks. He hadn't tried to contact her.

Maybe he should. He owed Deb that much. But no, it was easier not to. It might re-open the door and around they'd go again… inevitably with the same result—the choice between commitment and independence. He told himself to let it be. It was better that way.

It wasn't the first time either. There was Wendy. She and Brad had become engaged during the whirl of a university romance and after graduation they'd lived together several years. Wendy later claimed it was less than half that, saying he was offshore for three or four weeks at a time. In those early post-grad days everything about the job was new and exciting. Brad enjoyed the life, helicoptering to work, the bustle, the responsibility, the characters he met out on the rigs and service boats. The money was good too. Anyway, he told her, a land exploration job would be the same; possibly he'd be gone for even longer periods … and further away.

Wendy had accused him of being more in love with his work than with her. Brad told her not to be ridiculous but, deep inside, his doubts about committing to the next step grew. The spark he felt when partying with her in the capsule of free-wheeling university days had gone. He began to wonder if it had ever been love and whether he even knew what love was. Gradually he realised the relationship wouldn't work, but he shied away from broaching the subject. It was easier to retreat into his shell and escape to the rigs, vowing to tell her the truth during his next days off. In the end, the break was made for him. Wendy finally got tired of pressing for a wedding date and it was she who walked away.

Brad glanced across to reception and caught the girl watching him. She smiled. He got up and went over.

'I'm sorry the selection isn't up to much,' she said as Brad

Chapter 5 September 1987

approached. 'It's all donated. Women's Association mostly. No *Playboy* at all. That's what you oil people like isn't it?'

'Not all of us,' he lied. 'I've got a couple of books in the vehicle, but I didn't know how long this would take.'

'Could be a while yet. We had a rush on earlier. A smash on the highway. They're probably still getting through the backlog.'

'I thought Sister Frost looked peeved. It must be a tough shift.'

'Oh, the ice queen. She's always like that… Oops.' The girl put a hand to her mouth. 'I'm sorry. I shouldn't have said that. Sister Frost is really very good. I … it just slipped out… Please excuse me. I didn't mean it.'

Brad laughed.

'It's okay. I'm not going to report you. If she's good at her job, that's the main thing. Wingnut was a bit nervous, that's all.'

'Well, the doctors like her… think she's good I mean… at her job… oh.' The girl reddened and put her face in her hands.

Brad grinned. The receptionist was young and refreshingly honest. He told her again not to worry and that he was sure the sister was an excellent nurse. At that point an elderly man came up to the desk beside him.

'Can I help you sir?' The girl turned away from Brad, eager to end their conversation and attend to the newcomer.

Brad thought about going out to the Land Cruiser to get his book, his indecision vindicated a few minutes later when Sister Frost pushed through the swing doors and walked towards him. He watched her straighten her shoulders, the uniform firm across her breasts. Wingnut wasn't with her. Brad tried a jovial approach.

'What have you done with our roughneck?'

The sister gave him the faintest of smiles.

'We are keeping Mr Honeyman overnight, just for observation. There may be delayed reaction. It was a clean break, but we had to reset it. The splint was not adequate. It's a pity there is not more medical expertise at the rig.'

Brad started to defend Charlie, but Sister Frost brushed him aside.

'Mr Honeyman's knee, you'll be glad to know, is not a serious problem. No ligament damage, but there will be tenderness for a few days and he'll benefit from using a crutch. You can take him back to the rig in the morning as long as he keeps off his feet as much as possible.'

'Ah, no,' said Brad. 'He's no use out there with one only wing and a gammy leg. I've got his gear in the vehicle. He'll be on the afternoon plane to Perth tomorrow. His replacement will be aboard the incoming flight, so I'm dossing down in town tonight to carry out the exchange.'

'I see. Well, I'm afraid Mr Honeyman won't have a comfortable flight with that knee. The extra room in business class would help. I'm sure your company can run to that.'

Again Brad caught the sarcasm and saw the challenge in her eyes. Wow, he thought. It must have been a really trying day. He met her gaze. She would be very attractive if she lightened up a bit and smiled.

'I'm sure we can manage it,' he replied.

'Good. Mr Honeyman has requested some personal items for the night. If you could leave them at reception please, they will be brought to him.'

She turned to go.

'Okay. Well I may see you in the morning then.'

'Not tomorrow. I'm on the afternoon shift.'

He felt an unexpected twinge of disappointment.

'Oh. Good bye then, and thank you.'

Brad stood still a moment, appreciating her trim figure as she turned and moved away, then he went out to the vehicle to fetch Wingnut's gear.

(J.L. Stokes – Journal entry 12 November 1839)

... *I found our invalid so much recovered to-day that I determined on making a short march homewards in the cool of the early morning. We reached Tortoise Reach by 8 o'clock, A.M. where we passed the day. During our morning's walk I again had the luck to knock over a kangaroo. It was a female, and had a very young one in its pouch. It is worthy of remark that most of those I killed were does, with young ones of different ages, which afforded Mr. Bynoe the means of making some interesting observations on the manner in which they are brought forth, which will be found further on in the part of the work relating to Houtman's Abrolhos, where more opportunities occurred of arriving at a satisfactory result. Mr. Bynoe added here to his collection of birds, to which also, I was so fortunate as to be able to contribute a beautiful specimen of a rifle-green glossy ibis, common in Europe. I tried the water with a very roughly manufactured fly: the fish rose repeatedly at it, though there was scarcely a ripple, and notwithstanding my own want of success under these unpropitious circumstances, I feel perfectly satisfied that with proper tackle, and on a favourable day, this prince of sports might be enjoyed on the Victoria.* ...

Chapter 6

September 1987

Brad closed the journal and tossed it onto the bedside table. He found it easier to concentrate on Lieutenant Stokes' 19th century-style narrative in small doses. Besides, he was hungry. He didn't fancy staying in the motel room and ordering from the take-away Chinese menu in the information folder, so he decided to walk the few blocks to the main street to see what he could find.

Outside, the warm night enveloped him—a marked contrast to the air-conditioned room. Brad ambled along one side of the thoroughfare and back up the other, gazing into the shop windows as he passed. The main street had the country town feel that he enjoyed: a mix of clothing stores, a saddlery with assorted leather gear, a gift shop of local crafts, a hardware, newsagent, butcher, bakery, a second-hand book shop and several cafes that probably catered solely for lunch-time trade. Of the more substantial restaurants, only the Oriental Palace had lights on—the Chinese café offering the motel take-away menu. He turned away, deciding that a counter meal of steak, chips and a beer in the Grand Hotel made a better option.

Brad looked around as he ate. The pub had a more modern

decor than he had guessed from the outside façade. In the cavernous lounge a number of people were seated in front of a row of slot machines at the far end of the room, mechanically feeding coins and pulling handles. A few more patrons leant against the bar in conversation and a noisy group had pushed several tables together not far from Brad, celebrating a birthday or an anniversary of some sort. Nearby, two lovers fed each other morsels from a dessert plate and, past them, a woman sat on her own reading a book. Brad caught sight of a poster on the wall advertising a country disco for Saturday night. His imagination conjured the room full of Akubras, high-heeled boots, jeans and checked shirts whirling to the sounds of Slim Dusty. Ah… time for another beer. He rose and went to the bar.

Fresh glass in hand, Brad turned and rested his back on the bar counter. The party group had just burst into song, but the lovers seemed oblivious, holding hands across their table. He looked across at the lone woman. From this angle she seemed vaguely familiar. As if on cue she looked up from her book. Brad almost spilt his beer. Two hazel eyes framed by shoulder-length black hair stared straight at him. One corner of her mouth curled up in recognition. Brad took it as an opening—well, he couldn't pretend he hadn't noticed. He nodded and made his way over to her table, his mind struggling to find a deft greeting.

'Sister Frost – I'm sorry I stared. You look so different out of uniform… your hair down,' he finished lamely.

'Better, I hope,' she said. 'You're not staying at the Hilton?'

Brad let that pass and glanced down at her hand cupping a glass of red wine. He judged it was not her first.

'I'm warming it up. They always keep it in the fridge here.'

'Can I buy you another? It'll add a few degrees by the time you get to it.'

Chapter 6 September 1987

This time Brad was treated to a smile.

'Thank you,' she said when he returned. 'Today was a brute.'

Brad hesitated. 'I don't mean to intrude,' he said.

The nurse shook her head and pointed to a chair. He sat and sipped his beer. She watched him, but said nothing, forcing Brad to break the silence.

'I did hear something about a car accident along the highway,' he said cautiously. 'Were they badly hurt?'

'It was a head on. Two dead, four injured—three badly. One of them might not last the night.'

'Christ!' Brad was jolted as much by the cool, matter-of-fact tone as by the statistics. 'I don't know how you can do your job… to see that sort of thing on a regular basis.'

'It's not that regular. This was a bad one. Red wine helps.' She took a drink. 'Anyway I return the sentiment.'

'What do you mean?'

'How can you do your job?'

Brad frowned. 'I don't see the connection. Accidents like Wingnut's aren't every day. Anyway, I don't work on the drill floor. I just look at the rocks they bring up.'

'I'm talking about conscience. It's the bush that's the loser when companies like yours come in and trample all over it.'

Bloody hell, Brad thought. Where did that come from? He looked to see if she really meant it. Evidently she did—the hazel eyes held his gaze without a hint of irony. Brad decided to play it straight.

'Hardly that,' he said. 'The amount of ground cleared for the rig is minor compared to the vastness of the area and the road in is mostly on station tracks. We're not digging an open cut mine out there. When we've gone the bush will grow back and you'll hardly see a footprint at all.'

'Do you really believe that? Any intrusion leaves a permanent scar. And who knows what you're wrecking underground.'

'Whoa! Hang on. They're strong words. We're not wrecking anything. What gives you that idea? Anyway, there has to be a full environmental program approved by the government before any company moves rigs or equipment into an area. And we have… got approval I mean. It was in our hands well before the rig arrived. We wouldn't have done anything at all at the location without permission. It's all being done by the book.'

'What would governments know? Big money will always find a way.'

Brad sat back. 'That's pretty cynical,' he said. 'I'll admit the industry hasn't had the best reputation in the past. I can't defend the forests of derricks and pools of spilt oil littered around places like California and the Caspian Sea in the old days, but I can tell you that the regulations today are strict. That sort of pollution won't be tolerated. I prefer to think our program might bring benefits to the locality.'

'What, like finding oil you mean? That won't be for our benefit. It will only bring more companies in, more disruption.'

'It probably won't be oil. There's more chance around here that any find will be gas. That could be useful for the town—even a moderate discovery. It's a cheaper electricity generating fuel than the diesel the power station is using now.'

'Yes and that would mean pipelines and more ripping through the bush. It's an invasion whatever way you dress it up.'

The nurse drained her glass and took a long drink from the one that Brad had bought.

'Well, maybe it's not you exactly,' she continued. 'But you do work for them, so you're in the same camp.'

The last remark nettled Brad. It had echoes of conversations

Chapter 6   September 1987

with Debra after she joined an environmental group in Melbourne with other teachers from her school. Back off, he told himself. He finished his beer and got to his feet.

'Geologists study rocks and landforms, natural history. I like to think I know a bit about the environment and act responsibly. You ought to come and have a look before you judge us. We're not ogres.'

'You're inviting me out there?'

'Sure. Why not? Anytime you want.'

He said it without thinking. That didn't happen often and Brad was annoyed with himself. He turned to go. And yet, strangely, he meant it. Why? A chance to see her again. He stopped and faced her.

'May I know your name Sister. I'm Brad.'

She looked back at him in silence. Brad shrugged and turned to the door.

'Karen... It's Karen.'

'Well, goodnight Karen. I'll pick up our boy in the morning and we'll be out of your hair.'

Brad wished he could retract the barb as soon as he said it. He was still regretting it when he picked Wingnut up from the hospital the next morning. He considered leaving an apology and renewed invitation at the reception desk. In the end he did leave a note, but confined it to one of thanks for attending to Mr Honeyman. He made no mention of their after-hours conversation. The receptionist read the name on the envelope and grinned, the day's gossip in her hand.

Wingnut hobbled awkwardly to the Land Cruiser leaning on a hospital-issue crutch. 'Still on my L-plates,' he mumbled. 'Bloody knee hurts more than the arm.'

* * *

Attentive to Karen's advice, Brad did enquire about a business-class seat, but there were none available. Instead the check-in attendant put the roughneck in a row at the back of the plane next to two vacant seats so he could stretch out. Wingnut perked up when a shapely blond flight attendant ushered him out to the gate for pre-boarding. Brad waved him off and went to the arrivals hall to meet the replacement who turned out to be a nuggetty, jovial "call me Johnno" character with an iron grip. No tongs were going to slip out of his hands. They didn't converse much on the way to the rig. Johnno had worked in the Kimberley before so, apart from asking for a run-down on the personnel at Stokes-1, he was content to gaze out the window.

On arrival at the rig, Brad left Johnno with Ethan Williams to do the orientation and safety briefing and went to the mud-logger's hut.

'How's Wingnut?' Aaron asked as he walked in.

'Last seen with a grin all over his face in the care of a good-looking hostie. How are we doing here?'

'After all the kerfuffle, they finished the trip early this morning. Now back drilling, but still grinding away at the limestone. I wouldn't be surprised if they need another bit change before long.'

'Old Sourpuss is going to love that. Has he simmered down yet?'

Aaron shook his head. 'Word is he gave you the evil eye for just being there.'

Brad shrugged. 'I'm going to get something to eat.'

In the mess, he made a coffee and took half a dozen biscuits across to one of the tables. Lucy was running a damp cloth over

Chapter 6 September 1987

some tabletops at the far end of the room. She glanced at him, then looked away again without any acknowledgement and went into the galley. He heard her say something behind the partition and moments later Charlie stuck his head out, saw Brad and came over.

'Good trip for town?'

Brad looked at him warily. 'It was okay.'

Charlie sat down. 'I hear you date a nurse.'

'Jesus!' Brad exploded. 'How'd you come by that notion?'

'Ah… the Malteser knows everything.' The chef chuckled and let it lie as he savoured Brad's reaction. 'For me it is not so much mystery,' he grinned. 'It is small town. My food supplier see you in big conversation in pub.'

Brad was annoyed with himself for being pulled in so easily—the second time in twenty-four hours Karen had sparked an impulsive reaction.

'Hardly a date, and I don't think we hit it off anyway.'

Charlie leaned across the table.

'You know who she is, yes?'

'Sure. She's the Sister at the hospital who admitted Wingnut.'

'Yes. But more than this.' Charlie paused, teasing the moment. 'They say she is granddaughter of the old bloke who fires rifle near us. You unnustand.'

Brad stared at him.

'Now that explains a few things,' he said.

Chapter 7

October 1942

Arriving at The Depot, Ash's patrol found the camp at fever pitch. Reports had come in that morning about Japanese spotter planes flying low over Wyndham in B-Company's far western sector and over A-Company's base at the Roper River to the east. The planes had slowly circled, brazenly examining the camps and, in the case of Wyndham, the town's port and meatworks. Then they flew further inland, returning half an hour later and disappearing out to sea, presumably to land on aircraft carriers attached to the Japanese navy over the horizon in the Timor Sea. The coordinated episodes had revived speculation of imminent invasion, and not just among the Military. Hundreds of civilians from towns and properties around the northern coasts from Carpentaria to Cambridge Gulf were heading south. Reaction to these reports dominated the airwaves between The Depot and Nackeroo headquarters in Katherine.

Ash's ankle took second place when he fronted the Lieutenant to be quizzed on his findings. Had the patrol seen any aircraft over the Victoria? Had there been any signs of Japanese presence on the ground? Where would Ash

Chapter 7   October 1942

recommend strategic sites for camps and observation posts along the river? What would be needed for each? And, the Lieutenant looked at Ash's ankle for the first time, how soon would he be ready to go back out into the field?

'A written report in my hands this evening Corporal. And see the medic without further delay.'

The Lieutenant concluded the session abruptly and turned to the signals operator who had approached with another de-coded message from headquarters. Ash hobbled out, leaning on Gabriel's crutch. The swelling and pain had reduced, enabling him to put his foot on the ground, but he still needed the support to walk.

'Not a bad piece of handiwork,' the medical officer said admiring the crutch as Ash leaned it against the bench and lay down. 'Can't say the same about the ankle. I'd cut it off if we weren't so short of spares. Just a moment while I get a peg before we take the boot off.'

Ash knew that "medical officer" was an over-inflated term. He was a private who happened to have learnt some first aid. But there was no one else at The Depot better qualified. The Nackeroos, like all the outback towns and stations, had to rely on the flying doctor service for any critical cases. Ash's ankle was not one of them.

'Cut the crap and give me a verdict. I've got to get back out there or hadn't you heard the Japs are coming?'

The medic smirked.

'Touché. You had a lucky escape from what Stretch tells me. You could have been inside a croc by now.'

'Thanks to Gabriel.'

'So I hear. These Abos are good value as long as they are out in the bush.'

Ash choked back a rejoinder as the medic bent and probed his ankle.

'It's not broken. A bit late for a bandage. Anyway the foot could do with a good airing. You'll be okay. Keep off it as much as possible for a day or two. Now, out and take that stinking boot with you.'

* * *

Next day Ash was gratified to find the Lieutenant had heeded the recommendations in his report. Five Nackeroos, including a signaller and an Aboriginal tracker, with a corporal in charge, were to set up a base at Blunder Bay. Because Ash had pointed out the meagre supply of fresh water in the area, it was agreed this group would be without horses. Instead the patrol would be transported down river by the platoon's boat, *Pride*.

The Wyndham party had salvaged this 25-foot motor launch, found on its side at low tide beside the meatworks wharf. They'd stripped and rebuilt the motor, re-caulked and painted the hull, then carried it back to The Depot lashed onto the tray of a blitz wagon. Formerly named *Bondi*, someone had jokingly called the refurbished craft "The Pride of Sydney" and the name stuck. Joke or not, the bases along the river would soon be reliant on the little vessel to bring in provisions, equipment, relief personnel and the all-important mail.

The Lieutenant charged Ash with the job of establishing a base at Bradshaw. But there was a catch.

'No boat ride for you,' he said. 'We need a string of horses up there to patrol inland from the east side of the river. Set up food caches and stores around the area in case the Japs land and you have to go bush.'

Chapter 7 October 1942

The Lieutenant lowered his voice. 'You know there's a bloody scare on with these Jap observer flights. Well, I've also had reports about lights in the bush at night. Places where none of our blokes are. Could be anything… or nothing. Maybe just Aborigines from the mission; maybe stockmen from one of the stations, although it's late in the year for any mustering; could even be lightning as the Wet builds. The alternative… that there's an enemy agent out there makes my skin crawl, but we can't discount the possibility of a collaborator sending signals to the Japs. Just watch for anything out of the ordinary, anything or anyone suspicious. And that includes bush Aborigines.' The Lieutenant resumed his normal voice.

'Take Privates Greenwood, Middleton, signaller Jenkins and two trackers—your choice.'

Ash immediately requested Gabriel and then settled on Jimmy, an older man who had recently come into The Depot from Victoria River Downs station. He felt pleased to keep his patrol together, even though Sam and Stretch sometimes sparred like two yabbies in a tank. In any case, there weren't many permutations in a platoon strength at The Depot of only 24, all ranks. Bluey Jenkins was a more studious type, but Ash hoped he would fit in. A lawyer's clerk from Geelong southwest of Melbourne, with a shock of red hair, blues eyes and a freckled face, Jenkins was the youngster of the group. Like Ash, he'd never been on a horse until the training camp at Ingleburn, but he knew about radios and Morse code. His shoulders would carry responsibility for all communications from Bradshaw.

Radios and electronics were double-Dutch to Ash, even though he and all the other Nackeroos had been given a basic run-through while they were at the training camp. He left the organisation of the radio equipment in Jenkins' hands and was surprised when told eight pack animals would be needed for this alone.

'Christ. I thought you said the set was portable. Sounds like we're moving the whole bloody radio station.'

Bluey took him seriously. 'Well, we are in a way. We're going to need one animal for the transceiver and converter, one for the batteries, one for the battery charger, one for the drums of petrol to run the charger and another three, or better still, four more animals for relief. They can't carry their loads all day every day in this heat.'

Ash laughed at the earnestness. 'Okay, okay. I believe you. But it better be worth the effort. That's more feed we've got to carry or find.'

'Oh, it will. The FS6 radio is fairly old, but it is good when it's set up properly and you can do Morse or voice transmission if necessary.'

'Get on with it then. We move out in the morning.'

* * *

At the final count, the patrol took twenty-four animals, including eight mules dedicated to Bluey's signals equipment. Each of the Nackeroos had two mounts and the rest were pack horses to carry food and equipment. Stretch grinned as he looked along the line-up assembled outside the dilapidated, iron-roofed building that served as The Depot administration centre.

'All we need are a few covered wagons and we'll be set to roll to the Promised Land!'

'Let's just concentrate on getting this lot across the river,'

Chapter 7   October 1942

Ash said as he rode past to the head of the column and signalled the start.

He had enlisted the help of several of The Depot Aborigines for the crossing at Policeman's Point on a bend in the river just upstream from the base. A couple of the police trackers also turned up, although he suspected that they had come initially to watch the fun. The Victoria below the camp was about 500 yards wide and ran an eight-foot tide even though it was 100 miles from the sea. Ash timed the crossing for the ebb. The experienced Depot men led the straggly line of horses and mules into the water amid much shouting, flailing and shooting as a deterrent to the crocodiles in plain view along both banks. The horses seemed to sense the urgency, splashing through the shallows across the bar. The mules, though, needed more persuasion.

One in particular refused to budge. It just stood watching as its mates passed one by one. Finally the animal realised it was without company and bounded into the water assisted by a clout from one of the Aborigines. When it was halfway across Ash noticed a pair of nostrils gliding on the surface nearby. He shouted a warning and the men on the bank fired directly at the spot until the nostrils went under. The tardy mule rolled its eyes, but kept swimming until it floundered through the shallows and reached dry ground.

The packs containing the radio equipment, perishables, camping gear, extra firearms and ammunition followed across the river by raft. With the help of the trackers, the pack animals were rounded up, the loads strapped on and adjusted so that the weight on each was evenly balanced. Once again the errant mule refused to cooperate, aiming a vicious kick at

Bluey when he tried to position fuel drums on its back. Jimmy stepped in quickly to help.

'Proper grumpy bugger this one, Boss.' He grinned. 'Call 'im Always. He always kick and he kick all ways.'

'Well, he'll have to get used to the work Jimmy. You make sure he doesn't bolt and buck the load, okay.'

When all was settled Ash led the patrol out along the river flats heading north towards their date with Bradshaw station.

* * *

'It's even got beds and furniture… and running water! I'm going to like this place.'

The others smiled at Bluey Jenkins' youthful enthusiasm. It was the first time they'd seen a break in his serious demeanour. The patrol had followed the same route to Bradshaw as the reconnaissance journey three weeks earlier, although the slow pace of the column had meant two overnight camps instead of one. Bluey had spent most of the time riding beside the mules carrying the radio equipment, fussing over the animals, watching for any sign of imbalance in the loads and trying to steer them away from trees and other obstacles that might dislodge the packs. He'd paid particular attention to Always. The mule kicked at everyone who came close. No one was keen to saddle or unsaddle him—a task that had to be done at the beginning and end of the day and with each rest stop. Even Jimmy shied away from the job. Bluey persevered and by the third day, although sporting some dark bruises on his legs, he had formed a working rapport with the cantankerous animal. Proof of the relationship came when Always didn't hesitate in following Bluey across the Ikymbon River, the last obstacle before reaching Bradshaw.

Chapter 7 October 1942

The cattle station was still a going concern, although the owners had also bought the adjoining Coolibah property and shifted their headquarters to that homestead several months earlier. The Nackeroos were more than happy to make use of the empty Bradshaw homestead and outbuildings. After unloading they toured the surroundings, Bluey in the lead. The house had corrugated iron walls slung around a frame of heavy steel piping that also supported a gabled iron roof and wide verandas on all sides. Rough timber railings fenced off a neglected garden overgrown with shrubs and creepers. Inside the homestead they found a dirt floor and three rooms containing some home-made timber beds criss-crossed with strips of greenhide, other oddments of rough furniture and a wood stove. Several other buildings sprawled fifty yards away. Sam, with his farm experience, guessed they had been stockmen's quarters, a meat house, hay shed and, judging by the nails and a horseshoe lying in the dust, a blacksmith's shop. Best of all, as Bluey discovered, there was a large water tank kept full from a pipe lying on top of the ground and gravity feeding from the Yambarran Range about a mile away.

'The Timber Creek coppers said there was a spring up there, but I thought we'd have to lug water down. They didn't mention this luxury. I'm really going to like this place.'

'Yeah, well it's not a holiday,' Ash reminded him. 'The Japs could be here any minute. Where do you want to set up the radio?'

*　*　*

Bluey woke and sat bolt upright. The roaring noise seemed to be bouncing off the iron walls around him. He couldn't pin-point a source. Ash's warning about a Japanese attack flashed into his mind. Parting his mosquito net he reached for his rifle and groped his way to the door past the radio equipment and the pile of food rations. The noise was deafening. What the hell was going on? Stark naked, holding his rifle at the ready, Bluey staggered outside. The air was still. He couldn't see any movement. The noise lessened the further he went from the building. Puzzled, he turned full circle, gradually becoming aware of the mosquitoes homing in on his body.

'What's up Blue? Can't sleep?'

Stretch's voice came out of the shadows by a large boab across the yard where he had stationed himself for the first watch.

'What's going on? What the hell is that noise?'

'Frogs.'

Bluey caught the amusement in Stretch's tone and it dawned on him that somehow he had been set up. Earlier he had wondered about the others' preference for sleeping under canvas or out in the open. Stretch had told him that they didn't want to get in the way of his signals work. Bluey shrugged this off, thinking the real reason was they didn't want to be disturbed by the frequent tap-tap of his Morse key. He hadn't minded bunking alone. It was their problem. The rawhide bed was comfortable.

'What do you mean, frogs?'

Stretch laughed. 'The steel pipes holding up the house are full of the blasted things. Can't hear yourself think when they get going at night.

'You knew about this?'

'Sure. We copped it last time through. Welcome to Bradshaw.'

Chapter 7 October 1942

'Bastards.'

Next morning Ash was glad to see that Bluey had taken his initiation well. As soon as it was light the signaller moved his bedding into a tent beside the others, a wry grin on his face. He bore the itch of his numerous mosquito bites without complaint.

The post quickly settled to a routine, much of it keeping a watch on the river and the gathering and cooking of food. Ash set up a cook's roster. The job didn't require much expertise because the tins of rations hardly made for a varied menu. They had forgotten to pack fish hooks, but one morning Sam struck lucky by shooting a barramundi in the rocky shallows of the Ikymbon and that set the pattern for livening up their meals with produce from the land. Magpie geese and fish were added to the pot at regular intervals and Sam even made a passable bread that Stretch described as the bastard offspring of a pancake and a damper. Bradshaw's run still stocked cattle, but Ash issued instructions not to kill any. Even though the station owners wouldn't miss a beast or two he thought that, unless there was a dire need, the army shouldn't set a precedent. Surprisingly the patrol saw few kangaroos, but they did try to trap bush turkeys that roamed the area. There was little success until, a week into their residence, four Aborigines walked into the camp.

Gentle, but inquisitive, they looked at all the equipment, including the radio with its aerial slung up into the branches of a big boab. They also expressed interest in the weaponry, jabbering and pointing in particular to the two Thompson sub-machine guns. Gabriel and Jimmy followed them closely to make sure their curiosity didn't change from looking to touching and taking. One of the four spoke a little English and said that they were on walkabout from the mission on the Fitzmaurice River. They had heard the Nackeroos shooting and came to investigate. The mission pastor had told them to keep a lookout for 'Japanese men' and to report any to him, so he could tell the boss soldier. Ash, through Gabriel, asked them about the pastor, how many white fellas were there and how far to the mission. He learnt that the place was run by a 'Boss Moola and missus' and that it was 'little bit long way' from Bradshaw which Ash realised could mean anything up to 80 miles or more.

The Aborigine nodded sagely, then broke into a sudden smile, rubbed his stomach and pointed at a Tommy gun.

'You shoot turkey.'

Stretch laughed. 'There wouldn't be much turkey left with that fella—boom.' He spread and fluttered his arms to imitate an exploding bird. 'This one okay,' he added grabbing a shotgun.

The visitors were obviously disappointed, but they nodded and set off towards a patch of grass about an acre in area surrounded on all sides by bare earth. In a few minutes they had set it alight and stood quietly in the smoke. A short time later seven turkeys appeared, each coming from a different direction, greedily consuming dead grasshoppers and other insects overcome by the fire. Stretch quickly got the idea and with one blast scored two birds. Reloading swiftly, he managed to bag another two before the rest scattered and fled.

'Well blow me. Why didn't we think of that?'

He held out two of the birds to the Aborigines who accepted them and, without another word, walked off into the scrub.

Ash watched them go, staring at the bush long after they

Chapter 7 October 1942

had disappeared. Stretch came up carrying two turkeys in one hand, his shotgun in the other.

'What are you thinking Corp?'

'Could be nothing, but we'd better report this to HQ next sched. I'd like to know more about this missionary.'

* * *

'Here's your answer Corp. Took a bit of de-coding, but I think it's clear enough.'

Bluey held out a hand-written page.

Missionary Fitzmaurice River Pastor Hans Müller. Wife Gerda.

Müller born Germany arrived Australia 1920, now Australian citizen.

Founded FitzM mission 1925.

Interred Adelaide camp March 1940 under suspicion because nationality of birth.

Judged no risk. Released May 1940. Returned to FitzM same month.

No further action taken.

Major Stacy, Katherine NAOU

Bluey handed Ash a second slip.

'Here's one from The Depot. It came straight after.'

Suggest patrols inland and down river from Bradshaw soonest.

Vigilance essential. More lights—query signals—seen. Report findings.

Johnson, Lt. Depot NAOU

'Bloody hell, Corp,' Stretch burst out. 'That means those Abos today might have been checking us over. I thought they were a bit too interested in the radio. And the guns. They could be reporting to this pastor bloke right now.'

'Settle down.' Sam put a hand on Stretch's arm. 'The bloke's been cleared by our Ministry boys. They should know. Lights in the bush could be anything. We make enough light ourselves.'

'Yeah, but we all know Abos worked for the Japs here on the pearl luggers before the war. The Japs were probably planning an invasion from way back then, making maps of the coast under our noses. Their Abos were probably taught to spy, what to look for, signal where best to land, where all our defences are.'

'You're getting a bit carried away, mate. You'll be saying Gabriel and Jimmy are on their payroll next.'

'Now you mention it, Gabriel is from the mission isn't he?'

'That's enough!' Ash brought his hand down with a thump on the makeshift table. 'Empty accusations will get us nowhere. You know Gabriel's loyalty. We wouldn't survive long in the scrub without him. Another crack like that and you'll be on the *Pride* back to The Depot on a charge. And that's after I deck you. Tomorrow we spread out and have a good look around. Stretch, you're on the midnight watch tonight.'

* * *

Ash split the patrol into three parties.

He sent Sam and Stretch to follow the Victoria downstream for about six miles, then move inland to strike the western end of the Yambarran Range at a place known as The Tombs. It was supposed to be where Joseph Bradshaw, the founder of the station, was buried. Ash reckoned the craggy ridges would

Chapter 7 October 1942

provide a commanding view of the river to the southwest as well as a look at country to the north. They were then to head inland in a wide loop that would bring them back to the Yambarran Range spring on the northeast side and back to Bradshaw. Ash planned to take Gabriel, head directly to the springs and follow the southern flank of the Yambarran Range inland in a wide sweep to Mount Golla Golla and the upper reaches of the Ikymbon, then follow the river back to base.

The two parties would cover a lot of ground, marking any important features on the map, particularly water holes and springs. Ash also wanted each patrol to select a suitable place to set up a food depot that could be used if they had to abandon the post at Bradshaw. He reminded Sam and Stretch that if they did come across anyone or anything suspicious, the task was to observe without being seen. He didn't want any shooting or attempts at capture. Sightings were to be reported back to Bradshaw straight away, even if that meant curtailing the trek.

Bluey and Jimmy made up the third party, remaining at the homestead where Bluey could continue to monitor the radio traffic and make his scheduled transmissions. If anything vital was received from HQ he was to stay put and send Jimmy out to find them.

The patrols went their separate ways soon after breakfast. For the first mile Ash and Gabriel followed the well-worn path beside the water pipeline to the foot of the range, then they zig-zagged up the slope to where the early station owners had blasted a passage through the rock outcrop to the top. The day was oppressive, the humidity high as clouds massed in the north.

'Might be rains come soon Boss.'

'The start of the Wet, Gabriel?'

'Rains come then stop little bit, start again, all'a time. Proper big rain later, Boss.'

'Okay – well, let's get a look from the top while we can.'

They left the horses behind for the final climb and soon stood looking out at the vast Victoria floodplain, the river itself imprinted on the flat land in a series of wide curves till it merged with the haze on the horizon. The range unfolded on both sides in a giant wall of fractured rock, orange and brown in the mid-morning sun. The buildings of Bradshaw homestead lay below them, but elsewhere there was nothing made by man, just a vast raw expanse that Ash imagined unchanged for eons. A wedge-tailed eagle soared into view over the top of the range and skimmed along the line of the cliffs.

'That's the way to get around in this country,' he murmured, following the graceful flight. 'Now what's that?' Ash frowned as he noticed a patch of red that looked out of place on the otherwise green canopy of trees under the bird's path. The events of the last days led him to conjure a parachute caught and hanging in the trees.

Gabriel stared at the spot for a few moments.

'Kurrajong, Boss. Red flower.'

Ash didn't exactly doubt Gabriel, but he thought it strange there should be just one red tree in the whole landscape. The Japanese might not use the river access at all. It would be easier to drop a man by parachute.

'Let's take a look to make sure.'

Returning to the horses they set off along the base of the cliffs. The bush grew thick and tangled, forcing Gabriel to weave back and forth to find a way. Still, after half an hour Ash began to wonder if they had missed their target. By that stage he had no idea of how far they'd come.

Chapter 7 October 1942

'Kurrajong here, Boss. Seed good to eat. Make a drink, like coffee.'

There it was, straight ahead. The tree stood about 25 feet high, its base swollen, the trunk erect and tapering to the top. The bark was smooth and the branches spread symmetrically, covered with clusters of vivid red bell-shaped flowers. It made a startling picture, but not the parachute of Ash's imagination. He flashed Gabriel a chastened grin.

They continued to skirt the range, negotiating the slope, wary of loose scree and bushes that might snag the packs. Following a dry creek bed out onto the plain, Ash was all for making camp on a sheltered flat by the bank. Gabriel shook his head and pointed to the sky.

'Might be rain make big water quick-time,' he said.

The Aborigine led the way to a spot on higher ground where they unloaded the animals and made themselves comfortable without a fire. Ash didn't want to advertise their presence. Lying on his swag after a meal of tinned beef, lukewarm from a day in the pack and swimming in grease, he broached a subject that had been in his mind since the message from HQ the previous evening. He hoped Gabriel knew him well enough now to trust him.

'You know this missionary fella, Pastor Müller, Gabriel?'

'Yes Boss. He teach me little bit English. Before I go for stockman.'

'He a good fella?'

'Sometimes he work blackfella hard. Sometimes use stick.'

'Ah, on your backside when you don't learn lessons?'

Gabriel grinned. 'Yes Boss.'

'Did you ever see any Japanese men come up river to the mission… before this big war?'

'No Boss. But sometimes I think blackfellas come from finding pearl.'

'Blackfellas who worked on Japanese boats?'

'Yes Boss. I think might be. I be piccaninny then.'

'These blackfellas, did they talk to Pastor Müller?'

'I think, sometimes.'

'And did these blackfellas like the Japanese men on the boats?'

Gabriel shook his head. 'Might be work little bit too much.'

'So they wouldn't work for Japanese man now?'

Ash knew Gabriel would grasp his meaning.

'No Boss. Like that Nemarluk, he kill Japanese man in boat. Blackfella don't want Japanese man in this country. Might be help Australian fella win war. Might be blackfella allasame white fella.'

Ash sat back. If only equal rights could be true. But it was unlikely to happen, not for a long time ahead anyway. It would help if there were more Aborigines like Gabriel.

'Would you like to go to a school in the city, Gabriel? To learn like a white fella?'

Gabriel nodded.

'Yes Boss. Blackfella way good too.'

Ash left it there. He trusted Gabriel's judgement, satisfied the bush Aborigines who had come from the mission to Bradshaw had no sinister motive. The missionary's allegiance, however, was more problematic. Müller could still have connections to Germany… family, friends. He might still be patriotic, or he might be under some sort of pressure to act. Ash decided to meet the pastor face to face and make his own assessment of the man.

* * *

Chapter 7 October 1942

Ash and Gabriel arrived back at Bradshaw in pouring rain. The first showers began early that morning and become progressively heavier. The Ikymbon rose rapidly, the banks slippery and treacherous. The patrol was soon soaked and caked in mud as the horses sloshed through runnels of water flowing across the track. When they reached the homestead in mid-afternoon the thick cloud and constant downpour made it so dark that lamps had been lit. Water cascaded from the roof and the frogs in the pipes worked themselves into a frenzy. The yard was a mud patch strewn with fallen leaves and bark. As they unloaded the horses Bluey Jenkins emerged from the veranda wearing only a pair of baggy shorts and staggering under the weight of the radio battery charger.

'Welcome back Corp. Bloody roof leaks so I've transferred signals division to the out-buildings. It's not a hell-uv-a-lot better there, but at least I can hear myself think. And,' he added with a grin, 'later I have a surprise for you.'

Bluey refused to be drawn further, but remained chirpy even when Sam and Stretch rode in an hour later, dumping their sodden bedding on the dirt floor.

'Hey you blokes, don't drip all over the carpet!'

'What's got into you?' Stretch growled. 'You gone troppo or something.'

Bluey held his surprise until after evening meal and the radio schedule in which Ash reported the patrols' findings. His report was brief. Neither party had seen any sign of intrusion, but Stretch and Sam found several waterholes north of Yambarran Range. In a day or two they would return and set up a food depot nearby.

'Okay, now what's this all about?' Ash wanted to know when Bluey had finished tapping out the message in Morse and listened for the all clear. The signaller smiled and twiddled the radio dials.

'I was messing around the night you left trying to get the Australian radio stations this set is supposed to be tuned to,' he said over the whistling static.

'And what? You got this fuzz all night. Jesus! That's wonderful Blue.' Stretch threw up his hands in mock admiration.

'Just wait a moment. Ah, here we are. Get a load of this.'

Out of the radio came the unmistakable Glenn Miller tune *In the Mood*. The Nackeroos crowded round the radio, nodding and tapping fingers to the beat.

'Where's it coming from?' Sam wanted to know. 'Must be Sydney or Melbourne trying to entertain the Yanks.'

'No it's closer than that. Timor maybe. Only trouble is you have to put up with this too,' Bluey said as a woman's sultry voice came through the static—the accent difficult to discern, a hint of American:

"Hello boys, this is your favourite sister with the voice of truth. I am filled with sadness for you as you attempt the impossible. You cannot resist the conquering Japanese Imperial forces. They are now sweeping across New Guinea. Nothing can stop them. The Australian forces are retreating. But there is no escape. The way is blocked by the Imperial Japanese Navy which is victorious in the Coral Sea…"

'Christ, this is a Japanese station. What a load of bullshit!'

'Yeah. But you weed out the propaganda crap and just listen to the music. I can't raise any Australian stations. Must be something to do with–'

'Shut up,' Ash broke in. 'Listen. What's she saying now?'

"… sending a welcome to all soldiers in north Australia with a special message to you boys at Blunder Bay and Bradshaw. I know you are not there of your own choice, alone and far from your loved ones. Your superiors are making you stay while they are living fat and easy in the south. They have left you to be sacrificed. Imperial Japanese forces are coming soon. They do not want to harm you. Do not resist them. Go home now to your wives and girlfriends before it is too late."

The Nackeroos stared at each other in silence, oblivious to the rain pounding on the iron roof and the sound of an American swing band coming through the speaker.

Chapter 8

October 1987

Drilling supervisor, Ethan Williams poked his head through the door of the mud-logger's hut.

'You've got a visitor—Gabriel Fitz-something. Aboriginal bloke.'

Brad frowned.

'Well, not you especially, but I haven't got time. He wants to look around the permit.'

'Why? We okayed the rig site with the Aboriginal custodians and the authorities.'

Williams sighed, impatient. 'Yeah we did. But this bloke wants to go over the whole lease in case we decide to move the rig for a second well or maybe, God forbid, we strike something worthwhile and want to pipe it out.'

'What's the rush? There'll be no second well this year, if at all. Where's he come from? The government? Local landowners?'

'Jesus, I don't know. NWLC I think he said. I got enough to worry about without having to chase around after these blokes. Just make sure you keep him happy. I don't want any more delays. We're nearly out of time as it is. They're over by the mess.

Chapter 8   October 1987

'They?'

'Yeah. He's got a couple of mates,' Williams said as he withdrew.

Aaron Davey pushed a glass dish of cuttings under the microscope and grimaced at Brad.

'Sourpuss's in a mood this morning.'

'Not just this morning. He's been like a bear with his hibernation cut short ever since Wingnut's accident. Wanders round looking at the sky all the time as if he expects it to deluge any minute.'

'Well, we are behind because of all this tripping. And we're into October. I reckon Able is on his back.'

'Probably. I'd better see what this bloke wants.'

* * *

Brad walked across to the mess where three Aborigines were standing by a dust-caked Land Rover. One was young, with long straggling hair, surly expression and dressed in basketball singlet and shorts. He wore thongs on his feet. The second seemed more middle age, dark curly hair going grey at the edges and wearing jeans, a torn polo shirt and battered tennis shoes. These two were absorbed in watching the roughnecks manhandling a length of drill pipe into position on the drill floor.

The third was a much older man, although by how much Brad found it difficult to judge—could be in his sixties. He had an imposing, broad-shouldered stance, white stubbly beard and hair cut short back and sides. A tan Akubra shaded a creased brow and deep-set eyes; an open-neck, short-sleeved shirt was tucked into moleskin trousers that concertinaed over brown stockman's boots. The man caught sight of Brad and stepped forward, holding out a hand in greeting.

'I'm Gabriel Fitzmaurice. Danny and Lewis,' he added indicating his companions who looked around briefly before turning their attention back to the rig.

'Brad Dixon. What can we do for you? If you want to get closer to the action I can organise overalls and boots and some hard hats. Safety regulations, I'm afraid.'

'Maybe later for these fellas. But first we wanted to have a look around the permit… the supervisor said it would be all right.' Gabriel's voice was soft, educated.

Brad shrugged.

'Okay by me if he said so. There are no restrictions outside the rig perimeter, but where are you from? What are you looking for?'

'The supervisor didn't say? Ah, well I'm attached to the NWLC as a consultant. They want a report on all the petroleum leases in the Kimberley.'

'NWLC—North West Land Council?'

Gabriel nodded.

'But all the agreements are in place, for this drilling program anyway,' Brad said. 'They were sorted with you people and the government before we were awarded the permit. What's to report?'

'There's no problem with any of that. This is more an internal thing. The Council wants a proper formalised survey for the records. It's not a statutory organisation, so everything's been a bit ad hoc so far. No one's put it all together for them. I'm going over every permit, not just this one. Danny and Lewis are local, showing me around their part of the country.'

Brad was wary. The NWLC had been going eight or nine years—formed soon after the acrimonious confrontation

Chapter 8 October 1987

between a State Government bullishly backing oil explorers against Aboriginal landowners at Noonkanbah Station in the late 1970s. Surely the Council had got its act together by now. But then, maybe not. Aboriginal time frames were different.

'Okay,' he said. 'But it would help to know what you are looking for. Is there anything in particular you want to see?'

'Just a drive around. Lewis here knows the significance of the country. He was out here looking around where your people proposed running the seismic survey and again before you chose the drill site. I want to retrace those lines, get a feel for where they are on the ground rather than on a map. Why don't you come along? You'll see what I'm trying to do.'

Brad hesitated a moment, then agreed. What the hell. Williams said to keep them happy.

They headed out of camp in the Land Rover, Lewis driving with the youngster Danny next to him, Brad in the back seat with Gabriel. Before long, Lewis left the rig access track and took off through the scrub following the wheel tracks of an old seismic line. About a kilometre along he slowed, extended an arm out the window and jabbered something that Brad couldn't catch. Beside him Gabriel squiggled a few words in his note book, but made no comment. They carried on to the end of the line which was about six kilometres long and drove a kilometre across to the next. Again Lewis pointed. Brad looked, but saw nothing out of the ordinary—just a line of trees marking the bed of a creek. Gabriel made another note. On the third line they slowed twice, the three Aborigines absorbed in their vigil. Half the morning had gone and barely a word had been spoken to Brad by any of them. He shook his head and tried to keep the irritation from his voice.

'There isn't much point in me being here. I've no idea what I'm looking at, if anything.'

Gabriel said something to Lewis in the native tongue and turned to Brad.

'I'm sorry. I am forgetting. Let's take you to something we can show you.'

Lewis pulled the vehicle off the seismic line and headed towards a jumble of grey limestone blocks that poked above the tree tops. He parked about fifty metres from the outcrop and they got out to walk, picking their way around tumbled rocks, scrub and a stand of young boab trees. Brad noticed the rock at the base of the outcrop had been weathered and undercut to form a low natural shelter. Gabriel led the way, crouching as he went and pointing to the roof. The painting of a man spearing a kangaroo appeared surprisingly lifelike, particularly the outline of the roo as it rocked back on hind legs from the impact of the weapon that had just left the man's extended arm. The orange and white ochre figures were still sharp against the dark rock surface.

'A good panel,' Gabriel said. 'I like its simplicity. A single painting is unusual. Often there are dozens of images crowded together, some overlapping. There are more galleries scattered about the area but, for me, this is the best. You can understand we don't want it disturbed, or any of them.'

'Does this one have a special significance?' Brad asked.

Gabriel spoke to Lewis.

'No. It's just well preserved being out of the weather and too low for cattle to get in.'

'So not as important as the other places where you took notes. And yet I couldn't see anything there apart from trees and a creek bed, certainly nothing like this.'

Chapter 8   October 1987

Gabriel moved back out into the open, straightening his body with a sigh and rubbing a thigh.

'Not as supple as I used to be,' he said, leaning against the rock face as Lewis sauntered past heading to the vehicle to re-join Danny who had not bothered to visit the painting.

'How much do you know of our relationship to the land?' Gabriel asked Brad who came and stood beside him.

'The Dreamtime stuff you mean? I've read a bit.'

'Well, you might have read that sites of significance are geographic points on tracks followed by ancestor beings as they journeyed across the land performing various acts, some of creation, some of ritual. The harder part to understand is that the amount of area around each place, you can call it the sphere of influence, is open to discussion, even among our own people. The boundaries are not clear-cut. Women and children might be allowed to go to one point, initiates a bit closer and Elders closer again.'

'So how do you know what to tell exploration companies? I mean, if we can't see anything, how can we believe the boundaries you set?'

'Depends on the importance of the site, but mostly we'll settle on the outer limit.'

Gabriel stroked his beard, drawing his thumb and fingers down the furrows in his cheeks.

'Sometimes we make a problem for ourselves as well. There are sites that are secret. The locations can't be given to anyone who is not an initiate. Occasionally a site will be destroyed because no one is authorised to contact outsiders—companies, developers, even anthropologists—to say it's there. The result, unfortunately, is bitterness and suspicion. I don't know how we solve that.'

The admission surprised Brad. He looked at Gabriel anew, but saw no sign of scorn.

'I can see where mining an area might be a problem, like an open cut. But I don't understand the worries about drilling for oil. It's reasonably flexible and has a much smaller footprint. We can move the rig a bit to avoid a site of significance and drill a directional well. Why isn't that acceptable?'

'Sometimes it can be. But you have to realise that the Dreamtime tracks between places may be underground as well as on the surface. In some places the tracks criss-cross each other more densely than others. And also there is belief of special powers in the earth. If the ground is punctured and the powers are released it will bring sickness to the area.'

'Jesus. No wonder companies tear their hair out. The lawyers and anthropologists must love this Land Rights work.'

'It's important to us.'

Brad suddenly remembered who he was talking to.

'Sorry, I didn't mean to be flippant.'

Gabriel patted the rock he was leaning on.

'Blackfella law is like this rock. It never changes.'

Brad drew a breath to interrupt, but Gabriel forestalled him.

'Ah. I forgot. You are a geologist. A bad analogy. But you know what I mean. Our law is constant through from the time of the ancestors. White fella law is always changing, not the same for long. We just want acceptance of our law. Your law has the ability to change around it.'

'Maybe. But it's not that simple is it? Not now that politics has come into it. Look what happened with the oil field in central Australia—Mereenie—after the Land Rights Act was passed. You put in huge claims to the companies for royalties and compensations, even reimbursements of negotiating lawyers' costs and an option to convert to a large carried interest in the project. It was virtually a right of veto on the companies' activities.'

'Not so bad. Every negotiator starts with an ambit claim. It was worked out in the end, as you know. The field was developed and everyone is getting something.'

'Don't get me wrong,' Brad said. 'I'm not against Land Rights, but it's got to be fair. I think I understand about sites of significance and that they shouldn't be disturbed, but the underlying theme for you seems to be that land means all underground minerals and oil as well as the topsoil. The law says the minerals are the property of the Crown, so it's a national asset and should be shared by everyone.'

'White fella's law. Whose land was it in the first place?'

Brad suddenly saw he was moving out of his depth. He'd read a few newspaper and magazine articles, not the Land Rights Act. Some articles theorised about pre-Aboriginal inhabitants in northern Australia, so the blanket assertion that Aborigines are the only true landholders troubled him. He chose his words carefully.

'You have to admit that sometimes Aborigines use the Act as a sort of political rallying call that doesn't involve protection of heritage and sites of significance.'

'There is an element of that, especially with the younger generation. Danny over there is one of those disillusioned by the old teachings. Lewis is patient with him, trying to explain the importance of his heritage. But it's difficult. From the time the first missionaries and settlers arrived, European influence and laws have spoken against the blackfella values and way of living, forcing our people to accept the white fellas' rules. I saw and felt it when I was growing up, but with help I was able to fight against the trend.'

Gabriel frowned as he continued.

'For Danny and many of his generation it is harder. Modern communications have made them less isolated from the white world. The strict tribal laws have been supplanted in their minds with the European customs and privileges that they see around them. Danny gets angry because what he was expecting from that imposed life hasn't come to pass. He sees the big companies come in and take big profits, so he thinks it is okay to use the system to get royalties and have material benefits that white kids have.'

'Is that why he wasn't interested in this gallery? He didn't seem to be interested in anything much … except at the beginning. He couldn't take his eyes off the rig.'

'Well that's the other side of the coin you handed me. You can accuse Aborigines of riding the system, but equally there are companies who by-pass the Elders and go straight to the younger, more vocal people. Often the younger ones speak English so it's easier to speed through negotiations. But like Danny, they aren't necessarily empowered with the authority to speak for the particular clan. The company in question agrees to the young bloods' demands because, to management, time is money and they don't want to be held up in protracted talks. The company doesn't wait or try to understand the meaning behind the Aboriginal Elders' attachment to the earth or their cultural heritage. And that ends up in mutual distrust.'

Gabriel waved at the rock overhang.

'What's worse,' he said, 'is when the government itself uses its law to bulldoze any resistance—literally—ignoring all advice to the contrary.'

'You mean Noonkanbah?'

Chapter 8 October 1987

'Yes.'

'Yeah, well there were pros and cons in that one too, but I agree it wasn't the right way to go about it. No one wants to see that ugliness happen again. Hopefully we've moved on from there.'

'I hope so too,' Gabriel nodded. 'I've been accused by the young blokes of being too old, gone soft and conciliatory, but I'm trying to get across to everyone who'll listen that the core of the debate over land and resources is that Aborigines want their positions and responsibilities as custodians of custom and heritage to be recognised and respected. By everyone, including the politicians and the resources sector. And Aborigines want to be allowed to manage the dreamtime laws in the traditional way.'

'And the royalty money doesn't enter into it?'

'Of course it counts. But it's got to be earned and used in the right way.'

Gabriel pushed off from the rock support and started towards the Land Rover.

'Let's get back to work.'

'You know,' said Brad walking with him, 'I still don't really understand why you are going over all our ground again. You said yourself that Lewis was one of those who cleared it for the seismic survey and the drill site.'

'Yes he did. But the seismic lines are kilometres apart with a lot of country in between. He was concentrating on your work program of the moment. My question to you is: are you going to drill a second well and where will you locate it?'

'Christ! Consideration of a second well is way too premature and even if we were going to, I wouldn't tell you where we'd want to put it this far in advance. We have our secret sites too.'

Gabriel smiled and went on: 'And then there's the discovery, delineation wells, production facilities, pipeline routes. We need to have a complete account of where you can and can't go.'

Brad stared at him, eyebrows raised. It was beginning to sound like the conversation he'd had with Nurse Frost.

'What if you're not calling the shots?' Gabriel said. 'The NWLC might have to deal with another company out here. But, if we survey the lease properly now, it's all done and filed. It would make future negotiations smoother.'

'Hang on a minute, where's all this coming from?'

'Nowhere concrete. But it's reasonable to assume there will be a farm-in, particularly if you make a discovery. Your company is far too small to tackle the next steps alone.'

'You seem remarkably well informed for a Land Rights consultant, if I may say so.'

'Not really. No more than the next person who has anything to do with the industry. Your boss has a certain reputation.'

'Reg Able?'

'That's the man.'

* * *

Back at the rig by mid-afternoon, Brad took his two youngest guests to the store to kit them out with overalls, boots, safety glasses and hats to visit the rig. It took a while to persuade Danny of the need for boots and hard hat, but he liked the idea of the glasses. They were stylish, Brad admitted, with tapered eye guards at the sides as well as tinted lenses to combat the sun glare. He told Danny he could keep them as long as the drilling super didn't see him wearing them when he left.

Gabriel declined, saying he'd seen enough rig floors in his

Chapter 8 October 1987

time. Instead he went into the mess for a coffee. Brad escorted the other two onto the drill floor to the amusement of the driller and a filthy scowl from Ethan Williams. Over the din Brad explained what was happening and the driller even let Danny into the dog house for a close look at the levers and dials. After that they did a circumnavigation of the rig checking out the motors, mud tanks, pumps, and racks of drill pipe before heading to the relative quiet of the mud logger's hut. Aaron did his best to tell them what he did with the microscope and graph printouts, but in their eyes it clearly didn't match the action on the drill floor.

At the end of the tour Brad went into the mess and found Gabriel in conversation with Charlie. No surprise there, he thought. The Malteser would be siphoning as much information as he could get from the day's outing.

'Thank you for your company. I enjoyed our conversation. I hope we meet again to explore the topic further,' Gabriel farewelled Brad, shaking hands before getting into the Land Rover—the driver's seat Brad noticed. Lewis' job was obviously done for the day.

* * *

'Interesting bloke,' Charlie said as Brad re-entered the Mess. 'Good education. A firebrand once, I think.'

'Yeah? Maybe. He mentioned Reg Able was in the papers lately. I'm going to see if I can find the article.'

He moved over to the stack of papers and magazines at the back of the Mess.

'In "Scuttlebutt" column. *The Gazette*. Friday last week.'

Brad turned back and grinned.

'Maybe it's best if you just tell me all about it Charlie. Save me the trouble, unless you have things to do in the kitchen.'

'No, Lucy doing good out there. What you want to know?'

'Well, our NWLC friend seemed to think we were on the verge of farming out the Stokes prospect; maybe even selling out to a new operator. He seemed worried there'd be a discovery and he'd be dealing with a new company for the development and production phase. Any truth in that?'

'You know Able. Like I tell you one time before, he always looking for to deal. Always his way of doing the business.'

'Yeah, that's fine, but what's all this about a discovery? Why would Gabriel bring that up? Hell, we haven't even reached the secondary target yet, let alone the main game.'

'Ah. Maybe he read "Scuttlebutt".'

'What did that say? That we'd found oil?'

'No, not yet. But there is strong suggestion, you unnustand. It say oil and gas finds in Bonaparte before, but companies sit on it, waiting for oil price going up.'

'What? Is the paper reporting Able said this? That sort of rubbish is old hat. Conspiracy theorists have been spouting it for years.'

'It say Abel makes speech to investment peoples in New York. He said the Bonaparte has been place for oil since 1840s. But not much exploration wells compared to ones drilled for Bass Strait, so there is big potential for major discovery here. Stokes-1 is first real test of the region and in best place in basin onshore. Much better chances for development than offshore.'

'He actually said that?'

'I dunno. "Scuttlebutt" says it. But maybe lots of supposing.'

'I'll bet the old bastard didn't rush out to deny the reports though. Typical!'

'Something else.'

'There's more?'

'Yes. "Scuttlebutt" tell rumour that Able ready for signing Letter of Intent with big company for maybe future supply of gas to make power for new industry in Kimberley.'

'A gas discovery as well as oil. Sounds like the boss is hedging his bets. What industry would that be?'

'Paper talk maybe lithium. Also — how-do-you-say — elements of the rare earth? But no name for big company. Still for negotiations.'

'Jesus. No wonder Gabriel is wound up. Ha! No pressure on us either,' Brad added. 'Explains why Williams is so frazzled too.'

'You gunna reach target soon?' Charlie asked.

'Depends on this hard stuff, how soon we get through it. Maybe get to the secondary in a week—but the prognosis is all up the shit.'

'And that's not the only thing.'

Brad and Charlie turned at the sound of Aaron's voice. The mud-logger poured himself a coffee and sat down at the table.

'We just had a twist off,' he said. 'Old Sourpuss is ready to lynch the drill crew.'

Chapter 9

October 1987

Recriminations on the drill floor spilled over into the mess. Ethan Williams had not spared his wrath against the driller, Freddie Hawkins, for allowing the twist-off to occur on his watch. Hawkins, a tough, barrel-chested Queenslander from Roma, fired straight back, telling the Super to his face that he was at fault for pushing the crew to 'make hole' as fast as possible despite the resistance of the limestone formation.

'Bastard wanted to cut down the number of trips even though the bits were wearing to hell,' he told his table at the evening meal. 'Had to happen. Too much weight on the bit, too much torque for too long and bang—the pipe snaps.'

'There's too much rush,' a roughneck added. 'Word is that the next contract is enforcing delivery of the rig down south near Dongara in November whether we've finished here or not. That's what's putting the bindi up Sourpuss' bum. You ask me, they shoulda left drilling here till next bloody Dry.'

'Well, it's a fishing job now. That could take a week knowing this old rig.'

'Yeah, but do you know the best part? We're short a couple of fishing tools.'

Chapter 9 October 1987

'Bullshit. Can't be. We had a full suite at the last job.'

'Well we haven't now. I heard old Sourpuss ranting on about it outside the mess when I came in. They're gunna have to fly some gear in from Perth.'

* * *

Brad flicked the high-beam on and slowed down, cautiously scanning the edge of the track for roos and station cattle. He was errand boy for Williams, "volunteered" as the one least needed at the rig to go into town to pick up the fishing tools from the next day's plane. He hadn't done the trip at night and was surprised at the density of darkness outside the cone of the headlights. All the landmarks were blotted out and Brad had to rely on the odometer to know how far he'd come. There was no moon, the sky black with storm clouds that had rolled in that afternoon. Over to the west a sudden bolt of lightning jagged through the gloom. Charlie had told him there were often spectacular displays at this time of year—some rain, but mostly dry storms in the months leading up to the Wet proper. Often the mornings were clear again; no one sure when the continual downpour would begin. Some years the Wet didn't come at all. This year, though, the experienced hands at the rig were talking about an early onset. The air already felt like a damp blanket, thick and heavy.

* * *

Brad saw Karen Frost as soon as he walked through the pub doors. She was sitting at the same table as before, but with her back to him, talking to a blonde woman of about the same age.

His pulse jumped and part of his brain urged him to go over. Something about Karen attracted him. Her looks of course, but there was more—her directness and self-assurance perhaps. Still, he hesitated. He'd never been good with introductory lines and he was reluctant to chance his reception after the last encounter. Instead he went to the bar, rationalising that it was almost closing time. The barman may have even called last orders because some patrons were pushing back their chairs and saying good-nights. Sipping his beer, Brad couldn't help overhearing a conversation between two ringers slouching on stools nearby. In their early twenties, slightly built and tanned, he guessed they were jackeroos from one of the nearby stations. They both looked as if they'd made a night of it—the speaker in particular, Akubra pushed up high on his forehead, his torso swaying despite the stool and the support of the bar.

'You gunna come with me, or aren't you? There's two of um. Peesh a cake. Nurses. I sheen'm at the hoshpittle. Come on.'

'Where we gunna take them? Can't go to the motel. The boss is there. He'll skin you alive if he finds out.'

'I dunno. Their place. They're up for it. Bang like a dunny door, speshly the dark hair one.'

'You're too pissed. You couldn't do anything.'

'Wanna bet? Come on.'

Akubra got to his feet and steadied a moment, holding the counter before launching himself in the direction of Karen and her companion. His mate hesitated, then downed the dregs in his glass and followed. Brad watched their progress across the room as Akubra grazed several tables and almost tripped headlong on a chair leg. He righted himself and continued till he reached his target, yanked a chair out and sat next to Karen. His mate, obviously not wedded to the project, stayed on his feet behind

Chapter 9   October 1987

him. It was too far away for Brad to hear what was said, but clearly the approach wasn't subtle. He couldn't see Karen's face, but the blonde looked startled. Akubra reached an arm around Karen's shoulders and pulled her towards him. She let the arm linger for a fraction of a second before pulling back sharply and delivering a blow to his chest.

Akubra's expression changed from beery smile, to surprise, to anger, all in slow motion like a succession of screen advertisements in a cinema. He leant back looking at her, then in one movement closed his hand over Karen's wrist and tried to drag himself and her to their feet. The table rocked upsetting a glass of wine that rolled on to the floor, spilling its contents into Karen's lap. She resisted, using her free hand to slap his face. At the same time the blonde reached across trying to pull Karen's wrist free. Akubra's mate just stood there, unhappy with the developing scene, but not sure what to do as other patrons turned to see what the commotion was about.

'Let go you moron!' The blonde's voice, sharp and shrill, carried across the room.

Brad reacted on impulse. Arriving at the table, he brushed past the standing jackeroo and put a hand on Akubra's shoulder.

'Leave it pal. The lady doesn't want to go.'

He saw the startled look of recognition on Karen's face as Akubra twisted round to face him, but keeping hold of her wrist.

'Leave it!' Brad repeated.

'Pish off. Wosh it to you?'

Akubra tried again to get to his feet, pushing on the table with his other hand. He half rose, then overbalanced and fell back. He let go of Karen's wrist for the next attempt and stood upright, swaying slightly, but aggressive.

'You wanna make something of it?'

'No, I don't. And the lady doesn't either. Just leave her alone.'

Akubra pushed Brad in the chest. 'You gunna make me?'

'Just go away, will you. Stop bothering us you drunken halfwit.' The blonde's voice.

'Shut up bitch. Not intreshed 'n you.' Akubra turned to Karen. 'Wassamatta nursey? Not good enough for you? Not like banging your doctor frens?'

'Hey,' Brad said, grabbing Akubra's shoulders. 'There's no need for language. Cool it. Go home. No one wants a fight.'

Brad was conscious of people watching from other tables and he saw the barman approaching. He turned to Akubra's mate, still standing motionless.

'Take him out of here before there's trouble. Now.'

The mate looked blank, trying to assemble his thoughts. Then he nodded and took Akubra's arm.

'Come on Joey. Let's go. Nothin' for us here.'

'You pish off too. I'm stayin.'

'No you're not buddy. Come on. Time to go sleep it off.' The barman pushed past Brad and took Joey by the elbow, propelling the jackeroo in front of him. 'Time for you all to leave,' he added over his shoulder.

'Bitch,' Akubra spat out, but offered no further resistance as his mate took his other arm and the trio wended past the onlookers to the door.

Brad stood, awkward now, not knowing whether to stay. Karen had her head down brushing with a tissue at the red wine stain on her pants. The blonde raised her eyebrows at him.

'Thank you.'

'You okay?'

'My hero,' said Karen sarcastically, tilting her head and

Chapter 9 October 1987

batting her eyelashes.

He saw Karen's pupils were dilated. She was tipsy.

'What are you doing in town?' she said, straightening up. 'Another casualty, or has the rig stopped work?'

'Matter of fact it has for the moment. I'm here to pick up a part from tomorrow's plane.'

'Good.'

Brad wasn't certain if she meant it was good the rig had stopped or good that he was in town. He suspected the first, but was saved from asking.

'I'm Lorna,' said the blonde. 'It's a bit late to offer a drink, last orders were a while ago.'

'That's okay. I only came in for one beer. I'm Brad, from the dreaded Stokes-1 well.' He shot a sideways glance at Karen. She looked past him.

'Ah. You're the one. Karen mentioned she'd locked horns with an unusually well-mannered oilman. She didn't mention chivalrous too.'

'Oh, shut up Lorna,' said Karen and turned to Brad. She put the tissue on the table and gathered herself. 'I'm sorry. I think I need some deep breaths. Please sit.'

Karen patted the seat that Akubra had vacated. 'Lorna shares a house with me. She is also at the hospital. A pharmacist. We are... were... having a quiet night out to celebrate my birthday. I didn't want a fuss.'

'Are you really okay though? He seemed to grab that wrist fairly hard.'

'I'm more worried about the pants. Serves me right for wearing white near red wine.'

'Hardly your fault.'

Lorna changed the subject.

'What's wrong with the rig? Not that I'd know much about it.'

'A twist-off. When the drill pipe snaps in the hole. We're waiting for a part that can grab the fish that's left at the bottom.'

Lorna laughed.

'You rig people always have expressive names for things. I had a boyfriend once who called himself a roughneck. What's the one when you start a well?'

'Spudding.'

'That's right. What's it got to do with potatoes?'

'You've got to let us keep our mystique.'

The barman came back to the table.

'Sorry about that Karen. A couple of drinks and some of these bloody jackeroos think they're real tough stockmen. Hope it didn't spoil the party. You okay to get home?' The barman glanced at Brad.

'We'll manage,' said Karen. 'Walk will do us good.'

'Is it far?' Brad asked as the barman moved away.

'Nothing's far in this town.'

'Akubra seemed to know you were a nurse. I'd feel happier if I came with you both. See you to the door.'

'Thanks, if it's not out of the way,' Lorna said.

Karen looked at Brad, hesitating, assessing. She shrugged and nodded.

Outside, a few pub-goers were still saying farewells, but there was no sign of the jackeroos. 'Yuk. You can see where they've been though,' Lorna said as they steered around a mess on the footpath and walked on down the main street. All the shops were shuttered and dark. Past the hospital entrance and on a couple of streets they turned a corner and stopped outside a small brick house separated from the road by a concrete

Chapter 9   October 1987

apron on which a Volkswagen Beetle was parked.

'Want to come in for a coffee,' Lorna offered… or there's some beer? You didn't really get to finish that one drink did you?'

Brad looked at Karen who again hesitated before rummaging in her bag for keys. Inside, she immediately excused herself and walked down a passage to what Brad assumed were bedrooms and a bathroom. The lounge, where he stood, and the kitchen were one big space separated by a breakfast bar. The place was sparsely furnished with a three-seater couch and a couple of lounge chairs, several stools either side of the bar, a television and a small music system. A brick and plank bookcase leant against one wall.

'Compact.'

'We like it,' Lorna said. 'Beats the hospital quarters anyway. Now, a beer? You going to try again with a glass of red Karen?' she called down the hall.

A few pictures hung on plain white walls—one a bright green, yellow and blue tropical island beach scene, contrasting another of deep rust-red inland desert dune country. A smaller black and white photo hung over the bookcase. Brad moved closer for a better look and saw a group of grinning Aboriginal children assembled in front of an iron-roofed wood-paling church. The ground around was bare earth while a huge spreading gum tree to one side shaded the building.

'That's Fitzmaurice mission. Northern Territory,' Karen said as she came back into the lounge wearing jeans and carrying the white slacks which she threw onto the breakfast bar. 'I hope this stain comes out. They weren't cheap. Where's the salt?'

'I'll do it,' Lorna said, handing her a beer and a glass of wine.

'I'm going to have a water and then bed. Some of us have to work in the morning. Frosty here has two rostered days off,' she added in response to Brad's questioning glance.

He accepted the beer and turned back to the photo. The kids were larking about for the camera; all the girls in dresses, the boys in baggy shorts and singlets. Thin arms and legs and bare feet. Brad gazed at the figures, suddenly noticing one white face among them. A little girl, almost hidden behind the pack.

'My mother,' Karen said coming up behind him. 'She was brought up there. Her parents were the missionaries.'

'Your grandparents?'

She nodded, motioning him to a chair and sprawling across the couch leaving no doubt it was her zone. Her jeans stretched tight emphasising the roundness of her hips and trim waist. The arresting hazel eyes and a slight upward tuck in the corner of her mouth gave Brad a feeling he was being enticed and mocked at the same time. Beguiling.

'Lorna's playing matchmaker again.'

Karen's housemate put the salt back in the cupboard, pulled a face and waved goodnight.

'Does she need to? Must be plenty of suitors around town… and at the hospital.'

Immediately he regretted it, but Karen just twitched the corner of her mouth a little higher.

'Doctor frens,' she said mimicking the jackeroo. 'I thought you might pick up on that, and Dave the barman. Not considered the right sort. Most of them married, hence Lorna's efforts.'

'That leaves me out then.'

'Married?'

Chapter 9   October 1987

'No. Just not the right sort.'

Karen smiled—only the second genuine smile he'd seen in three meetings. He considered it worth the wait. Suddenly she changed tack.

'I meant what I said earlier.'

'About?'

'About the rig. That I'm glad it's been stopped from drilling. Maybe it won't get time to finish and have to ship out before the Wet.'

'That would delay the program, yes, but probably not stop it. There's always next season. The boss is a determined man when he's got an idea in his head.'

'I've heard about him. Sounds like a typical entrepreneur. Only cares about the next deal and stuff-all about anything else.'

'I wouldn't have thought Able would feature in conversations at the local.'

'We're not all country hicks, 'specially when it comes to operations in our back yard. A few of the doctors and business types in town are avid investors and follow the market closely.'

'Able's not listed though.'

'No, but there are plenty of companies surrounding him that are.'

'I guess you've heard then… I mean the rumour about the possible new minerals development?'

'Small communities thrive on rumours. Not everyone is happy about this one though.'

'I'd have thought a big development would be popular. Bring some cash and employment into the area.'

'You sound like the mayor.' Karen shook her head. 'We went down this path last time, remember. What's the cost to the environment? Ripping up everything just to get at something that'll boom one day and bust the next. Then we'll be left with a big scar in the ground and nothing else while the likes of the Able juggernaut move on.'

'The development could happen without Able's help. If we don't find gas to provide power, they'll bring some from elsewhere.'

'Yes but his gas is much closer. Maybe the economics won't work without it.'

'You've really got it in for us with this well haven't you? We're not even close to finding anything yet.'

'Don't take it personally. You're a pawn in the works. I'm talking about the possibility of a project and its aftermath. We lose something precious with all developments. The spin is that they're eco-friendly and sustainable... but they rarely are.'

Brad drank the last of his beer, wondering who Karen had been listening to. Her mind seemed so set. Or was it a ploy to unsettle him, a game? He didn't think so, but he did know he wanted to find out more about this woman, spend time with her. Karen was like no one he'd ever been attracted to before. Nothing like the compliant softness of Wendy and far more composure than Debra. What's more, he found it intriguing for Karen to have missionary grandparents on one side and, if the Malteser was right, the 'bush shooter' on the other. How much of that contrast went into her make-up? Now was not the time to find out. But when? A bold thought flashed into his mind. It was a risk if he'd read the signals wrong. Brad put down the empty stubby and rose to go.

'Well, this pawn is heading off home. Thank you for the beer. I'll tell you what though. I also meant what I said last time. Come and have a look at the rig. I'm not going to try and change your thinking, but at least you can see what I... we do out there. Why not come with me tomorrow... that is if you haven't anything else planned for your days off.'

The hazel eyes looked at him, appraising. She swung her legs off the couch, stood up and opened the door. Brad brushed past to the threshold.

'Well, think about it anyway. I'd like to take you.'

'A date?' The enticing uplift of her mouth, drawing him in. The tables turned.

'I only meant... well, yes dammit... a date.'

'Then yes, I accept. Tomorrow's free.'

There it was again. That full smile. He felt a rush of pleasure, a kid receiving a rare treat.

'Great,' he said, trying to keep the falter from his voice. 'The plane gets in at eleven. I can be round here at midday.'

Just past the VW he turned: 'Oh, and happy birthday.'

Chapter 10

November 1942

B-Company headquarters at Ivanhoe ordered the Nackeroo patrols at The Depot, Bradshaw and Blunder Bay on full alert after the Japanese broadcast. NAOU Command in Katherine immediately began an overhaul of operations to identify any breach of security. Codes and radio schedules were changed, voice transmissions restricted and the backgrounds of all signallers secretly reviewed. The tense mood eased when no internal leak was found, leaving Command to conclude that aerial observations by Japanese spotter planes had been the initial source. The Japanese had maps of the Australian coastline and could come to the same conclusions as NAOU about the best places for setting up observation posts.

Ash, though, wasn't convinced the spotter planes were the sole source of Japanese intelligence. The more he thought about it, the more he suspected there was another source—this one on the ground. The broadcast's specific mention of the Nackeroos' Victoria River bases narrowed the possibilities. He told himself a rogue operator had to be reasonably close, maybe mobile, maybe not. Where better to look for signs than the rugged, empty country to the north and east—the catchment

Chapter 10 November 1942

area for the Fitzmaurice Mission. Unfortunately the weather turned against them.

As October spilled into the first week of November the rain showers became heavier and more frequent, obliterating tracks and making the paths through the ranges slippery and treacherous. The rivers rose and so did the mosquito population. The cheesecloth nets over the Nackeroos' beds were no barrier to the insect attacks. Worse still, the increased presence of sandflies made any time down by the makeshift jetty on the Victoria a stinging torment. Bluey Jenkins felt it most, his fair skin covered in red welts from the bites. Sleep for everyone was hard to come by. The nights filled with sound—the pipe-amplified frog chorus, the bellowing of wild bulls, dingoes howling in the hills and the unnerving grunt of crocodiles in the river.

Everything was damp and stayed damp. Boots grew green fungus on their uppers and the soles became soft; clothes hung in tatters as the stitching rotted; saddles and packs went the same way and required continual repair. The men soon learned from Gabriel and Jimmy to tuck their wax matches, cigarettes and strips of emery paper in their hat bands, rolled in tight packages of water-proof canvas.

Confined to base with little to do besides repair equipment, prepare meals and make sure the animals didn't stray, the Nackeroos became bored and restless. The days dragged, tempers frayed, the atmosphere claustrophobic. The mood briefly lightened of an evening when Bluey tuned into what they now referred to as the 'Jap hour', the program of big band and popular American tunes transmitted from somewhere over the sea to the north. They jeered at the frequent propaganda items, but looked forward to the musical interludes. When over, the morose mood returned as everyone prepared for yet another restless night.

Ash realised some action was needed. Conditions on patrol would be uncomfortable, but probably not more than staying at the base. Besides, the rain would only get heavier and more constant as the Wet arrived, so he saw no point in further delay. Any enemy operative out there would be living with the same conditions.

The chance for a change of routine came when the *Pride* made its first call to the Bradshaw jetty with rations and equipment during the second week of November. Ash took the opportunity to send Jimmy, Sam and Stretch with a string of packhorses to establish a food depot at the waterhole that had been found on the east side of the Yambarran Range. Ash and Gabriel left Bluey at the homestead and boarded the *Pride* for a trip about 20 miles downriver to a place the crew had noticed opposite the junction of the Bullo and Victoria. They had marked it as a potential forward camp site, but hadn't been ashore to investigate.

The tide was ebbing when they pulled away from the Bradshaw jetty and mud banks began appearing in the river as the water shallowed. The skipper eased back the throttle and sent Gabriel to the bow to probe for the deeper channels while Ash kept a lookout on one side, the boat's "mate" on the other.

'We got stuck on one of those first time out,' the skipper said indicating a hump of brown mud in mid-river. 'Just our luck to strike a neap tide. We were still surrounded by mud and crocs two days later. Managed to get off on the third day, but I don't want to go through that again. So keep a sharp lookout.'

Ash scanned the mangrove-lined water's edge and the white-crusted salt flats beyond. In the distance he saw a smudge of taller vegetation that materialised as a stand of trees by a bend

Chapter 10   November 1942

of the river as they approached. The skipper cut the throttle and swung towards a small cove.

'You two go over the bow,' he said as he nosed into the bank. 'Whitey and I'll anchor out in the channel, otherwise we'll be high and dry. You've got an hour or so. We'll take you back on the incoming tide.'

Ash and Gabriel jumped ashore, landing on all fours to steady themselves on the slippery bank. They walked towards a grove of boabs, Pandanus palms, stringy barks and a type of tea-tree clustered about 100 yards in from the river. The trees were young and spindly, but close together so that their crowns provided good cover. Ash walked through the grove to the base of a low flat-topped hill, noting the additional shelter this would give for a camp as well as a lookout along the river. All the place needed was fresh water nearby. He turned to ask Gabriel and saw that the tracker had wandered off to the side along the bed of a dry creek. Ash watched him bend down and sift sand through his fingers.

'Might be little bit water here, Boss.'

Ash joined him and saw where an animal had scratched at the spot, scattering loose pebbles and leaves to the side. Gabriel dug down, enlarging the hole which quickly filled with water gurgling up from an underground spring. Ash shook his head in admiration. He would never have interpreted the signs on his own. He cupped a hand and tasted it... fresh and sweet. The spring was small, not enough for a horse camp, but it would support a forward staging point for walks inland and trips along the river bank.

'Well spotted,' Ash said to the boat crew when he and Gabriel were picked up for the return trip. 'You blokes have naming rights.'

'What about Bottle Glen on account of the boabs?' the skipper suggested. 'I've come to identify with those trees. They always look as though they've been planted upside down—as crazy as us lot hoping to hold back the whole Jap Imperial Army.'

At Bradshaw jetty, Ash arranged with the *Pride* crew to return in a few days with some building material and tools to transport the Bradshaw patrol back to Bottle Glen so they could establish a bush camp. Within minutes of stepping ashore his plans took on a new urgency.

Bluey looked up from the radio transmitter as Ash walked in.

'Hey Corp… you've just missed them. The bush Aborigines. Same ones. They came back looking for you.'

'What did they want?'

'I think I've got it right. They seemed to be saying they'd seen tracks down river from here. I couldn't get how far. They kept saying "little bit". I know that could mean anything, so I concentrated on the bloke that speaks some English and he said something about "near land in river". That'd have to be near an island, right?'

'Could be. The only island I know is Entrance Island, but that's near the Blunder Bay camp. They might have seen tracks made by our blokes.'

'I asked him that… well I tried to. I pointed at my boots and then at myself, but he shook his head and drew a boot print in the dirt. See, over there. It's much smaller.'

Ash went over to the marks scratched in the floor and put his own boot beside them. The outline was about two thirds the size, like a woman's foot. What would a woman be doing out there?

Chapter 10   November 1942

'Japs have got small feet,' Bluey said.

*   *   *

Ash didn't wait for the regular nightly radio sched to send the news to The Depot. He expected the Lieutenant would relay the message to the Blunder Bay base to investigate. But the message back said all the men at Blunder Bay apart from the signaller were on patrol to the west, heading for Legune Station and not expected back for a week or more. The job had to be done from Bradshaw. The Lieutenant also approved the establishment of a camp at Bottle Glen as soon as possible.

Ash spent the evening looking at his maps of the area downstream from Bottle Glen to the river mouth. Several mud islands in the stretch before Entrance Island seemed unlikely landing points, but further north in Queens Channel he noted the much larger Quoin Island that lay between the Victoria mouth and Keyling Inlet which was the mouth of the Fitzmaurice River. Ash assumed the bush Aboriginals hadn't crossed the Victoria, so the tracks they'd reported had to be on the east side. He narrowed his focus to a riverbank and coastline patrol. Even then, the task was enormous. There were a myriad of creeks and run-offs in a huge area.

When Sam, Stretch and Jimmy arrived back at the homestead next day Ash had his plan ready. He gave Stretch and Jimmy the job of constructing a shelter at Bottle Glen with the help of two Nackeroos from The Depot sent down on the *Pride* with materials and equipment. Ash would take Sam and Gabriel to continue as far down river as the boat could go in safety. The trio would then work their way on foot back up to Bottle Glen, scouting all the creeks they came across. Tracks the bush Aborigines had seen would be long since obliterated by rain and tide. But that didn't discount the possibility of finding other tracks and signs of a landing.

* * *

The first part of the boat trip past Bottle Glen meant negotiating the long stretch of water called Holdfast Reach. At the end of that the river narrowed and swung in the S-bend that Ash seen from Endeavour Hill during their first land patrol. This section was known as Whirlpool Bend for good reason, the *Pride*'s skipper warned.

'Worst part of the river, I reckon. They say five or six boats have been sucked down here.'

Ash saw why. The skipper kept as close as possible to the shore, steering the vessel around a rim of swirling water about 100 feet across. The centre of the funnel lay two or three feet below the level of the surrounding river. He watched a floating tree trunk, wrenched from the bank upstream, sink into the downward spiral. After a tense half hour, the *Pride* left the muddy river water behind and chugged into the clear sea water of Blunder Bay. They navigated the eastern branch around Entrance Island and hugged the shoreline of Queens Channel estuary leading to the Bonaparte Gulf. Another hour saw them approaching a narrow channel separating the mainland from a flat featureless hunk of land barely above sea level.

'That must be Quoin Island,' the skipper said. 'I haven't been this far before and I don't like the look of that strait. Too narrow. If I get caught in there the tide will rip us apart. I'm not going round the sea side either; too rough for this old tub. I'll put you ashore here. Keyling Inlet and the mouth of the

Chapter 10 November 1942

Fitzmaurice should be east northeast, not far overland if you want to trek across and then follow the coast back.'

Ash nodded and motioned for Sam and Gabriel to get the packs ready. The skipper steered into the sheltered mouth of a tidal creek and the three-man patrol scrambled over the side. They turned to watch the skipper swing the *Pride*'s bow around and head back up the channel to Blunder Bay on the incoming tide.

'Right Corp, what's the plan?'

'The skipper's idea makes sense. We'll start at the Fitzmaurice and work our way back. We'll make camp and start first light tomorrow.'

* * *

The whole region between the Fitzmaurice and the Victoria was Bradshaw station land and they trekked through grasslands criss-crossed by cattle tracks, steering clear of trees despite the shelter they offered. Gabriel pointed out that the cattle also used them for shade and to rub the itch from their flanks which left ticks behind that were only too willing to accept a human ride. Sam drew the only excitement for the overland sector when he came across the remains of a camp fire, the coals relatively fresh, but Gabriel assured him it was "blackfella cooking". If the Aborigines were close they didn't show themselves. That evening the patrol camped overlooking Keyling Inlet, a wide body of water similar to the mouth of the Victoria, where they found a welcome freshwater pool.

Next morning they descended to a narrow, sandy beach lined with sheltering trees, but found no signs of any human presence. Following the coast around the headland the beach disappeared and the sea crashed in against a line of rocky cliffs. No one could land on this part of the coast, so Ash led the way back up to the plateau and they skirted the area, keeping about half a mile inland. The going was rough, the only sign of life an occasional white-faced wallaby peering from behind boulders or bounding from one rocky crag to the next. In mid-afternoon the sky turned black as heavy clouds rolled towards them. That evening the storm broke with driving rain, thunder and the most vivid lightning display Ash or Sam had ever seen. They watched, mesmerised, as the jagged streaks lit the sky.

'Namarrgon come,' Gabriel said, his voice low.

'Who's that?' Sam asked.

'He lightning man. Make plenty noise. Bring big fella rain.'

'You're not kidding.'

In moments they were soaked, the swags sodden as they huddled together under their canvas sheets. They lay on the ground, boots on and rifles beside them. There was no hope of sleep. Each flash of light revealed rivulets of water everywhere. Sam swore and smacked at his leg.

'Creepy crawlies are enjoying this, anyway.'

Soon the others were scratching and slapping along with him. Standing, sitting, lying down; no position eased the discomfort. The rain finally stopped just before dawn and the long night gave way to a surprisingly cloudless morning. As the sun rose, so did the humidity. Their wet clothes steamed. Insects swarmed from the pools that had formed around them.

The men trekked through the morning in silence, the heat numbing their thoughts, until finally Gabriel pointed ahead to the flat expanse of Quoin Island. They were almost back to where the *Pride* had left them. Looking down on the water churning through the channel separating the island from the

Chapter 10 November 1942

mainland, they saw a jagged reef across the entrance, probably submerged in all but lowest tide. Obviously no boat could survive once caught in the rip. The skipper had been right not to make the attempt.

'The Japs are a lot of things,' Sam said, 'but I don't reckon they'd be crazy enough to ride that. If I was thinking of coming ashore without risking the river mouth I might have a go down there.'

He pointed to a small beach on the seaward side tucked into a cleft at the base of the cliffs. The way down was steep and exposed, but not impossible. No sign of occupation, but someone could be concealed where the sand ended in a stand of trees and rocks at the far end.

'No point in risking us all. I saw it first. Reckon I should go. Okay Corp?'

Ash nodded, dropping his swag and shrugging his rifle from his shoulder

'Take it slow. Signal if you see anything.'

Ash and Gabriel lay in the grass on the cliff top where they could see Sam working his way down the rough track. They kept their rifles trained on the trees below, alert for anything out of place. Sam moved carefully, testing each step and using his hands to steady himself. He reached the beach without mishap. The watchers on the cliff saw him unsling his rifle and walk in a half crouch towards the trees. He disappeared into the grove, but soon reappeared giving the thumbs up sign.

Ash relaxed. He hadn't really expected trouble. At the same time, an empty beach didn't mean there had been no Japanese landing. The cove lay opposite Quoin Island which fitted the bush Aborigines' description of "land in the river". Were they telling the truth? Why else would they come back to Bradshaw looking for him? Unless someone put them up to it… the German missionary perhaps? But why would he do that? To keep suspicion away from himself? No, that was too far-fetched. Yet Ash couldn't shake the feeling that something was amiss. He still didn't believe the Japanese radio broadcast was simply the product of a spotter plane pilot's information. It was too specific.

'Boss!'

Beside him Gabriel had risen to his feet, pointing at the beach where Sam was waving, beckoning them down.

* * *

'What've you found?'

Ash was breathing heavily after scrambling down the cliff path and hastening across the beach where Sam stood waiting.

'I reckon someone was here,' he said, pointing to tracks and signs of a fire under the trees. 'Not an Abo this time. Those are definitely boot marks. Hard to tell how big. But come and see this.'

Sam led the way to the rocks where a trickle of water splashed down the cliff face. The sand underneath had been hollowed out and lined with smaller stones to prevent the walls falling in, creating a shallow basin big enough to dip a canteen.

'That doesn't look like Abo's work either. Someone was here for a few days at least.'

Ash weighed the possibilities. One of the Nackeroos exploring out from Blunder Bay; a stockman looking for strays on Bradshaw station; a coast-watching sailor out from Darwin; or a Japanese observer. If it was the last, how did he, or they, get here? Surely a warship would have been reported by the boys at Blunder Bay. Landed from a submarine? More importantly though, had the Japanese moved on inland or gone back to the sub?

'Here Boss.'

They returned to the fire place where Gabriel had scraped among the coals and pulled out a blackened tin.

'A ration pack,' said Sam. 'Could be Jap. Could be one of ours too.'

'More Boss.'

Gabriel held up a scorched piece of waxed paper that he'd dug from one side of the coals. Ash held it up trying to decipher what remained of the printed lettering.

'Looks like S... U ... P. Then in the corner K-ra... or something.'

'Hang on. Let's have a look.'

Sam took the paper and studied it carefully for a few moments.

'I reckon it's "SUPPER. K-ration". I saw these when we were in Katherine. It's a bloody Yank ration tin.'

He handed the charred wrapper fragment back to Ash.

'I remember asking a big Negro truck driver what the hell supper was. There were crates labelled K-rations in his truck, but some were opened and they had three different coloured packs in them marked Breakfast, Dinner and Supper. He thought I was taking the piss. I reckon he was knocking them off to sell on the sly, or for favours, because he wasn't too pleased I'd seen them. Told me to get my dumb ass out of there. That's why I know it's a Yank tin. But what the hell is it doing here?'

Chapter 11

October 1987

Karen opened the door wearing boots, close-fitting jeans and a long-sleeve Khaki shirt, her hair tied back in a pony-tail.

'Will this do for a geologist's assistant?'

Brad nodded approval. He decided she would look good even in a boiler suit.

'We can find a hard hat and glasses if you want to go onto the rig floor. I didn't think to mention it last night, but you obviously know the sensible gear for a rig site.'

'I'm a country girl and I've been to plenty of cattle station call outs. I didn't think you'd want me out there in my uniform.'

Her grin took the edge off the jibe so Brad let it go and checked that the box of fishing equipment for the rig was securely wedged in the back before ushering Karen into the front seat. Within a few minutes he had negotiated the main street and turned the Land Cruiser onto the highway out of town.

'Sorry there's no air con in this thing,' he said as she wound down her window.

'It's okay. I prefer fresh air anyway. I hardly get any being indoors all week.'

'Yeah, well you might change your mind when we get off the

Chapter 11 October 1987

bitumen. There's a fair bit of dust to contend with.'

'I'm used to that too.'

'You must have done your training up here then. Nearest big hospital would be Darwin wouldn't it?'

'No I went down to Perth. Did a few years there, but couldn't wait to get out of the city. I slowly worked my way back up north with a bit of time in Carnarvon and Broome on the way. But you must be the one out of place—a city boy?'

'Yeah, Melbourne. That was home as a youngster and for uni. My parents have gone, but it still is I suppose, home I mean, although I go all over the place now.'

'Why aren't you the right sort?'

Brad shot her a puzzled look.

'Pardon?'

'What you said last night… not married and not the right sort. There must be a few lady skeletons around the country.'

'Oh, I don't know,' he said, taken off guard by the probe. He could feel Karen's eyes on him. 'I was engaged once… at uni. It didn't work out. After I graduated and got a job I was away too much. We just decided to unhitch. Well… she initiated it and I agreed.'

'And since?'

His life with Debra played out in his mind. How they had kept separate flats at first, but soon realised the unnecessary expense for Brad to rent a place that he'd only be in for a week a month, sometimes less. Often he'd only used it as a wardrobe to grab a change of clothes before heading over to Deb's flat. In the end he'd moved in with her. It made economic sense and she always made a fuss of him each time he returned from the field. She was a wonderful cook and a tigress in bed. For the first year all was rosy. They told themselves that the relationship benefitted from their weeks apart.

Then a management upheaval at work caused ructions down the line and Brad became enmeshed in big company bureaucracy. He resigned and joined a small geological consultancy that serviced onshore exploration. It meant he was posted interstate often and usually for the duration of the well. There were temptations resulting in one or two dalliances during his travels through other cities and towns. Debra sensed the deceit in him. She began to question whether he really wanted her and cared for her, or had the relationship become just a convenience for him. Brad wrestled with his failure to commit and the guilt that seemed to go hand in hand. The tears flowed and he promised that he'd take a longer leave after the Otway job so they could go away together somewhere quiet, intimate, away from phones and work.

Out of the blue, along came Reginald Able. Deb had screamed at him and slammed the bedroom door in his face. When she came out an hour later her manner lowered the room temperature by ten degrees. She told him to go if he must, but they were finished. And she meant it, of that Brad had no doubt. He didn't try to argue, knowing within himself that it was the release he'd wanted, but once again hadn't the strength to broach.

Karen looked across. 'Do I take silence to mean you keep a couple of lovers or a whole harem?'

Brad managed a smile. 'No. No harem. But, yeah, well, a couple of relationships… same story. Not engaged, but they ended the same way.'

'So there's no one waiting back in Melbourne?'

Brad detected a softer tone. Relief? Satisfaction? Or his ego willing it to be? Her expression betrayed neither.

Chapter 11   October 1987

'No, not now,' he answered, finally admitting what he knew was true.

'You must be a slave to Able then.'

'This job's first I've done for him. But I guess they're all the same. It's the nature of the work. Can't be done in a city office.'

'Are you good at it? Got a clear conscience with what you're doing?'

'What do you mean by that?' His response defensive.

'You said that first time in the pub that geologists care about the land. They know about the environment and act responsibly.'

'Oh, that. Yes I do care. I'm certainly not against conservation. I don't want to see things ripped up just because someone wants a development and has the money or political clout to push it through. There are ways to accommodate these things. Given some thought and good use of technology it can often work out, even if it's going to cost a bit more. Same for issues to do with Land Rights. But it's got to be a two-way street. There are too many radicals out there riding the environmental movement and Land Rights for what they can get. Most of them make pronouncements from their city towers. Or, if they do come out to have a look, it's only a quick trip for a day or two. They don't take the time to really get the feel of a place, weigh up the benefits of a project. God save me from zealots too.'

'Meaning me?'

Brad looked across. Karen wasn't smiling this time. He hastened to regain ground.

'I didn't say that. You've obviously got your opinions and strong values. And that's fine. All I'm saying is that a bit of understanding on both sides goes a long way. I met an Aboriginal bloke the other day. Gabriel Fitzmaurice. Working for the NWLC he said. He was interesting and reasoned. I learnt a few things about where the Aborigines are coming from. He made sense. I just reckon that if we talk about things openly, we can usually find a solution.'

'Might that be a touch naïve and sitting on the fence?'

'Yeah, well I've never been a political animal, so maybe it is naïve. I just get annoyed. Nothing's all black or all white. Are you really so against finding and developing mineral resources?'

'It's more a question of dishonesty.'

'I'm not sure I follow you.'

'Do I trust the so-called developers? How many times have entrepreneurial types like Able promised things when they know from the start the promises won't or can't be carried through? The only thing they're interested in about a resource is how much they're going to make out of it. They don't care how they get it. They probably don't even care about people like you who are working for them. You're just a tool. And when it becomes obvious the promises haven't been kept or the plan is changed, there'll be some excuse, something in the fine print. Or someone else's fault. But credibility is out the window as far as I'm concerned. So, yes I am wary.'

'I don't mind "wary". Everyone should be wary. That leaves doors open for talk. But it does mean people have a responsibility to listen and evaluate a thing from all sides. Negotiate. Maybe compromise.'

Brad slowed down as the green drum marking the rig road came into view.

'Ah. We turn off here. You might want to wind that window up now.'

Karen hesitated, but complied as soon as the dust from the front wheels curled up into her face and eyes. Brad couldn't

Chapter 11   October 1987

help the feeling of a small victory.

'I knew someone like that once,' she said. 'Compromise… of sorts. He was a real exponent of the natural order of things in the wild. Hated the idea of introduced plant species or feral animals like cats, pigs and donkeys. But he said there was not much that could be done about them in some of the areas up around here where access is limited. He used to say that eventually they'd all fit into the natural fabric. We'd have to accept there'd be sacrifices along the way.'

'That's sounds a bit like fatalism. I was talking more of things that can be managed. But I suppose it amounts to the same. He accepted things have to change; the environment moves on, it's not static. You trusted this bloke didn't you?'

'I did until he began seeing someone else behind my back.'

Brad's pulse jumped at this intimate detail. He let it lie and concentrated on the road. The corrugations seemed to be a lot worse than his inward trip. The box in the back began to knock against the door and dust seeped into the vehicle despite the closed windows. Up ahead the cattle yards came into view and the turn-off to the old loner's hut.

'Now there's someone who really doesn't like us.'

Karen looked out at the shack just discernible in the shadows against the limestone outcrop.

'Old Ash. Why do you say that?'

'He sneaks up at night and fires his rifle. Trying to warn us off, I suppose. He never stays around to talk to anyone. Gave me a helluva fright when I first got here. Ash. Is that his name?'

'Everyone calls him that. He's been out here for years, on his own mostly. Not many know his real name is Douglas Ashmore. He's my grandfather, but I suppose you've heard that by now?'

Brad nodded. 'The Malteser told me.'

'Who?'

'Sorry. The rig chef, catering manager… you'll meet him. I was waiting for you to mention it. So Ash must be grandfather on your father's side.'

'What makes you say that? Oh, my mother in the mission photograph at home.'

'Well yes. He doesn't fit the image of a missionary.'

'You're right. Ash was never one for the church. It's ironic, but he had something to do with mineral exploration in his younger days. He rarely talks about it. Something must have happened because he doesn't like talking to anyone these days. Everyone's an intruder. I suppose he thinks the rig's too close.'

'But you go and see him?'

'Not much. I did for a while when I got up here. But… well… we haven't a lot to say.'

'And your father?'

'Long gone. I hardly knew him.' Karen sighed. 'Look, I'd rather not talk about this now, don't want to spoil the day.'

'I'm sorry. I don't mean to pry. It's just that you said Ash was mostly on his own. I thought there might be other family or…'

'Oh that. Well there is someone who sees him a bit. Actually you've already met him. Gabriel. The Aboriginal from the NWLC.'

'Gabriel Fitzmaurice! You didn't say you knew him and here's me going on about Land Rights. You probably know more about why he was out at the rig than me.'

'We all have our secrets.'

'Okay. But what's the connection with your grandfather?'

'I think they knew each other during the war… World War Two, I mean. Gabriel said something about it once—working

Chapter 11 October 1987

with the Australian Army up around the NT. Said he owed his education to grandfather. He paid to send him to school.'

'Must have been a special friendship for him to do that. Fitzmaurice. It's an unusual surname for an Aboriginal. Did he have an Irish father?'

Karen looked across, frowning. 'Are you opening a file on him? Potential troublemakers for Able!'

'No. Just interested. Like I said, I found him a sensible bloke.'

'He told me that after the war it was hard for anyone different at high school. He was already ten years older than the other kids... and black. He needed a surname, so he chose the mission where he grew up.'

'He was at the Fitzmaurice Mission?'

'Sure. He's one of the older kids in the photo you saw. That was taken about 1935, just before he left to be a stockman.'

'So your mother would have known him?'

'I suppose so. She never said.'

'Well, it's an amazing coincidence.'

'What is?'

'That Gabriel is a common denominator for both sides of your family.'

Karen made no comment and they drove on in silence till Brad saw the top of the rig mast above the trees.

'There it is. Not far now.'

Karen seemed lost in thought and didn't look up.

'I can tell you something else for your Gabriel dossier,' she said. 'He was quite the activist for Aboriginal Rights when he finished school. He was one of the instigators of the Wave Hill Station walk off in the 1960s and he took part in other protests that followed.'

'He didn't say anything about it the other day. We did talk

about Noonkanbah though. He seemed quite pragmatic about that.'

'He probably is. I'm talking twenty-five years ago. I'm sure he's mellowed since then, but I'll bet, deep inside, he's just as concerned about your rig being here and about who might be involved in the future as grandfather seems to be… maybe I am too.'

* * *

Karen attracted some curious glances when they arrived at the rig; some lustful looks too. She took the attention in her stride, even waving when one of the men made a comment. The drilling supervisor was not happy.

'Jesus Dixon,' he hissed when out of Karen's hearing as they unloaded the fishing tools from the vehicle. 'As if we haven't got enough distractions. Make sure you read her the safety briefing. I haven't got time for it. And if you're going to take her onto the drill floor, stay out of the way. We got to get this fish out of the hole and it's going to be busier than ants on a sugar hit up there.'

Brad led Karen to the supervisor's office, apologising for the naked stares, but quietly pleased to be by her side.

'I'm a big girl. It's no worse than blokes coming in to the hospital. Most of them will be pussycats. Any from round here?'

'A couple of the roustabouts are local. The rest are from all over. The rig crew usually stays together. They just go where the rig goes. Now, have a read of this safety card. You'll be with me all the time, but it's the rules. Your boots are unlikely to have steel toe-caps, so grab a pair from over there. Should be some your size. Hat and glasses, then we're ready to look around.'

Chapter 11 October 1987

Brad tried not to sound like a tour leader. He felt nervous, like a kid hoping for praise and was gratified when Karen did seem genuinely keen to see everything that was going on. She put the drill crew on side by telling them not to hold back any swearing on her account and then asked the driller, Freddie Hawkins, to describe the dangers on the rig floor and exactly how Wingnut had met with his accident. Hawkeye was reluctant till Karen mentioned professional interest and said she'd looked after him at the hospital. In the mud-logger's hut, how much real interest Karen had in the microscopes and cuttings, Brad couldn't tell.

'Not quite five-star,' Brad said, showing her into his room in the Atco accommodation block.

'Not your average reading either,' she said picking up Stokes' journal from the table.

'You might be surprised to know that Able lent it to me. Said it gave the early exploration of the region. I'm looking at the entries on Stokes' journey up the Victoria River.'

'Able the history buff. There's a thing.' She put the book back on the table.

'Surprised me too. Not sure how yet, but I'm guessing the journal led him to the Bonaparte—certainly the well name. Now, what about a coffee? Not here,' he hastened to add. 'In the mess. You've got to meet the Malteser.'

Charlie bustled out of the galley as soon as Brad and Karen entered.

'Ah. New recruit. You can cook?'

Karen looked startled for a moment, then smiled. 'The odd damper here and there. That's all.'

The Malteser chortled and called out for Lucy to bring some pastries.

'We make just now for you and this rock man here. Please. Eat.'

Charlie the charmer, Brad thought to himself. He noticed that Lucy banged the plate unnecessarily hard on the table.

'Sorry,' she said narrowing her eyes at him before walking back to the kitchen.

Charlie didn't pay any attention. 'What you think of our home?' he asked. 'First time for a rig?'

'Yes, first time. I have seen a mine though.'

'Maybe the new one for Kimberley at Argyle, eh? All girls like diamonds, I think. Very beautiful.'

'Yes, and very expensive.'

'That's okay, Brad buy for you.' The Malteser was enjoying himself.

'Cut it out Charlie.'

'That mine's going to leave a very big scar though,' Karen said. 'Maybe it's not worth it.'

Charlie changed gears with ease.

'For a rig it is much smaller. And when we go, the bush will come back.'

'Spoken like an oilman. Except you hope to make a discovery. Then the disturbance will be much bigger and the scar won't heal.'

'Your grandfather says this disturbance?'

'No. I say it. Maybe my grandfather does too. I haven't spoken to him.'

Charlie sighed.

'I unnustand a little bit for him to be angry. But to shoot is dangerous.'

Karen nodded.

'Yes it is. I don't like that either. It is not the best way to negotiate.' She put emphasis on the last word glancing at Brad with the now familiar uplift to the corner of her mouth. 'But perhaps you won't find anything and the trouble for him will go away.'

'Then no more pastries either.'

'No more pastries. That would be a pity,' she added reaching towards the plate.

Charlie smiled and rose.

'Thank you. You are kind to the Malteser.'

At the galley door he turned and winked.

'I still think diamonds for you.'

Chapter 12

October 1987

It was late afternoon when Brad and Karen left the camp and headed back to town. They drove in silence, Brad anxious to know Karen's reaction to the visit, not daring to ask. He glanced across, but she was looking out the side window and he couldn't judge her mood. The silence extended for several minutes so it was a relief when she finally turned to him, smiling.

'Well, you've certainly got the chef in your corner.'

'Charlie? Yeah, I'm sorry about that. He likes to know everything that goes on, but he can be a bit familiar at times prying into personal stuff.'

'That too, but I meant about him playing the same company "little or no impact" line.'

Brad shook his head.

'There's a lot more to the Malteser than cooking. He's been right around the country a couple of times—seen a lot more of it than I have. He has a genuine love of the bush. He wouldn't be part of anything that destroys it.'

'I got that. Relax. It was instructive to see it all. Everyone just doing their job. I admit to being surprised about the smallness

Chapter 12   October 1987

of the area you need to knock down for the rig, but I reserve judgement on the big company tycoon types pulling the strings and what they plan for the future.'

'Not quite a gold star then?'

'No one gets that. Anyway, you have other things on your hands.'

Brad shot her a puzzled look. 'What's that supposed to mean?'

'The little girl in the mess.'

'Lucy? What about her?'

'She's got eyes for you, my lad. Charlie knows it too.'

'No way. She's Able's niece, out here for kitchen experience before going to some cooking school.'

Karen wagged a finger. 'All the more reason to watch out.'

Brad felt his cheeks flush. He gripped the wheel tighter and remained silent. Lucy. She had flirted with him and yes, he had responded. But was it so noticeable? Especially to Karen. He suddenly realised that it mattered what Karen thought of him. It mattered a lot—an unexpected, unfamiliar feeling. Brad concentrated on the road, the light beginning to fade as the afternoon cloud mass gathered overhead. As they neared the stockyards, Karen's voice interrupted his thoughts.

'Do you want to meet him?'

'What? Who?'

'Ash of course. We're nearly at his turn-off.'

'How do you know he's there?'

'Well his old jalopy is. That usually means he's around. Is it a yes?'

Brad hesitated, then decided: 'Why not?'

He turned the Land Cruiser off the road and followed the wheel tracks leading to the limestone outcrop and Ash's shack. As they came closer he saw that the hut was literally an extension of the limestone mass, with the rock face serving as a side wall. The other three walls were made up of rough-sawn timber boards. They were capped by a sloping corrugated iron roof, rusted and moss covered. The roof extended out at the front in an awning over the bare earth supported on three steel uprights that looked suspiciously like the drill pipe used as railings for the nearby stockyard. The front wall had one square window with a cracked glass pane. A vine twisted its way up the wall near the open doorway that was hung with vertical strips of canvas. A large water tank stood to one side next to a bucket shower held aloft by a rope over a pulley. A post-and-rail barrier enclosed the space around the building. Brad presumed it had been put up to keep the cattle out. An old wood-fired stove complete with flue stood in the yard along with a scattering of wooden and steel implements. A battered Bedford truck with a split windscreen and metal tray was parked nearby, rusty and mud encrusted, but obviously still used. Brad noticed a winch attached to a makeshift bull-bar welded across in front of the headlights.

As he pulled up alongside, a man came out of the hut, pushing the canvas aside. He stood under the metal awning looking at them, a rifle cradled across one forearm.

'Holy moly! Are you sure this is a good idea?'

But Karen was already out of the vehicle and walking towards the hut. Brad stayed behind the wheel, unsure whether or not to keep the engine running. He watched as she went up to the man and gave him a kiss on the cheek. It wasn't reciprocated. He couldn't hear what was said, but the man made an upward movement of his chin, then leaned the rifle against one of the veranda uprights and stood with his

Chapter 12 October 1987

arms by his sides. Karen turned and beckoned. Brad switched off and instinctively pulled the key. Half way out the door he changed his mind, replacing the key in the ignition before moving towards them. The man's eyes never left him, his face expressionless, waiting. Brad saw his feet were bare, his calves and thighs lean and knotted with muscle where they protruded from loose-fitting shorts. The collar of his short-sleeved shirt was frayed and stained.

'Brad, meet Ash. Ash, this is Brad: one of the men you shot up a week or so back.'

Brad glared at her, but she just gazed back, amused at his discomfort.

Ash looked to be well into his seventies, his face chiselled and sun-dried to the texture of leather, a dark cancer-like blemish on one cheekbone. He was probably handsome once. His stubbled chin jutted forward, a turkey gizzard below. He had a full head of unkempt grey hair that kicked up at the back of his neck and curled around his ears. But it was Ash's eyes that unnerved Brad—bright and blue, directed in an unblinking stare.

Ash unexpectedly stuck out a hand. Brad reciprocated and encountered a surprisingly firm grip. He had a feeling it was more a test than a greeting and wondered if he had passed.

'You from the rig?'

Ash's voice had a smoker's grating edge.

'Stokes-1 well. Yes I am.'

'Bloody invaders. Constant rumble and screech day and night. And for what? There's nothing there.'

'You might be right, but we don't know that yet.'

'Brad's the geologist on the well,' Karen said. 'He thinks it's more likely to be gas than oil.'

'There's nothing there. They've looked before. Found nothing. Why do you want to disturb the place again?'

'There was a bit of oil and some gas in a previous well, not commercial I'll admit, but...'

'So, why come back?'

Brad hesitated. It had been a long day. Did he really need this confrontation?

'That well was a fair way from here and it was twenty years ago. Technology has moved on. We can do things better now, see more before we drill, so it's worth another look.'

'You still won't find anything.'

'Brad's also into the early explorers of the region,' Karen put in. 'Stokes on the Victoria. I told him you were up that way in the war.'

'Stokes! He was the first invader. Then the Japs and now you lot.'

Ash's persistent goading wore Brad's patience and he reacted.

'The Japanese? There were Japanese air raids. I don't think they ever landed here, unless you mean the more recent invasion of Japanese electronic gadgetry.'

'So you know about the war, do you? Know what happened up here?'

The blue eyes seemed to grow more intense. Brad met the challenge.

'No. Only what I've read. My father served in the Middle East and then New Guinea. He talked about that sometimes. I know he came up against the Japanese on Kokoda. I heard some of those stories. But nothing about north Australia.'

Ash's eyes narrowed.

'Well then, you won't know the real story will you,' he said sharply.

Chapter 12   October 1987

Brad saw the clenched fists, suddenly realising he'd hit a nerve. Ash made an effort to stay in control. When he spoke again his tone had lost some of its belligerence. 'What's your father's name? I was in the desert too. Palestine. Egypt. I might know him.'

'Dixon. George Dixon.'

Ash shook his head. 'No, doesn't ring a bell. Still, it was bloody chaotic. Lots of blokes goin' in all directions. Never knew who you might end up in a shell hole with.'

Karen sighed and shifted her weight from one leg to the other.

'Doesn't look as if you're going to invite us in, but if you two are going to start swapping war stories some refreshment would be acceptable.'

Ash stared at her.

'Never was subtle, this one,' he said to Brad. 'There's no room inside. Anyway it's cooler out here. And there's no coffee. This isn't a George Street Café.'

'You better make that Collins Street. Brad's from Melbourne.'

'Not a lot of difference. They're all hang-outs for snooty toffs. You can sit over there if your feet hurt.'

Ash waved at a rough-sawn bench by the stove and turned to go back into the hut.

'Rum's all I've got. You can have it with water if you must.'

He came back out with a bottle of Bundaberg, a glass jar and two tin mugs.

'Straight,' Karen said. 'In the fancy jar.'

Brad tried to sound defiant. 'I'll take water, thanks. I'm driving.'

Ash flashed the ghost of a grin as he splashed a generous

slug into the mug and gestured at the water tank. 'Tap's over there.'

Brad filled his mug trying not to notice the flecks of grit introduced with the tank water and sat next to Karen. Ash leant on the stove, one arm extended to grip the flue.

'Dad was in Egypt. He came back when Curtin brought the AIF home. Then went straight to New Guinea. I suppose you were the same… except New Guinea.'

Ash just nodded and sipped from his mug. Brad persevered.

'Someone at the rig said there was an Army group up around here in the war called the Nackeroos. Were you one of them?'

'Who told you that?'

'Charlie Camilleri, the catering manager. He seems to know a bit about the area.'

'I'll bet he does, the fat old busybody. Did he put you up to this?'

'No. I'm just interested. I never did get much out of my Dad about his war.'

'Yes… I was near here for a couple of years.'

'There must have been a base in town.'

Ash laughed. 'Not this town, son. It wasn't built till the '60s. Close though. We had headquarters at Ivanhoe Station and a group at Wyndham. I was attached to another group over the border at Timber Creek if you must know.'

'So you'd have been on the Victoria River a bit? From what I've read it has a great history. Stokes thought it might lead to an inland sea.'

Brad cursed his careless tongue. He shouldn't have mentioned Stokes, but Ash just took another drink, then reached for the bottle and poured into his mug. Karen held out her jar. Brad put a hand over his. Ash shrugged.

Chapter 12   October 1987

'Up and down that bloody river more times than I can count. The brass thought the Japs might use it to get inland too. History repeating.'

Ash spat and reached into his shirt pocket, pulling out tobacco and papers. Brad marvelled at his skill in rolling the cigarette with one hand, the other still busy with his drink.

'You want one?' Ash proffered the pouch. Brad declined. 'You,' Ash said to Karen 'don't get a chance. Nurses should know better.'

'Sometimes with a drink.' She pulled a face. 'But not one of those.'

'Bloody brass didn't know what we should be doing. Typical. They had us out on patrols either side of the river too. We spent more time worrying about keeping ourselves alive than looking for Japs. Horses too. Watching where they fed so they didn't get walkabout disease or swamp ulcers or snake bite. Getting kicked in the guts by bloody pack mules. Wet all the time. Isolated. Mail from home every two months if we were lucky. And when the Japs did land we were supposed to let them come, stay behind and watch the bastards without firing a shot. Fat lot of good that would have done.'

'Like coast watchers behind the Japanese lines in New Guinea. They radioed the enemy positions, numbers, helped direct air strikes.'

'You are a bit of a history man aren't you? Not a war baby though, you're too young.'

'My brother was.'

'Was?' said Karen.

Brad looked at her.

'He died before he was one. Mum and Dad took a while to get around to me.'

'Oh.'

Ash watched the two of them through the last spiral of smoke rising from his cigarette. He ground the butt into the stove top.

'If it wasn't for the Aboriginals we had, I'd be history too. One of them saved my bacon more than once. I wouldn't have been able to do anything without him.'

'Gabriel?'

'Bloody hell! Are running a story on me? You sound like a blasted reporter. Did you tell him that Karen?'

'No, she didn't,' Brad lied. 'I've met him. He came to the rig.'

Ash looked at him, half believing, his eyes probing for the truth. He drained his mug and poured another, not offering the bottle this time.

'He taught me about it—the call of the land. His land. How to live from it and how to respect it, communicate with it.'

Ash fell silent, his face now less distinct in the failing light. He seemed to have drifted away, to have forgotten they were there. Brad looked at the sky and resigned himself to another journey to town and back in the dark. It was time to leave.

'What are you doing with this bloke anyway?'

Brad flinched at the abruptness, but Karen answered calmly.

'A roughneck broke an arm. Brad brought him in to the hospital. I've been out to see the rig, to find out more about it, where it happened.'

'You changed your tune. The ultimate greenie. You'd normally be out there with banners protesting the thing.'

'I wanted to see it. Doesn't mean I agree with all of it.'

'You're going soft on him aren't you? Sold out your principles.'

'I haven't sold anything.'

'That's not what it sounds like.'

Chapter 12   October 1987

Brad stiffened at the sneering tone. He stood up and banged his mug on the stove.

'At least she's had the decency to come and see the operation from the inside before making a judgement—not hide behind the sights of a rifle. You could visit too… if you've got the guts without that bottle.'

Ash didn't reply. Instead he turned and stepped towards him. Brad tensed. Ash was a head shorter and forty years older. Shit. He didn't want any confrontation. But Ash just gave him a wry smile and glanced at Karen who had risen from the bench, alarm on her face.

'At least you've picked one with a bit of spine for a change.'

Brad saw Karen go rigid, fighting for control. Her hands clenched, her face changed to a picture of cold fury.

'You bastard.'

She spat the words out and hurled the glass jar at the stove where it smashed into jagged pieces.

'I think we should go. This place has developed an almighty stink.'

Karen spun round and stalked back through the railings to the Land Cruiser.

'It's not my place,' said Brad as he moved past Ash to follow, 'but that was uncalled for. Thank you for the drink. I hope we next meet on more civil terms.'

Chapter 13

October 1987

Karen sat slumped against her door as Brad drove back along the wheel marks and turned onto the station road. Defiantly she wound down her window and faced outwards with her eyes closed, oblivious to the billowing dust. It soon speckled her dark hair and formed streaks of dirt on her cheeks and forehead. She cushioned her head against the juddering door pillar with one arm, the other folded across her chest with a clenched hand resting in her lap. She said nothing, her lips firmly pressed together, her jaw rigid.

Brad glanced across from time to time, not knowing what to say, how to break the silence. Did she blame him for what happened? Was she annoyed that he'd been there to see it, to hear the insults. He hoped not, but the thought worried him.

Ash was a bitter man, yet the bitterness seemed to reach beyond Karen, further back into the past. The Malteser had mentioned rumours of trouble during the war. Brad had detected a wistful stream in the old man too, a sadness, even a longing for something lost. He reflected on the fleeting change that came over Ash when he talked about Aboriginal relationship with the land. Yet there was no peace in him.

Chapter 13   October 1987

Something had left Ash deeply scarred and it soured the relationship with his granddaughter.

Brad breathed a sigh of relief as he passed the green drum and turned onto the bitumen. The juddering ceased and he loosened his grip on the wheel, suddenly realising from the ache in his shoulders how tense he had been over the corrugations. Karen, too, seemed to relax as the hum and clean air of the highway replaced the dust and vibrations. He looked across and saw that her eyes were open now, staring at the passing shadows. The evening air through her open window was pleasantly warm. Brad enjoyed this part of the night when the land began to send the day's heat back into the atmosphere. It was a time to revive and refresh. Checking the road signs he saw they were not far from town. The whole journey had been made in silence and again he wondered how to break it, or if he should.

'He's not really my grandfather.'

Brad stared at Karen, unsure if he had heard correctly, her voice a strangled whisper.

'Take the turn-off to the Little Bungles,' she said more clearly. 'I want to go to the top.'

Although puzzled, Brad did as she asked without comment, steering the car towards the prominent landforms on the edge of town. The banded domes were dark brooding sentinels on either side of the winding track that led to a lookout near the top. He parked and turned off the headlights. When his eyes adjusted, the whole township spread out below, the street lights making dotted lines surrounding the muted glow of houses with blinds drawn.

Beside him Karen stirred and moved into the centre of her seat. Brad instinctively lifted his arm around her shoulders, meeting no resistance as she gave a sudden sob and buried her face against his chest. Within moments her body was racked with gasping spasms as tears flooded down her cheeks. Brad held her gently against him, stroking her arm. The extent and suddenness of her emotion alarmed him. The sobs seemed endless, releasing a pent-up hurt deep within her. He yearned to help, but did not know how.

Gradually the tears slowed and Karen's breathing became more regular, her body resting against him in synch with the rise and fall of his chest. She lifted her head to his shoulder, sniffing back the moisture in her nose, but she made no attempt to sit up straight. Brad reached down to his pocket and offered a crumpled handkerchief.

'Best I've got, sorry.'

'My hero … again.' Karen half laughed, half sobbed as she wiped her eyes and nose. 'I apologise for this. I must look a mess.'

She did—dirt and mascara streaked cheeks, swollen eyes, hair straggling loose from the pony-tail. Brad saw a different Karen from the self-assured, independent "ice queen". Still alone, but less confident, reaching out. He squeezed her arm and waited.

'I knew what he'd be like. I shouldn't have asked you to go in, but you were talking about him. Even Charlie mentioned him, so I just thought …'

'It's okay. I shouldn't have reacted that way either, kept my mouth shut. I think he's a troubled man. Something is haunting him. What did you mean "He's not really my grandfather"?'

'Oh, just that he's been my sort-of guardian since I was about twelve, but not my grandfather. He disappeared some time during the war.'

'Disappeared? You mean killed in action overseas?'

Chapter 13   October 1987

'No. He disappeared near here. I'm not talking about my father's side. I never knew anything about that grandfather. I mean my mother's father, the pastor at the Lutheran mission on the Fitzmaurice River, the place in the photograph.'

'What happened?' Brad took the handkerchief and gently rubbed a streak of dirt from her cheek.

Karen sighed and tilted her head to look at him. She'd shied away from his questions about family earlier in the day. Her memories, many of them anyway, were painful. But somehow she felt comfortable in Brad's presence. No one else, not even Lorna, had witnessed such a release of emotion. She always fought to maintain composure and yet tonight she'd let the tears flow without thinking and without restraint. Karen saw in Brad's eyes that his concern was genuine and she felt his warmth and tenderness towards her.

'I've never found out the full story,' she began. 'I've tried, but there's no one to ask. My mother told me once that there was a lot of unpleasantness around then… during the war, I mean… even before that. Grandfather was born in Germany. My grandmother was too. They came to Australia after World War One, around 1920 I think. Grandfather was in the church, a pastor. Germany was broken. They wanted to start a new life, find peace. Grandfather began somewhere near Adelaide. Other Germans had already immigrated to South Australia, Lutherans, so he found a position in the church there. But he wanted to work with the Aborigines, get more into missionary work, so he took grandmother and they went to central Australia, to help at Hermannsburg. They were there for about year. Then grandfather thought he could do more by going out on his own. He saw an opportunity up in the North. That's when he founded the Fitzmaurice Mission.'

'What? You mean from scratch? That must have taken some courage. It would have been very primitive up here then.'

'Well, yes. It was about 1925, frontier stuff. There were cattle stations. Bradshaw was closest. The nearest town was Timber Creek, more of a police post really.

'Why did he want to be so isolated?'

'I suppose he saw a cause, to try to bring what his calling told him would be a better life for the Aborigines up here before they were influenced by anyone else. Why do any missionaries go where they go? Anyway they managed on their own. You saw the mission church in the photo. I was told grandfather built that with his own hands. Grandmother helped with the school. Gabriel was one of the first children brought up there, but there were lots of others. Grandfather got jackerooing jobs on the stations for a lot of the boys; the girls were given work in the homesteads. My mother was born at the mission. No doctor, just an old gin acting as a midwife. Luckily grandmother came from hardy stock in Germany. God, I hate to think what it would have been like though… all alone, going through it…'

Karen's voice trailed away.

'When was that?' Before the war?'

'Well before. 1930. Mother grew up as just one of the kids—well, there's that photo again. It's the only one I have of her as a child. It looks like a carefree life, for her anyway. But it turned sour when World War 2 broke out. Even before that, she said, when things looked dark in Europe. She didn't know or understand about it, but she did pick up the change in grandfather and grandmother. She learnt later that there were suspicions and snide comments going around the stations and the towns like Katherine. Darwin too. A whispering campaign that grew louder. The whole country was in it by 1940. Anyone

Chapter 13 October 1987

who was German, or Italian, was targeted. Suddenly they were suspected of being collaborators and a security risk, even if they'd taken Australian nationality, which my grandparents had back in the 1920s. It didn't matter to the authorities.'

Karen paused again.

'Were they interned?'

'Only grandfather. They came to the mission and just took him away. Mother told me it was a terrible day, burned in her memory. She was ten. Soldiers and someone with a piece of paper that he read out. Grandfather had to go with them. They said he was a spy. It didn't help that he had taken the family back to Germany in the mid-1930s, just for a short time. That always puzzled me. Why do that? Mother didn't remember much about it. She was too young. I found out later it was a church summons, something to do with grandfather renewing contacts, reporting his progress. They soon came back here, but the trip was on his record and five years later it was interpreted as him receiving instructions from the Third Reich to spy in Australia. I have tried to find out more about that visit to Germany, but any church records over there for that time are long gone. What I did find was a vague reference in a police file that seemed to say the opposite—something about grandfather being beaten up by Nazi thugs. But it was just a line in a report that mentioned his name and didn't take me any further. My mother didn't know anything. The details would have been kept from her. She just remembered her father got sick for a while.

'Anyway, back here in 1940 the government hauled him down to a camp for internees in South Australia. Grandmother stayed at the Fitzmaurice to look after mother and keep the school going. The authorities couldn't find anything incriminating in grandfather's record, maybe the church spoke for him, so his internment was mercifully short, two or three weeks. When they let him out, he came straight back to the Fitzmaurice. He probably shouldn't have, but the mission was his life. He didn't want to abandon it.

'The whispering campaign began again when Japan entered the war. Mother said there were all sorts of fears and suspicions flying around when Darwin was bombed, then Broome and Wyndham. The army came up and there were soldiers at Katherine and Timber Creek. They said a Japanese invasion was likely. There were rumours about lights at night to guide the Japanese troops ashore. Mother remembered her parents being shunned. No one would speak to them—the whites that is. The Aborigines still did, but they were mostly detached from it all anyway. Except some who worked with the army.

'Like Gabriel,' Brad said softly.

'Must have been. Then, mother told me, grandfather went out one night and never came back. He just disappeared, and the mission boat was gone too. She was old enough to ride by then and she went out looking for him along the river and the coast every day for weeks. Grandmother took the mission truck out too. They thought he might be lying injured somewhere. But there was no trace. No one came to help. Worse. People said he'd gone off to board a Japanese ship or submarine; proved he'd been a spy all along.

'Grandmother stood the strain for the rest of the war and a few years afterwards, I suppose because she had to look out for mother. But it must have scarred her. Soon after Mum's twenty-first birthday, grandmother took her own life.'

Karen began sobbing again, softly this time. Brad tightened his embrace. Below them, some of the house lights of the

Chapter 13 October 1987

town had gone out, leaving dark patches within the lighted street grid. The night air, still warm, fanned through the open window.

'I'm sorry,' she whispered. 'I'm making a fool of myself.'

'No you're not. Don't worry. You don't have to say any more.'

She sat up straight and retrieved the handkerchief, feeling stronger as the long-suppressed burden lifted. 'But there is more I want to tell you.'

Brad kept his arm loosely round her shoulder.

'Only if you're sure. Say if it's none of my business, but I am puzzled about where Ash comes in. And what about your mother and father?'

'Mum and father were married in the late 1950s and had a couple of years together. I don't think they were very happy. Mum always said she was damaged goods. I never understood what she meant. But later I realised it was the stigma of the war and growing up with all that hate before and after my grandfather's disappearance. Just not knowing would have been unbearable. And then suddenly grandmother's suicide. It's hell having to endure all that.'

Brad noticed the present tense, wondered, but didn't interrupt. Karen seemed calmer, more composed.

'Father was a station stockman, but I never knew him. He left soon after I was born. Later I did try to find him, but it was too late. Apparently he'd been thrown from a horse and killed. Mum married again. Well, she didn't actually go through the ceremony, just found Bert and went to live with him, taking me along—me under sufferance on his part, I think. I don't really know how they met, but we went to Cloncurry in northwest Queensland where he owned one of the pubs. We lived in some of the rooms above the bar. Not exactly salubrious accommodation. I went to the local school with kids whose parents owned the town businesses and a few from some of the stations round about.

'I think that pub's where Mum learnt to drink. Or, at least, that's where it was easy to drink without it being talked about. She tended the bar all day. I suppose it was friendly having a glass with the customers, which sometimes became two and three. Bert didn't like it though. I remember some terrible rows upstairs after closing time. The walls were very thin. I'd lie in bed with my hands over my ears trying to block out the shouts and screams.

'Then Ash came into the picture. He must have walked into the bar one day and recognised Mum somehow from her childhood days at the mission during the war. It might have been from her maiden name. She'd gone back to that—Müller—showing her German ancestry. It was her way of dealing with the past, defying it almost. I always kept my father's name. I was nine or ten then. She told me Ash had been up in the Northern Territory in the army. Apart from being a cattle town, Cloncurry was also a hub for mineral explorers. Of course, you'd know that.'

'Mm… copper, silver, lead. Mt Isa up the road… and Mary K uranium.'

'Well, that's why I think Ash had something to do with an exploration group. He was out in the bush a lot with the survey teams. He knew about cars and trucks, the mechanical side I mean. Maybe he was a foreman or team leader or something.'

Brad nodded. 'Could have been senior field assistant in charge of vehicle maintenance.'

'Anyway, after that first time, he'd come into the pub to see Mum whenever he was in town. There'd be gaps of several weeks

Chapter 13 October 1987

or so when he went bush. He was always kind to me. I remember him taking me to the pictures once or twice. Cloncurry had this funny little open-air theatre. It was just four walls and no roof and a bare earth floor with a big screen at the front and you sat in canvas fold-up deck lounge chairs. Another time he took Mum and me to the big rodeo in Mount Isa. I don't think there was anything going on between Ash and Mum. I mean, I thought he was old. You know how anyone over thirty looks old to a kid. He was probably in his mid-fifties. Mum was mid-thirties. I never saw them in an embrace or anything. Maybe he heard about grandmother's suicide and just thought he'd look out for Mum. For me too. He was always bringing me rocks and plants and insects and things he'd found in the bush. That's when I first got interested in the natural environment.

'What did your stepfather, or whatever you called him... Bert... think of all that?'

'He never had much time for me, so he was glad when I was out of his hair doing something with Ash. But the rows with Mum got worse. I remember there was a huge one when Ash took Mum for a day-trip to Mt Isa to do some Christmas shopping. It had been raining in the catchment area for the Cloncurry River, so they probably shouldn't have gone but Mum wanted to get a present for me that she couldn't get locally. It was meant to be a surprise, that's why I didn't go. I don't know if you've been to Cloncurry, but every time the river came down in flood it cut the Mt Isa road. That's what happened. Mum and Ash were stuck on the other side for three days. Bert went off his trolley. It's not as if Mum and Ash could get intimate or anything. There was a whole line of cars and trucks at the crossing waiting for the river to go down; a pop-up community sharing food and talk the whole time. I think he was just annoyed at having to serve behind the bar without help. When they did get back he went right off at Mum. Told Ash to find another drinking hole too.

'Things got worse after that. Mum started drinking more and more heavily and the rows seemed to go on all night, some of the day too. I used to dread going home after school and stayed out as late as I could, going for walks by myself into the bush surrounding the town. It came to a head when Mum went on a real binge one day and ended it with pills. Like mother, like daughter. I was twelve.'

Karen went silent a moment, leaning her head against Brad's arm and closing her eyes. Then she opened them again and turned to him.

'That's when Ash took charge, became my guardian. I don't know what happened legally. I don't suppose Bert put up any fight. Next thing I know Ash sent me to Perth, to boarding school. Don't ask me how he afforded it. I don't know. I guess he thought that Perth was as far away from Cloncurry and the hurt as he could send me, make new friends, start afresh. He came down to see me every now and then, maybe a couple of times a year. But he wrote to me, mostly about the bush and the places he'd been working. After a while, though, I got the impression he was tiring of mining and exploration. Just occasional references in his letters, like saying the company had trees knocked down instead of going around them, and that there was unnecessary erosion along mine tracks and in sample pits left bare after rain, rubbish left at camp sites. He came to Perth much less often and when he did come he wasn't the same jovial companion he'd been in Cloncurry.

'Then I heard that he'd actually got out of the industry and had gone native in that shack of his and we began to lose touch.

Chapter 13 October 1987

He was getting older of course, in his sixties and I suppose I didn't help. I went a bit wild in my teens, discovered alcohol, smokes and other drugs—not the hard stuff, thank God, but I made all the mistakes you'd expect. He didn't approve, as you can imagine. After I finished high school I wasn't sure what I wanted to do, but I did have a childhood memory of the Royal Flying Doctor Service. John Flynn founded it in Cloncurry in the 1920s and the town was proud of that. We did a school project on it once. I sort of liked the idea of nursing so that's what I did. A few hiccups along the way with bad relationship choices. That's what Ash meant tonight about me picking spineless liaisons. And he was right. That's what hurts. I still like a drink too. I try to remember my mother's problem, but sometimes it's a release after a really shitty day… and one leads to two and three… then it ends up as doctors and nurses or something worse.

Karen paused briefly.

'Luckily last time a hero came by and whisked me out of trouble.'

Brad had been listening, but looking out the windscreen at the town below when he heard the change in Karen's tone. He turned his head. She was smiling, her cheeks still smudged, but her eyes dry and shining.

'Now you know me better than I know myself,' she said softly. 'It's time I got to know more of you.'

She leaned closer, nudging his arm further round her shoulder till his fingers felt the softness of her breast.

'Mr Dixon, is there a rug in this company vehicle, by any chance?'

'No… but there's a tarp in the back.'

Brad's heart raced as Karen kissed him lightly, teasing, the fragrance of rum still on her lips, her hand slipping down his chest to the waistband of his trousers.

'Will you go and spread it out. I don't want you to have to explain to the boys in the shower block how you got gravel rash on your back.'

Brad thrilled at Karen's touch, her skin like silk, her lips exploring his body until he flamed with desire. She straddled him, her breasts rising and falling, her hands slowly coaxing, her thighs pressing, drawing him deep inside her. The intimacy unexpected and sensual, the surprise adding to his pleasure as she shed her inhibitions and they climaxed in a frenzy of passion. Afterwards they lay together in silence knowing words would break the spell. The night air cooled their bodies, a sliver of moon intermittent as clouds passed overhead. Eventually Karen rose.

'We'd better go before the ants decide I am breakfast.'

'They won't if I get there first.'

Brad reached out, but she cuffed his arm away and began putting on her shirt and jeans. Reluctantly he did the same, then folded the tarp and threw it back into the Cruiser.

Chapter 14

December 1942

Ash gazed out to sea, the charred K-ration label in his hand. He shook his head.

'Foot prints too scuffed to identify, a man-made water catchment, a camp fire and a Yank ration tin. All in the middle of bloody nowhere. Jesus. None of it adds up to anything that makes sense. The only thing we know for sure is that someone has been here, an American by the looks of it.'

Sam pulled a face.

'Where would a Yank come from?'

'Christ knows. It could've been a downed flier. The Yanks would keep that quiet, but you'd think our Blunder Bay boys would report something.'

'If they'd seen it. It's a fair way from there with the haze and all.'

'Well whoever it was, he's not here now.'

Ash shouldered his rifle and started back with Gabriel across the sand to the cliff track, but Sam went over and stared at the coals for a few moments.

'You planning to wait for a tram?' Ash called.

'Just wondering,' Sam said as he caught them up, 'is there

any way a Jap could have captured Yank rations?'

Ash shrugged.

'It's possible, I suppose. Not likely from New Guinea. That's mostly our blokes. Maybe from the Philippines when they ran MacArthur out. But Japs wouldn't eat western food. Jesus, we struggle with the stuff they send us ourselves. They'd be into rice and dried fish or something like that.'

'I didn't mean for them to eat it. Maybe they planted it for us to find, so we'd think Yanks had been here. Throw us off the scent.'

'Why would they do that? We could easily check. You'd reckon if they were scouting around, they wouldn't leave anything. They wouldn't want us to know they were here at all.'

'Yeah. Maybe. But what about that Jap-sized boot print the bush Abos reported?'

'I've been thinking about that, wondering if they've sent us on some wild goose chase. I'd like to talk with them again. Bluey mightn't have got the story straight, or they were just playing us.'

'Why would they do that?'

'I don't know. What do you think Gabriel?'

'Same I tell you before, boss.' The tracker waved an arm towards Quoin Island. 'This place Nemarluk country. He cross here for going to that Port Keats. Blackfella here allasame him. Don't like Jap man.'

'Who's Nemarluk?' Sam asked.

'A renegade black back in the '30s. Big strong bugger apparently. Killed some Jap fishermen up around here because they stole Aboriginal women, or so it's said. He was caught by the troopers, but escaped. Finally recaptured just over there on the other side of the Victoria, Legune Station land. The

Chapter 14   December 1942

police from Timber Creek got him. They put him in Darwin gaol. He died there, a couple of years ago I think.'

'But all that was way before the war. What's it got to do with anything?'

'What Gabriel's saying is that Nemarluk is a bit of a hero, 'specially round here. A sort of black Ned Kelly, a resistance fighter against occupation of tribal lands. The local bush Aborigines don't really like any of us, but they don't like the Japs most.'

'So they wouldn't make up a story just to spite us?'

'You don't think so, do you Gabriel?'

'No boss.'

'That's good enough for me,' Ash said. 'I'd still like to talk to those Fitzmaurice mission boys again, but right now we've got a trek ahead of us and we keep our eyes open. The sooner we report this the better.'

They climbed back up sweating and swearing, burdened with their packs and rifles that continually snagged in shrubs on the slope. The midday sun beat down, yet the cliff track remained slippery from the night's rain. At the top a gentle breeze offered some relief as they rested, taking a swallow from their canteens. Ash estimated it would take two full days to trek back along the Victoria to the new forward base at Bottle Glen.

He almost wished he was back in the Middle East. At least there he knew the enemy was present. Casualties, bomb craters, strafing by fighter planes. He could deal with it. On the Victoria there were none of those things. It was if they were operating in a vacuum. Yet Ash believed the threat of invasion was still real. He remained convinced someone was out in the bush preparing the way. What he couldn't reconcile was the puzzle of the beach camp and its hint of American involvement.

The patrol splashed across the creek emptying into the cove where the *Pride* had left them two days earlier and set off across the tidal flat beyond. Ash, in the lead, concentrated on the ground ahead of him, looking for the best path, wary of breaking through the salt crust.

* * *

Although the mornings were clear, afternoon storms had become a regular occurrence. They slipped and slid their way beside the river, only moving away from the banks for the evening camps when Gabriel mentioned that crocodiles often came inland at night during the wet season. They saw no sign of human presence, arriving at Bottle Glen bedraggled and exhausted.

Ash brooded over the Fitzmaurice Aborigines' tip-off and the puzzle of the beach camp. He needed to visit the Fitzmaurice mission to talk to them. He also wanted to meet the Lutheran pastor and his wife who held sway over the local Aboriginal population. Ash decided to make his full report to the Lieutenant at The Depot in person, so he could flesh out his concerns following his abbreviated radio message.

The Glen camp was not as salubrious as Bradshaw, but Stretch hadn't the advantage of being able to adapt existing buildings. Even so, Ash was amazed to see one of the sheds made from sheets of corrugated iron. Stretch told him they'd been ferried up from The Depot on the *Pride*, but he was cagey about the origin.

'Best you don't ask, Corp. All the timber came from the Glen though.'

In the second hut, the timber was so raw that the forked

Chapter 14   December 1942

uprights planted in the ground had begun to sprout. A wide square of canvas had been slung over the ridge pole, while the sides of the hut were made of brushwood collected from the surrounding bush. Stretch and his team had also built a fireplace, made a rough-cut table with a few seats and they'd dug out the spring, shoring up the sides for easy access. An improvised bucket shower hung in a nearby tree. Stretch flung his arms wide, mocking the pose of a property agent keen for a sale.

'Not the Savoy, but the location is excellent: a river view, plenty of shade, running water, the occasional water taxi, fishing, big game croc hunting plus mossies and sand-flies on call twenty-four hours a day. What more could you want?'

* * *

When the *Pride* arrived Stretch, Sam, Jimmy and Gabriel climbed aboard with Ash for the return journey up-river to Bradshaw where Bluey had maintained a lone vigil and kept radio contact for the past ten days. Ash continued on to The Depot to make his report and receive further orders.

He found the atmosphere at The Depot strangely subdued when he arrived. Everyone walked around with morose expressions and barely returned his greetings. Even the medical orderly had lost his playful banter. Ash wondered if there had been bad news from the front lines in New Guinea or a Japanese advance at one of the other Pacific battle zones. He threw his swag into the bunkhouse and hurried to the Lieutenant's office, fearing the worst.

'You could call it a disaster,' the platoon commander said, wearily returning Ash's salute and motioning him to a seat. 'And I'm the one to blame apparently. Your blokes at Bradshaw and the others on the river won't be happy either when they find out.'

'Sir?'

'We had a supply truck in this morning from Katherine. The load included a dozen crates of beer. As you can guess, the blokes took those off first only to find at least half the bottles broken. The drivers said the road in had been atrocious and the breakages must have occurred in transit. Pretty thin story because every one of the broken bottles was without a metal cap. The bastards had obviously had a piss-up along the way. I refused to accept any of it; sent it back and radioed Katherine HQ the reason. Everyone now blames me for not letting the full bottles stay. 'Course if I had, none of that would have left the base. The regulation two bottles a week per man wouldn't have gone far and you blokes out in the field wouldn't have got any. Then I'd have been in your gun sights.'

The Lieutenant grinned. 'They'll get over it. I bet the next load will be intact whenever it gets here. Now, tell me more about this beach landing you uncovered.'

Ash related the details, including the bush Aborigines' story about the supposed Japanese boot print that had initiated the patrol. The Lieutenant heard him out.

'I've had HQ check with our Yank friends at the airfields near Darwin. There was no downed pilot in the Victoria region, or a pick up. Well, that's what they say anyway. I guess we gotta believe it. Doesn't solve the mystery, I know. You still think there's an operative out there don't you?'

Ash nodded, remaining silent as the Lieutenant continued.

'I'm inclined to agree, or at least I think there's a lingering possibility. But I've got bad news for you.'

'Apart from the beer.'

Chapter 14   December 1942

The Lieutenant smiled. 'Yes, apart from the beer. The brass don't want you anywhere near that mission. They say the pastor has been thoroughly checked out. They don't want the army to be seen to be persecuting him. I reckon the Church has done a bit of leaning on someone in Canberra. I don't know that; only my guess. They did hint that Müller could start to turn the local Aborigines against us. Not actively. That would be treason. More subtle like non-cooperation, not reporting things. We need their eyes even if the reports are not always reliable. And they make the best damn trackers I've ever seen. Anyway, that's the official line. No bothering the missionary.'

'And unofficially?'

The Lieutenant sucked at his moustache. 'There's some rugged country out there. I suppose it's possible a patrol in that direction could lose its way or have some problem that needed help from the closest outpost.'

'I'll try not to get lost Sir. I'll take Gabriel in case it does happen.'

'Good idea. Keep me informed. Oh, by the way, is your signaller coping all right?'

'Jenkins? I haven't seen him for a couple of weeks. Fine when I left. Why do you ask?'

'Just that some of his transmissions have been a bit garbled in the last few days.'

'He has been on his own at Bradshaw while we've been on patrol and Stretch setting up Bottle Glen. But that's not new. We've been away before.'

'Some blokes handle it better than others. Keep an eye on him.'

'I will.'

'All right Corporal. Sorry about the beer. Hopefully there'll be some waiting for you when you get back.'

Chapter 15

December 1942

'No bloody beer! Christ, I'd like to get my hands on those bastards in Katherine. I bet they get down to the pub every night. Wouldn't know a bloody day's work if it hit them in the face.'

'Settle down Stretch. It's not the Q-store's fault. If you want to rage at anyone, try the drivers. And be careful with that. I was one in the Middle East.'

'Yeah well Corp, you were in a war zone. Some real action. No time to sit on your arse and have a piss-up. I'm getting jacked off with this bloody charade out here. What are we doing? There's no bloody Japs, nothing to do except build tin shacks in the middle of bloody nowhere and wander round the bush like a bunch of overgrown boy scouts. And on top of all that, only water to stop a thirst. Jesus, a man can't even trust his own side to get him a proper drink.'

Ash let it ride. There was no point inflaming the situation, but Stretch's outburst added to his growing concerns about the morale at Bradshaw. Stretch was bursting to see some real action, disillusioned that his expectations in joining the Nackeroos hadn't materialised. More than once he'd lamented not joining the troops in New Guinea to have a proper go at the enemy.

Bluey didn't seem to be holding up well either, but for different reasons. Sam told Ash that they'd found Bluey with the radio in pieces, babbling about the set having got wet and that he needed to keep every bit of it clean. Sam checked and couldn't find any leaks in the roof, at least not where the radio was set up, so Bluey's motivation for taking the equipment apart was odd. But they'd gone along with it, gently urging him to put it all together again to catch the evening schedule.

'I think he's worried that he is on his own out here with all of us depending on him for the only link with HQ,' Sam confided. 'He has to be sure the set is in perfect order. That Jap radio broadcast aimed at us has got under his skin too. He's jumpy, worrying about a Jap patrol coming through and him being here with the light on at night a sitting duck. Bluey's a city bloke. I reckon the bush and the isolation has got him a bit spooked.'

'Well, we can't play mothers and fathers. He's a big boy now. He's got to grow up. But I hear what you're saying. The Lieutenant mentioned him as well. Something about his messages getting a bit mixed up. HQ haven't changed the code again have they?'

Sam shook his head. 'Not to my knowledge, but then, I wouldn't know Arthur or Martha about it. Bluey seemed to be on top of that last change. Maybe in his state he's mixing the new cypher with the old one somehow. Christ, I hope not. He's right about one thing. We do rely on that bloody radio.'

'Stick close to him will you. Maybe jolly him along a bit. And while you're at it, keep an eye on Stretch as well. He's getting a bit toey.'

Chapter 15 December 1942

'Christ, I didn't sign up to be a nursemaid. Anyway, why me? Where are you going to be?'

'A little errand to the Fitzmaurice. Something I want to check out and to see if those bush Aborigines are back.'

Sam studied Ash, wanting to know more, but the corporal's stony expression told him that was all he'd get. He changed tack.

'Why don't you take Stretch with you?'

'I thought about that, but I can't rely on him being civil if we meet the pastor. I'll take Gabriel. He knows his way around the mission.'

* * *

Ash and Gabriel left at first light next morning. They took a spare mount each, but decided against a pack mule. Instead they divided their swags, food and equipment between all four horses. They headed due north over the Yambarran Range, descending on the other side along a cool and silent gorge, green with creepers draped over the undergrowth. The gorge floor had a covering of tall bamboo-like grass with jointed stalks and wispy leaves that brushed their thighs as they passed. Water lay in shallow pools along the creek bed. The dark, reddish cliffs towering on either side were pock-marked with caves. If accessible, they'd make ideal observation posts. But the cliffs were sheer.

'Could anyone reach those caves Gabriel?' Ash asked.

'Might be wallaby, Boss. Jump 'longa ledges.' Gabriel pointed at the fissures in the rock face.

'No people then.'

'Might be for my people in old times. Place for drawing spirit totem. For talk. But not now Boss. Too big boot.'

Gabriel grinned and pointed to his army-issue footwear—incongruous lumps of leather ill-fitting on his narrow feet and thin ankles.

Ash laughed. He got the point. No Europeans or Japanese would be able to scale the cliffs without ropes and pitons. He was intrigued by the thought the caves might contain galleries painted by Gabriel's people, stories in ochre about the world around them.

'One day Gabriel, when the Japs have gone, I'd like to come back without boots and you can show me these paintings.'

Gabriel glanced across, but detected no sarcasm in the remark. The corporal was among the many Nackeroos who accepted him as a member of The Depot platoon, but Ash was one of the few white people he'd encountered with a genuine interest in Aboriginal lore and a thirst for knowledge about the land. Gabriel harboured a hope that Ash's respect could continue after war ended and the other soldiers had gone.

'Little bit I show you better place, Boss,' he said quietly.

Moving out of the gorge they came to a knoll of creviced sandstone marking the end of the ridge that capped the Yambarrans along the skyline to the east. Ahead lay a rock-strewn slope before another drop to a wide grassy plain. Gabriel led the way, letting his horse pick its own path down through the maze of boulders until they reached level ground. Once there the heat and humidity increased suddenly, as if someone had turned a dial to high. Yellow grass, stiff as straw, stretched in front and to the sides, interrupted here and there by straggly acacia, the occasional boab and stunted white-trunked eucalypts with lime-green leaves. The plain was ringed by sandstone and limestone ridges, the strata dark against a hazy, faded blue sky.

Chapter 15 December 1942

'My country, Boss,' Gabriel said as Ash halted and slowly absorbed the scene, wrapped in a silent blanket of moist air.

'You were born in this place Gabriel?'

'That way Boss.' The native pointed at the line of hills in the distance. 'Mission there. Might be we see tomorrow.'

Ash was content to keep the horses moving at walking pace across the plain as he gazed from side to side, mesmerized by the stillness around him.

'You had a magnificent backyard to play in,' he said. 'Lots of big space,' he added when he saw Gabriel's puzzled look.

'Not for piccaninny, Boss. The Missus shut door for piccaninny at night. And after lunch, door shut for little bit.'

Ash nodded. He could understand the night curfew, but the missionaries must have enforced a mid-afternoon rest as well. He looked across as Gabriel suddenly chuckled.

'What's up?'

'We naughty buggers sometime. Go out when Missus not looking. Jump on piccaninny cow. He buck strong, but we hold that fella tight to stay on.' Gabriel grinned at the memory.

'You learn to ride that way? On the mission calves?'

'Yes Boss. Horse later when I go for stockman work on station. Big ride for muster. Plenty dust. Catch cow, push that fella over, give him fire iron.'

He mimicked the actions of chasing strays, roping and branding. Ash laughed as he caught Gabriel's obvious enjoyment of the action of the annual dry season muster. He could picture the hard riding, ducking under low branches, dodging obstacles hidden in the long grass. Probably plenty of spills too.

'Exciting times. You must have travelled plenty of this country on the muster.'

'Not here Boss. Veeardee.' Gabriel pointed south.

Ash frowned. Then the penny dropped. 'Ah. VRD – Victoria River Downs.'

'Yes Boss. But Veeardee Boss man say no work in big rains, so muster finish I go walkabout. I come to my country.' He waved an arm at the surrounding plain. 'Good place; my place.'

Ash was surprised that station managers actually encouraged their Aboriginal workforce to go walkabout during the Wet. But he realised that must have been when Gabriel acquired the knowledge and traditions of his race. The pair continued across the grasslands with Gabriel recounting his youthful awakening. He went into more detail about the features around them when Ash spoke of his interest in learning how to survive alone in the bush: knowing where to find water; the habits of native animals; the gathering of bush foods like seasonal fruits and following wild bees to their hives in tree hollows and raiding the sugar bag or honey; learning which plants could be used as medicine and which contained the poison to stun fish and bring them floating to the surface.

The afternoon clouds had rolled in when they rode onto higher ground—rocky again as they approached what appeared to be a massive overhang that offered shelter for the night. After attending to the horses Gabriel beckoned to Ash and walked further in under the roof.

'Might be something for you, Boss.' He grinned and pointed at his feet. 'Okay for boot.'

There was no need to stoop, even where the ceiling met the wall. Outside, the rock face had weathered to a dull grey, but the underside of the overhang was a fresh orange of fine-grained sandstone crossed at intervals by coarse bands of mottled conglomerate.

Chapter 15   December 1942

'Here Boss.'

Ash saw that the ceiling and wall were covered with a myriad of paintings in ochre reds, whites and charcoal blacks. He recognised kangaroos, lizards, a crocodile and turtles. Among these, daubed in clusters, were human-like figures with round heads, spikey hair and circles for eyes, tubular bodies with stubby arms and hands with fingers, legs and feet with individual toes. The thick body of a serpent surrounded the whole mural, its head raised and forked tongue extended as if protecting all the creatures within its domain. Ash stood spellbound.

'First my people,' Gabriel said.

'Ancestor beings?'

'Yes Boss.'

'And the big snake is the creator, guarding them?'

'Yes Boss, I think.'

Outside, shafts of sunlight suddenly speared through a break in the clouds low on the horizon, bathing the plain in a golden glow. The ridge around them turned crimson. Ash stood watching the silent tableau, wondering how many others had done so before him; undoubtedly the painters of the mural behind him, but perhaps other tribespeople who just came to gaze at their country from the vantage point above the plain. Ash wanted to ask if this was a sacred place but, when he glanced across, he knew that speech would be an intrusion. Gabriel, with his back to Ash and rifle across his shoulder, stood tall and motionless in the overhang entrance looking out at his heritage—a modern guardian silhouetted against the blazing sky.

Then the moment was gone. The clouds closed in, the sunlight disappeared and the colours quickly faded into dark shadows. Ash turned to look a final time at the mural. He watched as the painted figures were extinguished one by one in the gathering dusk until only the serpent's head and its forked tongue were visible. Then that, too, succumbed. He turned back to the entrance and saw that Gabriel had already gathered fuel and lit a fire to ward off the spirits of the night.

* * *

The mission was a Spartan affair. The two main buildings—a wooden church and what Ash took to be the mission residence—were set back a little from the banks of the Fitzmaurice River where Pandanus palms and thickets of mangroves grew in tangled profusion. The church was a plain building with the branches of a large river red gum leaning over a high gabled roof of corrugated iron, a simple cross attached to the top. Faded white paint on the paling walls was coated with red dust. Beside the church stood a smaller oblong hut with open windows on each of the long walls and a single narrow door at the front. The mission house lay across the clearing in the shade of a huge Milkwood tree, its lush canopy reaching over and brushing one side of the building. The iron roof, not as steeply gabled as the church, extended well past the thick mud-plastered stone walls to form a wide veranda on all four sides. A set of stone steps gave access to the front door. Further from the river, on the outskirts of the mission, stood several rows of small square huts with brush sides and roofs of closely woven tea-tree. A group of Aboriginal children playing in the dust nearby stopped their game and stared as Ash and Gabriel rode into the clearing and dismounted.

Ash went up the house steps leaving Gabriel with the reins.

Chapter 15 December 1942

Before he reached the front veranda a woman came around the side rubbing her hands on an apron that she wore over a full-length black dress buttoned in front right up to her throat. Her hair was grey, pulled back tightly from her face and clumped in a bun at the back of her head. Dark eyes regarded Ash with a mixture of curiosity and displeasure as if she had been taken from important household business.

'Frau Müller? I am Corporal Ashmore from the NAOU. I am sorry to arrive unannounced. I have come to speak with the pastor… your husband. Is he about the mission?'

'We do not use that form of address, young man. Our home is here for a long time. We do not refer to the Fatherland since… since the troubles.' Her voice was deep, the guttural accent still strong despite her years in Australia. 'What do you want from him? He is to be questioned again?'

'No… I… My apologies Mrs… madam…' Ash stopped, flustered.

'The Aborigines call me Missus. That will do.' She spoke the words to Ash, but directed her gaze over his shoulder. Suddenly recognition shone in her eyes and she smiled. 'Gabriel? Is that you? Such a long time. Are you working for the army now?'

'Yes Missus. I be tracker for Nackeroo.'

'I'm not sure Boss Moola will be pleased to hear that. We forbid all mention of the war here.' She looked back to Ash. 'Is this official business? We were told there would be no more trouble.'

Ash framed his reply carefully, disclosing as little as possible about the NAOU presence in the region.

'Partially, yes, madam… missus. I am interested to speak with one of the mission Aborigines. I don't have his name but he speaks a little English. He visited our base and was headed back to the mission. I would like to talk to him again. And to meet the pastor.'

'A number know some English. We only speak that here, apart from their own language so I don't know you who you want. The adults come and go as they please, not like the children who it is my responsibility to see remain in school.'

She waved her hand in a shooing motion at the group of young faces, bolder now, with mischievous grins and clustered around Gabriel, touching saddles and bridles and rubbing the horses' necks.

'The pastor deals with the older men. He may know who you mean. You will find him in the church. There is a sermon to prepare.'

Ash nodded, touched his hat and began to move away.

'You can leave the horses under the tree. There is a rail there. As long as you keep them away from my garden.'

Ash glanced around the side of the house and saw a cultivated plot, green with vegetables, some fruit trees including several banana plants. A hose lay coiled on the ground, connected to a pipe that ran beside the house in the direction of the river.

'Good tucker there, Boss.'

'They probably eat better than we do. Garden's an idea though. Maybe we could get Bluey interested.'

The interior of the church was as plain as the outside. A central aisle with five rows of wooden benches either side led to a simple altar covered by a white cloth embroidered with a yellow cross. A wooden cross was fixed to the wall directly behind it. Several paintings of the nativity hung from the walls in the spaces between open windows. Pastor Müller looked up from the lectern where he was flicking pages and making notes.

Chapter 15 December 1942

He frowned as Ash and Gabriel started to walk down the aisle, his German accented voice sharp in rebuke.

'I do not allow those in here!'

Ash suddenly realised he had his rifle slung over his shoulder, caught at a disadvantage already.

'I'm sorry pastor. It has become such a part of me, I hadn't realised.'

'So you say. No. Leave it on. I will come out.'

Müller came towards them. A tall man, slightly hunched, wearing a white open-neck collarless shirt, long black trousers and scuffed black boots. His face was tanned a deep brown with puffy pouches under his eyes, bushy unkempt eyebrows and a prominent nose. He wore his receding silver hair short, pushed back from his forehead without a part, his mouth almost hidden by a straggly white moustache and goatee beard. Like his wife, Müller was quick into defence.

'I am to be questioned again? I was assured there would be no more. Where have you come from?'

The pastor looked down towards the river where a sleek two-masted lugger with a gleaming white hull was moored beside some planks along the bank.

'You have no boat?'

'No,' Ash replied. 'We have ridden overland. But you have a boat I see. For the mission?'

'Of course for the mission. We sometimes brave the rock bars in the river and the entrance tides to go out to Darwin. There are things we cannot grow, like fuel for the boat, the water pump and for the truck.'

He pointed to a dilapidated old Ford with spoked wheels, no doors or windscreen, parked behind the church. His voice took a bitter edge as he continued:

'We go when we must. Now Darwin is not such a pleasant place. I am called a Kraut to my face, even that old word Hun. Ach, such long hatred. They say I teach German to the children, tell them Germany and the Axis will win this war and to be prepared. Now you, the army, comes again to persecute Gerda and me. We are Australian citizens since a long time. We do nothing. We do not speak of war.'

Ash kept silent. Why then did the mission Aborigine tell him the opposite—that Müller asked the Aborigines to look out on their walkabouts and to report signs of unusual movement, people, to him? But the old man had shifted his attention to Gabriel, a puzzled look on his face that slowly changed to recognition.

'Gabriel! At first I did not know you. You are in the army now? A great pity to waste your time serving this nothing government. It has no intention of defending us here, or any communities in the north. Oh yes,' he said, turning back to Ash, 'we hear the radio news. Not so isolated we miss that the government has made a line across the country. They will fight for the cities in the southeast, but leave us on our own up here when the invasion comes.'

Ash stared back at him.

'What makes you so sure the Japs will come? They have their hands full in New Guinea. We will stop them there.'

'Perhaps'. A faint smile. 'Perhaps not. They have Timor now. The Australian soldiers are withdrawing. And that puts only empty sea between us—Japanese sea, by all reports—a mere four hundred miles. Ach, yes. They will come when they are ready. And what will you do? Fight them like Leonidas and his three hundred Spartans at Thermopylae? There is no narrow pass here. The whole north is an open door.'

Chapter 15   December 1942

'Why are you still here… if you are so sure we cannot stop them?'

'Why? My work is here. Who else will care about the mission? Who will teach the children if we leave the school?' He pointed to the small building beside the church. 'The government? No! There is no interest. The white community, station managers? No! They are only interested in cheap labour. They give drink and tobacco instead of wages and take the women. Who will help the Aboriginal people fight the temptations of civilisation? Pah! Syphilisation.' He spat the word.

'And the Japs will be better? They will help and understand?'

'Maybe yes. Perhaps not. But what would you have me do, you three hundred Spartans?'

Ash shrugged. 'Maybe they are better off left alone. They know how to live in this country better than you, or me or anyone else.'

'They need spiritual guidance. Christian values.'

'I think you delude yourself. Gabriel has shown me more about the spirit in this land—his land—than any of your Christian values can impose. Such things have no place here.'

'You are like all the others, the government, to mock, to say the Aboriginal people cannot be taught or assisted.'

'Maybe you should let Gabriel and his people make up their own minds and not interfere.'

'They must be educated first. How else can they survive to make their own world if that is what they want?

'Perhaps. But why do they need your religious dogma?'

Pah!' Müller turned away, then swung back. 'What do you want here? Why did you come?'

'Papa, Papa. Mutti says to ask the men to come and have something to eat and drink.'

Ash looked around as a child of eleven or twelve came running up, her dark hair flopping on her shoulders, the hem of her dress swirling about bare legs and feet. She stopped abruptly when she saw the rifle on Ash's shoulder. Then shyly sidled over to her father and took his hand.

'No Frieda. I think the men are leaving now.'

'But Mutti says it is all prepared and laid out.'

The pastor scowled at Ash, but patted the child gently and gave her a smile.

'Ach. Well then, we cannot waste it, can we? Tell Mutti we are just coming.'

Müller watched his daughter skip back to the house. 'My wife is the hospitable one. Perhaps she is glad to see you again Gabriel, despite your new friends.'

'Missus always good to me Boss.' Gabriel grinned.

'I would have thought,' Ash said as they walked across the clearing, 'that you have a very good reason right there for moving south. At least send the girl and your wife.'

'We have talked about this. Gerda will not leave. She is dedicated to all the children. And Frieda. How can I send her alone?' The pastor looked down at the ground. 'What terrors she would face in a city on her own. Children can be more hurtful even than adults. I cannot do that. She is better with us. We will together face what comes.'

The missus was waiting for them on the step. Ash unslung his rifle and stepped aside to hook it on his saddle, but stopped when he saw the native children still skylarking around the horses. Temptation might be too much. He wanted no accident.

'Lean it by the door,' Müller said. 'They will not come up on the veranda.'

His wife nodded and ushered them into the house where a

Chapter 15 December 1942

table was set with plates and cups beside a large platter of cut watermelon and another with slices of cake.

'Please, sit,' she said. 'You will take coffee?'

Ash felt awkward and out of place. It was the first china he'd seen in months. Fresh fruit obviously from the missus' garden and cake from her oven, her demeanour much changed from her first greeting. Gabriel too hesitated at the door, unsure of his status in the white domain. But Gerda called him in and he stood by the table looking around the room nervously. At her mother's prompting, Frieda came over and touched his hand.

'You can take some watermelon. I grew it in the garden. It's sweet.'

'Thank you missy. Might be I have for outside.'

Gabriel took a piece of the proffered fruit and retreated to the door, clearly more comfortable on the veranda. Gerda sighed, but made no move to call him back.

'You should not do that. You know they are happier that way,' Müller said to her, reproval in his tone. 'Even our Spartan might like to be outside.'

Gerda threw him an angry look, but made no reply. Instead she spoke to Ash.

'Did Hans know if those boys had come back?'

'I haven't had a chance to ask.'

Müller looked across at his wife and then a questioning glance at Ash.

'We were debating other things. Who did you want?'

Ash explained again about the four mission Aborigines visiting the camp and his wish to see them.

'You come from the Victoria way?' Müller asked.

Ash hesitated.

'I see you do. Well the Aborigines do not say where they will go when they walk off. They don't know themselves exactly. But, yes, four did leave about two weeks ago. Jacob's country is across that way. He is not back here yet. What do you want with him?'

'Just trying to clarify what he told one of the men… the whereabouts of a waterhole in the area.'

'You came all this way for that? This I don't believe. There must be more. What else did he report?' Müller's voice rose, sharp.

Ash sidestepped the question.

'We patrol a large area and it is important to note significant features. Sources of water may be vital, not now perhaps, but when the Wet finishes, yes. Who better to help with this than the Aborigines who know the area?'

'You have Gabriel.'

'We do. But there can never be enough information, enough connections. You will know that from your own work. You have a radio here?'

'Of course. It is important for flying doctor reception.'

'Yes, Pastor Müller, and you use it to keep informed. You said so earlier. No doubt you transmit mission news as well. The Spartans, as you call us, also follow all sources of information. Have you something of interest that you can tell us?'

Müller glared at him.

'Pah! I have no wish to play games with you. I said all there was to say to interrogators in Adelaide. Why do you want to bring another persecution to my home?'

Ash was about to deny the intention when he caught a strong aroma of coffee wafting into the room, a smell he hadn't experienced for a long time. He glanced through to the kitchen

Chapter 15 December 1942

where Frieda was helping her mother with a pot on the stove. The girl smiled at the look of approval on his face and held up a wrapper. Ash stiffened, his expression turning to one of surprise as he saw the lettering on the packet clearly marked: K-ration. Müller noticed the change and followed his gaze to the kitchen.

'The Americans are more generous with their supplies than Australians,' he said. 'A product of my last visit to Katherine. A donation to the mission. They do not sit in judgement as do others.'

Ash recovered quickly.

'No doubt fallen off the back of a truck. Light-fingered Yank soldiers are keen when the gift costs them nothing. I salute your good fortune.'

Ash enjoyed his coffee. Instant it may have been, but it tasted infinitely better than the Australian ration with its aroma of stale peanuts. He made it last as long as he could. Müller suspended hostilities while his wife and daughter were in the room, but after finishing his cup there was no mistaking the haste of his exit on the pretext of returning to work on his sermon, leaving Gerda to make the farewells. She delivered them with a final plea.

'Please forgive my husband's anger,' she said. 'Hans is not himself since the... the attack, you know... back in Germany.'

Ash raised his eyebrows.

'No. What attack was that? When in Germany?'

'We went back just a year before the war began. A holiday. Hans was to see old friends in the church. Also we wanted to show Frieda a little of where we came from, such a difference from here. We didn't know it was going to be like that or we would never have gone. Hitler, the Nazis... so cruel... so full of hatred. Hans was attacked. I don't know why. He was damaged in the spine. It still pains him, but he is too proud to show that.

'So, you see we cannot go back. Hans… I too… feel some sadness with that, but this is our home now. He is hurt to be persecuted also here. So you will please tell them to stop this. I ask you to stop, if not for us, for Frieda. She is just a child like these others here. The hate and the fight is not theirs. My wish, and Hans', is that it will soon be over.'

She shooed the crowd of giggling children from the horses and then stood watching as Ash and Gabriel mounted and rode out of the clearing.

* * *

Ash decided to make a wide sweep back to Bradshaw, away from their outward track. They would benefit by reconnoitring new country and might even be fortunate in running into the mission Aborigines. A long shot, but possible unless they didn't want to be found. Ash left the course to Gabriel and began mulling over the pastor's words. Despite his wife's pleas and excuses, Müller had given the impression of being anything but a loyal Australian—bitter towards the government and his treatment; expecting the Japanese to invade; not taking any opportunity to leave; in fact, wanting to stay. Did he think that being German in origin would render the family safe under Japanese control? Did he want the Japanese to come? Was he helping them? The radio could as easily be tuned to Japanese frequencies as it could monitoring and transmitting on the flying doctor-outback station network. And there was the American K-ration pack. Surely that was a coincidence too far. Not only that, but the mission had a boat that was quite capable of ocean sailing. It

Chapter 15   December 1942

wasn't far from the Fitzmaurice to the Victoria by sea, closer than to Darwin, a journey Müller had undertaken a number of times, he had said. Spying on and reporting the Nackeroo positions and strengths would be possible.

And Frau Müller herself? A tough woman behind the concerns for her husband and child. Had Ash seen the true Gerda when he first arrived, aggressive, defensive, perhaps something to hide? Was the change to a more hospitable guise an attempt to throw him off the track? Overall, his suspicions had been raised, not allayed by the visit. Ash formed his thoughts into the report he would make to the Lieutenant. The missionary should be treated as a potential collaborator, despite the government clearance he had been given. He should be watched somehow, his movements noted. But, even as he envisaged this, Ash realised the impossibility of the task.

They spent two days on the trek back to Bradshaw, the last night camped near the Tombs at the end of the Yambarran Range overlooking the Victoria. The following morning they descended to the flood plain and rode to the homestead along the river bank. Well before they arrived at the base Gabriel suddenly stood up in his stirrups craning forward.

'Big noise there, boss. Might be trouble.'

Ash could hear nothing at first, but as they drew closer the crisp crack of a rifle shot pierced the morning air. Ash unslung his weapon and took the lead, moving warily through the scrub until he could see the homestead buildings. Several figures were grouped beside the water tank near the old house. Ash recognised Stretch and then Sam, but the third man with his back to him was a puzzle. It wasn't Bluey, he could tell that. As Ash dismounted and walked into the yard the man turned— the Lieutenant!

'Corporal. We have a problem. Signaller Jenkins has absconded. There is evidence he has been signalling the enemy.'

Chapter 16

October 1987

Brad drove out of town puzzled and deflated. Karen was a world of contrasts. He wanted to stay and make sure she was alright. But she had said no and stepped quickly to her door without looking back. Irrational thoughts whirled. Did she regret already her intimacy with him? Was he dismissed as a moment of weakness not to be repeated? The doubts churned his gut. At the green drum he eased off the accelerator along the station road, slowing to walking pace as he passed Ash's turn-off. The hut was in darkness, not even an outline of the limestone outcrop distinguishable in the gloom. He drove on. Three kilometres before the camp, the glow of the rig lights appeared above the tree canopy—a beacon now less welcoming than before. He entered the compound contemplating plausible excuses for another trip to town. Before he'd even opened the Cruiser door, Ethan Williams was in his face.

'About bloody time you got back. Where the hell have you been? Jesus. Talk about the vanishing man. This is not a holiday resort. If you want to bang your nurse, do it on your own time.'

Brad could see the drilling super was just getting started. He cut him off.

'What's the problem? You said you'd be fishing all day.' He looked at his watch.

'I know what bloody time it is. Some of us are more dedicated to the job than others.'

'And the fishing?'

'Yeah, well after the first two tries I gave it up. It wasn't going to work and we don't have time to waste. It was quicker to side-track.'

'What, going through all the limestone again?'

'We did. Must have hit a fractured zone or something. Straight down in no time and then out into easy street. Drill's dropping like there's no tomorrow now.'

'Shit. A drilling break. What depth are we at?'

'950 metres.'

'Any reason for the change? It's too soon.'

'Jesus, how would I know? I've told you before. You're the bloody rock doctor.'

Brad brushed past before Williams could say more and headed for the mud-logger's hut. As he pushed open the door Aaron swung around in his chair to face him, a smirk plastered from ear to ear.

'Well look what the cat dragged in. Have a good time? Hope you gave her one for me. By the way, old Sourpuss is gunning for you.'

'He found me. What's going on? How did the side-track get through so fast?'

'I think we must have deviated through a more porous zone, fractures anyway. Look at the cuttings. And, there's something else. I reckon the fish must have been right at the bottom of the formation. When we got back to that depth the bit went into a new formation almost straight away. Check the microscope.'

Chapter 16   October 1987

Aaron stood up to make way as Brad leaned down to peer through the lens.

'Looks like a conglomerate.'

'Yep. I'm betting my boots we've hit the top of the Carboniferous.'

'Shit! We shouldn't be anywhere near that yet. It's much too early on prognosis.'

'Well, there it is. Pressure's up a bit and the gas readings are a tad above normal too. They've had to increase the mud weight just in case.'

Brad went over to the well prognosis chart pinned to the hut wall. He smoothed the creases and traced his finger along the drilling line, looking across the graph to correlate the depth on the vertical axis.

'According to this the Gibb River Sandstone secondary target should be 150 metres below the top of the Carboniferous. When we get there Able wants to core.'

'What, all the way through? That'll slow us back down to a crawl.'

'Yep. Specific instructions. He wants as much info out of this well as possible. In the meantime, keep an eye on those gas levels and watch for any more drilling breaks. No telling what we might run into. I'll go and tell the super about the coring program.'

Aaron laughed. 'Better you than me.'

Brad pulled a face. 'I'm not flavour of the month anyway. One more irritation isn't going to make much difference. I'll be back to give you a breather soon as I clean up a bit.'

* * *

Brad walked over to the rig and climbed the stairs to the drill floor wondering how best to tackle Williams. The coring program required fitting a special bit and a core barrel behind it and that meant stopping the drilling and tripping out of the hole to attach them. Then they'd have to re-run all the drill string to the bottom. Depending on the thickness of the Gibb River sand there might need to be several trips up and down to change the barrel and make sure they retrieved core from the whole section. It was a slow operation. Drillers, he knew, just wanted to make hole as quickly as possible. The last thing Williams needed as the rig's end-of-contract deadline approached was another interruption. Brad's cushion was that the drilling super couldn't buck Able's orders.

Freddie Hawkins was watching the monitors in the dog house, a contented look on his face, obviously enjoying the easier drilling. His grin broadened when he saw Brad at the door.

'Well if it isn't young Romeo back from the nest. Nothing like a good shag to start a shift.'

'Ah, leave it out will you. I got enough stick from Williams.'

'Yeah, well you shouldn't parade her around like that. We'd all like a piece. It's almost worth busting an arm to go and check her out in person. You know you owe Wingnut big time.'

Brad admitted it with a nod. Hawkeye realised that Brad had not come to pass the time.

'You want Williams? He's over by the mud tanks. Be back shortly. The bastard's been on our back for hours now. You obviously know he cut the fishing job short. Good decision as it turned out. What have you got for us this time?'

'Good news and not so good news, depending on how you look at it.'

'Spit it out.'

Chapter 16 October 1987

'We've adjusted the well prognosis. On the new info, the secondary target should be just over 100 metres further down …'

'And?'

'And when we get there we're going to need a core right through it. Boss's request,' Brad added hastily as Hawkeyes expression darkened.

'Bloody marvellous. We are going to spend the Wet here at this rate.'

'They'll fly you out… if it happens.'

'Yeah, but I can't do much without the bloody rig, can I? Not many jobs vacant on any others at the moment. You gunna tell Sourpuss or are you leaving it to me?'

'Tell him I'll be in the mud hut in half an hour if he wants to see me. We've got coring gear here haven't we?

'Yeah. Stuff's over there.' Hawkeye thrust his chin in the direction of the pipe racks. 'How much core we gotta get?'

'Best guess, could be two or three trips.'

'Shit!'

On that note Brad waved a half salute, went back down the stairs and made his way to the accommodation block. He yawned. It had been a long day. He hadn't been up this late at the rig before, but he knew it would still be a while yet before he saw his bed. So… a shower to freshen up would help and then over to relieve Aaron.

'Nice to see you back.'

The girl's voice came from the shadows beside the mess where she had accommodation separate from the men's quarters.

'Lucy! Christ, you gave me a fright. What the hell are you doing up at this hour? It's after two.'

She stepped out into the glare of the lights. Brad saw she

was dressed in tight jeans and a T-shirt, sandals on her feet and her blonde hair swinging loose around her shoulders. Only once before had he seen it freed from the constraints of her kitchen cap. Her dimpled cheeks rose in a smile.

'Couldn't sleep… I was waiting for you.'

'Me? Why?'

'Did you have a good time with her?'

'I don't think that is any of your business.'

'You can have a better time with me… finish what you started.'

Lucy stepped forward and put her arms around Brad's neck, pressing her body close.

'Cut it out Lucy. I haven't started anything. You're just a girl.'

'So you have noticed. Come inside and I'll show you more.'

She brought one arm slowly down his side, slipping a hand on his chest to pull at the buttons of his shirt. Her lips brushed his neck and cheek. Brad hesitated: aware; paralysed; tempted. Karen's breath was still warm on his body. He could not demean the passion they had shared. His thoughts were only of her. Brad reached across to pull Lucy's arm away.

'Please stop this. Before someone sees.'

'Come inside then. No one there to see but me.'

'That's a bad idea. Lucy I'm not going to. Please don't be foolish. No!'

His voice was louder than he intended and he looked around quickly, wondering if they could be seen from the drill floor or the office cabins. Lucy came forward again and placed her hand on his belt, fingers undoing the buckle. Her tone harsher, sarcastic.

'Perhaps you like an audience. You showed her off to everyone.'

Chapter 16   October 1987

'Enough! Please.' This time he wrenched her hand away. 'It is not going to happen.'

Her slap to his face was fast and hard; her face suddenly contorted in anger.

'You won't be so smart when my uncle hears. And he will. You won't be here long after that, so you'd better clear out to your precious nurse while you can... you bastard.'

Brad stood, hand on cheek, as Lucy swung on her heel and disappeared back into the shadows. The door slammed. Damnit! This he didn't need. He looked around. No one was about, the rumble of the rig the only sound. He moved off towards his room, walking slowly, his head spinning. Lucy could make trouble for him. It will be her word against his that something happened between them. She could also report him for bringing Karen to the rig. That he couldn't deny or defend. Well, yes he could defend it if need be. Public relations in the community, showing that oil people weren't ogres killing the environment. Worse will be the poisonous atmosphere between the two of them in the mess. Charlie will pick it up straight away even if no one else does. Shit! Now he really did want to be elsewhere. Karen had warned him to look out for trouble; he'd walked straight into it.

In his room Brad pulled himself together, stripped off his clothes and, with a towel around his waist, went to the shower block where he stood motionless for a long time, letting the water beat down on his skull. He felt better in fresh jeans and shirt, the tiredness at bay, ready to sit the well and wait to see what the geology held in store. On the way out he noticed Stokes' journal on the table and scooped it up. Maybe the old explorer could divert his mind from both Karen and Lucy for a while.

(J.L. Stokes – Journal entry 14 November 1839)

... When the morning of the 15th broke it was discovered that one of the men belonging to the watering party had deserted during the night. He had been guilty of this offence once before, in order to steal the spirits which had been buried for the use of my exploring party. What however could have induced him to take this step a second time—risking, without any apparent motive, the danger of being left on a strange, and almost uninhabited coast, it would be difficult even to suggest. Parties were immediately despatched in quest of him, and at length, after an arduous search, he was found behind a large sandstone rock on the side of a hill; having revisited the spot where the provisions had been concealed for the use of my party, in the hope of obtaining possession of his god the rum-keg. He had evidently prepared for desertion: clothing, biscuit, and fishing tackle being among the stores with which he had made off. ...

Chapter 17

December 1942

'Say that again! Messages to the Japanese?'

Ash gaped at the Lieutenant in disbelief. He glanced at Sam who simply nodded. Stretch didn't look at him, keeping his eyes on the ground. Ash thought the Queenslander looked sick, his tall frame stooped, his head bent. Shock maybe. He turned back to the Lieutenant.

'What evidence? Where is he? I heard a shot.'

The Lieutenant stepped away from the group towards the veranda of the homestead beckoning Ash to follow. He gestured at a bench under the iron overhang.

'Sit down Corporal. The story is not pretty.'

'I'd prefer to stand Sir. Horse riding still doesn't really agree with me.'

Ash lent against one of the steel pipe uprights, propping his rifle against his thigh, butt on the ground and waited. The Lieutenant sighed and looked along the veranda as if seeking a way to begin.

'It's a mess, Corporal, a bloody mess.'

The Lieutenant lapsed into silence again and, as if on cue, a frog started to croak. Ash kicked the pipe with his heel.

'It would help if I knew what has happened… Sir.'

'I dare say, Corporal. Truth is I'm not overly sure myself. It appears that Signaller Jenkins has been tuning in to a radio frequency used by the Japanese.'

'Yes Sir. He found the Jap Hour. Sorry… that's what we call it. It's a propaganda program laced with American big band music. It lightens the mood and you get a laugh out of the bullshit the announcer sprouts in between tunes.'

'I know about it, Corporal. It's the program that broadcast the specific positions of our camps here on the Victoria.'

'I reported that. The Brass thought the information came from spotter planes together with an educated guess.'

'But you didn't agree.'

'No Sir. I have a gut feeling there is someone out there in contact with the enemy. The information was too precise… But Bluey? It's one thing to listen in to a Jap program that's meant for us anyway. Doesn't mean he transmitted anything. He's one of us. That's not credible.'

'I'm afraid it is.'

The lieutenant pulled a folded paper from his shirt and handed it across. Ash read the short note written in pencil, all in capital letters:

I HAVE HONOUR TO REPORT TO IMPERIAL COMMAND AUSTRALIAN SURVEILLANCE ON VICTORIA WEAKENING. NO SUPPLIES POSSIBLE IN MONSOON. RIVER OPEN FOR ENTRY GLORIOUS IMPERIAL FORCES. REISEN

'Where did this come from? What's it got to do with Bluey?'
'He wrote it on his pad. It was by the radio.'
'Who found it?'

Chapter 17 December 1942

'Private Greenwood.'

Ash scanned the paper again, frowning.

'But it's bullshit. Our surveillance isn't weakening. Why would he write that?'

'It has the ring of truth I'm afraid. With all the rain, the *Pride* is already having trouble getting back up the river. The inflow from the catchments is becoming too strong. When the Wet sets in properly, supply by boat will be impossible.'

'I didn't know that. Why would Bluey?'

'You haven't been speaking to the boat skipper lately. He has. The skipper said so. This message clearly states we'll be vulnerable in the Wet. It would be just like the Japs to launch an invasion when the rains set in, when we least expect them. They will have all the equipment needed to cope with the quagmire up here. Track vehicles, plenty of manpower. The lot. We'll be left floundering.'

'Shit. I still can't believe it. But what's reisen? Sounds German to me.'

'It is. Means something like, "setting out on a journey," so I'm told.'

'The missionary, Müller, he's German.'

'The word is also the name the Japs call their Zero fighter plane, again so I'm told.'

'Yeah, but you'd have to speak Japanese to know that, and especially to send messages to them. Know the Jap codes too.'

'Private Jenkins does speak Japanese.'

'What! He never said anything about that. You sure?' Ash was incredulous, staring wide-eyed.

'Yes Corporal. I am sure. It's one of the reasons he was brought into the NAOU. The Command thought it might be useful for behind-the-lines surveillance when… if the Japs came ashore. There was no need for anyone else to know.'

Ash fell silent. Out in the yard Gabriel unsaddled the horses. Sam moved up to help him. Stretch languished behind, kicking the dirt, head still down and shoulders hunched. Ash frowned.

'What's the matter with Stretch? He looks crook. Come to think of it, begging your pardon Sir, but what are you doing here? I mean, how did you know about all this and get here so quickly? What's happened to Bluey?'

'Whoa, whoa Corporal. One at a time. Bit of luck really. The *Pride* happened to pull in here soon after Private Jenkins took off and Private Greenwood found the note pad. The skipper battled back up river to The Depot with the news and I got aboard for the trip back. What I found is a sorry story. Private Middleton is not sick. More like hung over. He's going to be shipped back to Katherine and carpeted. I doubt he'll be back.'

'Why? What's he done this time?'

'It seems Private Middleton has been supplementing his beer rations and making his own… well I don't know what you would call it… cocktail to be polite. Some concoction of dried fruit from the ration packs mixed with native fresh fruits no doubt pointed out by Jimmy or Gabriel. No, I don't hold them responsible,' the Lieutenant added hastily as he saw Ash about to protest. 'Middleton has taken advantage of their knowledge. He scrounged some sugar and yeast from somewhere and brewed the stuff in the bush behind the homestead here. I found the barrel this morning and put an axe through it. You didn't know about it Corporal?'

'I had no idea.'

'No excuse. You should know your men better. I could bring charges against you for… negligence, incompetence, dereliction of duty. But that wouldn't solve anything.'

Chapter 17   December 1942

He waved an arm at Stretch mooning about in the clearing.

'He went on a binge last night. You can see the after-effects. That's how I know about the stuff. The point is, Private Jenkins got into this moonshine too. He must have found the stash a while ago and has been helping himself. Probably in the times he was here alone. I'm told he's not a big drinker, so I can only imagine what it did to him. I mentioned to you there were concerns about his work.'

'Yeah I asked Sam to keep an eye on him. I just thought he was getting spooked by the bush. City bloke alone. So what happened? Did this stuff push him over the edge into the enemy camp?'

'God knows. It might have, or he could have been feeding the Japs information all along. No one here, easy to do if you know the language. Apparently the Japs don't use conventional Morse. They've got something called a Katakana system. Double Dutch to the likes of you and me, but a signals operator would know about it.'

Ash took this in, shaking his head. How did he miss the signs? There must have been some. Well, there were. Bluey's erratic behaviour. He thought he had that covered. But a Japanese informer? Christ, how would anyone pick that up unless they caught him at it?

'But Sir, why did Bluey bolt now? More to the point, why did he leave this message lying around? Doesn't make sense.'

'We won't know that until we get hold of him. But my guess is he joined Middleton in a bender last night. Possibly took more than usual. You can see the effect on a seasoned drinker.' He inclined his head in Stretch's direction. 'I haven't got any sense out of Middleton yet, but perhaps Jenkins goes manic. Maybe he thinks we're on to him and takes off. Strange thing is, Private Greenwood says that wild mule has gone too—the one that kicks anyone who gets close.'

'Always? Bluey was the only one who could handle him. He couldn't have been too pissed if he took him along.'

'Maybe, maybe not. Anyway he hasn't got far. Jimmy began tracking him this morning before I arrived, up in the range by the spring. Jimmy wasn't being very secretive about it, just following the trail on Private Greenwood's orders. Jenkins took a pot shot at him. That's the shot you heard when you were coming in.' The Lieutenant stood up. 'Now you know as much as I do. We need him caught and brought back. Alive. The intelligence boys need to question him. I want you and Greenwood to see to it. Take Gabriel. I'm going to tear strips off this other miserable bastard. See if he can put some light on what happened last night.'

'Sam wasn't involved? Drinking, I mean.'

'No. Says he knew the other two were. Couldn't miss it, I suppose. But he figured they were just easing tensions and left them to it. Take some fresh horses and make sure you bring him back intact. That's an order.'

* * *

Ash's party followed the water pipeline to the foot of the Yambarrans, aware that Bluey could be watching their progress if he was still near the spring at the top. There was not much Ash could do about that, but as soon as they began the climb he directed Gabriel to go ahead and scout to the side of the zig zag track using all the cover he could find. Ash and Sam continued on the path until they reached the pass near the summit. There they dismounted, secured the horses and

Chapter 17 December 1942

cautiously made their way through on foot

Ash put himself in Bluey's shoes. Would he stay nearby? No, more likely he'd take a chance and make a break, try to go across country, perhaps to the mission on the Fitzmaurice. Maybe steal the boat and rendezvous with a Japanese submarine in the Gulf. Ash had a sudden thought. What if Bluey was already working with the Müllers? He'd go there for help, use the mission radio to set up a rendezvous. The German could take him out and return to his post. No one would be any the wiser. Reisen could be a joint call sign—German and Japanese—what could be more fitting for the pair of them working together?

Behind him Sam hissed. Ash saw him pointing at Gabriel signalling on the rocks above. Suddenly a shot rang out and the tracker dropped out of sight. Shit. Bluey hadn't made the break. It didn't mean that he wouldn't try later, though. Ash beckoned Sam closer.

'I'm going to see if Gabriel's okay, then try to get around to come in from behind. You get as close as you can this way and find a position to watch for me. If you can't see me, wait fifteen minutes and then start firing. For Christ sake don't hit him. The Lieutenant wants him alive. The frontal diversion should give me a chance to rush in and nab him. I'll send Gabriel back to you.'

Ash found Gabriel crouching behind a rock fingering a hole in his shirt sleeve and a graze on his arm.

'Close one, Boss. He allasame bad Jap man?'

'Looks like it. We need to get him. Go with Sam the front way.'

Ash took his bearings. The spring flowed from a fissure in the rock into a man-improved pool containing the inlet for the pipeline to Bradshaw. Bluey would have a rock wall shielding him on one flank and open ground around the pool on the other. He'd be covering the frontal approach through the pass, hopefully not paying much attention to the track behind him. Ash moved off in a wide arc, keeping his body hunched so as not to break the skyline. The crouched posture soon made his thighs ache, but he kept moving until he was between Bluey and the track to the mission. Slowly he picked his way back up the incline. A whinny just ahead stopped him. Hell! He had forgotten about the mule. With luck Bluey would think the animal had heard someone coming from the front, not behind.

Ash moved forward again, flattening himself behind a boulder at the side of the track. Gradually he raised his head to peer over the top. Bluey lay facing the front as he'd hoped, his rifle barrel resting on a small pile of stones, the butt into his shoulder. Always was saddled, tethered beside him, the mule restless, whinnying softly. Ash mentally measured the space across to Bluey. Too far. He wouldn't make it half way across before being heard. Ash scanned the track beyond the spring. There was no sign of Sam or Gabriel. He stretched a cramped leg, inwardly cursing as a dislodged stone flicked out onto the track, clinking on other stones as it went. Always swung around to face him, whinnying loudly at the disturbance. Bluey looked up at the mule, then lifted his rifle from its rest and pointed it along the track to where Ash was hiding. There would be no hope of surprise now.

At that moment several shots rang out in quick succession. Bluey whipped around and fired at the noise. Ash had only seconds to act. Leaving his rifle behind, he scrambled to his feet and sprinted across the open space, his boots pounding on the earth, his chest heaving. Despite the gunfire Bluey heard him and jerked his rifle up trying to get Ash in his sights.

Chapter 17   December 1942

Ash leapt the last few yards, twisting in the air and landing heavily across Bluey's legs. The rifle went off beside his ear, the muzzle brushing his cheek as he rolled up over Bluey's chest and wrestled for a hold of the weapon. Bluey squirmed, grunting loudly under the weight and using the rifle butt to pound Ash's shoulder. Ash pressed his forearm down across Bluey's throat, his other hand still grasping for the barrel. The young signaller's strength surprised him. Bluey wriggled free, working the bolt and forcing the barrel around to point at Ash's chest. Ash thrust at the weapon in desperation, knocking it away as Bluey pulled the trigger. The shot went skywards and the recoil knocked him off balance. Ash pushed hard and Bluey fell sideways under the mule's belly.

Already spooked by the gunshots, the animal lashed out with its back legs. One hoof caught Bluey in the chest, the other in the side of the head. The signaller groaned and lay still. Always kicked again, this time swishing the air inches from Ash's face. He wrenched himself from under Bluey's body and rolled away just as Sam and Gabriel ran up to help. Gabriel grabbed for the mule's bridle, twisting and skipping to stay away from the vicious kicks. Sam took Bluey's legs and dragged the signaller clear. He went back for the rifle, then leaned over Ash who lay propped on an elbow gasping for breath.

'Jesus Corp, I thought you were a gonner. You okay?'

Ash nodded. 'Bit winded. I don't know where he found the strength. How is he?'

'Not good by the look of him.'

Ash swore. He got up, wincing at the pain in his shoulder and went across to Bluey. The signaller's eyes opened as he knelt and cradled the battered head in his arms. Blood oozed from a point just behind his ear. Bluey's voice was barely audible.

'It's you Corp… I thought you were the Japs… been chasing me all day. I had… to fight them off. Think I got one…'

'What the hell's he talking about,' Sam said, kneeling opposite. 'Bugger's off his head. Blaming us now.'

Ash frowned. 'Quiet Sam. Get me some water will you.'

He looked down at Bluey and wiped blood and dirt from his face.

'What were the Japs chasing you for Blue?'

'To get back… the code. Their code… I worked it out. Thirsty… so thirsty.'

Ash took the canteen that Sam had brought and splashed a little on Bluey's lips. The signaller coughed and groaned moving his arms to hold his chest.

'How did you work it out Blue?'

'Kat… a… kana chart. Intercept'd lots messages… lots of nights… from Reisen. Every night Reisen. Compare them to… work out code. Then the Japs come… Brad…shaw… to get back code. Had to… get away. Keep code safe.'

Bluey closed his eyes, the effort exhausting him. Ash could see he was going.

'Who is Reisen, Blue? Do you know Reisen?'

The dying man moved his head slightly.

'Did you know Reisen, Blue? It's very important.'

Bluey opened his eyes again. 'No,' he whispered. 'Just messages… intercept on Jap radio… many messages… Worked out code.'

The eyes closed, his breath shallow now, coming in gasps that rattled from his chest. Suddenly he lifted his head and grasped Ash's arm, his voice clear.

'Did you get the message? On my pad. Reisen's last message. The Japs are coming.'

Chapter 17   December 1942

Bluey's head fell back and his body went limp as the last breath expelled from his lips.

* * *

'I believe him Sir,' Ash said after he had related the story back at Bradshaw.

He and the Lieutenant watched as Bluey's body was untied from Always and lowered to the ground; the mule inexplicably quiet, allowing Sam and Gabriel to handle him without fuss.

'I think Stretch's booze last night took hold, skewed his mind. Hallucinating. He really did think we were the Japs. He thought that last message was being played out. And I think he did crack the code, sitting all those nights alone, comparing the messages, looking for clues to the words. He wasn't transmitting. He was intercepting and interpreting.'

The Lieutenant sighed. 'A brilliant mind, finely balanced. We misunderstood him Corporal. It's a great pity he didn't write the code down. No notes… nothing that we found. It would have been a coup for the intelligence boys.'

'All in his head, Sir. He would have destroyed any jottings so the Japs wouldn't know he'd cracked it. But there's one thing I am sure of, more than ever now. Reisen's still out there and I've got a good idea who it is.'

Chapter 18

October 1987

Brad rubbed his eyes, gritty and sore from peering through the microscope. The early morning light filtered in through the single dust-smeared window of the mud hut. He yawned and arched his back, arms above his head. It had been six hours since he took over from Aaron. The drilling had made good progress and for once the Super was happy—well, as content as Williams would ever be. The bit had passed through the top Carboniferous formation in five hours and then encountered an underlying shale layer. The cuttings flushed to surface in the drilling mud suggested the shale would be an adequate seal for the Gibb River Sandstone beneath it. Whether there were any hydrocarbons in the reservoir remained to be seen.

The seismic survey run across the permit a year earlier had identified the Stokes prospect as a combination of two potential traps. The shallow structural component appeared to be a relatively simple anticline. That was the secondary target and the moment of truth for this trap was fast approaching.

The more contentious stratigraphic trap lay much deeper. It had been interpreted as a Devonian-age reef completely surrounded and sealed by impervious shales. The reef reservoir,

Chapter 18   October 1987

known as the Mitchell Limestone, was Able's primary target, his big gamble. He had committed to pay one hundred percent of the cost for the Stokes-1 wildcat which seemed to Brad to be a huge risk. The man must be very sure of a positive outcome. A rattle at the door signalled Aaron's return. He came in sipping a coffee and holding out a second mug to Brad.

'Thought you could probably use this. Jesus, I was right. You look as if the tide's been out for months.'

'I feel it too. It's a long time since I've stayed awake around the clock. I've lost the stamina of uni days.'

Aaron grinned. 'Well you will make a steeple chase out of it. Where are we at in here?'

'Drilling through shale at the moment. At this rate I reckon we're going to be at the top of the secondary target within the hour. If you can take over, I'll alert the Super to get ready to pull out and start the core program.'

'Great. Let the fun begin. Oh, if you're going in to breakfast keep out of Lucy's way. She looks as if she's been up all night too. She gave Hawkeye a real mouthful just now and all he did was ask for extra bacon.'

* * *

Brad freshened up with a quick shave and shower. Rush hour had passed by the time he walked into the mess. He joined a queue at the servery only three people long as Lucy doled out portions of eggs, hash, beans, bacon and tomato onto the proffered plates. Aaron was right. She banged the ladles about and dished the food mechanically without the usual cheeky grin and comment. She had obviously been crying, her eyes red and her face blotchy despite the make-up. Brad told himself there was no reason to feel guilty. He hadn't flirted any more than the younger blokes on the rig crew. She had no call to take it so seriously. The rationale didn't quell the sinking in his stomach. As his turn came Lucy stiffened and her eyes narrowed as if she had been steeling herself for the moment.

'Serve yourself,' she hissed, bouncing the ladle and tongs on the counter and walking away into the galley.

The roustabout ahead of Brad looked back in surprise, eyebrows high. 'You must have really pissed her off,' he said. 'At least I got breakfast.'

Brad was last in the queue, so no one else seemed to have noticed. He flipped eggs and bacon onto his plate, then put a slice of bread in the conveyor-belt toaster and surveyed the room while waiting for it to brown. A few off-shift drill crew lingered over coffee. The three latecomers ahead of him took a separate table listening to the roustabout who pointed back his way, no doubt describing Lucy's performance. Brad didn't see the Malteser in the far corner until he lowered his newspaper and signalled.

'Good morning mister rock man,' Charlie said as Brad sat down. 'You are making a core today I hear. This is good news?'

'Your sources are on the mark Charlie, but I can't tell you whether or not it is good news. Not yet. It has been part of the well program from the start. You're not angling to go insider trading are you?'

'Me? For you to say such things? But the Malteser would not mind if news was good, you unnustand.'

Charlie winked, then suddenly grew serious.

'Ah, my young Brad. It is as I feared. You know this too.'
'What?'
'Ha! Do not pretend. I speak of Lucy.'
'She is upset.'

Chapter 18   October 1987

'Of course, she is upset. You think I don't know this? Today all in this room sees her upset. I am asking you now. Do you know why?'

Brad stopped eating and looked Charlie in the eye.

'Yes… at least I think so. Last night—late—she… she wanted me to… to go with her… to her room.'

'And?'

'And I said no. Really, I did. I said no.'

'And she slap you, yes?'

'Yes. How did you know that?'

'The Malteser knows everything.'

'You mean you saw us?'

'Of course. I see everything for this rig.'

'Why did you ask then?'

'Ah, the Malteser's little test for you, my friend. I have seen this will come. Lucy is young. She has impressions she cannot hide so good. I see her eyes when you bring your nurse.'

Brad nodded. 'Karen saw that too. I didn't even realise.'

'Yes. Karen she is good for you I think. She likes you also.'

'I hope so. I… well, I just hope so.'

'Now. Lucy. I know you are not for blame. Not too much. Oh yes, I see you play a little,' Charlie added when Brad began to protest. 'Also some others.' He glanced at the young roustabout. 'But Lucy choose you because a rock man is more important than a drill man. For her she thinks it is true. But I cannot have this in my kitchen. It is engine for the camp. A faulty part, like in a truck, makes performance not so good. So, I have decided Lucy must finish and go home.'

Brad grimaced, pulling in air through his teeth.

'You know she will make trouble with her uncle, she threatened that. Now she definitely will.'

'This is not so much a problem. I will tell my friend Reg Able the truth. He will know. He send Lucy up here because of same troubles in the city. He asks the Malteser to fix. Well I cannot fix all things all the time. But you don't tell this to anyone else, unnustand? My—how do you call it?—my reputation is for keeping safe.'

Brad laughed at Charlie's admission, feeling a weight lifted off his own mind, despite the lingering guilt.

'Yes Charlie. I unnustand very well.'

'Good.' The Malteser folded his paper, stood up and put it on the stack on the magazine table. 'Now I go back to the kitchen to make… ah, preparations. But you will tell to me soon how this core making is going, yes?

* * *

Brad knelt by the first barrel of core laid out in trays in the shade of an annex to the mud logging hut. He had marked the trays in sequence of well depth and now brought over a hose to wash off the drilling mud. The drilling supervisor detoured across on his way to the rig floor.

'Got what you want? Better be worth it. You realise all this is taking time we don't have.'

Brad suppressed his irritation.

'Probably at least two more barrels to come. Able needs all the info possible. Tell your blokes what's come out so far is a good job. I appreciate their patience. And yours.'

'Okay. I will. I dunno how you can get anything from these things anyway. Just looks like bloody rock to me.'

'What we've got is similar to the same formation in the old Victoria-1 well. A good correlation so far. The logs detect

Chapter 18 October 1987

increased gas in the mud, but there's no oil staining I can see. Not in this section anyway.'

Bending down intent on the core, the rumble of the rig in the background, neither of them noticed the arrival of the vehicle until it pulled in across their line of sight to stop outside the office hut. Williams looked up at the battered Bedford truck.

'Who the bloody hell's that? Oh, Christ! It's our Abo land custodian again,' he added as Gabriel Fitzmaurice climbed down from the passenger side. 'Don't know the driver though. What do they want?'

Brad recognised the truck immediately.

'That,' he said quietly when Ash stepped out and came into view around the bonnet, 'is our night-time shooter.'

'You know him?' Williams incredulous.

'Yep.'

Brad stood up and walked across to meet his visitors. He noticed Ash was wearing boots this time, but without socks, the same frayed shirt and shorts, stubbled chin.

'You invited me,' Ash said. 'Gabriel visited last night and said you were a good listener, not like some other oil company blokes I could name. He said you were genuine, so I thought I'd take you up on it. Here we are.'

Brad laughed. 'You certainly picked your timing well.'

'Good news?' Ash waved at the trays of core. When Brad didn't answer he went on: 'I know what core is and what it can say.'

'Ah, yes. Karen told me you were in the mining game a while back. So you'll know I can't let you look at it.' Brad caught Gabriel's questioning glance. 'It's nothing exciting. We're a long way from the primary target yet. But I can show you round the rig and the general layout.' Then, unable to resist, he added: 'It's a lot different in daylight.'

Ash acknowledged the dig with the ghost of a smile, his blue eyes penetrating, assessing. He made no reply, but Brad suddenly felt uncomfortable. The look reminded him of Karen's frank appraisal when they first met. Ash was not a relation, but she had learned something from her guardian. Gabriel, too, remained silent, watching the interplay between them.

'We've both seen enough rigs in our time,' said Ash. 'This one looks as if it's been around a while. Able doing it on the cheap?'

'You'd have to ask him. You know he's in for the whole hog in this well? That's not peanuts.'

'So I heard. But he'll lay off a big percentage when the time comes, preferably before the well finishes.'

'What makes you say that?'

'He can sell anticipation better than reality. That's always been his game.'

'I think he really believes in this one.'

'That'd make a change. I've told you before, there's nothing here. I'm trying to convince Gabriel to stop worrying. They can't develop a dry hole. Able's just playing everyone along.'

'How can you be so sure? I agree it is wildcat country, but there've been good indications. I'm not writing it off yet. Anyway, a discovery could be a good thing if handled properly. Maybe Gabriel and the NWLC would like the royalties that flowed from a development.'

Brad glanced across and Gabriel smiled back.

'You know we've already had that discussion Brad and I've given you an answer,' he said quietly.

Chapter 18 October 1987

'Well, I wouldn't hang my hat on anything Able's in,' Ash went on. 'He's a manipulator. He uses your geologist-speak to inflate the prospects so he can fleece the market. What have you told him now the core's cut?'

Brad refused the bait. 'Sounds as though you've got it in for the man.'

'We've crossed paths before. Cost me money I didn't have, the bastard. Not in oil. He's got his fingers in mining too, probably more so.'

'In Queensland?'

Ash pursed his lips. 'I see my granddaughter has been talking. Yes, in Queensland.'

'Look, I know Karen's not your granddaughter, so cut the act.' Brad looked Ash in the eye. 'Why did you really come here today?'

Ash studied him for a moment. 'Like I said, you invited me.' Then he produced a wry smile. 'And I wanted to check you out. I'm not so old I can't tell when she's got her eye on someone. We don't see things the same way these days, but I can't buck my guardian duties... and I don't want her hurt any more than she already is. She tell you much?'

'Some. Look, if you don't want to see round the rig, come and have a coffee. Both of you. You know the rig's dry, so I can't offer any hard stuff.' Brad gestured towards the annex. 'I've got time. The core can wait.'

Ash patted a shorts pocket. 'I carry my supplies with me. But no, I won't indulge here. I respect some rules. Anyway I'm not sure I can be civil to your catering man.'

'Charlie? He's all right. One of the best blokes in the camp.'

'He might be, but he's friends with Able.'

'I don't think Charlie's got any illusions about Reg Able.'

'Possibly not. But let's leave it at that.'

'Well,' Brad said as Ash and Gabriel turned back towards the truck, 'will we see you boys again?'

Ash swung around, his blue eyes staring. 'As you know, there's rum at my place. Come by. If the truck's there, I am.'

* * *

The full suite of core cut through the Gibb River Sandstone was arranged in trays in the correct depth order and labelled by next day. Brad spent time in the annex carefully making a detailed geological description. He was encouraged to find one six metre-thick band of continuous, good quality reservoir at the bottom of the sequence. It corresponded with an excellent gas show seen in the logs and he had no hesitation in including a recommendation to come back and test this zone once the hole had been drilled to its planned total depth.

Brad was not surprised when he received a return fax from the Melbourne headquarters of Able Exploration congratulating everyone on the promising result, but urging the rig crew to run casing through that section and get back to drilling without further delay. Reg Able made it plain he wanted to go straight on to his primary objective, the Mitchell Limestone reef anomaly on the seismic charts that lay another 2,000 metres below. Ethan Williams seized on the faxed instructions and immediately began cracking the whip.

The move back to routine drilling took some of the pressure off the geological team and Brad found himself with time on his hands. He could not switch off completely. The well had already thrown up enough surprises for them to be wary of the downhole geology. He and Aaron still had to monitor

Chapter 18   October 1987

the program, keep an eye out for drilling breaks, describe the cuttings and file reports. But after Ash's visit to the rig he began thinking more and more about Karen. He wanted to see her, allay his doubts. There were so many things he wanted to ask, to know more about—just to spend time with her alone, away from rigs and hospitals and prying eyes. He wracked his brain, searching for an excuse to go into town, in vain. Even Charlie could not manufacture one for him.

The only time a vehicle left the camp Charlie himself was in the driver's seat, taking Lucy to the airport. Brad gladly missed that trip. The girl had been taken off kitchen duties for her last two days and she had spent the time in her room. Even her meals were delivered there. Charlie had said no more to Brad about the incident, nor Able's reaction to his niece being shipped back south. There was plenty of talk among the rig crew though. Brad let it lie, shrugging off any knowledge about Lucy's behaviour. When she left, the subject fell by the wayside.

His yearning for Karen grew stronger. Despite the "business or emergencies only" rules for the rig's satellite phone, the Malteser relented one evening, plugging it into the connection in the kitchen where Brad wouldn't be seen. He rang twice. No one answered at Karen's home, then at the hospital he was told she was too busy to take the call. He hung up without leaving a message, afraid it would be ignored.

The days of the second week in October fell into a humdrum of time spent either in the mud loggers' hut or in his room, punctuated by meals in the mess. Brad avoided social contact with others on the rig, preferring his own company during off duty hours. There, unable to sleep one night, he reopened Stokes' journal and read a passage that set in motion the sequence of events that would change his life.

(J.L. Stokes – Journal entry 20 November 1839)

… *I went ashore to collect a few geological specimens: the sandstone which prevailed everywhere was in a decomposed state, but there was a very decided dip in the strata to the south-east, of about 30 degrees. On the east side of Water Valley, I found the same kind of slate, noticed before at Curiosity Peak: but what most interested me was a bituminous substance found near the bottom of the wells recently dug, and 23 feet from the surface of the ground. It was apparently of a clayey nature when first brought up, but became hard and dark upon exposure to the air, and ignited quickly when put into the flame of a candle. The sides of Water Valley were very precipitous, and nearly 300 feet high: a growth of palms marked the spot, and served to indicate our wells. …*

Chapter 19

October 1987

Brad stared at the page, savouring the sudden thrill of discovery. He read the passage again, going over every word. There could be no doubt. The short paragraph contained what had to be the oldest written reference to finding oil in Australia. 1839. Not the gusher of Texas legend at Spindletop, but oil nonetheless. Now he understood. John Lort Stokes recording oil in what was to become known as the Bonaparte Basin. Brad sat up, laughing to himself. Stokes-1 had been inspired by a few handfuls of bituminous substance found in the bottom of two shallow wells dug on the banks of the Victoria River in search of fresh water nearly 150 years earlier. Reg Able's drilling program would have to be the ultimate long-shot in the tradition of the old-time wildcatters. Of course, Brad realised there was much more to the Stokes-1 location than that; for one thing, the modern seismic survey had identified drillable potential. But when it came down to it, the original rationale for the well stemmed from a piece of regional history that was recorded in its day merely as an interesting curiosity. Brad began to regard Able in a new light.

He leaned back against the bedhead and closed his eyes, trying to visualise the scene of Lieutenant Stokes examining the tacky substance that had been shovelled from the wells. Did it smell like tar? Is that why he thought to see if it would burn? Someone must have had a candle handy. But that seemed unlikely during the day. Perhaps they took a sample back to the ship and the flame test came later. While Stokes was making his examination, the *Beagle*'s crew may have been filling the water casks, a far more precious commodity than oil on that voyage. Brad let his imagination wander, the book resting face-down on his chest, the fake-wood panelling of his sparsely-furnished room expanding and then dissolving into the vast emptiness of the Victoria floodplain. The pantomime was taking place a century and a half ago, about 200 kilometres away to the northeast as the jabiru flies. Not very far really.

Brad's eyes flicked open. He sat up again as an idea formed in his mind. Were there still traces of Stokes' water wells in the small valley that opened out onto the river? It would be fascinating to find out, to go and have a look for them. Even if they couldn't be found, it would be interesting to see the general area, to put the whole story in context, physically. Water Valley probably didn't have that name now, but it might be possible to deduce the location. Holdfast Reach was a name still on the maps.

The more he thought about it, the more Brad liked the idea. There would be time once the well results were in. Another thought occurred to him. Douglas Ashmore had been stationed on the Victoria River during the war. He, surely, would know his way about. The countryside wouldn't have changed that much in forty years. Ash might even know of Water Valley or, at least, the general region. Brad wondered if he could get the old bloke to talk about his Nackeroo days.

* * *

Chapter 19   October 1987

Ash was leaning under the open bonnet of the old Bedford when Brad pulled up to the cattle fence outside his hut. He noticed the same crumpled shirt pulled out from the waistline of baggy shorts, the legs of which were hiked up on the old bloke's thighs showing the division between tan and white skin as he stretched into the engine. Bare feet again too. Ash probably only wore boots when he left his property. Brad got out and walked across.

'Trouble?'

Ash came out from the engine holding a spanner, his fingers greasy and a streak of dirt on his forearm.

'Nah. Just needs a thump every now and then. That yours?' He waved at the faded green Land Rover with its spare wheel strapped to the bonnet. 'Old two-door, long wheel base, split windscreen. Doesn't look your type.'

'And what's my type?'

'You look more a Range Rover bloke, padded seats, plush interior.'

Brad shook his head. He'd been in Ash's presence for less than a minute and already the old bloke had him on the back foot.

'Actually, it's Charlie Camilleri's. He lent it to me. I can't take one of the company Land Cruisers unless I'm on company business.'

'So. A social call.'

'You invited me. Something about a rum. So here I am.'

'Nothing happening at the rig then?'

'No, just drilling ahead. I've got an hour or two and fancied a drive.'

Ash deviated to the water tank to wash the muck from his hands and arms and then held aside the canvas strips on the door. Inviting him in this time.

'I suppose you want to drown it again?'

'Please. I can't go back to the camp under the weather.'

Brad stopped just inside the threshold and looked around. A single room furnished with an iron-frame bed in the far corner and a sturdy wooden table placed under the window. Its machine-turned legs and two delicate high-backed chairs seemed out of place. Bare limestone made up the whole of one side wall, the rock covered with a curtain of faded blue fabric. There was no ceiling between the overhead beams and the corrugated iron roof. The other walls were simply the rough inside surface of the timber boards nailed onto the outside of the hut. Several pieces of linoleum covered parts of the timber plank floor. An assortment of cooking implements, including a frying pan and a large saucepan, hung from hooks fastened to the underside of a shelf that ran along the length of the wall opposite the window. Bottles and jars and a kerosene lamp sat on top of the shelf. Below that stood a doorless cupboard stacked with tins of food. He saw no fireplace or stove but then remembered the old wood-fired stove outside in the yard. Probably too hot to cook inside in such a confined space.

Ash handed him a tin mug containing a good slug of rum and indicated a canvas water bag hung from a hook near the door next to a rack holding a .303 rifle and a shotgun.

'Add what you need.'

'Is that your old army service rifle?' Brad asked, eyeing the .303 as he splashed water into his drink.

'I never gave it back. Use it to get a bit of beef occasionally. Station manager is okay with that as long as it's not too often. In return I keep the dingoes down.'

'You wouldn't have had much use for it when you were on

the Victoria though, would you? In the Nackeroos, I mean.'

Ash narrowed his eyes as if he suspected a trick question. He took a swallow from his mug.

'There were plenty of crocs about.'

'Right.' Brad recognised the "do not go there" sign and sipped his drink as he continued to look around the room. On a battered trunk by the table a little wooden figure caught his eye. He went closer and saw that it was of a naked young Aboriginal child smiling coyly, head to one side and a finger of one hand in the corner of its mouth. Exquisitely carved, the facial expression was one of shy curiosity and innocence. Propped up next to it was a framed photograph that looked vaguely familiar. Brad searched his memory, then stepped back, suddenly recognising it as the one Karen had on her wall in town—her mother as a child among the mission kids. Ash saw his reaction.

'You've seen that picture before, haven't you?'

Brad recounted what he'd been told about the Fitzmaurice missionaries—Karen's real grandparents; he placed emphasis on the word—the suspicions of spying, the grandfather's disappearance, the suicides, the father's desertion.

'She hasn't left much out. She must trust you.'

'I think so… well, I hope so anyway.'

'I suppose you've come for the rest', Ash said.

Brad again caught off guard. 'Well … no… not exactly, but yes I'd like to … to…,' he stuttered, fumbling for a word, '… to understand. I …' He broke off, feeling awkward.

Ash studied Brad's face, silently assessing. After a long pause he sighed and sat back, a decision made. 'Alright,' he muttered and reached for the bottle, pouring himself another slug. Brad put a hand over his mug and shook his head, noticing the change in tone as Ash began to conjure up the past.

'I went to the mission in late 1942 to check it out. I took Gabriel because he knew the place. He'd grown up there. That's him in the back row, far right.'

Brad leaned in to examine the photograph as Ash moved on.

'The Nackeroo Command at Timber Creek had been getting reports of unexplained lights in the region at night. The Jap invasion threat was very real then, to us anyway because we'd be in the front line when they came. If someone was sending messages, we needed to find him. The missionary, Müller… Hans Müller was his name, had been interned earlier because of his origins, so he was a prime suspect. But Karen probably told you that.

'I met Müller and his wife there… Gerda her name was. The child, Frieda, she got to me. Her innocence and trust in her parents and her life at the mission, insulated from the bloody war going on outside its boundaries. When her father disappeared, I went back and gave her that carving. I hoped she'd be able to use it to hold on to the life she'd been leading, or at least have something to remember those innocent days.

'I got the carving back when she died.'

Ash drained his mug and reached again for the bottle. Brad remained silent, waiting for him to continue.

'I didn't think we'd ever meet again when I gave her the little piccaninny. It was a farewell gift. After the war I went back home to Melbourne and hooked up with an ex-fiancé. Stupidest thing I've ever done. The Yank she'd dumped me for had gone home and she was… available. We got married and I got my old job back as a garage mechanic. I can't remember which soured first. It was pretty much even. Anyway a year later I was out of both and I went to work with a mining company that sent me to Western Australia, helping the field crews out,

Chapter 19   October 1987

maintaining the vehicles and any other engines around the place. A few other companies followed, much the same work. Took me all over the country during the '50s and into the '60s. Money was good and not much to spend it on. Then in the late '60s I wound up with a mineral exploration company in northwest Queensland. It was owned by an up-and-coming entrepreneur named Reginald Able.'

Brad looked up sharply. 'You worked for Able?'

'Yeah. Same bloke. There aren't two of them, thank Christ. Well, Able's mob had a base in Cloncurry. First time I walked into Bert Pope's pub in the town I saw Frieda… behind the bar of all places. I knew her straight away. She'd grown up of course, her hair style was different and her face had a few lines, but there was the same mouth, nose. And her eyes, a devastating hazel colour… yes, just like Karen's.

'It took a few nights in the boozer before she accepted me as a friend, not just one of the customers to string along and drink with. Bert didn't like her drinking, but he liked the customers she brought. God knows how she ended up with him. She never said. But she wasn't happy, I know that. She tried to hide the marks where he belted her, but I could see them under the make-up. Sometimes I thought me being there made it worse because Bert twigged a relationship. We never got intimate. I was getting on a bit and there was twenty years between us, but I don't think that mattered to her. Got the sense she wouldn't trust someone a third time. Never met her first husband. Another bastard from what I gather, buggered off soon after Karen was born. So Frieda and I just talked, much as I wanted more.

'I took Karen to a few things in the town too and some day-trips into the bush. Bert didn't want her around and anyway the pub was not the sort of place for a young girl. Frieda was grateful, I think. She had to stay behind the bar most of the day and night. I wanted them to come away with me. The three of us. Go interstate. I liked the West. We'd have got by. But it didn't happen.'

Ash tilted the bottle at Brad's mug. This time he let him splash some in and rose to top it up from the water bag. When he sat down again Ash was gazing out the window, both hands on the table clasping his mug. He seemed to be in another world, another life. The silence stretched to a minute or more before Ash stirred, took a drink and looked across the table.

'I was away in the bush a lot. You'll know that. It's part of the job. There was one trip that was going to be longer than usual. Up at a place called Mt Cuthbert, an old disused underground copper mine they were re-evaluating near Kajabbi about 100 kilometres northwest of The Curry. I had to go out and make sure the pumps kept working. There was a lot of water to pull out, and keep pulling out, because the moment the pumps stopped the mine would flood again. So it was a long job—a couple of months.

'Before I went I'd talked Frieda round to the idea of her leaving Bert. I was going to quit the job as soon as I got back and we were going to take Karen out of school, then just up stakes and go. We didn't tell Karen. She wouldn't have been able to keep it quiet. About six weeks into this job I got an urgent message. Frieda had killed herself with pills and booze. Karen had found her. Jesus, after all she'd been through. I don't know what pushed Frieda over the edge. I thought we had it all worked out to leave. I suspect Bert found out somehow, threatened her and she had no one to turn to, took the only way out she could see. I'll never know for sure, but it damn near

Chapter 19 October 1987

killed me to realise I wasn't there when she really needed me. If it hadn't been for Karen I might have done something stupid.'

'And that's when you sent Karen away, to a boarding school in Perth she said.'

'I couldn't bear to see her life ruined too. It would have been if she'd stayed there. So, yes, I sent her as far away as possible. It's also when I got the wooden piccaninny back. Karen found it when she was packing her mother's things. Frieda had kept it all that time. She'd wrapped it up and put my name on it. I knew then she was telling me that she had decided to leave—just not with me and Karen. I couldn't throw the job as I'd planned. I needed the money. Boarding school is not cheap. Even then I didn't have enough, so I borrowed from Able.'

'Oh, shit.'

'There's your connection right there son. He gave me enough rope for a while. Then he called it in, plus interest. Cleaned me out. Your mate Camilleri was running the camp at the time, wheeling and dealing in stocks and shares on the side. He still is I bet. He reckoned he could get me out of debt if I put a few dollars here and there on shares he recommended. I was desperate, so I did. You can guess the result. Bloody disaster. In the end I just chucked it all in and walked out. Came here, right out of everyone's way. I still owed Able and I expected him to set his lawyers on to me. But it didn't happen. Maybe he thought I wasn't worth the trouble the publicity would bring.'

'Does Karen know about…,' Brad trod carefully, '… about your Able connection?'

'Not from me. And if you tell her, I won't be shooting in the air next time. She and I don't see eye to eye on enough things already.'

'Is that what you've got against this well? Just because it's Able?'

'That's got something to do with it.'

'But not all?'

Ash scrutinised Brad for a few moments, the suspicion returning. 'You said you weren't here on company business.'

'I'm not. It was an observation. I wondered if perhaps you were sympathetic to the concerns of Gabriel Fitzmaurice and the NWLC. You said yourself he opened your eyes to the Aboriginal concept of the land during your time with him in the war.'

'Has he said something to you?'

'About you? No, not to me. But he did mention to Karen some time ago that he puts his secondary education down to you.'

Ash sighed and Brad detected another breach in the old bloke's defensive wall.

'God knows I owed him that much. He saved my life. He was indispensable. Not just to me. To the whole section. All the Aborigines in our unit were a godsend, not just Gabriel. But I had most to do with him.

'We talked a bit when out on patrol. He had a notion that because he and the other Aboriginal trackers were treated as equal to the white soldiers in the army and had an important role in our defences against the Japs, that it would continue to be all dandy for his people after the war. I knew it wasn't going to happen. The Aborigines would be back to second class as soon as the last shot was fired, but I couldn't bring myself to tell Gabriel that. He was naïve, yes, but he was also intelligent… and loyal.'

Ash fell silent for a moment, drifting in the past.

Chapter 19 October 1987

'He stood by me through a bad patch there for a while at the end. Pulled me through. He didn't have to. I didn't deserve it.'

Another silence before Ash breathed in deeply and continued.

'The least I could do was fund him going to high school. I thought with that bit of a start he could make his way, maybe even make a difference for his people. I was able to scrape up enough after the war. There were concessions I could call on and the Lieutenant who'd been in charge of my unit in Timber Creek had a bit of influence, so Gabriel went off to Brisbane. He found it hard, but he got through.

'Karen mentioned he became involved in the early push for Aboriginal Rights, the strike at Wave Hill.'

'There were other walk-offs too in the late '60s, but Wave Hill was the first. Gabriel was a station hand in that region before the war, so he knew the conditions the Aboriginal stockmen worked under. After the war nothing changed—next to no wages, lousy accommodation, food. There was none of the equality he had hoped for. The granting of equal pay in the mid-60s was supposed to make a change, but the station owners got around it and Aboriginal pay rates stayed well below that of the white stockmen.

'So yes, Gabriel did get involved. He helped get the Australian unions to back the strike and give it national attention. The publicity was all about wages and conditions, but underlying it all was the simple fact that the Aborigines wanted their land back. I suppose you could call him a radical in his day. He's mellowed since, but he's still fighting the bulldozing tactics of some governments and companies.'

'You kept in touch all that time though?'

'Not after he left Brisbane. I knew what he was doing,

especially when his name popped up in the protests, but I didn't see him again for twenty years or so. I was wrestling my own demons then as I've already told you. But I never forgot those days on patrol along the Victoria and the things he showed me.

'I saw the minerals game as an escape to the freedom of the open spaces at first. I'll admit the money was good too. Then I began to see everyone, governments, the corporates, financiers, miners—all in a rush to make a buck and cut corners to get it. There were people who cared about the damage left behind, but none of them had a voice. All the talk was about helping the economy and providing jobs. It all began to look short-sighted. No thought for the long-term. That's another reason I pulled the pin.

'Gabriel found me here through his connections with NWLC. You've met him. He's determined, but he's fair. So I'm on his side. Call it Land Rights if you like. To me its prevention of rape. My beef with Able just reinforces it. Gabriel and Karen are the only ones who know the land connection. Everyone else thinks I'm just some nutter with a rifle. But now you know the story too, so am I right to trust you?'

Brad returned the stare. 'I meant what I said. I'm not on company business. But I think you'll find that Charlie knows too. He was the first to tell me you were Karen's grandfather. Not quite right as it turns out. But he'll know you from your time in Cloncurry dabbling in his stock market plays.'

'Only if he sees me. That's why I didn't go into the mess the other day. He didn't know why I was in debt to Able, so there was no link to Karen.'

'Well, okay, but I do think you might be wrong about Able and this particular well. He is following a dream.'

'Bullshit!'

Chapter 19 October 1987

Brad was startled by the sudden vehemence and flashing eyes, but he ploughed on.

'So am I in a way. Although my dream's more recent. Can I tell you about it? The other reason for coming today is to ask for directions.'

He began to relate finding the passage in Stokes' journal, but Ash put up his hand.

'I've read Stokes. I know the passage. Don't tell me. You want to look for those wells.'

Brad nodded and Ash sat back smiling.

'Bugger me. You are a romantic. But there'll be nothing to see after 150 years. So what's the point?'

'I don't expect flags and an X on the spot. I'd just like to see what there is to see of the area. Maybe to get a feel for what Gabriel showed you,' he added.

Ash studied Brad's face. When he spoke again his tone was flat, almost as if the old bloke was resigned to something inevitable.

'Won't be easy getting there with the rains coming. When are you going?'

'When the well's finished I'll have a bit of time.'

'Come back then. And don't give me any more crap about Able and his dream. All that says is that he wants to feed his bloody ego and hook in some other sucker to pay for it.'

Chapter 20

October 1987

Brad sat at the stockyards corner for several minutes, the Land Rover out of gear, engine idling. He thought about Ash's doomed relationship with Karen's mother, shattered because of one last job. He pondered the man Ash had become. Lonely. Bitter. At war with himself. Living on regret. Brad didn't want that. He wanted stability, trust—mutual trust—companionship and love. His mind went back to the night with Karen, when she unburdened herself to him. He saw her pain then, and now it was there again in the story Ash had told. She too was fighting demons of the past. But would she share that battle? Would she let him in to help her leave it behind? The intensity of his longing surprised and unsettled him. He was stepping onto unfamiliar ground.

An approaching vehicle broke into his thoughts, the engine note changing as the driver shifted gears. The vehicle slowed at the stockyards and Ethan Williams lifted a finger from the wheel in the traditional outback greeting to a fellow motorist as he passed. Brad remembered the drilling super saying he would be freighting a sample of the Stokes-1 core from the airport that morning to a laboratory in Melbourne for detailed analysis.

Chapter 20 October 1987

Brad waited till the dust settled, then put the Land Rover into gear and turned to follow Williams into camp. He would have to finish this job, but he was determined to tell Karen of his feelings and hopes as soon as he found an opportunity.

* * *

'You fraternising with the enemy again?'

Williams threw the remark out the open door of his office as Brad walked past to the mud logger's hut.

'Just trying to find out his problem and short circuit any more trouble. Even bullets fired into the air have got to come down somewhere.'

'And?'

'And what?'

'Did you find out his problem?'

Brad had found out a great number of Ash's problems, but he wasn't going to tell Williams.

'He's mainly concerned about the proximity to his home and what will happen if we find something worth developing.'

'Chance would be a fine thing,' Williams retorted. 'I can't see us finding anything this side of the Wet now, despite what Able wants. Your shooter will have plenty of time to shift house out of the way. Or he might prefer to stay and be the first one connected to the natural gas line the developers put in. I can see the headlines now. First gas to service a fruitcake living in a dunny shack in the wilderness.'

Williams guffawed. Brad didn't join in. He was more interested in the well's progress.

'You seem to be making hole pretty fast. Where are we?'

'We're nearly at 1,500 metres. Yeah, it's chewing up the rock.

Able's pushing me like hell to get to the primary by the end of next week. He hasn't managed to get a contract extension on the rig, so far anyway, and I just don't see us getting finished by the end of the month with all the testing and completion work.'

Brad shrugged. 'Lap of the gods then.'

As he walked on towards the mud hut, he calculated he'd be finished up in a couple of weeks at the latest. With luck he could find an excuse to get into town to see Karen even before that.

'Still in one piece I see.' Aaron grinned as Brad walked in. 'What's the old buzzard like?'

'Never mind him. The drilling super says we're at 1,500, but he's still grousing about not having enough time to finish the job.'

'Maybe he's got money in the Malteser's little sweep,' Aaron said.

'Sweep? What sweep?'

Aaron Laughed. 'If you spent more time at the rig you'd know Charlie's got a bet going on what depth we'll be at when the Wet hits or the rig contract expires—whichever comes first.'

'Jesus, that man must eat gambling chips for breakfast. So what is the current status?'

'Seems to be back on track. We're 500 metres below the Gibb River. Gas reading's still up a little. They're tripping at the moment. The Super wants to change to the twelve and a quarter inch bit to try to get the rest of the way to the primary target in one hit. Ambitious, but …'

Aaron broke off as an alarm suddenly sounded on the rig. 'Shit!' Look at the pit level monitor. It's way too high. They've got a kick.'

Chapter 20   October 1987

'Christ! How the hell did that happen?'

'They must have been pulling out too fast.' He pointed at the gauge. 'The bottom hole pressure's too low and formation fluids are coming in.'

Brad ducked outside leaving Aaron to watch the gauges. He saw the roughnecks scurrying around the drill floor. Williams was in the dog house shouting instructions to activate the blow out preventers. 'Do it now. The longer we leave the well open the worse it's going to get. For Christ sake, don't argue. Just shut it in.'

Williams stormed down the rig stairs, pushing past Brad to get into the mud hut.

'We're gonna have to circulate this bastard out,' he yelled at Aaron. 'Gimme a rundown on the pressure data.'

He grabbed a calculator as Aaron began reeling off numbers for pressure limitations of the blow out preventer stack, the wellhead, the casing and the mud pumps. Brad watched, staying out of the way. His knowledge of kill procedures was minimal, but he realised they had to compute the right weight, density and circulating pressures for the heavy 'kill' mud that would be pumped down the well.

'Okay,' Williams said putting down his calculator, his tone calmer. 'We go with the two-step program. I hope to Christ it works or we'll kiss the well goodbye, probably my ass too. Keep an eye on those downhole readings,' he said to Aaron. 'Let me know immediately if anything changes. You, Dixon, come with me. You can be my message boy. About time you made yourself useful.'

Brad followed the Super outside and up onto the drill floor where Hawkeye was waiting in the dog house, anxiously watching the gauges.

'Here's what we're gonna do,' Williams said. 'Open the choke, keep the pump strokes even, no more than 50 per cent of normal rate. Go easy.'

The driller was a picture of concentration, the roughnecks and roustabouts standing by, tense. No one said anything, strain etched on their faces and fists clenched. Minutes ticked by.

'Shit!' Hawkeye spat it out. 'Pressure's rising. We're not holding it.'

'Fuck. Shut it down.' Williams turned to the drill crew. 'We need more mud weight. Let's go.'

Brad watched as the men sprang to life hauling sacks of barytes to the mud tanks and tipping the powder into the hopper. They worked as a team, two bringing the sacks over, one slitting the necks open and one hoisting the contents into the hopper. Williams was busy with his calculator.

'Right. Let's try it again. Just enough choke till it equals the annulus pressure. Incoming mud pressure same as in the drill pipe?'

Hawkeye nodded.

'Okay, keep it constant. Steady with the pumps.'

Once again the rumble of the motors took over, the drill crew unmoving, actors in a frozen pantomime, Hawkeye's forehead shiny with sweat. Williams joined him in the doghouse, staring at the instruments. Five minutes went by before the Super finally spoke.

'I think we've got it this time.'

There was no change in his tone, but Brad sensed Williams relax a little and saw the driller roll his shoulders to ease a cramp. He suddenly felt out of place, surplus to requirements, wondering why the Super wanted him there.

Chapter 20 October 1987

'Are we in the clear?' he ventured.

Williams stared at him, unsure whether he was being facetious.

'Jesus, Dixon, you're worse than a mistress at a wedding. We aren't out of the woods yet. This first circulation is just to get the formation fluid influx out. We still have to kill it by running a second circulation with even heavier mud. If everything's okay at the end of that we can count ourselves lucky and get back on course. If not I'll be sending Able my resignation before he gets in first. Your presence is no longer needed, if that's what you mean. You can bugger off and leave it to the workers.'

* * *

The Malteser was not a happy man either. Brad noticed the glum expression on the chef's face as soon as he walked into the mess.

'This rig has jinx,' he said as Brad poured himself a coffee and sat down opposite. 'First we have accident, then we fish. Now we have blowout. I think this well is no good.'

'Charlie, it's not a blowout. It hasn't gone that far. The Super has it under control. But there are sure to be recriminations. Hawkeye's crew was on duty when it happened. Someone got sloppy and Sourpuss is far from pleased. But that's for him to deal with. It shouldn't affect you… or your little wager.'

Charlie shrugged, but his face didn't change, despite Brad's dig.

'Come on. This is not like you. What else has happened? Is there trouble because you sent Lucy home? Or maybe I'm the one in trouble.'

'No, I don't hear about Lucy. I worry for my money.'

'Your money? What money?'

Charlie pushed across the table the paper he had been reading. 'Maybe you have portfolio.'

Brad saw it was open at the financial pages.

'No way. I'm not into shares Charlie, you know that. I wouldn't trust anything to the whim of the market. Anyway, what's the problem? It looks like it's still booming.'

Brad pointed at the headline announcing that one of the country's high fliers had just bought another company for a sum in the billions of dollars. But Charlie shook his head.

'Too much. The big boys they go crazy to buy each other, buy up everything to grow, but there is nothing for underneath. They sell junk bonds to get the money for the buying. Or they have… how do you call it?… hairy loans from the banks. Easy money.'

'But that's not particularly new is it? From my small understanding, it has been a bull market for a couple of years. The stock market is way up. That should be good for your shares shouldn't it?'

'I think maybe now it is too hot, too good for the truth. Now I think is better to sell something to have cash for later.'

'Well, I'm certainly not the person to ask Charlie. Sorry.'

The Malteser reached over and took back the newspaper, tucking it into the fold of his tunic. A semblance of cheer returned to his face as he did so, as if his worries were folded away along with the article.

'Okay. I unnustand my problem is not for everyone. I think anyway, you have more important puzzles for your head.' Seeing Brad's frown, he went on: 'You wonder how to go to see your nurse. For you it is serious, yes?'

Chapter 20 October 1987

'Does it show that much?'

'Ah, my young friend, I have said this before. The Malteser sees everything. For you she will wait.'

Brad's reply was cut off as the mess door banged open and Ethan Williams stalked into the room.

'God, there are days when I wish this wasn't a dry camp. I could murder a Jack Daniels.'

'My kitchen has best instant coffee in the Kimberley,' Charlie said, his humour restored. 'For you I get it myself. But you first must tell me that the rig doesn't explode and the Malteser with it.'

'We're still stabilising the well, but we are over the crisis. Shouldn't have happened in the first place. Comes of trying to push things too hard. Able's hell-bent on getting a result before we lose the rig.'

'We nearly did lose it.'

Williams glared at Brad. 'I wouldn't get too smart.'

'It wasn't meant to be a crack. I've never seen anyone move so fast to get on top of it. That'll go in the daily report.'

'It won't need to. You can tell Able in person. I just got a fax saying he'll be coming up for a look the day after tomorrow in his private jet. He wants you to pick him up.'

Brad caught Charlie's wink from behind the Super's back. He had just been handed a cast iron reason to get to town.

Chapter 21

January 1943

Ash couldn't remember a more miserable Christmas than 1942. Even during his teens in the Depression years in Melbourne when his father struggled to put food on the table, there was always some treat unearthed from somewhere. The two Christmases he spent in the Middle East were passable too: pantomimes with the Red Cross nurses, songs and jokes, a special slap-up meal in the mess. But the 25th of December 1942 at Bradshaw on the banks of the Victoria River brought no joy, just unremitting rain, uncomfortable heat and the constant presence of mosquitos and sandflies. Food supplies from Nackeroo headquarters at Katherine were not getting through because the road to Timber Creek was one long line of bogged trucks interspersed by surging water that no longer kept within the banks of creeks and channels. The *Pride* had been retired for the Wet. The boat didn't have enough engine power to fight against the flow down the Victoria to get back upstream. On top of that, Bluey's death and Stretch's departure for disciplinary hearings were still raw wounds for the Bradshaw patrol.

Stretch hadn't been replaced, but Gordon Heath, a

Chapter 21   January 1943

twenty-year-old Sydneysider, had joined the group as the new signaller. He'd spent his first few months in the Nackeroos in Katherine where he had earned the nick-name Pebbles because of the thick lenses in the spectacles that he never took off. His pass through the Army's medical he put down to his expertise with Morse code. Weedy, fair-skinned and with an aversion to firearms, Pebbles cheerfully pointed out to Ash that he could hardly see a target even with his specs on, let alone hit it. 'But put me in front of a Morse key and I'm your man,' he said with a satisfied grin.

Ash and Sam made him welcome and tried to put on a reasonable spread for a Christmas meal. But there was only so much they could do with tinned cabbage and dehydrated potatoes. Gabriel and Jimmy were able to contribute some bush tucker in the form of seeds and fruit, along with a goanna that they threw in the fire whole and presented to the table when the skin was black. Ash decided then and there that for New Year he was going to break a rule and bag one of the station cattle that still roamed near the homestead.

The Nackeroos spent Christmas Day listening to the frog chorus and the rain belting down on the iron roof. They could barely hear the music of the Jap hour that evening over the din. The downpour continued all week. There was little else to do but roll thin cigarettes from the rapidly diminishing stash of tobacco and re-read the damp pages of newspapers and magazines brought on the *Pride*'s last run several weeks before.

Ash had brooded over Bluey's intercepted message since the day the Lieutenant showed it to him. In fact he'd memorised it, including the obsequious tone and Imperial bullshit:

I HAVE HONOUR TO REPORT TO IMPERIAL COMMAND

AUSTRALIAN SURVEILLANCE ON VICTORIA WEAKENING. NO SUPPLIES POSSIBLE IN MONSOON. RIVER OPEN FOR ENTRY GLORIOUS IMPERIAL FORCES. REISEN

Looking out at the downpour, he realised how accurate it was. Their supplies were dwindling and the conditions made any meaningful surveillance along the river virtually impossible. The Japanese could tie up at the Bradshaw landing and come in for tea before the Nackeroos spotted them. More importantly, who was Reisen? It would have to be someone who knew the area, someone who was holed up close by. Ash had his prime suspect. He wanted permission to go back to the Fitzmaurice Mission straight away and bring in Hans Müller for questioning at Army headquarters. The Lieutenant was inclined to agree with him and put in the request for action, but orders came down from Command to leave the Pastor alone. Ash suspected the influence of the church in political circles, but the Lieutenant thought it was more likely to be that the intelligence boys advising Command simply didn't believe there was a threat from the Fitzmaurice.

'The Army has three scenarios regarding invasion points,' he told Ash. 'We don't figure directly in any of them.'

'Oh yeah. And what do the brass think they know?' Ash couldn't keep the sarcasm from his voice.

'Given the onshore logistics, Command believes the Jap Navy might try the Gulf of Carpentaria near Normanton in Queensland; or the McArthur and Roper Rivers here in the Territory. But I personally think the third scenario has more going for it.'

'What's that?'

'The Japs might try to come in through Cambridge Gulf

Chapter 21 January 1943

and land at Wyndham. There's more infrastructure there and they could build up the airfield to accommodate squadrons of bombers and fighters. That would put them in easy range of the west coast as well as Darwin. They could consolidate and bring in troops in a simple hop from Timor without much resistance seeing the Yanks are concentrating on New Guinea and the western Pacific.'

'Yeah, maybe. But what about the message that Bluey picked up? Clearly it pinpoints the Victoria. At the very least you've got to say it's a fourth possibility.'

The Lieutenant nodded.

'I agree we shouldn't discount it, but HQ's intelligence people believe that message was a blind—something to occupy us while they come in somewhere else. Maybe even several places at once for all we know. Just keep a sharp look out. I'm giving you authority to do what you think's necessary to watch the east bank of the Victoria, but don't go near that mission again. That's an order.'

Ash looked out at the sheet of water flowing across the homestead yard and came to a decision. The rain had been virtually non-stop since the Lieutenant left on the *Pride*'s last trip back to Timber Creek and it obviously wasn't about to let up any time soon. They'd have to go out in it regardless, but Ash wasn't going to patrol anywhere on an empty stomach.

'Hey Sam, grab your rifle. Let's go and get some beef.'

Chapter 22

October 1987

'Hello. You're back again.'

The hospital receptionist gave Brad a cheeky smile as he approached the desk.

'No injuries to report this time? Shall I page Sister Frost for you then?'

Taken aback by her impudence, Brad only had time to nod before the girl picked up a microphone on the desk and her amplified voice came through the tannoy: "Sister Frost to reception, please. Sister Frost."

Brad had called at the house earlier. He knew Lorna wouldn't be there because she worked a normal day shift at the pharmacy. He didn't know Karen's shift rotations, but he thought there was a chance she might be home. When she wasn't, he debated whether to wait or to try the hospital. His impatience to see her meant the latter course won. Now he wasn't so sure. He hadn't expected such a public announcement.

'Thank you. Very perceptive of you,' he told the girl who smiled sweetly in return. Another gem for her gossip circle.

Brad positioned himself to one side of the desk where he could see both corridors leading off the reception hall. He

Chapter 22   October 1987

wondered which one Karen would come from when, suddenly, there she was bustling into the room just as he had first seen her. Neat blue uniform, those startling hazel eyes, dark hair pulled back from her face, but businesslike with slightly furrowed brow as she searched among the people near reception. When Karen caught sight of Brad she stopped in surprise and a smile flitted across her face, quickly replaced by her professional look as she saw the receptionist watching.

'Mr Dixon. How good to see you. Come this way. How is Mr Honeyman?' As they moved over to the central seating she lowered her voice. 'What on earth are you doing here? Has something happened? Is Ash all right?'

It was Brad's turn to be surprised.

'He's fine, as far as I know. There've been some issues at the rig. The boss is flying in tomorrow and I'm picking him up. But it's really you I came to see. I've been thinking a lot about you and I... well I've missed you.'

It was said, but now he felt foolish. His face was hot and he sensed that Karen was not about to let him off the hook easily.

'Have you, indeed. Well, you've certainly picked your audience.'

'I'm sorry. I didn't want to hang about outside the house.'

'You'd have been waiting a while. I'm on afternoon shift. I'm not off till about 11 tonight.'

'Could we get a late supper?'

'Where on earth at that time in this town?'

'Well, I could get something, bring it around and get it ready.'

'Lorna's on leave. Her mother in Perth is sick. So no one to let you in.'

'Oh. Well I can stay in the motel till you're finished here.'

'Persistent fellow, aren't you.' She smiled. 'I'm never sure of the exact time I finish. Can't have you loitering in the street, though. The neighbours are likely to call the police and that wouldn't look good on your CV. I'll have to trust you with my keys. Wait here a moment.'

'I think the receptionist is on to us,' Brad said when Karen returned.

'You've made Fiona's day. Just don't jangle these on your way out of here. We don't have to give her concrete proof. I've got to get back to work.'

Brad felt a light pressure on his arm. 'I've been thinking about you too,' she whispered. Then she was standing. 'Goodbye Mr Dixon. Thank you for letting me know.'

* * *

Brad showered and changed at the motel, taking his time. A glance at the Oriental Palace brochure told him the restaurant was open till 10.30 on Saturdays. Reheated takeaway was not his ideal for a late supper, but he didn't have much choice. He entered the Palace right on closing time, earning an exasperated look from the waitress. The food was in his hands within a few minutes and the window blind pointedly pulled down as soon as he was back in the street. Brad walked the few blocks to Karen's place via the pub bottle shop and let himself into the house feeling like a burglar who'd stolen the keys. He even checked for curtain twitches at the neighbours' windows. Once inside he put the food in the oven and set it on low, grinning inwardly at his domesticity.

He regretted not bringing anything to read. Television didn't appeal so he wandered over to scan the bookshelf—a few crime novels, a biography of Flying Doctor founder John

Chapter 22   October 1987

Flynn and one of Howard Florey, the man who made the first penicillin. He also noticed TGH Strehlow's *Journey to Horseshoe Bend* and pulled it out to read the cover notes: the story of the last journey of the author's father, Carl Strehlow, the Lutheran pastor who had headed the Hermannsburg Mission in Central Australia in the early 1900s. Brad understood Karen's interest. He glanced up at the old photo of the Fitzmaurice Mission on the wall above the bookcase. The black and white print was grainy, but looking closely now at the young white girl who was Karen's mother he could see the likeness, especially around the eyes and the lift of her cheekbones. And Gabriel. Top right Ash had said. The youth would be about fifteen Brad judged, probably not long before he left to become a stockman. His face was thin, his expression more subdued than the other children as if he already felt the weight of the second-class status imposed on his race in the world outside the mission.

Brad became so absorbed in the photograph that the knock on the door gave him a fright. He frowned; maybe a neighbour had seen him enter and come to check? He hesitated a moment, thinking about his explanation before a second knock propelled him to the door.

'About time. Have you been pocketing the silver?' Karen laughed at Brad's blank expression. 'You had my keys, dopey. How else was I supposed to get in?'

Brad registered the VW Beetle in the driveway. 'I'm sorry. I didn't even hear the car.'

'Remind me not to rely on you for security.' She threw her bag on the couch and leaned forward to kiss him briefly on the cheek. 'Mm. Something's cooking.'

'Not original I'm afraid. But I did bring a red.'

'Anything's better than the hospital mush,' she said pulling out plates and glasses.

They ate side by side on the couch, not saying much, concentrating on the food, the plates balanced on their knees with the cartons from the Oriental Palace and the opened bottle of red on the small coffee table in front of them. When Karen had finished she poured another wine and turned towards Brad, clearly something on her mind.

'You've been to see Ash again.'

'Wow. Word gets around fast.'

'Not really. I went back after our visit. I was still upset and I wanted to tell him he was… well rude and obnoxious and that I wanted an apology and that you deserved one too. He said you'd already been out there. Why did you do that?'

Brad picked up the change in her tone.

'He came out to the rig first. Then he sort of invited me.'

'He went to the rig? I didn't think he'd be seen dead anywhere near it.'

'Responding to my challenge to him, I suppose.'

'That's a first. You must have hit a nerve that I couldn't. Anyway, what does sort of invited mean?'

'He wouldn't accept a drink in the mess. Just said he had stronger stuff at his place if I was interested.'

'And you were?'

'Yes, actually I was. Not about the rum. I wanted to ask him about the Victoria River.' Karen looked puzzled. Brad hastened to explain. 'You know I've been reading Stokes. Well there's a passage I came to where the explorer finds oil in some water wells along the river. I've decided, seeing I'm up here reasonably close, I'd like to try and find them. I thought Ash might know about the area seeing he'd been there during the

Chapter 22   October 1987

war. Remember he said he'd been up and down the river many times.'

'So you talked about the war?'

'Yeah, a bit.'

'What about my grandfather?'

'Yes. He came up.'

'What did Ash say about him?'

'He was a bit vague really. He just mentioned that his unit was on the lookout for Japanese infiltrators and collaborators. I got the impression the subject was off limits, so I didn't pursue it. Anyway, I was more interested in the geography of the river. He did say he was fond of your mother though—as a child… and then later.'

Karen leant closer and gripped his forearm.

'So he did go to the mission.'

'Yes. He said your mother, he called her Frieda, seemed a happy child. He has that same photo in the hut.'

'You went inside?'

Brad nodded. Karen was silent for a while, her hand still resting on his arm. When she spoke again, it was a whisper, almost as though talking to herself.

'I don't believe grandfather was a collaborator. I've been trying to find out. War records in Canberra have a file, his internment at a camp in South Australia on the Murray River. There is no proof of any contact with the Japanese or anyone else. He was let out within a month. They wouldn't do that if he was suspect, would they? What if it was the opposite? What if he was sent back to the mission to find out if there were any spies in the area?'

'As a spy for the Australian Government, you mean?' Brad raised his eyebrows. 'That's a stretch, surely.'

'Maybe. Oh, I don't know. Someone may have found out. It might explain his sudden disappearance. There's nothing in the records. But there wouldn't be. I just can't believe grandfather's religion, his faith, would let him betray his country. He was Australian by then. I've been reading a book about the strength of one Lutheran missionary's values. It was unshakeable.'

'Strehlow you mean? At Hermannsburg? I was looking at that in your bookcase.'

'Not just stealing the silver then.' She gave him a rueful smile. 'I'm sorry. I didn't mean to be sharp before. It's just that Ash gets me going. We used to have fun when I was younger, in Cloncurry. He talked to me then, showed me things. Now he doesn't let me in at all, always baiting me. And then you come along, I let down my guard and blurt it all out. I haven't let anyone in like that for a long time. It just felt right… at first. Then I began to wish I hadn't said so much. I was angry with myself the other night, not with you. I'd spoiled our day and I thought you might see me as weak, or neurotic… or worse… just someone who is cheap. It worried me because being with you that night was truly wonderful… and, well, it unexpectedly mattered what you felt about me.'

Brad began to speak, but Karen put a finger to his lips.

'No, let me finish. Then, when I went out to demand an apology from Ash, I heard you'd already been there and I was angry again… no… more like disappointed that you could go behind my back. I thought, that's it. The end. Then today you turn up at the hospital and I was glad to see you. I really was. Even Fiona noticed that. Now tonight you tell me you had an invitation from Ash to visit. Inside his hut as well. I've never been in there. I'm jealous. And I shouldn't be. I just don't know where I am with him… or you. Oh God, what a mess.'

Chapter 22   October 1987

Brad slipped an arm around her shoulders, drawing her to him.

'Please don't think that. There's no mess that I can see. I've been in relationships before that, deep down, I didn't care about. But not with you Karen. Please believe what I said at the hospital. I've missed you so much. From the moment we parted that night I've been wracking my brains for ways to be with you again. I think everyone at the rig can see it. Lucy certainly did.'

Karen shot him an enquiring glance. Brad told her what had happened and Lucy's departure from the rig.

'I'm half expecting a hard time from Able when I pick him up at the airport tomorrow. Maybe even the sack. Lucy threatened to tell him I'd made all the advances. He specifically requested me to pick him up at the airport. But, you know, I don't give a damn about that. It's you I want to be with.'

Brad kissed her cheek. 'If you remember, even Ash made a comment about us being an item. And that was before we… made love.' He squeezed her arm. 'I admit the visit to Ash's place was partly to satisfy my curiosity about the man. It was after I told him I knew he wasn't your grandfather.'

'You told him that?'

'Yes. At the rig. He was fishing for my intentions I think. I wanted to know why.'

'Did you find out?'

'Not really.'

Karen studied Brad's face, weighing the denial. 'I'm almost certain there is something,' she murmured. 'Something Ash is hiding from me. What is it?'

Brad's stomach lurched. Much as he loved Karen, he

couldn't betray Ash's confidence—for her sake as well as for Ash. He deflected the question, trying to keep his voice steady.

'There's nothing that I saw. Not much of anything really. The only things to do with the war period was that old photo and a little wooden carving that meant a lot to him. He'd given it to your mother. I think he said you found it among her possessions addressed to him … oh, and he's still got his .303 army rifle. But then, everyone on the rig crew knows that; he's fired it around the camp often enough.'

Brad wasn't sure that Karen was satisfied. 'You know,' he added, 'I think Ash is a man fighting himself, not you. I think he loved your mother and because of that he loves and wants to protect you… And he's not the only one.'

Karen put her head on his shoulder. 'Brad,' she said quietly. 'Can I come when you go to the Victoria?'

'Of course. That would be perfect. A chance to be on our own. But it's just a geological whim of mine. Are you really interested in some ancient water wells that probably aren't there anymore?'

'Not really. But it's the region where Ash was during the war. And maybe you could take me to the old mission on the Fitzmaurice, or what's left of it. It's not far away. I'd like to see it. Where mother was happy and where grandfather put his faith. It would mean a lot.'

Brad lifted her chin and kissed her, feeling her lips part and their tongues meet in a lingering, teasing dance. Then she pulled back, the hazel eyes shining, inviting.

'Will the company accountants mind if they pay for a motel room you don't sleep in?'

'I'll make sure they won't find out,' he murmured as his fingers explored the top buttons of her uniform.

Chapter 23

January 1943

Pebbles looked up from the clicking Morse key when Ash and Sam came back to the homestead carrying a haunch of beef between them. The signaller held up his hand to silence their boisterous chatter as he concentrated on the message coming through. The others caught the concerned look on his face as he scribbled on his pad.

'What is it?' Ash barked as Pebbles signed off and turned towards them.

'There's been a reported sighting of an unidentified submarine in the Carpentaria Gulf near Mornington Island and another of a ship putting troops ashore near Normanton. We are to go on full alert and wait further instructions. C-Company is checking. So far the reports are unconfirmed.'

'Shit! It's finally happening.' Sam looked at Ash. 'What are we supposed to do now Corp? Carpentaria is a bloody long way from here.'

'Like the Lieutenant says. We stay alert. Doesn't mean the Japs have focused on one point.'

Ash looked at the bullock's blood down the front of Sam's shirt. His was just as stained.

'We're not wasting this beef at any rate. Ask Gabriel and Jimmy to get a cooking fire going in the corner over there. We can grill it all and at least have a decent meal tonight. After that we clean all the weapons thoroughly and divvy up the ammo. I'll set surveillance watches for the night later. There's no point in moving out along the river this late in the day. Pebbles, you stay by that radio. I want to know the moment anything else comes through. Did the Lieutenant say when the reports were made and who made the sightings?'

'Reports are from last night Corp, but nothing about who from. Who's out there around the Gulf anyway? I thought everyone had buggered off south.'

'Same as here. Station people are still around and there are a couple of missions over on the eastern shore. The rest are defence force including our C-Company boys. There'll be bush Aborigines scattered about too. It wouldn't surprise me if one of them made the report. Maybe reliable, maybe not.'

As the Nackeroos went about their individual tasks, Ash pondered the best way to set up surveillance. He was a man down with no replacement for Stretch. He was equally determined that Pebbles should not be left alone as Bluey had been. Ash worked away at the barrel of his rifle with a rag and the pull-through, mulling over the few possibilities open to him until the smell of grilling meat became impossible to ignore. The beef was tough, but the taste more than made up for that. They ate their fill and a bit more, savouring the feeling of a full stomach for the first time in a very long while.

'Best tucker this restaurant's put out since I've been here.' Sam leant back and patted his shirt front, emitting a loud belch. 'Pardon my French.' He grinned. 'We gotta have Bradshaw beef on the menu again soon. But we don't want uninvited guests.

Chapter 23   January 1943

How are we going to tackle that possibility Corp?'

Ash puffed out his cheeks and rubbed the stubble on his chin.

'We don't have many options. Pebbles has got to man the radio. So tonight you and Jimmy take the first watch; Gabriel and I will do midnight to dawn. Tomorrow we're going to have to split up. We need to get into position further down river. I reckon the Japs are more likely to make a landfall closer to the mouth and come inland from there rather than risk being seen this far up on the water. I'm going to take Gabriel and Jimmy down to Bottle Glen to set up there. We won't have a radio. That's the reason for Jimmy being with me. I'll send him back with a report for the Lieutenant once we've had a look around. Sam, you stay to watch Pebbles' back. You can also do surveillance during the day from the spring up on the Yambarrans, especially if there is any break in the rain. Pebbles, I don't want any down-time on that radio while you're in control, so make sure the batteries stay charged. If the Japs do get this far, put it out of action and destroy any code books you have.'

'Don't have any Corp. It's all in my head.'

'In that case, don't get caught. You and Sam use the horses to get back to Timber Creek if you have to retreat. The Lieutenant will need to know what's going on.'

'Are you going to ride down to Bottle Green?' Sam asked.

'Yes. Why?'

'The salt flats down there will be a quagmire by now. You'll never get through.'

'You got a better idea?'

'Yeah. Why don't we build you a raft? The current will take you there in no time. If you stick close to the bank you should be okay and there'll be three of you on the poles to steady her. It will be a one-way trip, but horses will be a liability at the Glen even if they do get there safely. What do you reckon?'

Ash contemplated the scheme. He wasn't a strong swimmer. He knew Gabriel was, but he didn't know about Jimmy. The Victoria was flowing at close to its peak and the current would snatch anyone who fell overboard. On the other hand, if they could keep close to the bank as Sam suggested, the current would be more subdued.

'I can't say the thought thrills me, but yes, I suppose it can be done. The raft will have to be sturdy though. That river won't give a second chance.'

'Okay,' Sam responded. 'I've seen some old 44-gallon fuel drums behind the outbuildings and there's plenty of timber and rope about.'

Ash mulled it over some more. The construction would delay them, but the trip itself would take an hour or less, whereas horses could be floundering around for days. And Sam was right, the Bottle Glen camp wasn't suitable for maintaining horses.

The short delay enabled Ash to receive word about the reported Carpentaria landings. C-Company patrols had found no traces at all of any Japanese occupation around the supposed sightings. The Commander was sure that no one had come ashore. That didn't negate the possibility of submarines and ships out in the Gulf, but there had been severe electrical storms at the time of the reports. Vivid imaginations could conjure up all sorts of shapes and lights at sea in those conditions. The news reinforced Ash's conviction that Bluey's intercepted message from Reisen was genuine. The boffins in Katherine might dismiss it as a red herring, but he couldn't. He sent a message to the Lieutenant informing him of his intended move to Bottle Glen.

Chapter 24

October 1987

The airport was almost deserted when Brad arrived—no one at the check-in desks and only one person at a car rental booth doing some paperwork. A cleaner wearing a fluorescent vest wheeled a trolley, picking up paper cups and wrappers discarded after the early morning flights to Perth and Darwin. A girl in the food kiosk was making sandwiches.

Reg Able's Lear jet was due to land about midday, but Brad had made sure he was early. One of the perks of private aircraft is that you can keep away from commercial airline schedules and arrive with a minimum of air traffic congestion, crowds and fuss. But it also means there is no notification of flight arrival times on the airport screens. It was better for Brad to wait for Able than the other way around.

Sitting at the airport Brad let his thoughts drift over his last few hours with Karen. It troubled him that their passionate night had been soured in the morning by his appointment at the airport. Karen was annoyed that Brad wanted to leave the house soon after breakfast even when he explained he'd have to return to the motel to shower, change and check out by 10 am. She accused him of being at Able's beck and call. The well was still a bone of contention between them. Brad couldn't decide whether Karen's dislike of Reginald Able was the main reason for her antagonism towards the drilling program, or whether she disapproved of oil exploration in general.

He thrust that aside and instead began to anticipate the next time he would be with her—on the trip to the Victoria—no rigs, no Able, no hospital, just the two of them free to be themselves for three or four days. Brad didn't hold out much hope of finding Stokes' wells, but he looked forward to exploring with her the countryside that the early navigator had described; probably little changed since that time. He wondered how much of the church in Karen's photograph would still be there, or the other buildings for that matter. As far as she knew, the place had died with her grandfather's disappearance, left unoccupied, shunned, because people, the authorities, even the church hierarchy were convinced of the man's treason. On the face of it there could be little doubt of that. No other explanation made sense. Brad understood Karen's need to go there, but he feared for the effect the place might have on her.

The scream of jet engines startled him. He looked at his watch: 11.57. Able was bang on time. Brad got to his feet and went to the arrivals gate as the sleek aircraft with its twin engines and swept-back wings taxied towards the terminal. The high-pitched whine faded as the captain shut down. The fuselage door folded out and down, extending steps to the ground. A slim redhead in a tailored uniform alighted and stood waiting at the bottom. Brad smirked. Of course Able would have a hostess on board even when he was the only passenger. It went with the image.

The man himself appeared at the top of the steps, dressed much as Brad remembered on his first meeting—in his

Chapter 24   October 1987

travelling clothes: casual shoes, jeans and an open-neck shirt, this one with short sleeves as a concession to the heat. His grey-flecked hair was cut short on his skull, which drew attention to his beaked nose. At the bottom of the steps he said something to the redhead. Brad saw that Able was by far the shorter of the two. The girl shook her head and the boss walked on towards the terminal. At the half-way point he stopped and opened his brief case to pull out a grey oblong object with a short antenna attached. He poked it and held the device to his ear. Brad guessed it was one of the new mobile phones. Trust Able to be one of the first to have it. He didn't look happy about it though as he poked it again, frowned and brought the thing down to his side. Inside the arrivals area Able caught sight of Brad.

'Bradley. Good to see you. I need a phone. This overpriced brick won't work out here in the sticks.'

Brad indicated a line of public phones along the back wall.

'Not a pay phone. I want some privacy. Where's the airport manager's office?'

Brad didn't know, but the girl at the car rental booth directed Able up the stairs to offices at the back of the building.

'Grab my bag will you. Just the one. The vehicle out front? I'll be with you shortly.'

Brad exchanged a glance with the girl and did as he was told.

* * *

Reg Able said little as they sped along the bitumen. He pulled some papers and a pocket calculator from his briefcase and busied himself punching buttons and making notes in the margins of the printed pages in his lap. Brad kept his eyes on the road. Why had Able specifically asked for him to do the pick-up? He might as well have hired a chauffeur.

They soon reached the green drum turn-off and left the highway. The car juddered along the gravel station track. Able had trouble working the calculator and keeping the papers from sliding to the floor. Brad grinned to himself as the boss soon gave up and looked out at the black soil plain rolling away on either side of the road.

'You read Stokes yet?'

The question caught Brad by surprise.

'Some. I've got to the part where he finds oil in water wells on the Victoria, which I presume is why you lent it to me.'

'What do you think about that?'

Able's eyes were on him, the trademark penetrating stare. Brad decided to hedge for the moment, to see where the boss was going.

'Well, Stokes doesn't give us much to go on. He could have found anything, even some sort of vegetable biomass. I'd put Stokes' find down as historical interest. Mind you, I have read elsewhere that the formations in the Victoria River area do contain rocks capable of generating oil and gas, but they are old, Proterozoic I think.'

Able brushed over Brad's answer, eager to deal an ace.

'There's a later, more detailed report of an oil seep near the Bullo River. An official sworn statement too. Dated 1904. A prospector found oil oozing from the side of a gorge about seventy kilometres from the Victoria junction. There's even a record of it being analysed down in Melbourne and found to contain oil comparable to petroleum deposits in Borneo.'

'I haven't heard of that report, but I'd reckon the close proximity to the Victoria would make those rocks Proterozoic too.'

'So, not the same as here.'

Chapter 24   October 1987

'We are looking at much younger formations at Stokes-1. Devonian and Carboniferous. That's not to say hydrocarbons couldn't have migrated into them from older rocks. But the Victoria is a fair way from here so there's no way you can make any direct correlation. It doesn't negate your program though.'

'I'm glad to hear it.'

'There's oil and gas offshore in the Bonaparte Gulf and some sniffs onshore as you know.'

'So it's okay to keep dreaming?'

Brad caught a hint of sarcasm. When he looked across, Able was smiling. Brad felt like a fish on a line. The boss continued.

'I've got a lot riding on this Bradley and not a lot of time. You and I both know the main target is a Devonian reef play and that it's never been tried in the Bonaparte. But that's not enough to generate the interest I want for Stokes-1. I need to have a catchy story: History pointing the way to the present. A nineteenth century explorer providing a clue to unlock modern day riches. What could be better? It doesn't really matter if the rocks are not exactly the same. We don't have to dwell on that. It's the overall impression that counts, especially if there is even a hint that the dream might turn to reality.'

'But any geo will see through that sort of hype.'

'Probably. But it's the media I'm after. I am not making anything up. The story of Stokes' find on the Victoria has been out there for a hundred and fifty years. Not many people other than historians have read his journals, so it's not widely known. All I'm doing is alerting everyone that oil has been discovered in the region. The precedent is there. It's a great story, the sort of thing the magazines and TV programs love. When they tell the tale it will create a groundswell of interest in the exciting potential of Stokes-1.'

Brad drove in silence for a moment or two recalling Ash's scorn for Abel's dream. What was his comment? "You can sell anticipation easier than reality." Brad frowned as something else occurred to him.

'Why are you telling me all this? I'm a contractor last time I looked, not a bound employee.'

'All the better for being independent, although I should remind you about the confidentiality clause in your contract. It's simply that you have read Stokes' journal and know the story. All you have to do is say exactly that if anyone asks. I'm guessing you are sufficiently intrigued to want to go and see the place where the wells were dug. Am I right?'

Brad looked at him, taken by surprise for the second time. 'Yes.'

'That makes it even more credible then. I'm not asking you to lie. Well, maybe a white lie.'

'Who is going to talk to me anyway?'

'The media. They'll run with what I give them, but maybe want to embellish it with a comment from the man on the spot.'

'What if they ask about the geology of this well?'

'You tell them all technical statements about Stokes-1 have to come from me. No exceptions. Easy as that.'

Brad felt uncomfortable. He didn't want to be part of Able's spin.

'I can't say I'm happy about any of this, but I am still puzzled. What did you mean by not having a lot of time? I presume by all this story telling that you've got a deal going, but the well is still a long way above the primary target. Why the short fuse?'

'Ah, there's the question. I suppose there's no harm in telling you. I've been around the financial game a long time now and I've seen a few ups and downs. Mostly ups in the last decade

Chapter 24 October 1987

and that could be a looming problem. Over the past week the stock market has become a little too hot for my liking. I've a feeling in my water that something's going to blow. And I mean big time. That won't do me or any other investor any good. Deals could be dumped or postponed, value lost. I nearly cancelled this trip because I'm out of touch up here.'

'The phone call at the airport?'

'Yes. Nothing's happened yet.'

'No wonder the Malteser was so glum.'

'You've talked to Camilleri?' Able's tone was sharp.

'Not in detail. He's worried about his shares. Also about the slow progress and problems with the well. Has he got something riding on your deal?'

'Charlie's his own man. But he's right about the well problems. We should have been all done by now. Williams and his crew will be lucky to get a job from me again. Give me your take on what's been found so far.'

Brad ran through the well status, filling in more detail than his faxed reports, noting in particular that the well had come in high to prognosis, but that the secondary reservoir zone was promising. Able listened, staring out the front windscreen, not even noticing the stockyards or Ash's hut as they passed. Brad wondered what the boss would say if he knew who was living there and undoubtedly watching as the Land Cruiser went by. Brad had to admit that the old bloke knew Able a lot better than he'd given him credit for. As he turned into the camp he wondered if Ash would be abroad with his rifle that night.

* * *

A stony-faced Ethan Williams followed Reg Able up the steps to the drill floor. It was clear he had received a bollocking from the boss who made straight for the drilling Super's office as soon as Brad parked the vehicle. Although Able had a reputation for treating employees well, he expected one hundred and ten per cent effort in return. That meant no stuff-ups and it was obvious he held Williams ultimately responsible for the well falling behind schedule. The kick had been circulated out by the time Able arrived, but Williams elected to keep the well shut in pending the boss's instructions. After addressing the drilling crew and then visiting Aaron Davey to go through the well logs, Able gave the order to resume drilling. By late afternoon the rumble of the rig engines again permeated the camp.

The Malteser directed Brad to put Able's bag in the separate accommodation that Lucy had vacated. Brad was relieved that the Boss had not mentioned his niece's departure. Either Lucy hadn't carried out her threat or Able had chosen to ignore it. Charlie may have smoothed the path too. In any case, Brad guessed that they had more important concerns of a financial nature on their minds when he saw the two of them in deep conversation in the mess soon after the resumption of drilling. Being a Sunday, stock markets around the world were closed, so there was not a lot they could do but wait to see what the new week's trading would bring.

Able remained taciturn and preoccupied during the evening meal which he ate with the Malteser at a separate table to everyone else. His presence put a dampener on the atmosphere in the mess, the usual buzz of conversation missing as everyone lowered their voices and avoided looking his way. Perhaps noticing this, Able finished his meal quickly and rose to leave. On the way out he stopped by Brad's table.

Chapter 24   October 1987

'I'd like a meeting with you, Davey and Williams first thing tomorrow. Let's say eight in the Super's office.'

* * *

Able was on the rig's satellite phone when Brad, Aaron and Williams arrived, so they helped themselves to the Super's coffee supply and waited. Able completed his call and reached for the coffee that Aaron offered.

'Good morning gentlemen,' said Able. 'There are some decisions to be made and I need all your inputs, so sit down and let's get on with it.'

He came out from behind Williams' desk and perched on the front of it rather than take a chair. He gazed pensively at the floor in front of the desk for a few moments. Brad noticed dark pouches under his eyes.

'Some years ago I visited the Canadian oil fields and I met a geologist who showed me around, in particular the Leduc oil field in Alberta. It was a major find in its day. This fellow told me onshore northwest Australia had look-alike plays, buried reefs of Devonian age. He couldn't understand why no one was aware of them or, if they were, why they had only been given a passing glance. Since then of course we know oil has been found in reef deposits in the Canning Basin out from Broome. But no one… no one has bothered to look for them in the Bonaparte. That, gentlemen, is why we are here. The Stokes prospect is going to prove to everyone that we have a Leduc too.'

Brad knew this was drawing a very long bow and he wondered if Able really believed it. More likely it was the same hype that he was planning to spin about linking it to Stokes' discovery on the Victoria River. Yes, the Mitchell Limestone reef target was a valid prospect when looking at the original seismic data, but the drilling had already shown interpretation of overlying formations to be inaccurate.

'You may be wondering about the urgency for completing this well.' Able paused as if still deciding how much he would reveal. 'The approaching wet season and the end of the rig contract are obvious reasons, but there is another factor… and I'd prefer this doesn't become common knowledge.'

Again he paused.

'It has largely been forgotten that in the 1950s the Western Australian Government provided an incentive for petroleum explorers by guaranteeing that the first 40 million barrels of oil produced from a new onshore discovery in the State would be free of excise tax. That provision has lain dormant for thirty years. If anyone does remember it they have probably assumed that it had a sunset clause and has long since expired. It hasn't, but… '

'So why the bloody rush,' Williams muttered.

Able glared at him.

'I haven't finished. As I was going to say, I have it on good authority that some people in the Energy Department have suddenly rediscovered this part of the Oil and Gas Act and they are advising the government that the tax incentive is no longer necessary. They are suggesting the legislation be repealed in the first session of Parliament next year and the Minister is considering the move. If that is the case then coming back next year to finish the well will be too late.'

'Even if the spud date of the well is before any repeal date?' Brad asked.

'I'm afraid so. It's the date of the discovery that counts. It may not happen, but why take the chance?'

Chapter 24 October 1987

'And the tax break is only for oil?'

'That's correct Bradley. In the 1950s the focus was on oil discovery. Gas was second prize. No one could do anything with it, especially in isolated places. It just wasn't a commercial proposition. So there you have it. The quandary. What I want from you people is the exact state of the well and the likelihood of making it down to the Mitchell oil target before we have to release the rig.'

'Can't you break the contract?' Williams wanted to know.

'Of course,' Able replied irritably, 'if I'm willing to pay the day rate plus two hundred per cent for each day past the contract date. That's roughly one hundred and fifty thousand dollars a day. You do the math. With the likelihood of being caught here for the Wet, that's five months if we're lucky. In my book that's twenty-two or three million give or take.'

Brad did some quick sums in his head: forty million barrels excise free, oil price around US$44 assuming it didn't change in the next year, minus development and production costs. If Able was so sure there'd be an oil discovery he'd be way ahead, even after paying the rig penalty rates. But, of course, Able wasn't sure. No one could be. That was not the game he was playing. The boss gave Brad a knowing glance, reading his thoughts.

'I'd rather find out what we have before I go down that road,' he said quietly. 'My question stands. Where are we now and will we reach the Mitchell before the end of the month?'

'The well prognosis puts us about 1,500 metres above target at the moment,' Brad ventured, 'but I wouldn't hang my hat on that. We were wrong in the early part of the well. It could be less… or more.'

'Today's the nineteenth,' Williams put in. 'Allow three days to rig down, pack up and get the trucks out of here, that leaves nine days. Two hundred metres a day is possible, but if we hit more hard limestone on the way down, we're stuffed. So, say seven days to get there if everything goes well. That leaves minimal time for any evaluation—logs, tests. And we'll have to plug before we leave. Whichever way you look at it, it's too tight. I don't like it.'

'We'll also be leaving without testing the secondary target,' Brad added. 'We got some good gas indications there that are worth a look.' He looked at Aaron for confirmation. 'A pity to leave that hanging.'

Reg Able sat in silent contemplation for some time while the others watched, wondering which way he'd jump. Finally he blew out his cheeks and spoke.

'We go for the main prize. But I want everyone on the ball. It's on you,' he added looking at Williams. 'No more mistakes. Right. Thank you gentlemen. I have some calls to make.'

Chapter 25

January 1943

Gabriel, Ash and Jimmy—the three buccaneers as Sam dubbed them—arrived safely at Bottle Glen. The voyage had its tense moments, skirting half-submerged trees where the current spun the craft 360 degrees. They needed their combined strength to pole themselves to the bank. The trip only took an hour, but Ash was exhausted by the time they disembarked.

'Might be we sail to Darwin next Boss,' Gabriel said with a grin as he leapt into the shallows with a mooring rope to secure the raft to a slender boab near the water's edge.

He and Jimmy unloaded the provisions and gear while Ash walked up to inspect the camp. The buildings had withstood the torrential rain and storms with fewer leaks than the homestead at Bradshaw, although the surrounding ground was carpeted with leaves and branches stripped from the overhead foliage. The volume of water rushing down the creek had collapsed the stonework around the spring, so Ash set to work cleaning out the muck.

By late afternoon the camp had been set to rights, but they quickly found the sand flies welcomed their presence. When the mosquitoes joined in at dusk, Gabriel built up the fire and the trio huddled in the smoke generated by the damp wood. A short time later Ash gave up the fight and retired to his swag, preferring the stifling heat under the cheesecloth netting to the mosquitos' whining attacks on his face and neck.

He lay sweating, his mind churning the possible ways to keep watch along the river and what he would do if they sighted the Japanese. With Gabriel and Jimmy's help he was sure they could melt away into the bush and shadow an enemy force if it came ashore. It would be more difficult if the Japs stayed on the river and worked their way upstream. Ash knew he wouldn't be able to keep abreast of them even if they were slowed by the strong current. His best bet then would be to send Jimmy back to Bradshaw, cutting overland across the meanders. If Jimmy could reach Pebbles and Sam before the Japanese, a radio warning could be sent to the Lieutenant.

An even more difficult scenario would be if the Japanese put a force ashore as well as advancing on the river. It would be impossible to keep tabs on both parties unless he and Gabriel split up, something he didn't relish. He doubted his ability to last more than a few days on his own.

Ash dozed fitfully as rain splattered on the shelter's canvas roof and crocodiles grunted somewhere along the river.

He woke at dawn, momentarily disoriented by the new surroundings and the strange quiet. The rain had eased. Gabriel and Jimmy looked up from the fire when Ash emerged, dishevelled, and made for the creek to wash. He wondered if the two Aborigines had left the fire at all during the night. Gabriel held up the long body of a snake as he approached.

'Good tucker boss.'

Ash declined, but Gabriel just grinned and threw it in the fire where it crackled and twisted in the flames.

Chapter 25 January 1943

'Bin bush blackfella here in the night, boss,' Gabriel said casually as he poked the blackening reptile.

'You saw him?'

'No. But he bin watching.' He waved his stick at the dense undergrowth past the spring. 'Might be he bin camping longa waterhole before boss.'

'Do you think he is still around?'

'Yes. Might be.'

Ash pondered a moment. Why would the Aborigine hang around? Perhaps just to cadge tobacco. Or maybe he had something to tell them. Another set of eyes on the river.

'Do you think you and Jimmy could find him, bring him to talk to me?'

'Might be we try boss.'

* * *

Ash spent the morning on the hill immediately behind Bottle Glen. It was a relief to find a place away from the insects that plagued the camp. The rain had cleared and he looked out over the stretch of river leading to Holdfast Reach. The river itself was swollen and brown with sediment gouged from the banks. In places the water foamed as it rushed past half-submerged obstacles embedded in the mud. Elsewhere all was still. The land seemed as empty and forbidding as ever.

'Boss.'

Ash turned to see Gabriel leading an older man towards him. He was naked except for a string around his waist and a cloth headband holding a mop of greying hair back from his lined face. His broad chest was creased with tribal scars, his arms and legs long and lean. He stood tall and straight and his eyes met Ash, unblinking.

'This man bin watching us,' Gabriel said.

'Is he on walkabout from the Fitzmaurice Mission?'

'No Boss. He proper bush blackfella. He bin with that Nemarluk one time ago.'

'One of Nemarluk's old brigade! Well, he'll be no friend of the Japanese. Can you ask him why he watches us?'

The man's eyes had not left Ash's face and when Gabriel put the question, he answered directly in English: 'Boat bin come longa river.'

'A boat! When?'

The man held up one finger and pointed at the sky.

'One day? Does he mean one day?'

'Might be boss, I think.'

'He's not talking about our boat... the raft, is he?'

'Boat bin come longa river,' the man repeated, still looking at Ash. 'Little bit.' This time he pointed down Holdfast Reach towards Entrance Island and the river mouth.

'How many people?' Ash asked, trying to keep his tone matter-of-fact.

The man just shook his head. Ash frowned. He tried again. 'Japanese man?'

Again the man shook his head. Ash and Gabriel tried several other tacks, but it became apparent that the bushman didn't know the answers. He had seen a boat, maybe yesterday, somewhere down river; that was the extent of it. Ash didn't doubt the boat sighting, but he was sceptical about the time as well as the location. The man could even be talking about seeing the *Pride* when it was up and down the river before being taken out of service a month earlier. But he could not ignore the man's statement. The old fellow had made a point

Chapter 25   January 1943

of coming to tell them, so that must give some credibility to a recent sighting.

Ash realised he would have to investigate. Should he take the raft further down river knowing he couldn't bring it back again to Bottle Glen, or should he walk? It had been hard going when he traversed from the cove near Quoin Island with Gabriel and Sam. Conditions had become a lot worse since then. Time might be important. No, the raft it would have to be. He turned back to the bushman who was still watching him intently.

'Thank you. We will go to look at this boat.'

Ash reached into his shirt pocket and pulled out several cigarettes he had rolled that morning. The man took the proffered smokes, nodded and turned on his heel. Ash watched him walk down the slope, then suddenly step off the path and disappear into the bush at the base of the hill. He wished he felt as confident in the surroundings.

Chapter 26

October 1987

Brad looked at his watch. After midnight. His mind was too active to sleep. When he began the Bonaparte project he relished being part of something different, historic even, if there was success. Now he couldn't wait to finish the job and get away. Disillusion with Reginald Able was part of it, but there was a wider picture too. For the first time in his career he had begun to question the values of the resource industry and his own role within its corporate structure. Geology was still fascinating, but he was turning against the rootless lifestyle, here today, somewhere else tomorrow. He wanted to spend quality time with Karen, in one place, for weeks… months. He pulled on a T-shirt and stepped out into warm night air.

Brad pushed through the mess door and was surprised to see Able and the Malteser sitting together at a table at the back of the room. Neither looked as if they'd been to bed. Charlie was still in his chef's tunic. Able wore the same shirt he'd had on during the day. Both had sombre faces. They weren't speaking and didn't look up as Brad walked past to the coffee station. He glimpsed a half-empty rum bottle before Charlie swept it out of sight in the folds of his tunic. Brad pretended

Chapter 26 October 1987

not to notice. The rig was supposed to be dry. Rules for most, but not for all. Brad made his coffee and turned back towards them trying to sound casual.

'Can't sleep either?'

When he received no answer Brad took the hint. He grabbed a random magazine and a handful of biscuits and walked past them to a table nearer the door. Clearly he was an intruder. A stubborn streak kicked in and he remained where he was, munching the biscuits and flicking through the pages of the magazine. It was an automobile monthly, a subject in which Brad had zero interest. He could only concentrate on the pictures and even that was a struggle. He forced himself not to glance at the back of the room, straining to hear anything being said. But the conversation had ended. Brad flinched at the sound of a chair pushed back abruptly. Suddenly the boss stood next to him.

'Bradley, you're a historian. Remember today: Monday 19 October 1987. It's a black day that will have lasting repercussions.'

Able continued to the door where he looked back briefly before exiting into the night.

A moment later Charlie came over, sat his ample frame opposite Brad and put the rum bottle on the table.

'Some for you?'

Brad pushed his mug across. 'I wouldn't say no. Anything to liven up this god-awful coffee.'

Charlie poured a generous slug, splashed some more into his own and drank.

'Okay,' Brad growled. 'Are you going to tell me what's going on? It must be serious to break this golden rule.' He indicated the bottle.

'Yes, my Brad. Is very serious. The US stock market, she crash. Europe also. Free fall. Twenty percent already in America. This is maybe five hundred billion dollars lost, billion I say and the day is not finished, you unnustand. I worry about this happening. You remember I said this to you. The market is too hot. I sell a little before, but I will still lose much.'

'And Able too?'

'Oh yes. For him it will be very bad.'

'He doesn't know how much yet?'

'No. He must wait till openings of Australian market tomorrow… ah today, you unnustand. For us it will be the black Tuesday. Sure to follow America down, maybe further even. And nothing to do about it. Reg Able must wait. Me also.'

'What triggered it all? I mean, I know you said the market was overvalued, but why today… sorry, yesterday? Why not last week or tomorrow?'

'Too early for knowing, I think. Maybe too much computers in programs for trading. Maybe the insider trading too. Suddenly someone says sell. For why, I don't know. Then someone else worry about that. Thinks maybe they know something, so better to sell also. And someone else and someone else and so it goes. This mind of the market has no reason, it follows like herds of the sheep. This is the risk. Sometimes it goes up and then we smile. Now it goes down we cry… and drink the rum.'

Charlie shared the last of the bottle between the two mugs. Brad nodded his thanks.

'Yeah, well it's certainly not my scene. Why trust a bunch a greedy geeks who don't give a shit about anything except lining their own pockets, and pulling fast ones to do it?'

'Ah, my Brad this is strong language for you I think. Maybe

Chapter 26 October 1987

you are not happy also. You don't sleep. You have the lady for your mind, yes?'

Brad smiled.

'Charlie, you have missed your vocation. You should have an expensive office and a couch.'

'The cook he sees more, I think. Many peoples come to the rig to run from some problems. That's okay. The Malteser likes to watch, to see this thing or that, maybe to talk, you unnustand.'

'Yes I do. And you are right. I do think of the lady. Soon it will resolve, I hope, when this job is finished. That may be quicker than we thought if Able has taken the bath you say he has.'

Charlie sat back and stroked his chin.

'I think Reg is not finished yet. He has some more… how do you call it? …irons in the fire.'

Chapter 27

January 1943

Gabriel untied the raft from its mooring and pushed out into the shallows, nimbly leaping aboard before the craft swirled out into the current. Ash and Jimmy were already in position with their poles to prevent them moving too far into the river as they eased away from the camp site into the long straight stretch of water that led to Holdfast Reach. It was well into the afternoon and the light dimmed as storm clouds banked up along the northern horizon. Ash had toyed with the idea of sending Jimmy back to Bradshaw from Bottle Glen with a message for the Lieutenant outlining his movements. In the end he decided to wait to see if they found the boat and determined its importance.

Ash knew from his maps that the Victoria was a mile wide at this point, but it looked to be vastly more from his position low down on the water. The west bank was barely visible. The river's width meant the force of the current lessened and they were able to control the raft more easily. Even so, Ash had no wish to be on the river at night. He planned to put in to a sheltered anchorage at the mouth of a large creek that he remembered from previous trips about halfway up Holdfast

Chapter 27   January 1943

Reach. After about an hour, it was not the inlet that caught his eye but the unmistakable shape of a boat's twin mastheads swaying gently above the mangroves lining the river bank.

Ash realised they would be seen by anyone on board if they went past.

'Quick, into the bank,' he hissed, motioning Gabriel and Jimmy to help pole the raft as silently as possible towards the shore. The high-water level had half submerged the nearest mangroves so they were able to pull right in amongst the branches and tie the craft securely. Ash slung his rifle across his back and signalled the others to follow. Adrenalin surging, he worked his way through the mass of stems and roots across the narrow neck of land to the inlet shore. The others heard his sharp intake of breath. There in the lee of the hills sat a lugger at anchor, its gleaming white hull rocking slowly in the current, the name *Frieda* printed on its bow.

Ash recognised the vessel immediately. 'I don't need to go to the mission Lieutenant,' he muttered. 'The mission has come to me.'

Chapter 28

October 1987

News of the market rout in Australia began filtering through the rig camp as the Melbourne and Sydney stock markets opened. The Malteser had a radio on in the mess where listeners heard that the share market bubble had not only burst, but blown everything to bits. One commentator had coloured the story by calling the phenomenon "a global tsunami that traders had watched seeping towards Australia as sunrise crept remorselessly around the world."

Brad had seen the advance of that tsunami himself, played on the faces of Charlie and Able just hours earlier. Listening now over his breakfast plate, he heard that the Australian market had started in negative territory by opening twenty-five per cent down on the previous day's trading. Some of the bigger stocks were three quarters of the price traded the day before. Small stocks didn't trade at all because no one was in the market for them. The largest volumes traded were in industrial and resource stocks as panicked foreign investors quit Australian shares to shore up their cash reserves back home.

Mention of the hit on resource stocks didn't sound good and a number of conversations in the mess speculated about the possibility of a downturn in the industry that would put jobs in jeopardy. A few, worried about the more immediate future, asked Brad about the fate of the Stokes-1 well still grinding its way into the earth outside; a question that echoed his own, especially in the light of Charlie's parting comment overnight. He shrugged and tried to make light of it.

'Geologists, believe it or not, don't have the ear of management. But I'm bloody sure we'll have an answer before the morning's done.'

Tired from his sleepless night, Brad went back to his room to await the outcome.

Chapter 29

January 1943

The Nackeroos crouched quietly in the mangroves, watching for any movement on board or along the creek. Had the lugger passed Blunder Bay base unseen? What was Pastor Müller doing here? A final check on the Army's positions before sending an all clear to the Japanese Navy? Ash's anger rose. He would put an end to it.

With daylight fading he made a decision.

'Jimmy, you stay and keep a sharp lookout. If anyone comes to the boat, you come and find us. Gabriel, we go along the inlet and find his tracks. I'm not going back till we finish him.'

Gabriel noticed the malicious edge to Ash's tone. He'd heard it before, at the mission, then again after finding the radio message that Bluey had intercepted, and most recently when they interrogated the bushman at Bottle Glen. It troubled him, but he was in no position to argue.

They set off, Gabriel leading and Ash trying to emulate his noiseless steps. Nothing stirred in the boat as they passed. Water slapped against the hull and thunder rumbled in the distance. Gabriel studied the ground, then pointed to boot prints in the silt that led upstream. Ash lost the marks when

Chapter 29   January 1943

the shore became rocky, but Gabriel pressed on. The creek soon narrowed and the tracker squatted to examine the ground more closely. He pointed to the other side of the stream.

'He cross here Boss.'

Ash nodded and waded across. Gabriel resumed his squat on the northern side for a few moments before moving slowly up the side of a gentle rise. At the top, he dropped to his stomach and motioned Ash to do the same. They wriggled forward until they could peer into the next valley. The hillside sloped down to a wide grassy floor bordered by straggly acacias and low scrub. On the far side the plain ended in a sandstone cliff about 300 feet high. In the dying light, Ash saw dark patches of caves and overhangs in the wall. There was movement among the trees at the base of the cliff. Ash pointed. Gabriel shook his head.

'Wallaby, Boss.'

They watched the animal move out from cover to feed on the grass. Gabriel rose to a crouch and made his way silently down the slope. Ash followed, gingerly at first, but then more confidently as he gained his night vision. They reached the bottom and made their way around the base of the hill to the trees, by-passing a wide, but shallow depression that seemed strangely out of place, almost man-made, in the flat valley floor. Ash paused to look at it, but Gabriel kept moving towards the tree-line and beckoned him to follow.

Once there they retreated into the shadows and sat on their haunches, listening. Gabriel slowly moved his head in an arc to sweep the whole valley. He tensed and put a hand on Ash's shoulder, pointing at the sandstone cliff. Ash peered into the gloom. At first, he only saw the deeply etched rock face. Then he noticed a faint glow in one of the dark patches. It flickered and brightened to a yellow light. A lantern. As they watched, the light was lifted higher to shine down onto a bulky box-like object. The figure of a man bent over it rubbing a hand across the top. A radio set! Ash was certain. With an aerial probably slung along the cliff. How did he get up there? There must be a narrow wallaby track along the ledges—treacherous and slippery, but possible for a fit man and perfect to conceal a hideaway.

Ash watched transfixed. Rage and loathing swept through him. The man was transmitting to the enemy. It had to be stopped. He jerked his rifle around and off his back, jarring the butt on the ground with a dull thud. Out in the valley the wallaby caught the movement and spooked, thumping away in rapid bounds. In the cliff cave the man heard the sudden commotion and looked up, the light full on his face revealing the prominent nose, straggly moustache and goatee beard of Pastor Hans Müller. Ash no longer had doubts.

The crack of a single rifle shot echoed through the night. The figure on the cliff dropped out of sight. And then silence.

(J.L. Stokes – Journal entry 7 December 1839)

…*With my mind fully occupied by all we had seen of late, I hurried on without waiting, and reached the observation spot, just glancing towards the cliff, which presented nothing to the view except the silvery stems of the never-failing gum trees.*

I had just turned my head round to look after my followers when I was suddenly staggered by a violent and piercing blow about the left shoulder: and ere the dart had ceased to quiver in its destined mark, a loud long yell, such as the savage only can produce, told me by whom I had been speared. One glance sufficed to shew me the cliffs, so lately the abode of silence and solitude, swarming with the dusky forms of the natives, now indulging in all the exuberant action with which the Australian testifies his delight. …

Chapter 30

October 1987

Brad tossed the journal aside. He couldn't concentrate on Stokes' problems now. He had too many of his own. One of them was Reginald Able's plan to link Stokes' historic water wells to the drilling less than one hundred metres from Brad's room. Whichever way he cut it, the charade failed Brad's concept of ethics. Able said to consider it a harmless white lie, a diplomatic untruth. But there was nothing well-intentioned about this unless you counted Able's intention to line his own pocket. The stock market crash only made the deception more necessary. Able would use fantasy to lever himself out of trouble. Bugger it! If he was asked for confirmation of the Victoria River correlation, by the media or anyone else, Brad would put the whole story into its proper geological perspective.

A thump on the door made him jump.

'Super's office, now,' Aaron said as he stuck his head into Brad's room. 'Methinks changes are afoot.'

'What have you heard?' Brad asked as he joined the mud logger outside.

'Not much. The boss has been on the sat phone since six this morning, so the Super says. Completely taken over old

Chapter 30   October 1987

Sourpuss' office. Kicked him out to make the calls. Probably to his brokers. I reckon he'll be liquidating assets; collecting as much cash as he can.'

'Probably. But it wouldn't surprise me if he's put in a few "buy" requests as well.'

'Why? Have you heard something?'

'Not really. I just think he's a canny bastard. He'll be looking at bargain prices for stocks where the value will return once the panic eases.'

'Well aren't you the knowledgeable one. I thought you didn't have a bar of share trading.'

'I don't and won't, especially after this fiasco. Finance bloke on the radio was calling it worse than the Friday in 1929 that sparked the Great Depression.'

'Cheery thought. But you must have had a whisper. Tell me.'

'Well, it's just something Charlie said about Able and more irons in the fire.'

* * *

Ethan Williams had partially regained his office when Brad and Aaron arrived, but Able still commandeered the chair behind his desk. The Super lounged against a filing cabinet pretending he was unconcerned.

'Good morning gentlemen,' Able said. 'A lot has happened in the twenty-four hours since our last gathering. I don't have to spell out the market blood bath that is still going on as we speak. Bradley, I will require your services once again please. I need to get back to Melbourne today… before I have to sell the jet.'

Able smiled at his own jest. Brad thought it might be close to reality.

'Ready as soon as you like.'

'Good. You'll all be wondering about Stokes-1 so I'll get straight to the point. Ethan, I want you to stop drilling immediately…'

'But…'

'No, hear me out. I'm not shutting you down. On the contrary, I want you to come back up the hole and run some flow tests on the Gibb River secondary target. ASAP.'

'But why?' Williams frowned. 'Wouldn't it be better to keep going? No one is going to need the rig now with the industry probably going into meltdown.'

'First of all we don't know that. But if it does become reality there'll be all the more reason for the contractor to enforce the penalty clause if we retain the rig over the due date. He'll want to screw as much money out of me as he can, especially if his next contract falls over, which it very well could in this climate. I might be able to bargain with him. That's one of my tasks when I get back to Melbourne. But I can't rely on it, nor do I have the luxury of time. No, I want a test in the Gibb River. I have no time for maybes in the Mitchell. I need to add value to the well and the permit right now.'

* * *

The trip back to town was a virtual repeat of Sunday's drive from the airport to the rig. Able remained silent for much of the way. Brad let him brood and kept his eyes on the road. He was as much surprised as Williams about the change of plan for the well. It intrigued him that the boss had been forced to abandon his hype about the Mitchell Limestone primary target. If he was as convinced of success as he had made out

Chapter 30   October 1987

at the beginning, he would surely have pressed on with the drilling. They might not have time to run tests on any oil found, but the logs would show if it was there or not. Surely that would give him a chance to sell the anticipation of a commercial discovery—his sort of deal. The upside for Brad with the new plan was that it let him off the hook. There would be no need for fables about correlation with the historic water wells on the Victoria. Thinking of which:

'It might not be the best time to ask,' he began hesitantly, 'but would you mind if I took three or four days away from the rig after the test program? I still would like to try and find Stokes' water wells while I'm up this way. I find the whole thing intriguing and…'

'You really don't want to back up my theory on that do you?'

Brad gripped the wheel tighter.

'I'll be honest. No, I don't. You might be right, but it's too much of a stretch with the meagre data we've got. But I do thank you for introducing me to Stokes' journal. It's a great read. His descriptions are so vivid.'

'So were his perceptions of the future,' Able cut in. 'You might want to re-read a passage written before he found that oil. An entry back in October 1839. You'll find it interesting in the light of some of the opposition to my exploration program in the Bonaparte.'

Brad looked across in surprise and Able smiled.

'Oh, I'm not so isolated in Melbourne that I'm ignorant of what has been said up here. But to answer your first question, I have no objection at all to you making that expedition… and taking your pretty girlfriend.'

Able let that sink in a moment, his smile becoming a smirk.

'In fact, you might have a great deal of time on your hands if the market doesn't right itself. But you will know that yourself. I confess to you that I have lost a bundle today. I am going home to retrieve what I can.'

Brad didn't trust himself with a reply beyond a thank you. He was relieved they had reached the bitumen and he drove the rest of the way to the airport without saying a word.

The Lear jet was waiting on the tarmac when they arrived, the captain and the tall hostess too. Brad handed Able's bag to the ground crewman. The boss proffered his hand and they shook, firmly.

'Good bye Bradley. Make sure you get me a good result in the Gibb River test. Drop me a note about your adventure to the Victoria when you return the journal. Oh, and give my regards to Douglas Ashmore when you see him next.'

Chapter 31

January 1943

'Got the bastard!'

Ash jumped up, waving the rifle above his head. 'We got 'im, Gabriel. We got 'im...' He stopped short when he saw Gabriel had not moved, staring back at him. 'What's the matter? The bastard had it coming.'

'Yes Boss.'

'Well, what's the problem? He was a traitor for Christ's sake. Against me... and you. Vermin.'

Ash spat the word out, but Gabriel looked away. A different Ash stood in front of him—manic, obsessed. A man who wasn't going to listen. Suddenly Ash was like other domineering and contemptuous white men he'd known, on the cattle stations, in Katherine and the one time he'd been in Darwin. The transformation shocked him, but he stood his ground.

'He teach me Boss. When I was piccaninny.'

It was Ash's turn to stare, his euphoria deflating. Now exasperation in his tone.

'Don't be so dim. He was bringing Japanese here, Gabriel. Here... to take our country. Don't you understand that?'

Gabriel kept his eyes averted. For the first time in Ash's

company, he felt his place as just a tracker, useful for keeping the white Nackeroos alive in the bush, nothing more.

'Might be, Boss,' he said quietly.

'Shit!'

Ash kicked the ground. He caught something new in Gabriel's attitude. It was disapproval. It sobered him, although Ash felt no guilt for his action. He was a soldier. It was war. Müller had taken Bluey's life, even if indirectly, and the pastor was clearly aiding the Japanese invasion. That risked thousands of Australian lives.

Gabriel looked at him as if he had broken a bond between them. Christ! Müller was the enemy. He was sending messages—probably in the middle of one. What did Gabriel expect him to do? Wait for him to finish? Ash fought to keep his pent-up hatred as the fury of the moment dissipated.

'Might be not dead fella, Boss. Better to go look.' Gabriel practical, his voice barely audible.

Ash stared at the tracker, still motionless in the shadows. Sudden doubt crept into his mind. He turned back to the cliff and saw the lantern light still flickering, marking the cave about half way up the face. There was no sound, no movement; out in the valley the wallaby would be watching, ears alert for any new disturbance. Ash went back over the moment he had fired.

It had been a single shot. The pastor had gone down, but had he been hit or had he just instinctively ducked? Ash had to know. Gabriel was right. He would have to go and see, to make sure. But how to get to the cave? Would Gabriel help him now to find a path up the cliff?

Chapter 32

October 1987

Brad called in to see Karen before leaving town, but she wasn't at home. He thought better of running the gauntlet of the hospital again. Instead he left a note under her door explaining that he had to get back for the last critical phase of the well program, but that the trip to the Victoria was a goer. He wrote that they could probably start out in less than a week's time and he couldn't wait to be on the road with her. But he made no mention of Able or his knowledge of their relationship, or of Able knowing that Ash was living near the rig. How could he without relating the tangled web that Ash had told him in confidence? He had been floored by the boss' revelations and the calculated way he had delivered them. Brad told himself it was probably just as well Karen had been at work. She would have sensed his hesitance straight away. Ash's secret had become a burden—more than that, a deception that he no longer wanted to carry. He vowed to tell her. But not yet. He needed to think; to pick his time.

Brad drove back to the rig in a daze.

The camp, when he arrived, was not a happy place. Aaron filled him in as they sat together in the mud logger's hut looking through the logs of the Gibb River reservoir section.

'Old Sourpuss is fuming. I don't think that man is happy unless he's not, if you know what I mean. Anyway he's dirty on Able because he'd prefer to be drilling ahead. He doesn't think that a test program should be done until we get down to the well's programmed total depth.

'Hawkeye's on shift in the dog house at the moment and he's more concerned about getting the rig out of here before it's rained in. He is sceptical, but he also reckons the industry will be in chaos so he's pessimistic there'll be a job waiting for the rig anyway. Sort of an each way grouch.

'The drill crew are worried about their own job futures. And Charlie is mooning around the mess saying his shares have gone south and he's lost his shirt. He reckons there won't be any new rig catering jobs either.

'So all in all a pretty contented bunch. What about you?' Aaron added. 'You weren't beaming when you came in either.'

'Ah, don't ask,' Brad said. 'But it's got nothing to do with the rig. In fact I'm at the stage where an enforced holiday will be a good thing. How come you're not bothered by all the goings on?'

'That's because I've jagged a job on one of the production platforms doing development wells off the west coast starting in November. I'm pretty sure that'll still be on because the big boys have already invested too much to pull the pin now.'

'Jammy bastard. When were you going to tell me?'

'I could say you were never here to tell.' Aaron winked. 'No. I just got it confirmed a few days ago. Haven't had a chance since and, anyway, I didn't want to while Able was here.'

'I don't think it would have made much difference whether he was physically here or not. That bloke's got eyes and ears everywhere.'

Chapter 32   October 1987

'That sounds like the voice of experience.'

'It is,' Brad said. 'But let's not go there. When does Williams reckon he'll be ready to set up the first test?'

'They're still pulling out of the hole at the moment. Able wants a full production test on that five metre zone we picked out on the logs… here at the bottom of the Gibb River.' Aaron stabbed a finger at the log chart. 'So they've got to go back in, set the packers to isolate it and perforate the casing. Best estimate Williams will give is tomorrow afternoon some time.'

'Let's hope it's worth it.'

'You're not kidding. I reckon Able must be pretty desperate to want to go straight to production testing. Sure, it's the best part of the reservoir, but it's not that good. I've seen better log results.'

Brad grunted. 'Desperate is not quite the word I'd use. Not for Able. The man's a gambler with his back to the wall. I reckon he knows he's going to take a hit on whatever deal he has going here and he's making a calculated ploy to claw something back.'

'Still sounds desperate to me,' Aaron said. 'But he's set the scene. There's not a lot we can do about it now.'

* * *

Around noon on Wednesday 21 October Ethan Williams signalled that he was ready to begin the test program on Stokes-1. Everyone in camp gathered beside the rig where they could get a good view of the flare pit. Even the off-duty drilling crew roused out of their beds. There was still a "why are we doing this?" attitude among most of the participants, but deep down everyone sensed that the result would have a bearing on their immediate futures. Besides, anything was better than the grim tidings that continued to come from financial markets and the corporate world. The radio news was bad from start to finish of each bulletin—companies defaulting, banks in trouble and requesting government bailouts, suicides among investors who had borrowed heavily to participate in the boom and now had crippling debts. In the United States there was even a report of a killing spree as an irate stockholder, blaming his losses on a broking firm, entered the office and began shooting indiscriminately. The stories were full of anger, mostly at the authorities that had somehow allowed it to happen. No one took responsibility for their own greed.

Brad, standing with Aaron, wondered how Able was faring in his Melbourne office. He had been told of the test schedule and had demanded to be contacted the minute there was a definitive result.

'Open her up,' Williams yelled.

The crowd fell silent, waiting, eyes glued to the end of the flare line. Nothing happened at first, but then the line began shaking and there was a sudden spurt of liquid that continued in bursts for several minutes.

'It's drilling mud,' Aaron said. 'Probably went into the formation when we increased the mud weight. It should clean up, but we might be waiting a while. Let's hope it hasn't completely clogged the gas flow.'

A number of bystanders began moving away.

'Bloody dud,' one of the night shift roughnecks muttered. 'I'm going back to bed.'

In the end it was a nervous wait of fifteen minutes before the first gas appeared, spluttering through the pipe with the remains of the muddy water, and another minute or so before

Chapter 32   October 1987

the flow became constant enough to light the flare. The flame shot out a metre past the end of the flare line and blazed strongly. Williams left the valves open until he was sure no more liquid was being emitted and then shut the test down.

'Only so so, but better than a kick in the bum,' he said. 'We'll let the pressure build up for a couple of hours and then give her a proper go.'

*   *   *

Brad sat back from the typewriter. The test result was good, but not immediately commercial. There would need to be more evaluation and probably another well, or at least a side-track to better understand the reservoir. It could make an additional development project if the underlying Mitchell Limestone primary reservoir contained a worthwhile discovery. But they'd have to wait. The ball was in Reginald Able's court.

Brad had telephoned the results through to Melbourne as soon as the test had been completed. Able wanted it confirmed in writing. In the meantime, Able instructed Williams to suspend the well and stand by.

```
FAX TO ABLE EXPLORATION
MELBOURNE
1700 HOURS WEDNESDAY 21 OCTOBER 1987
ATTN: R. ABLE
FROM: B. DIXON
SUBJECT: TEST RESULTS STOKES-1 BONAPARTE BASIN
PERMIT EP 12.
GIBB RIVER SANDSTONE RESERVOIR INTERVAL 1,545
M – 1,550 M
```

INITIAL FLOW OF DRILLING FLUID AND FORMATION WATER. CLEAN-UP TIME 15 MINUTES

FIRST GAS TEST 10 MINUTES DURATION. GOOD FLOW, ONE METRE FLAME DWINDLING TO HALF METRE BEFORE SHUT IN.

PRESSURE BUILD UP FOR TWO HOURS

SECOND GAS TEST ONE HOUR DURATION. STRONG FLOW, ONE AND HALF METRE FLAME THROUGH HALF INCH AND THEN ONE INCH CHOKE. NO APPRECIABLE PRESSURE DROP DURING TEST.

GAS FLOW AVERAGE 1.5 MILLION CUBIC FEET PER DAY. MINOR CONDENSATE ACCOMPANYING FLOW ESTIMATED TO BE ONE BARREL PER THOUSAND CUBIC FEET.

RESERVOIR QUALITY: GOOD POROSITY AND PERMEABILITY.

Brad fed the sheet into the fax machine thinking it might be his final act in the service of Able Exploration. There was one week left on the rig contract and the market was collapsing. The time had come for his excursion to the Victoria.

Chapter 33

January 1943

'Gabriel, you think I can get up there to look… without taking off my boots?'

Ash's tone had lost its sharp edge. Gabriel heard uncertainty and attempted humour in Ash's voice now, more like the normal Boss. His eyes had lost the crazed glint.

Gabriel rose and stood beside him. 'Pasta Moola go up. Might be we find his track, Boss.'

They advanced slowly, staying in the shadows of the tree line. Ash kept his rifle at the ready, his eyes on the cave, watching for any movement that would mean Müller was still alive. If the pastor was armed, Ash realised they would be sitting ducks on the cliff face. It was a chance they had to take.

At the base of the cliff Gabriel motioned Ash to stay put while he scouted along the edge. The tracker moved so silently that Ash was startled when, after a few minutes, he suddenly reappeared at his side.

'This way, Boss. Okay boots.'

The track proved to be a series of ledges weathered into the bedding planes of the rock strata—narrow, but wide enough to negotiate with care. Ash slung his rifle across his back and reached up to haul himself onto the bottom ledge. Gabriel led the way, slowly zig-zagging upward, weak moonlight between scudding clouds just enough for them to find hand and footholds.

'Müller would have done this in daylight,' Ash muttered. He willed himself not to look down or to think about the possibility of an ambush. Instead he concentrated on copying Gabriel's every foot and hand position. There was no rain, but the rocks were still wet and slippery from a storm earlier in the day. The rifle strap cut into his shoulder, the weight of the weapon pulling him outwards so that his hands began to ache with the strain. Fortunately there were several places where the ledge widened and he took these chances to flex his fingers and catch his breath. Finally, after half an hour of effort, they breasted the threshold and crouched down in the cramped space of the lantern-lit cave.

Ash screwed up his eyes to let them adjust to the flickering flame after the darkness outside. He heard the hum of the radio and turned towards it. The lantern sat on top of the transmitter illuminating Gabriel's face as he bent over it, but the space behind the bulky set lay in shadow.

'Where is he Gabriel? Is he dead?'

'Here Boss. Pasta dead. Something more.'

'What?'

Ash scrambled across, taking a moment to process the scene. 'Oh, Christ. No!' The shock set him back on his heels. He closed his eyes and slumped against the wall. 'It can't be.'

Chapter 34

October 1987

The drilling supervisor registered no surprise when Brad told him he was using the well suspension as a chance to do a bit of sightseeing around the region.

'Able said you'd be off as soon as the test was completed. He also instructed me to say that you can't use a company vehicle. We're going to need them all to get the drilling crew out of here. How long are you planning to be away?'

'Four or five days. Hard to tell.'

'Yeah. Well there might not be much here by the time you get back. God knows what's going on in Able's scheming brain. I sure as hell don't. The whole bloody program's been a cock-up from the start if you ask me. I may still be here; I may not. If not I guess I might see you round the traps somewhere.'

Williams shook his hand briefly and turned back dismissively to the report he was writing.

Brad's immediate problem of a lift into town was solved later that evening when he asked Charlie if a rental car company would deliver a vehicle out as far as the rig.

'This is not a worry,' the Malteser said. 'I go to town tomorrow for private business, you unnustand. You come with me to get car there. A nice one for the lady yes?'

* * *

The Malteaser turned the Land Rover onto the road away from camp. Brad looked out the passenger window.

Charlie glanced across. 'A last look at rig for you?'

'Nearly, I suppose. I've still got some gear here that I'll pick up on the way back. Why? Are you dismissing me too?'

'No my Brad. I am thinking you dismiss yourself from this job.'

'Well, I didn't get much encouragement from Able. Williams and the rig boys are probably out of here too. And Aaron.

'Ah, the mud boy. He goes to good job offshore I think.'

'Jesus Charlie, is there anything you don't know? What are you going to do when everyone's gone?'

'This depends for my shares.' He nodded at a manila folder on the seat beside him. 'I go to make calls. The bank is for more private phone, you unnustand.'

Brad left it there, not wanting to know about the Malteser's portfolio woes.

The stockyards came into view. Brad looked across the other side of the road at Ash's hut. No truck. He wondered where the old bloke was this time.

'No more shooting eh,' said Charlie as they passed. 'Maybe he get me another time.'

'What on earth do you mean by that?'

Charlie shrugged and tapped the folder. 'Is a long time ago. He is not so good with the shares. I make a mistake to tell him, and poof! His money is gone. Maybe still he is not happy with me for that.'

Chapter 34   October 1987

Brad sat rigid.

'You knew Ash was here all along, that he was the one shooting around the rig.'

'At first, not so much. But then I see him. At the rig, in the old truck. He comes to visit you I think. He is older now. Well so is the Malteser. But I know him from before in Cloncurry and I stay out of the way.'

'So it was you who told Able that Ash was here. I bet you told him I was seeing Karen too, didn't you?'

'Ah, that one I tell to explain to him you have not some interest in Lucy, you unnustand.'

'Bloody hell Charlie. You don't need to worry about another rig contract, or your shares. You could join ASIO. Your espionage skills are second to none!'

'Ah my Brad, you have the sense of the humour. The Malteser will miss that, but I think for you it is good to be with your lady. You will invite me to the wedding, yes?'

Brad laughed. It was impossible to be annoyed with the big busybody. 'If we get that far, Charlie, yes, if we get that far.'

Outside Karen's place, the Malteaser clambered out to enfold Brad in a bear hug. The Land Rover wobbled under Charlie's weight when he climbed back into the driver's seat. He gave a final salute and drove off to his appointment at the bank.

Karen opened the door and embraced him on the step, her lips pressed against his and her eyes shining.

'I thought you'd be here today and I'm all prepared with days off and everything.'

'I didn't realise you were clairvoyant as well as beautiful,' Brad laughed as she led him inside.

'I'll admit I had help. Ash told me.'

'Ash!' Brad couldn't keep the surprise from his voice.

'Yes, he's been watching the rig and saw the flare, so he knew the test program was going on. Your note said you'd get away as soon as it was over, so when he came and told me I guessed I'd see you today.'

'Wait a minute. Ash came in to town… here? That must be a first. Why on earth would he do that?'

'Well, you told him you were planning the trip and he reckons you'll need a guide, especially if we run into any wet weather.'

'Ash wants to come with us?'

Karen caught the note of disappointment and took his hand.

'It's all right, isn't it? I mean he does know the whereabouts of the old mission and on the Victoria you don't know exactly where to go. He says we'll need to get a boat. There are no roads to that part of the river.'

Brad rubbed the back of his neck. 'It's not quite what I had in mind.'

'Oh Brad, I'm sorry if I've butted in to your plans. I know you have been in a lot of outback places, and I'm not doubting your experience. But the bush can be unforgiving up here. I really think we can benefit from his local knowledge, even if it is forty years old.'

'You've made your peace with him then?'

'Yes, I have. I couldn't believe it when he was here on the doorstep. So unexpected. And I… oh I don't know how to say this… but somehow the way he sounded, it was strange.'

Brad put his arms around her. It wasn't at all how he'd planned it. But he had to admit he had no firm idea where to begin his search on the Victoria. Stokes' journal just called the place Water Valley and it was somewhere along Holdfast Reach. It hadn't even occurred to him there may not be roads

Chapter 34 October 1987

into the area. Ash knew the river intimately. It wouldn't have changed much in forty years.

'Okay.' He kissed the top of her head. 'You are probably right. I admit we could use some help. We'll have to hire a vehicle though. I don't qualify for a company car on this trip.'

Karen looked up at him with a guilty grin.

'Ash says his truck will be best.'

'What, the old Bedford? He must be joking.'

'No. It has a winch and high clearance, room for extra fuel and ... well, he says it will be fine.'

'I see. And just where and when will we join him and his jalopy?'

'He will pick us up from the motel in the morning. Oh, and he also said to tell you if you were not convinced about him joining us, that he was still responsible for me and that I would need a chaperon.'

Karen burst out laughing at the mix of surprise and indignation on Brad's face.

'But that's tomorrow,' she added. 'We can be together tonight.'

Chapter 35

January 1943

Ash sat with his head in his hands, rocking backwards and forwards as the enormity of his mistake took hold.

If only he had waited, climbed up to the cave to confirm his suspicions instead of firing impulsively. Müller couldn't have escaped. He had nowhere to go. Now the pastor was dead. Because of him. Ash had taken a life. He'd killed Frieda's father. He shuddered as the cold of guilt and remorse spread through him.

How could he face his comrades? The Lieutenant had backed him. And Gabriel, the man who had been a friend, trusted him enough to show him his world and teach him to respect the land and what it could provide. Ash had surely shattered that trust.

His body heaved as great sobs rose within him, jerking out in a succession of low-pitched moans. The demons crowded his mind. He could not go on.

Chapter 36

October 1987

The Bedford drew plenty of attention when it pulled up outside the motel. So did Ash when he climbed down in his baggy shorts, frayed shirt and boots without socks. The only concession to town etiquette was an attempt to tame and comb flat his straggly hair. Brad came over with the bags and heaved them onto the back tray before turning to grasp the old bloke's hand.

'I can see by the boots that you are in travel mode.'

Ash tightened his grip, acknowledging Brad's acceptance of his presence. Then he busied himself with roping the bags firmly in place while Karen hoisted herself up and moved to the middle of the bench seat, making room for Brad next to the passenger side door. He draped an arm across the back of the seat so that his right hand lightly touched her shoulder.

'Careful of my chaperon,' she said to him in a stage whisper, moving closer as Ash seated himself behind the wheel. The driver feigned deafness and pulled the truck out onto the street. Within a few minutes they were on the highway heading east towards the Northern Territory and Timber Creek. For a while no one spoke. Brad enjoyed the novelty of the old vehicle, gazing ahead through his half of the split windscreen.

'This is good cruising speed for the old bus,' said Ash. 'Timber Creek in about three hours I'd say.'

'Does it see much bitumen?' said Brad.

'Have some respect—she, not it,' he answered patting the wheel. 'Hardly ever. This might even be the longest stint since I've had her. Reliable though if you look after her.'

'All roadworthy then.'

Ash gave him a faint "game on" smile.

'I see you've stopped the well. Will the rig be there when we get back? The test flare didn't look very strong,' he taunted.

Brad refused to be drawn so early in the trip.

'We haven't found another Moomba, if that's what you mean. If I had to guess I'd say the rig will still be there, probably for the duration of the Wet. But I doubt if the crew will. Have to wait and see.'

'Okay, here's the rules,' Karen broke in. 'No talk about rigs. No work at all. We're on a voyage of discovery… and some family history. I would like to know how this old bus, sorry, she, is going to get us anywhere near the Fitzmaurice when there are no roads and no river access unless we come in through the mouth in the Bonaparte Gulf. I've done my homework.'

'I told you that you'd hooked yourself one tough-minded lady here son.' Ash winked. 'It's a good question, but it has a simple answer. We fly in.'

'What? How?'

'Helicopter. I did some phoning back there in town. The Lieutenant in the Nackeroos in charge at Timber Creek stayed in the Territory after the war. Moved to Darwin and is still there. I spoke to him last night. Reminiscing. It so happens that his grandson Garry is a chopper pilot and runs a charter company out of Timber Creek. There's not much on at the

Chapter 36 October 1987

moment and he can give us a ride to the old Fitzmaurice Mission site and back. This afternoon.'

'All three of us?'

'Yes. A Jet Ranger I'm told.'

'Wow!' Karen said. 'You must have got on well with your Commander for him to set that up.'

Ash shrugged. 'We were both older than most of the blokes and we saw eye-to-eye on a few things. This is not on the free list, but I am paying mate's rates.'

'I should pay our share,' Brad chipped in quickly.

'Not for this one Brad. It's something from me to Karen. A bit like our early trips into the bush round the Curry. And it's long overdue.'

'I... I don't know what to say,' she said. 'But thank you. God, it's...'

'It's not a lot of time really. An hour there. An hour on the ground and an hour back.'

'Are you planning the Victoria by chopper too?' Brad asked.

'No, no. I think you'll experience that better by river. We'll overnight in Timber Creek, then drive to Bradshaw and borrow a boat from there.'

'Borrow?'

'I told the manager I'd been stationed there in 1942/43 and wanted to have a final look around. You can chip in something for the fuel if you like. Anyway, that's the plan. I hope you don't mind that I've cut in on your trip. Just saw a chance to get out there again.'

* * *

The chopper rose with a sudden crescendo of whipping rotor

blades. Karen stiffened and gripped Brad's hand tightly, then slowly relaxed when the noise eased to a steady beat as they flew over the tiny township and out along the winding ribbon of river. Brad had flown in helicopters many times, but he never tired of the juddering lift-off and the slow rolling out of the panorama below. From this altitude, in this part of Australia, the geology sat up and looked at him. The sweeping curves of sedimentary layers etched into the landscape and the flat-topped mesas with green vegetated scree slopes fell away on all sides as they coasted over a wide plain marked with straggling tributaries to the main river.

'Bradshaw Station coming up.' Garry's voice came through the static in the headsets.

Brad looked down to see a sprawl of buildings beside the light brown oblong scar of the homestead airstrip, the scrub of surrounding trees and the thin sliver of the Angalarri River as it made its way to the junction. The much broader Victoria wound past just beyond the homestead yards, while ahead lay the steep slopes of the Yambarran Range. This was the country that Stokes had walked all those years ago. Brad marvelled at the stamina of the man and his crew, and more recently of Ash and his platoon of Nackeroos. From his high perch the country looked majestic and benign. He could only imagine the harsh reality the explorers faced on the ground.

Brad heard Karen's voice in the headphones, asking about another large river snaking across the yellow grassed plain in the distance.

'The Fitzmaurice,' said Garry as they flew towards it. 'Not as wide as the Victoria, but a lot of rock bars across it that can wrench the bottom out of a boat so I'm told. At low tide the rocks stick up and become waterfalls. Whirlpools and big

Chapter 36   October 1987

crocs too. Good fishing for barramundi if you can get in there. Usually boats come around the coast from Port Keats. Ah, there's what we are looking for. Those old ruins just ahead.'

Garry set the helicopter down on the flats overlooking a bend in the river. They got out and were hit by a wall of hot air.

'Be close to forty degrees,' the pilot said cheerfully. 'Not much here now, but Grandad said you'd have seen its heyday Doug.'

Ash nodded. 'It wasn't elaborate. Just a church and school about here and the main residence over there.' He pointed to a square of crumbling stone walls and some sheets of rusted corrugated iron. 'The Milkwood tree is still there though. Shaded the whole house.'

He wandered across for a closer look, but Karen stayed where she was, gazing at a row of wooden stumps eaten almost to the ground by white ants. An equally decimated bench lay on its side nearby.

'Careful of snakes in the rubble,' Brad said as he came up beside her.

'I'm just trying to imagine the church in my photo. Somehow I thought there'd be more, but I suppose a timber building wouldn't last long. That bench might be one of the pews, or maybe one of the seats in the school. My mother and the other children in the photo must have been standing right where we are now. And this is where she grew up, looking out over the river. It's so quiet. Isolated. You can only really appreciate that when you see it from the air. Nothing for hundreds of kilometres in any direction. I wonder if she was ever lonely. I know there were plenty of Aboriginal kids to play with, but I mean lonely for a European playmate. She never really said much to me, except that very few whites came near the place because of the rumours about Grandfather. She would have ridden out there alone looking for him when he disappeared. God. How would you find anyone in such emptiness?'

Brad put an arm around her shoulders.

'Frieda, your mother, invited us in for tea,' Ash said as they joined him. They walked towards the main house, some of its walls still standing. 'I remember she offered us some watermelon. She was so proud. She'd grown it herself. There was a garden just over there beside the house. They pumped up water from the river. She helped your grandmother bake a cake too and we had some of that. Or at least I did. Gabriel didn't feel very comfortable in the house, so he went onto the veranda. It went right around the house and there were stone steps up to it. That would be that pile over there.'

'Do you think she was happy here? My mother?'

Ash gazed through the gap where the door had been, opening into the front room and then the kitchen beyond that. He was back forty-five years. The food on the table, the smell of coffee and then the sight of the American ration packages. The abrupt way the missionary left them. Ash had been sure then. Very sure.

'Ash?'

'Sorry. Frieda? Yes I think she was happy as kids go. She was certainly bright and cheerful around us. I saw it as a happy innocence. And the little Aboriginal kids were a mischievous bunch too. They all got on well together by the look of it. Black and white didn't matter to them at that age.'

Garry was sitting in the shade of the chopper looking out at the river when they walked back.

Chapter 36   October 1987

'All done? Desolate place now. Granddad said the missionary disappeared. Big mystery. They never found him did they?'

'No,' Ash replied softly, almost an undertone. 'They never did.'

Chapter 37

January 1943

Gabriel was startled by the sudden intensity of Ash's reaction. He had seen similar depths of emotion in his own culture when there was a death within the community at the Fitzmaurice Mission, but never among white people. Even the death of the Nackeroo signaller, Bluey Jenkins, had been met by his fellow soldiers with stoic detachment. If there was grief on the stations where he had worked, then it was hidden from view. Now, though, Gabriel saw the boss had something broken inside.

Ash knew what he'd done. Müller's body lay across a dead Japanese soldier. There was a bullet wound in the pastor's skull and a sword in the Japanese man's chest. The sequence of events was clear.

Ash raised his head and pulled at the gun strap around his shoulders. In the dim light his eyes caught movement in front of him and words floated to him from somewhere in the distance.

'Better we go down now, Boss.'

Gabriel crouched beside him, gently prising his fingers from the rifle and guiding Ash to the cave entrance away from the two bodies lying in the shadows.

Chapter 38

October 1987

The combination of low tide, the Bedford's high clearance and Ash's steady progression in low gear meant they easily forded the Victoria at Policeman's Point, just upstream from the Timber Creek store. For the next hour the truck ground its way along the Bradshaw Station tracks with Ash spinning the steering wheel to and fro in an effort to avoid the ruts. Rain had fallen recently and he skirted numerous mud patches by following wheel-track detours into the surrounding bush made by previous vehicles. The Bedford's bench seat was hard and uncomfortable. Karen, in the middle with less to hang on to, jolted the most. She moved closer to Brad so as not to impede Ash's frequent gear changes. They forded several small running creeks until they finally left the breakaway country and drove across the flats to the Angalarri River with Bradshaw Station on the far side.

'This whole stream was called the Ikymbon when we were here in the war,' Ash shouted over the roar of the engine as he engaged low gear to cross the ford. 'I don't know why it's changed. There's a new homestead now too, not the old pipe-framed place that we used as a base. The manager told me it is still there though. I wouldn't mind having a look at that before we get the boat.'

He drove past the new buildings, watered lawns and spreading shade trees that they had seen from the air the previous day, until they came to what looked like a derelict tin shed overgrown with scrub. The corrugated iron roof was mostly intact, held up by a framework of iron pipes, but half the cladding on the side walls was missing. The building had an earth floor strewn with lumps of concrete and other debris. Weeds and shrubs intruded through the gaps in the walls and a very large double-trunked boab tree had grown so close that one of its trunks rested on the roof. Ash looked at the ruin in silence for a while, lost in his memories. Then he shrugged and turned away.

'It was no great shakes when we were here, but it was still luxury compared to some of the other bush camps the Nackeroos had to endure. I suppose the worst part was the blasted frogs. They never shut up. Drove us mad, along with the mosquitoes and sand flies. Probably still there, the bloody things. We had big Horse flies too. They were bad.'

'How long did you spend here Ash?' Brad asked.

'On and off the best part of a year 1942 into 43. We did a lot of patrols out into the ranges and up the river, so we weren't here all the time, except the signaller. He had to stay with the radio equipment. One bloke went mad through the solitude. Thought the Japs were coming and took off into the bush. Killed in the end. He…'

Ash stopped short. He hadn't thought about Bluey in years. Or Stretch or Sam. Or the replacement signaller… he'd forgotten his name anyway. The Lieutenant was the only one who'd kept in contact. The others could be anywhere by now…

or dead. He looked at the big boab. They'd all carved their names into the trunks. They should still be there…

'We'll wait by the truck,' Karen said gently. 'Leave you alone for a bit. There's no rush.'

Chapter 39

January 1943

Ash offered no resistance as Gabriel lay the weapon to one side and coaxed him to his feet. He stumbled to the cave entrance in a half crouch. Ash remembered little about the descent along the narrow ledges to the base of the cliff except Gabriel's guiding arm across his shoulders and whispered words of encouragement. He heard them again when they reached the bottom and he slumped against the rock.

'Okay now, Boss. Better you stay here. I go back for rifle.'

Chapter 40

October 1987

Ash gunned the motor as Brad cast off from the Bradshaw landing. The eight-metre launch sped away from the bank into the middle of the river where Ash turned the bows downstream and eased back on the throttle. He didn't need full revs for the ebb tide and the station manager had reminded him of the treacherous mud banks that could easily catch them unawares. How different this vessel was from the *Pride* of his day, or that bloody raft. In this sleek launch they'd be down river in no time.

At the junction with the Bullo River, Ash pointed out the little cove on the opposite side of the Victoria as Bottle Glen, describing it as just another interim camp he'd used. But he waved away Brad's offer to pull in and have a look. This part of the trip belonged as much to the young geologist as it did to him.

Brad had quizzed the Bradshaw manager about Stokes' wells. The manager didn't know of a place called Water Valley on today's maps but, if it was supposed to be opposite where the *Beagle* had been anchored in Holdfast Reach, he said it would most likely be in the vicinity of Lalngang Creek. He recommended the inlet as a safe place to pull in and tie up out of the strong Victoria current. They could have a good look round the area from there. When he'd pointed to the spot on the map, Ash recognised it immediately. The place was so etched into his memory that when he steered the launch slowly in through the mouth of the Lalngang stream, he half expected to see the mission lugger tied up to the mangroves in the lee of the ridge that overlooked the waterway.

It was too late in the afternoon to go exploring. Brad curbed his impatience and applied himself to the task of unloading the gear to set up camp under the lip of the ridge. The searing edge had gone from the day's heat by the time they had finished and gathered wood to light a fire. Brad relaxed beside Karen, sipping a beer and watching the rocks around them turn a rust red, then deep crimson as the sun dropped to the horizon. Later, in the flickering light of the flames, they heard the grunting of crocodiles down on the river banks and listened as Ash related more about his wartime experiences.

'You know,' the old bloke said, 'the station managers encouraged us to break as many croc eggs as we could find. They reckoned it was a good way to cull the numbers because the big buggers would take cattle when they came down to drink. Just leap out and grab a bullock by the nose and drag it under. Saw crocs on the Nile too, when I was in Egypt. The Middle East was a completely different war…'

It was as if Ash wanted to unburden himself of a lifetime. Brad didn't mind. Somehow it felt right with Karen nestling into his shoulder and Ash yarning on the other side of the fire. The old bloke was different in this setting. The antagonism of the first meetings had gone. Ash had made his peace with Karen. Maybe he was now making peace with himself.

Chapter 41

January 1943

The lantern was guttering by the time Gabriel returned to the cave and he had to work quickly. He scraped away as much as he could of the thin layer of dirt on the floor to form two hollows. Then he levered the pastor's body into the one where the ceiling sloped down to meet the floor at the back of the cave and pushed earth and loose rocks over it, taking time to fully cover the bloodied head.

Gabriel paused over the body of the Japanese man. He wondered what had brought the pastor and the soldier together. It was obvious there had been a fight, probably not long before he and Ash arrived and saw the light in the cliff. The sword was still buried deep in the man's chest. Gabriel left it there. He couldn't bring himself to pull it from the corpse. Instead he piled the remaining earth and rocks up around it.

At the cave mouth Gabriel picked up the rifle and turned for a last look just as the lantern flame went out. He stepped onto the ledge leaving the radio humming in the dark.

Chapter 42

October 1987

Brad led the way to the top of the ridge and looked out over the wide valley beyond. In a few places patches of bare salt-encrusted earth permitted no growth, but most of the floor was covered in yellow grasses and clumps of spinifex. A dry creek bed ran along the near side, its catchment marked by dark staining that extended in a web of runnels down the rocky slope on which he stood. Green-topped acacias nestled in straggly groups around the base of the slope, interspersed here and there with boabs and grey-trunked melaleucas. On the far side a cliff rose about a hundred metres above the plain. From where Brad stood, the face appeared to be marked with dark blotches that he thought were caves. The largest just the sort of place where Aboriginal artists might have daubed their depictions of tribal life on the roofs and walls. He decided to climb up later and have a look, but first he wanted to explore the valley floor.

Brad had memorised Stokes' description of Water Valley in the journal. He had also found a drawing of the camp site made by Captain Wickham. It was a loose photocopied sheet that Reg Able must have inserted in between pages at the back of the

Chapter 42 October 1987

journal. Brad tried to fit it to the scene before him. The broad stretch of water that the *Beagle*'s captain had named Holdfast Reach in retrospect after losing his anchors in the muddy river bed shimmered in the morning sun. Brad pictured the vessel moored in mid-river. It would have been a short row across to the shore where the sailors pitched their tents. Perhaps the little creek had water in it then and this enticed them to choose the spot to camp in the shade of the trees. There was no sign of the huge multi-trunked boab that they had inscribed with the name of their ship. He couldn't see anything resembling a well either, nor the Pandanus palms mentioned as marking its site. Much would have changed since Stokes' time. Yet he felt confident he was in the right place. Most of the main features matched the word and pen pictures, especially the line of the high cliff against the sky and the way the slate interbedded with the sandstone. Brad waited for Karen to come up alongside him before beginning his descent into the valley.

Further back Ash moved slowly, picking his way carefully across the loose scree, his mind crowded with thoughts of dusk forty-five years earlier. He had tried for years to suppress the details of that night, but as he breasted the ridge top, the scene immediately fell into place. He remembered lying on his stomach peering over the edge; the wallaby and the movement near the edge of the valley; Gabriel squatting down silently among the trees; the light in the cliff cave; the crash of his rifle; the climb… his ascent to hell.

Ash shuddered. His demons circled. He willed himself to stay calm, to think clearly. He furrowed his brow and set off down the slope towards the others, recalling his movements all those years ago.

When Ash stepped onto the valley floor the others had

already moved away through the long grass towards the centre, casting their eyes back and forth as they went. He kept closer to the base of the hills to more precisely retrace his former path. There had been something else that night, something which had seemed out of place. He dismissed it at the time. It seemed important now, relevant to Brad's quest. It was along this way he was sure, something unusual, something man-made… Man-made! The memory flooded back. He remembered skirting a wide, shallow depression in the dark that had seemed different to all the other landforms in the area. And there it was right in front of him near the first group of trees—a rounded basin-like dip in the valley floor three or four metres wide and two metres deep.

'Brad. Karen,' he called. 'Over here.'

* * * *

Brad stood on the depression rim and clapped Ash on the back.

'You must have second sight. How on earth did you stumble on this so quickly? It's got to be it. One way to find out.'

Brad dropped down into the centre of the dip and scraped away the top layer of salt-encrusted soil, then dug deeper with a hefty stick he found lying under the trees. Reaching down he scooped some of the exposed dark oily clay material into one hand and brought it to his nose. He beamed up at the others and held out his hand like a schoolboy at show and tell.

'Smells of kerosene. Looks like pitch. I'd say this is a Eureka moment. Bloody marvellous. Celebrations tonight.'

They sat together in the shade of the trees reconstructing the *Beagle* camp site in their imaginations; Karen as caught up in the excitement as Brad.

Chapter 42 October 1987

'The tents would have been somewhere here under the trees, the boats pulled up above the high tide mark down by the river. They'd probably have to roll the water barrels along the flat to the well and back again. How many barrels would there have been? They might have constructed a windlass frame for raising and lowering a bucket. I wonder what the water inflow would have been like—fast, or a slow seep. They were here for a couple of weeks.'

Brad rose to his feet and brushed his hand across the seat of his shorts.

'I reckon this would be a prime spot for some of the Aboriginal people too. Wouldn't surprise me if this valley was a favourite camping place for them. They would have dug their own wells. Maybe that's how Stokes knew where to look. Anyway I'd like to go to the cliff cave up there. It will have a marvellous view out over the river and there might even be a painting gallery.'

'Are you sure that's a good idea?' Karen asked. 'Won't we be intruding?'

'I don't think so. We wouldn't touch anything. Look at all those places they've found in Kakadu. Everybody's allowed to go there. I reckon it will be fine. Come with me. It'd be the icing on the cake for today, a good end to the whole trip.'

Karen nodded and stood beside him, but Ash turned away.

'I'll never get up there. You go. I'll head back to the boat and pack up. We need to be on the river back to Bradshaw before three unless you want to spend another night out here.'

Chapter 43

January 1943

Gabriel led the way directly across the valley floor back to the mission lugger. There was no longer a need for stealth or vigilance so he kept the rifle slung over his shoulder. Ash made no comment or demand for the weapon. He merely followed in morose silence, his brain tormented with self-reproach. He had betrayed everyone's trust in his relentless pursuit of Müller, and he had been wrong. Now he shrank from the consequences. He could not front the Lieutenant after what had happened. A gross abuse of command. Certain demotion and disgrace. Possibly Court Martial. Unless he could do something. Something big to thwart the coming invasion. His mind grasped at desperate possibilities. He must do it. He had no other choice.

By the time they reached the boat, reality and fantasy merged. Ash had formed a wild plan and convinced himself it would atone for his tragic blunder. At dawn he would sail out into the Gulf and intercept the Japanese on his own. But first he would need help to navigate the lugger down the river.

* * *

Chapter 43   January 1943

'Gabriel, Jimmy… get aboard and be ready to pull up the anchor when I start the motor.'

Ash's mood—the rapid shifts from highs to lows and back again—made Gabriel uneasy once more. For now the voice was firm… in control, yet the manic stare of the previous night had returned. Gabriel signalled to Jimmy to obey the command. He had already hidden the rifle among the rocks onshore, but he remained watchful.

'Might be we go to Depot, Boss?'

'No. We head downstream a little bit. Wait for my signal.'

Ash clambered over the gunwale and entered the compact wheelhouse near the stern. He had no experience of boats, but as he switched on the ignition and heard the engine kick into life he told himself the task would be little different from driving a truck in the Middle East. He had a mission to accomplish. It didn't need a manual.

'Up anchor!'

Ash swung the wheel to point the bow towards the mouth of the creek. He avoided the mangroves crowding the narrow opening and motored out into the Victoria. Immediately the current snatched the craft and swept it downstream. The deck lurched, throwing Gabriel and Jimmy violently against the rail where they hung on grimly, water sluicing over them. A whoop of laughter came from the wheelhouse. Gabriel turned to see Ash grinning as he brought the lugger round onto an even keel. Whirlpool Reach lay ahead and Ash steered closer to the bank, remembering the course the skipper of the *Pride* had taken to avoid the treacherous maelstrom. The vessel answered the helm slowly, bucking and rolling in the grip of the conflicting currents.

Gabriel and Jimmy staggered along the slippery deck to take shelter behind the wheelhouse screen. Ash directed them to keep a lookout as floating trees and other flood debris kept pace with them on either side. Jimmy shouted a warning as he saw a large branch suddenly dip into a vortex. The jagged end spun and reared up, striking the port side with a juddering thud. Ash opened the throttle and powered away before it could strike a second time. Several more glancing blows were felt below the water line, but the motor did not falter. With a final surge they were through the turbulence and rounding the tight S-bend that led into the relative calm of Blunder Bay.

'How about that for a ride?'

Ash felt exhilarated, adrenalin pumping as he steered through the eastern chute past Entrance Island into Queens Channel. He was ready to tackle the Gulf. Gabriel noticed the euphoric tone and grew anxious. Something was very wrong with the Boss. He had made no attempt to stop and make contact with the Nackeroos at the Blunder Bay camp. Instead, by following the eastern bank he seemed to be deliberately avoiding it. Gabriel suddenly realised that Ash did not intend to return. Instead the Boss was embarked on some sort of insane mission of his own. Gabriel reached for the wheel. It would be suicide to go out into the Gulf.

'We go back now, Boss? Better we stay Blunder Bay camp I reckon. Might be radio talk to big boss at Depot.'

Ash shook his head and pushed Gabriel's arm away. It was time for him to go on alone. The dark shape of Quoin Island loomed ahead and he headed for the place where the *Pride* had landed himself, Sam and Gabriel for their overland trek to Keyling Inlet.

'Gabriel, you and Jimmy must go ashore here. Go back to Bradshaw. Tell the Lieutenant there will be no more signals. Say I have gone to stop the Japanese soldiers coming. You got that?'

Chapter 43   January 1943

'No, Boss. I think better you come back.'

Gabriel spoke softly, appealing for reason, but Ash turned on him. 'That's an order Gabriel. You hear? Take Jimmy and go. Now!'

Gabriel hesitated. It was not his place to disobey, but he saw it was not the true Boss speaking. The Boss in front of him was sick, broken in the head. The Boss had been his friend. He could be made well again. Gabriel could not let him go where death was certain. Nervously he placed a hand on Ash's arm.

'Boss. We go back now. Japanese man dead. Soldiers don't come.'

Ash reacted in sudden fury. He turned from the wheel and pushed Gabriel in the chest. Gabriel staggered back, catching his heel on the raised door jamb, grabbing wildly for a handhold. Ash followed him out of the wheelhouse and pushed again, sending Gabriel sprawling on the deck. As he raised his fist to strike a third time, Ash caught sight of Jimmy standing wide-eyed by the rail. At that moment the lugger jolted to a halt, throwing both men off-balance as the bow ploughed into a submerged mud bank. Within seconds the current swung the stern around. The momentum wrenched the bow free and spun the vessel out of control towards the narrow tidal race between Quoin Island and the east bank of the channel. Ash made a lunge for the wheel, at the same time yanking the throttle lever to full power. Even as he did so, he knew it was too late. The helm failed to answer and he couldn't hold on as the wheel spun out of his grasp.

The stern hit the rocks first, ripping the propeller from its shaft. The engine screamed. Then the jagged reef bit into the bow, splintering it like matchwood. Water swept over the stricken vessel driving it, broadside on, further into the constricted passage. The hull groaned and shuddered in the unrelenting onslaught. The last thing Ash heard was grinding and cracking as the timbers split and he was catapulted into the river.

Chapter 44

October 1987

Brad carefully studied the cliff. It was not as steep as it appeared from a distance. He noticed a narrow track of sorts worn into the rock. It zig-zagged up the face using the horizontal bedding planes as steps—a highway for a rock wallaby, but possible for humans as well.

'Are you sure?' Karen looked up apprehensively.

'Yes, as long as we're careful. It's wide enough and there are plenty of handholds.'

Brad and Karen made steady progress, leaning into the wall and watching the placement of each step.

They paused to catch their breath and to look out across the valley. Brad watched the distant figure of Ash labouring up the far ridge and disappearing over the top in the direction of the boat. He checked his watch. Just after midday and hot, the sun high in the sky. It would be cooler in the cave which he could now see just a little further ahead.

Brad eased himself over the lip and then moved further inside to give Karen room to follow. At the entrance the roof was high enough for a small person to stand, but he was forced to stoop. It was easier to drop to his knees. He waited a moment as his eyes adjusted to the dim light, then scanned the rock above, quickly disappointed to find none of the paintings that he had hoped to see. It was not an Aboriginal galley after all. More like an animal's lair. The floor was covered with sand, fragments of rock and scattered scraps of bone and dried animal faeces—maybe dingos used the place. Or had.

'What's that box thing over there?'

Karen moved past him to the far side of the entrance where an oblong object lay covered in dirt. As she brushed her hand across, the top fell open and hung, lopsided, down one side. Inside she saw two large knobs set in a metal plate separated by a glass-fronted dial, all surrounded by switches and sockets. One had a piece of wire attached. The dial had a single needle pointer and some markings arranged in an arc on the face underneath it.

'Must be some sort of detector machine,' she said. 'Like an old Geiger counter or something. It's got a metal plate on the side.' She rubbed with her finger. 'There's some markings, but they're scratched. I can't make them out.'

Brad peered over her shoulder.

'It's been here a while. They look like Chinese characters. No. Christ! It must be Japanese. You know what I think? This is an old Jap radio set.' His voice raised, excited. 'Bloody hell. It must be from the War. Someone sending messages from here, or near here. Hiding in this cave… '

'Brad.'

'They'd never be found… who'd think of looking for them up here?'

'BRAD!'

The sharpness of Karen's tone suddenly registered as she gripped his arm.

Chapter 44 October 1987

'What?'

'All these bones around the floor… they're human.'

Brad stared at her. 'What makes you say that?'

'Look there.'

Brad followed her eyes along the wall to where the skull lay half exposed in the dust, its eye sockets staring at the roof.

'Shit. This might be an Aboriginal resting place.'

Karen moved down and began scaping the sand and dirt away, exposing neck vertebrae and then further down a part of the upper arm and rib cage.

'Ouch! Bugger.'

'What is it? Are you okay?'

'Something sharp here stuck in the ribs. Hang on, I'm trying to scrape around it. It's long, like a strip of metal. Ah. There's some sort of handle… Oh my God! Brad, it's a sword.'

Brad knelt beside her, grasped the hilt, gently pulled the rusty blade clear of the rib cage and held it up to the light. It was long and thin and slightly curved at the end. A single-edged weapon. The binding on the hilt had partly rotted.

'Careful, it might still be sharp,' Karen said as he tested the edge with his finger and rubbed at the rust near the hilt. 'Can I see?' She took the sword from him and held it horizontal, weighing it across her two hands.

'He must have been killed with it,' she whispered.

'Can you tell if the skull is Japanese, Asian?' Brad asked. 'I mean, could he have been killed with his own sword? It's a Jap sword. All the officers had them in the War.'

'I don't know. I'd have to see the whole skeleton to even guess.'

'It could have been hari-kari, a suicide I suppose. The Japanese did that rather than be captured.'

'You mean like that ritual disembowelment? The sword is in the wrong place for that. It was through the side of the chest. Look, the tip of the blade is broken. It might have hit a rib. It would have been very difficult to do that yourself.'

'It's amazing. I can't believe we've stumbled on this. It's a sort of spy nest crime scene. I wonder what happened here.'

Brad sat down to get the weight off his knees, stretching out his legs to ease the cramp. As he did so his boot struck something in the rubble on the floor at the back of the cave. He scraped his heel across to move it out of the way and heard Karen gasp. He glanced at her, then quickly down to his foot, immediately pulling it away in fright as he saw the dirt falling away and another skull staring back at him.

'Christ. What's going on? We must be in a cemetery.' He got back on his knees and began to scrape the rest of the muck away. 'Well, there's no doubt about how this one died,' he said as he pushed his finger through the round hole in the side of the skull a few centimetres above the hinge of the jaw bone.

Karen joined him. She brushed the dirt away from the base of the skull to expose the neck vertebrae and shoulders. Brad moved out of the way and watched her gentle probing, a nurse's touch. He saw her hands stilled for a moment, then her fingers moved along and behind both sides of the neck manipulating something. Slowly she pulled the chain and pendant clear and held it up. Her eyes suddenly widened and a look of open-mouthed horror came over her face.

Chapter 45

January 1943

Gabriel and Jimmy dragged Ash out of the water and laid him on his side. His eyes were closed; his breathing shallow. It was a miracle he had survived. He had resisted fiercely when Gabriel reached him, fighting his rescue. Gabriel had been forced to strike him under the chin or Ash would have drowned them both.

Now he and Jimmy sat in the sand waiting for the Boss to stir as the late morning sun dried their tattered clothes.

* * *

Ash sat up slowly and looked around. The thin strip of beach under the high cliff looked vaguely familiar. His head ached. He fingered the bruise on his chin, rubbed dried blood from the stinging cuts on his arms. He glanced up as a shadow passed over him.

'You drink this Boss'.

He accepted the scalloped shell and drank in gulps, the cool water eased his throat and cleared the haze from his mind.

Ash lay back and closed his eyes. The pastor returned to haunt him.

Chapter 46

October 1987

'It's my grandfather. I know it is. Oh God, to find him like this. Here, after all this time.'

Karen sobbed quietly, her head against Brad's shoulder, her hand clasped tightly around the silver pendant.

Brad held her gently.

'How can you be so sure?'

Karen opened her fist and showed him the small silver cross in her palm.

'It's a Luther rose set in a cross,' she sniffed.

'There must be millions of them. Why do you think this one belonged to your grandfather?'

'Because this one's a special design. See, the rose seal is in the centre of another cross. Look at the arms.' Karen wet a finger with her tongue and rubbed an arm of the cross. 'What do you see? You should know as a geologist.'

Brad took the pendant from her and examined it, adding his own spit and shining it on his sleeve. He recognised the flash of fiery red and blue.

'The arms are inlaid with opal.'

Karen nodded. 'I've never seen it before, but my mother

Chapter 46   October 1987

told me about it once. She said grandmother had it made from Coober Pedy opal for grandfather when they were young and helping at the Hermannsburg Mission. Mother said grandfather always wore it.'

She sobbed. 'All this time I've been wanting to find out what happened. Believing he couldn't have been a traitor. Now I've found out the truth and I wish to God I hadn't. All those horrible stories… people were right. They all knew. Maybe grandmother and mother too.'

Brad couldn't find any words to say. He felt apprehensive. Something was not right.

'What do you think happened?' Karen whispered. 'Did someone find them sending messages? Just kill them and leave them. How could anyone do that, whatever they'd done?'

'I don't know,' he said quietly. 'It was war.'

Suddenly a sharp report rent the air. Brad stiffened. A gunshot. He'd heard that sound before, and not so long ago. He eased Karen's head from his shoulder.

'Can you manage the track down? I think we'd better get back.'

Chapter 47

January 1943

Gabriel kept a close watch on Ash during the two days they camped in the trees at the end of the beach. He was relieved to see no return of the mania that had scared him in the hours after finding the bodies in the cave. Ash had been quiet, composed even. He seemed to have resigned himself to his fate.

On the third morning Jimmy led the group up the steep path to the cliff top and set off on the long trek to Bradshaw. From the heights they looked down at the tidal race where the lugger had struck. There was no sign of wreckage. The vessel's back had been broken. It had sunk beneath the surface and the currents had done the rest.

'The pastor has disappeared,' Ash said softly. 'No one knows where he went. Do you understand me? No one can ever know.'

Gabriel looked across and caught a fleeting dread in Ash's eyes. In that moment he understood the immense burden the Boss had inflicted on himself—one that he would carry forever.

Chapter 48

October 1987

Another vessel was tied up beside the Bradshaw launch when Brad and Karen breasted the ridge and made their way down the slope to the Lalngang Creek camp. Brad quickened his step. From the other side of the stream he saw a figure emerge from the mangroves, staggering a little as it stepped over the tangle of roots at the water's edge. Brad splashed across the ford and ran the last stretch to the boats, Karen close behind. The man lowered a drooping bundle from his broad shoulders and gently laid it on the ground. He looked up as they approached and Brad recognised the dark skin and white stubbly beard on the face of Gabriel Fitzmaurice. He glanced down at the bundle on the ground, fearing the worst. Karen made a sobbing wail as she rushed past them both to kneel by Ash's still body. She tore at his shirt, her nurse's training urging her to find out if there might be hope to save him. But then she saw the shattered jaw and the tangled mass of brain and bone at the back of the old man's head. Brad saw it too and went behind a boat to be violently sick—great shuddering heaves that seemed to come from the depths of him. When there was nothing left, he stumbled round to lean on the bow, his head throbbing and his mouth bitter with the taste of bile.

Gabriel squatted next to Karen talking softly as she remained kneeling, head bowed over Ash's body. He signalled to Brad and together, with a hand under each shoulder, they lifted her and set her down on a rocky outcrop away from the corpse. Brad noticed for the first time the .303 rifle that Gabriel had propped up against the side of the second boat. Gabriel saw his glance and nodded.

'I hid that once a long time ago, but gave it back later. There were heavy penalties in the Army for losing a rifle.' He sighed. 'It was beside him in the mangroves. He wanted to do it in there out of sight and where the crocodiles would find him. He wanted to leave no trace. I couldn't let that happen, no matter what he'd done.'

'How are you here Gabriel? Did you know this would happen?'

'Yes,' he answered, pushing the Akubra back from his forehead. 'Yes, Ash told me of this trip and what he was going to do. He made me promise to follow and find you to explain. He thought of a letter to you, Karen, like he did in the old days, but he'd got out of the way of writing. This was the best way he said, so there would be no misunderstanding.'

'Tell me why,' Karen said, her voice barely a whisper, her face white and strained. 'Why did this happen? What for?'

'The cave,' Gabriel said. 'You been up there? Ash thought you probably would. He knew the spot. I did too.'

Gabriel hesitated.

Karen sat stony-faced looking at him. 'Ash shot him, didn't he?'

'Yes,' Gabriel said. 'He was so angry. So sure... and so wrong.' Gabriel came closer and put a hand on her shoulder.

Chapter 48 October 1987

'Your grandfather wasn't working with the Japanese signal officer. He was tracking him, probably over a couple of months. I don't know why he didn't report it. Probably he didn't trust the Army after he'd been interned and all the station people and the Nackeroos were still suspicious of him. He must have finally caught the man in that cave, surprised him sending another message. Maybe then he would have contacted the authorities to warn them. We'll never know. But he was a good man, Karen… a good man, not a collaborator.'

'So all this was covered up?" said Brad. 'You told no one about it?'

'Ash told us to forget all about it. It never happened. The pastor had just disappeared. So yes, I said nothing. At first I suppose because I was ordered not to. Then, when the war ended, my people went back to being treated like dirt. I didn't owe white Australians anything. So I kept silent out of loyalty to Ash. He was one of the few who had respect for my culture. I told myself it would do no good to bring it all up again.'

'So Ash coming back to the mission to see my mother, and then being in Cloncurry and looking out for me… that was just his conscience. Nothing else.' Karen spat the words out.

'No, in his way he loved your mother, Karen, I think from the first moment he saw her as a child at the mission. And from that he loved you. But he couldn't tell you. He lived with his private hell for more than forty years. One small moment of madness that destroyed so many lives. He did his best to repair the damage, but he knew it would never be enough. I think, inside, he died that night along with your grandfather. In the end he begged for your understanding… and for your forgiveness.'

'Why now? Because he knew I'd finally find out his deception? He didn't even have the guts to tell me to my face.'

'No. In the end he didn't. I know he thought about telling you many times. Why now? I can't answer that exactly, but he did say he had finally met someone else who would fight for you.'

* * *

The wonderful few days spent with Karen and Ash evaporated on the trip back. Gabriel had absolved Brad from anything to do with the authorities, telling him he would make the arrangements. He said Brad should just take Karen back and see that she was all right. Brad tried to talk to Karen, but she mostly sat alone on the far side of the bench seat, clasping her grandfather's pendant.

He wanted to hold her, to tell her he was there, to keep her from more harm. But he let her be. There was nothing he could say that would mend her wound. He could only hope her pain would ease.

Outside her house, Karen asked him not to come in. 'Really,' she said. 'I just want to be alone.'

* * *

The Malteser raised an eyebrow when Brad drove into camp in the Bedford. His eyes were full of questions.

'Don't ask,' Brad said. 'Not yet.'

'Okay. But better you have this.'

Charlie handed him a fax which he scanned without emotion. Nothing he hadn't expected. Able told him his services had been terminated. All the company's assets, including the interest in the Stokes-1 permit, had been sold to a big American independent headquartered in Baton Rouge, Louisiana—Zydeco Energy. Brad had heard the name. Able wittered on about it being a give-away price in the circumstances and that he'd had no choice. He admitted that originally he'd had been angling for Zydeco to farm-in. But that went by the board with the crash. Able had lost his bargaining power. He couldn't afford to wait or haggle. He said that the test results in the Gibb River reservoir had been the only reason he'd got any cash consideration at all. The sniff of gas had been enough to keep them interested. When the crisis blows over, and it will, Abel's fax said, the Americans will come in and finish the well. They think there is potential, especially at the bargain basement price they paid. But Abel was sorry, Zydeco had their own geologists on staff. Brad would not be needed. The footnote read: "Give the Stokes Journal to Charlie Camilleri. He'll send it on to me."

(J.L. Stokes – Journal entry 21 October 1839)

… *I left here a paper in a bottle, giving an account of our proceedings, and should have been sorry to think, as Wallis did when he left a similar document on a mountain in the Strait of Magellan, that I was leaving a memorial that would remain untouched as long as the world lasts. No, I would fain hope that ere the sand of my life-glass has run out, other feet than mine will have trod this distant shore; that colonisation will, ere many years have past, have extended itself in this quarter; that cities and hamlets will have risen on the shore of the new-found river, that commerce will have directed her track thither, and that smoke may rise from Christian hearths where now alone the prowling heathen lights his fire. There is an inevitable tendency in man to create; and there is nothing which he contemplates with so much complacency as the work of his own hands. To civilise the world, to subdue the wilderness, is the proudest achievement to which he can look forward; and to share in this great work by opening new fields of enterprise, and leading, as it were, the van of civilisation, fills the heart with inexpressible delight.* …

Chapter 49

November 1987

Brad closed the journal for the last time. Was Able trying to tell him something by recommending that passage? That the wilderness was there to be subdued, developed, and that he would be back some day in the not-too-distant future to do so. It would be just like him. For now, Zydeco Energy had the ball in its court. Zydeco had bought the Stokes prospect, signalling they would continue the operation, if not now, then soon. The likes of Gabriel Fitzmaurice, the Land Rights and environmental people, they would all have to deal with a new invader.

Brad opened his door and stood on the boardwalk. The rig filled his view. It was silent now. It would remain in place for the next few months. The first storms had come and there was no hope of trucking it across the black soil plains. Ethan Williams and the drill crews had departed, the lucky ones to new jobs in what remained of the industry; others to find work in farms and towns until conditions improved.

The Malteser was still on site, catering for the few care and maintenance people who looked after the rig during the Wet. Charlie was biding his time, reassembling his decimated portfolio. Brad knew that he, like Able, would bounce back and be off on another adventure. He would draw new lines on his map in the mess.

Brad spent his last days on the rig thinking about Karen and the trip to the Victoria. He yearned for her smile, those enticing hazel eyes, her touch. He respected her wish to be alone. At least, he told himself so. In fact, deep down, he was afraid. Ash's relationship with Karen had been eaten away and ultimately destroyed by secrets. All but one exposed by his death. But that remaining one now belonged to Brad alone. How could he tell Karen it was Able's money that put her through school, helped give her the chance to shine; the man she despised so much. Certainly not now, on top of everything else that had happened. Yet if he did not tell her, how could any relationship between them survive? He would be following the same path that Ash had taken. So he had made his decision. He would go back to Melbourne, for a while at least. He would give Karen the time that she needed and then ask her to be with him. And he would tell her Ash's last secret so that there was nothing left to stand between them.

Brad packed his bags and said his goodbyes. He gave Stokes' journal to Charlie as instructed. For once the Malteser asked no questions and made no comments about his plans—just another bear hug and his word to keep in touch.

Brad drove the Bedford out onto the road to town. He had promised to leave the old truck there for collection. The Nackeroo Lieutenant's chopper pilot grandson Garry had expressed an interest in having it and he'd make a donation to the hospital fund for the privilege. Brad thought Ash would approve.

Brad smelt smoke in the air through the open window as he approached the stockyards, but it was not until he reached the

Chapter 49 November 1987

turnoff that he saw the still-smoking remains of Ash's hut. He wrenched the truck around onto the two-wheel tracks that led to the old bloke's former home. The posts and rails to keep the cattle out were still intact, but the hut itself had been reduced to charred rubble. Not a stick was left standing and the limestone outcrop that had formed one wall was scorched black. Even the water tank had dropped onto its side, the wooden stand demolished by the flames. Brad got out and picked his way through the mess. There was nothing to salvage. Some of the iron pots were still warm, so the fire could only be a day old at most. Undoubtedly it had been deliberately lit, but who could have done it and why. He kicked at a half-melted tin mug, sad that Ash's life now really was a pile of ruins.

Brad noticed the roughly-fashioned cross in the far corner of the yard beyond the old wood stove as he walked back to the truck. It was made of two lengths of eucalypt bound together with twine. One limb of the cross had been carved with the word ASH; the other with three words PROPER GOOD FELLA. Coming closer he saw the freshly dug earth and smiled to himself at the way Gabriel had "dealt with the authorities." The few locals in the area might wonder about the fire, but no one at all would be any the wiser about events on the Victoria. As he turned away Brad noticed a small oblong tin box by the side of the grave. He opened it, unrolled the hessian wrapping and saw the shy, innocent expression of the little wooden piccaninny looking back at him. Ash's gift to Frieda and now his final bequest to her daughter. He rewrapped the carving and put it on the seat beside him.

There was no answer when Brad knocked on Karen's door. His spirits sank. He had already been to the hospital to be told that Sister Frost had taken compassionate leave.

Dear Karen,
I tried to find you. I want so much to see you and talk to you. This note is not the same. I just want to be with you and to say I will wait for you no matter what.

   I love you
   Brad

He folded the paper and placed it on the little tin box and left them both in the porch where they'd be sheltered from the coming storm.

* * *

The airport grew crowded as flight time neared. The incoming plane landed and passengers disembarked into the arms of welcoming family and friends. Brad watched through the terminal windows as airport handlers unloaded the luggage and then turned to the outgoing cases. He did not see Karen until she stood beside him.

'Hello Brad. I got your note.'

She was dressed casually in denim shorts and a light blouse, her hair tied back in the pony-tail he liked so much. He scrambled to his feet to look into the hazel eyes; there were dark lines underneath them. She smiled.

'I'm sorry about your job,' she said, 'even if I'm happy the project has stopped.'

'To tell you the truth, I don't mind either. I've lost my appetite for it. Unfortunately someone else will soon be here to start it up again. You'll have to get used to American accents in town.'

'Brad, I've come to give this back to you.' Karen placed the tin box in his hands. 'It's too painful a reminder right now. Will

Chapter 49 November 1987

you keep it for me? I will come and get it when I feel ready.' She stretched up and kissed him lightly on the lips. Then she turned and walked towards the exit.

'Promise?' he called after her. But she kept walking. He wondered if she hadn't heard him over the noise of the flight announcement and the crowd.

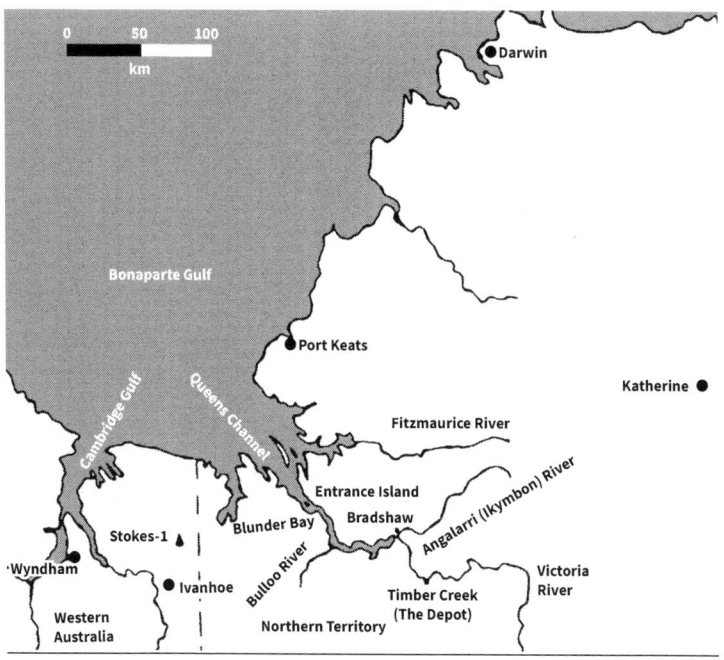

The area covered by B-Company of the North Australia Observation Unit during 1942/43

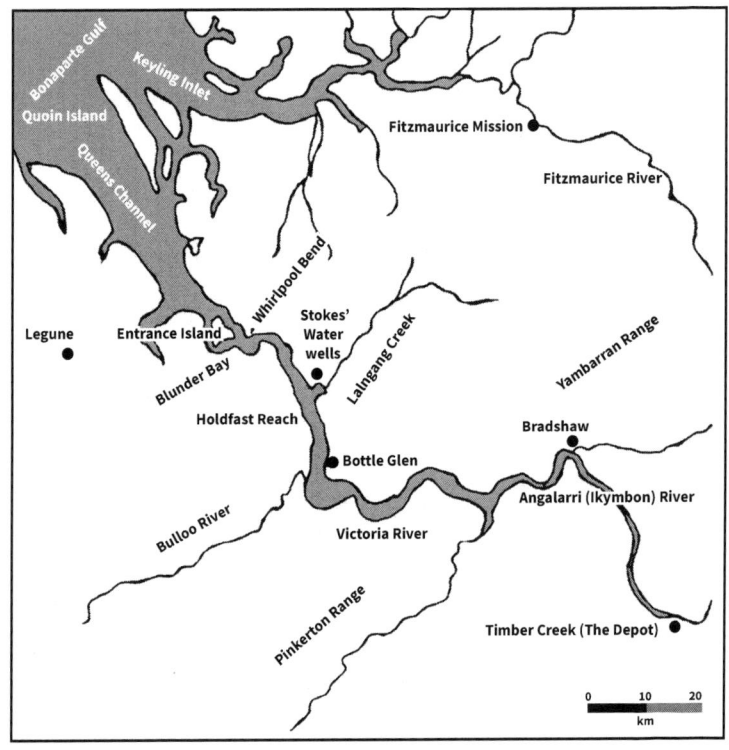

The Victoria River region patrolled by B-Company's Timber Creek platoon during 1942/43

Notes & Acknowledgements

All characters in the story are fictional with the exception of 19th century explorer John Lort Stokes and his commander on HMS *Beagle* Captain John Clements Wickham; along with references to Australian WW2 Prime Minister John Curtin; North Australia Observer Unit commanding officer Major William Stanner; and the 1930s renegade Aboriginal warrior Nemarluk.

Although there have been a number of oil and gas exploration wells drilled onshore and offshore in the Bonaparte Basin since 1960, the Stokes-1 wildcat well of this story is a fiction. Similarly there are and have been missions of several denominations established across northern Australia, but there is no Lutheran mission on the Fitzmaurice River and never has been.

There are reports of Japanese landings/sightings on northern Australian river banks and beaches during WW2, but no evidence of significant enemy incursions. However, the Japanese air raids on Darwin, Broome and Wyndham in 1942, the midget-submarine attack in Sydney Harbour in the same year and the many Japanese 'spotter' plane flights over northern Australia towns and army bases were very real, spreading fears of imminent invasion and prompting the formation of the NAOU. Tokyo Rose, a generic name given by Allied troops in the South Pacific during World War II to female English-speaking radio broadcasters of Japanese propaganda, also sought to erode morale.

The Nackeroos of B-Company NAOU did occupy bases at The Depot (today's Timber Creek), Bradshaw Station, Bottle Glen and Blunder Bay on the Victoria River during 1942 and 1943. I am indebted to the memoirs of former Nackeroos B. Wright, Ray Thatcher, Peter Newman, Morrie Vane and Lance Mac Smith, and particularly to Lance's daughter Mary Mac Smith, who provided invaluable background for the fictional characters and events in the story.

Extracts from J. Lort Stokes' journal are taken verbatim from his *Discoveries in Australia; with an account of the coasts and rivers explored and surveyed during the voyage of H.M.S. Beagle, in the years 1837-43*, published in London in 1846 and reproduced in 1969 as No.33 in the Australiana Facsimile Editions by the Libraries Board of South Australia in Adelaide.

Finally my thanks to Yannick Thoraval, Peter Simpson and Christopher Beck for their penetrating critiques of the story and their sage advice on its structure; to Mark Zocchi and his team at Brolga Publishing for their faith in the manuscript and their skills in readying it for publication; and to Elaine Grant, always my first reader and sounding board, whose encouragement, love and support kept me going through the many periods of frustration and doubt that the project would be completed and find a home.

RW August 2022

ORDER

THE
INVADERS

ISBN: 9780648697084	Qty	
RRP	AU$24.99	.....
Postage within Australia	AU$5.00	.....
	TOTAL* $_____	
	* All prices include GST	

Name: ....

Address: ....

....

Phone: ....

Email: ....

Payment: [ ] Money Order   [ ] Cheque   [ ] MasterCard   [ ] Visa

Cardholder's Name:..

Credit Card Number: ....

Signature:..

Expiry Date: ....

Allow 7 days for delivery.

Payment to: Marzocco Consultancy (ABN 14 067 257 390)
               PO Box 452
               Torquay Victoria 3228
               Australia

BE PUBLISHED

Publish through a successful publisher.
Brolga Publishing is represented through:
• National book trade distribution, including sales, marketing & distribution through Simon & Schuster.
• International book trade distribution to:
   - The United Kingdom
   - Sales representation in South East Asia
• Worldwide e-Book distribution

For details and enquiries, contact:
Brolga Publishing Pty Ltd
ABN 46 063 962 443
PO Box 452
Torquay Victoria 3228
Australia

markzocchi@brolgapublishing.com.au
(Email for a catalogue request)